# Belle St. Marie

## A Novel by

### KAY MOSER

**THOMAS NELSON PUBLISHERS**
Nashville • Atlanta • London • Vancouver

Copyright © 1996 by Kay Moser

All Rights Reserved. Written permission must be secured from
the publisher to use or reproduce any part of this book, except
for brief quotations in critical reviews or articles.

Published in Nashville, Tennessee, Thomas Nelson, Inc.,
Publishers, and distributed in Canada by Word
Communications, Ltd., Richmond, British Columbia.

**Library of Congress Cataloging-in-Publication Data**

Moser, Kay.
  [Celebration]
  Belle St. Marie : a novel / Kay Moser.
    p.   cm.
  Previously published as: Celebration.
  ISBN 0-7852-7539-8
  1. Plantation life—Louisiana—Fiction.
2. Grandmothers—Louisiana—Fiction.   3. Women—
Louisiana—Fiction. 4. Louisiana—Fiction. I. Title.
[PS3563.O88395C4  1996]
813'.54—dc20                  95–45859
                                   CIP

Printed in the United States of America.
1 2 3 4 5 6 7 — 02 01 00 99 98 97 96

This book is dedicated to you
—the reader—
in celebration of your
God-given worth.

# PROLOGUE

With an open wooden box of fragile, old papers in her lap, Elinore D'Evereau sat on the front verandah of her Louisana plantation house, Belle St. Marie, and stared down the oak-draped, winding driveway. Around her finger she twisted a silver tendril of hair that had escaped from her graceful, upswept hairstyle. Her mind was far away, drifting back over the generations of D'Evereaus who had called Belle St. Marie home since the late eighteenth century. At the same time she was worrying about her granddaughter, Rachel D'Evereau, a college student now. "My bright, beautiful, unbending Rachel," she murmured. "What will become of you? You certainly haven't had it easy."

Elinore pulled an old Civil War diary from the box and stroked it gently. "I suppose I shouldn't be surprised. None of the D'Evereaus ever had it easy; we all learned the lessons of life the hard way. Well, Rachel, maybe someday when you're older and more willing to learn, these old diaries will help you. As for now, all my fretting won't do you a bit of good. I best get my errands run." She returned the diary to the wooden box and firmly closed the lid. Then she rose from her favorite wicker chair and stood for a moment, staring down the drive. "Generation after generation," she sighed, "the D'Evereaus have marched off to wars down that drive, or left with their newly married husbands to bear their children. Or in these so-called modern times they have left to make their fortunes grow or just to take on the world. Looking outside for the answers when they're all inside us. That's you, dearest Rachel, storming the world like a soldier, demanding peace. Someday something will make you look inside, and you'll find the truth."

She turned suddenly toward the screen door, "Now, that's enough, Elinore," she scolded herself, "get on with your errands and leave Rachel in God's hands where she belongs." Carrying the wooden box, she crossed the center hall and ascended the elegant staircase. She opened an ordinary looking door on the second floor and struggled up the steep steps to the attic. After placing the box on an old trunk, she allowed her hand to linger on it for a moment as she reassured herself, "I can trust that Rachel will find these diaries, when she's needy and ready." Turning away from the precious papers, she descended the two flights of stairs, her heart lightened by her faith, her eyes deep pools of serenity. "I'll be back soon, Lovey," she called to her housekeeper as she walked out of the front door of Belle St. Marie *for the last time*.

# ONE

## FOURTEEN YEARS LATER

The man lunged at Rachel and pinned her arms to her sides the instant she stepped outside the back door. Her heart beat wildly as she gasped for air and fought to make her numb mind work.

Turning, she struggled to wrench herself loose from his arms. Then suddenly she realized that he wasn't restraining her at all. He was leaning on her. She jerked her head back and stared up into his face, and there she found the drunken, dazed eyes of her husband, Collins.

"You scared me to death!" she screamed as she pushed him away from her. The enormous adrenalin flow continued to surge through her body as her fear turned to fury.

"Where have you been?" she shouted. "I've been up all night. Where have you been?" He swayed toward her, obviously on the verge of passing out there in the doorway.

Rachel grabbed him, held him up as best she could, and helped him drag himself into the den and on to the couch. There he collapsed, just barely able to sit up, and stared at her with glazed eyes. As she opened her mouth to blast him out, his eyes showed a glimmer of perception, and he slurred some words.

"Shocking, isn't it, Darling?" He laughed sarcastically. "Absolutely disgusting for anyone to lose control like this!

Not at all the thing to do. Not at all like you." He leaned toward her, leering as he laughed. "You never lose control, do you, my darling Rachel?" He wagged his finger at her as if he were correcting a child. "Never, never, never!" Then his voice turned icy cold, taunting, "You always land on your feet, don't you, my Darling?"

Before she could respond, his eyelids sank, and he would have fallen forward to the floor if she had not caught him and pushed him over on his side. "Oh no!" she wailed. "He's unconscious! What am I going to do?" She glanced at his feet which were still on the floor. "Leave them there!" she ordered herself. "Let him wake up with a half-broken back. Serves him right!" She turned away and walked back to the door, picked up her scattered briefcase and keys and started out. She got to the point of locking the door behind her before she stopped herself and went back.

As quickly as possible she dragged his leaden legs up on the couch, pulled off his shoes, and went to the bedroom for a blanket. "Why am I doing this?" she demanded of herself. "Heaven knows where he's been, who he's been with." Then she stared down into his face, and there she found her answer, there under the two-day beard and the swollen features. He's still Collins, she thought. In spite of every awful thing he's done, he's still Collins. My Collins. And I guess I still love him. She sighed and paused long enough to tell herself, "You belong in a loony bin, Rachel D'Evereau Greyson. You're nuts!" Then she picked up her things for the third time and left.

As she slid into the driver's seat of her car, she remembered Collins' crumpled figure on the couch and tried to calculate how long he was likely to sleep. I better call that smart-mouthed secretary of his, Shawna whats-her-name, after my first class, she decided. Then I'll come home at noon and check on him. If I'm going to be an idiot, I might as well be a total one! She inserted the key and turned it, but the car made only a clicking noise, followed by total silence. She tried again and again. Nothing but the click. Frustration and anger burned through her as she recognized the undeniable sign of a dead battery.

"Not now!" she cried, "not today!" She felt like beating her head against the steering wheel but settled for slamming her fists against it instead. Then she glared at her watch. Thirty minutes until my first class. No time to get the car fixed. I'll have to call a neighbor.

Grabbing her things, she jumped out of the car and started toward the house. Then she saw Collins' car parked in front of the house, one front wheel over the curb on the grass. "He was driving!" she gasped. "He didn't even call a taxi this time. When I get him sobered up—no, I can't think about that. I've got to get to the university. I'll take Collins' car! Heaven knows he's not going to need it." She headed for his car, started it, and drove quickly down the street.

When she did, the breeze through the open windows sent a stack of envelopes floating around the front seat. Several ended in her lap.

Angrily she slammed on the brakes and gathered up the envelopes to secure them. As she hurriedly stacked them, she noticed that the top one was an electric bill. I pay the bills, the thought raced through her mind. What's he doing with an electric bill? She glanced at the name and address and froze, paralyzed by what she read.

The horn of another car sounded nearby. She forced herself to take her eyes off the envelope, looked around and saw the other car. She was blocking its path. Hastily she drove out of the way and stopped at the curb.

She brought the envelopes into view again, and as she shuffled through them, she moaned over and over, "no, no, no, no." Something in her was dying.

Mrs. Shawna Greyson. The envelopes were mostly addressed to Mrs. Shawna Greyson at an address Rachel recognized as an exclusive condominium complex close to Collins' office. A few envelopes were addressed to Mr. Collins Greyson at the same address.

A fury like she had never known seared through her veins. She whipped the car around and roared back down her street. When she reached the front door of her house, she jabbed the key into the lock and banged open the door. Even from the entry she could see Collins snoring on the couch. Slowly she walked to his side and stared down at him. I want to kill him! she thought. I want to kill him, but not while he's asleep!

Turning abruptly, she stomped to the kitchen where she filled the mop bucket with cold water. When she returned to the couch, she threw half the cold water in Collins' face.

"Wake up!" she screamed. "Wake up, you lousy liar!"

Collins bolted to a sitting position, his head swaying, and tried to focus on her. "What the—"

"You're having an affair with Shawna, aren't you?" she yelled at him. "You're living with her at the North View Condominiums, aren't you?"

"No—" Collins stammered.

"Don't you lie to me! I found your utility bills in your car!"

Collins stared at her in confusion, obviously trying to force his hung-over mind to work.

"Say something!" Rachel screamed. He was silent. "Say something!" she yelled again as she threw the rest of the cold water in his face.

"Okay, okay! It's true!" Collins shouted back at her as he wiped water out of his eyes. "But you have to let me explain," he began as he tried to rise from the couch.

"Don't bother! How many times do you think I'll

stand for this?" Rachel shouted as she shoved him back on the couch. He was so weak and befuddled he fell backwards and sat there staring up at her.

Much to his surprise, Rachel jerked up the telephone book, fumbled through it, and grabbed the phone. "This is Rachel D'Evereau Greyson," she spoke sharply into the receiver. "I want a cab to meet me in twenty minutes at the North View Condominiums, No. 12. Do you have that? Twenty minutes."

"What are you going to—" Collins began.

"Get up!" Rachel interrupted.

"Now, Rachel, we need to talk—" Collins tried again.

"I've done all the talking I'm going to do. Get up!" Still he didn't move, so she reached down and slapped him across the face with a strength born of pure wrath.

Collins struggled to his feet and tried again to talk to her.

"Move!" she yelled as she shoved him toward the door.

"Rachel, for heaven's sake—" he pleaded outside the front door.

"Move!" she yelled repeatedly as she shoved him down the sidewalk. She kept pushing him, and he kept stumbling forward until he reached the passenger side of his car. She opened the door and ordered, "Get in!" Motionless, he stared at her in confusion. "Get in!" she ordered and pushed him down onto the seat. "Put your feet in," she commanded. He was too hung over to argue, so he pulled his feet in, and Rachel slammed the door.

When she slid behind the steering wheel and started the car, he asked nervously, "What are you going to do?"

"You'll see," she warned as she turned the car around and started down the street.

"Rachel, what are you going to do?" Collins demanded, his nervousness turned to panic now.

Rachel stared straight ahead in stoney silence until she

had maneuvered the car onto the freeway and was driving at high speed. Then she glanced over at him and spat out, "I'm going to deliver you to your wife!"

The taxi driver arrived at the condominium just as she pulled into the parking lot. When she reached Collins' condominium, she slammed on the brakes, jumped out and yelled at the taxi driver, "I'll be right with you!"

Then she jerked open the passenger door of Collins' car and commanded, "Get out!"

"Rachel, please, let me—"

"Get out, Collins!"

Reluctantly he stood up, but he was so unstable he had to steady himself for a moment by clinging to the car.

When she saw that he had his balance, she ordered, "Walk!" and pointed to the front door. He began to shuffle along, but he was too slow for her taste, so she grabbed his arm and dragged him to the door. Once there, she rang the doorbell.

Several minutes later the door was opened, and there stood Shawna. Her expression turned to terror.

"Don't worry, Shawna," Rachel spoke with detached coolness, "I'm not here to claw your eyes out. I wouldn't risk breaking a fingernail on the likes of you! You want to be Mrs. Collins Greyson? Fine! Here's your husband!" She shoved Collins at Shawna, turned her back, and walked away.

When she reached the taxi cab, the driver was standing by the passenger door. "What's going on?" he demanded.

"Nothing," Rachel responded nonchalantly as he opened the door for her. "Just delivering some drunk home."

The driver closed the door, hurried around to the other side and started the cab. "Where to, Lady?"

Rachel gave him her address, and he drove her out of

the condominium complex. She didn't look back. Collins had done enough this time. She was finished.

On the way home she thought over the names of lawyers she knew and settled on one to handle the divorce for her.

When she entered her house, the phone was ringing. It was the secretary of the Education Deparment at the university; she had forgotten all about her classes, and her colleagues were worried about her. Mentioning only the trouble with her car, she reassured the secretary she would be in as soon as possible. When she hung up, she called the local garage to come start her car. Then she called and made an appointment with the lawyer she had chosen.

Finally there was nothing left to do but wait for the auto mechanic. Standing next to the phone, she surveyed the den where an hour before she had still been able to find love in her heart for Collins. It looked perfectly normal to her except for the large water spots on the couch. But they were drying fast.

By the time the mechanic came to look at her car, she was eager to get to work. She definitely did not want to stay home and think. Reassured that her car only needed a new battery and would be in working order by 5:00, she called a taxi and rode to the university. On the way she made up her mind that she would absolutely refuse to be upset or to break down in any way. She was determined that her professional life would go on. I must make this work, she insisted, it's all I have left now. Collins can never mean anything to me again. Never! Oh why do I feel so numb about that when I should be so determined? she demanded and then answered her own question.

It takes a long time for loss to sink in, to be felt. I should know that from living through Justin's death. Rachel shuddered. My little brother and Viet Nam. Tragedy guaranteed. Justin dead, mother breaking down. Seven years ago I stood by that gaping hole in the red clay of Louisiana and watched it swallow up Justin's coffin. The soldiers folded the flag that covered the coffin and gave it to me. I will never forget the feeling of that cloth in my hands as I heard the first clods of clay hit the top of the coffin. And there was Daddy, watching silently, broken-hearted but proud. Very proud. I stepped toward him, "This belongs to you." I shoved that taut bundle of flag into his diaphragm. "Take it! You killed him for it. You sacrificed him to uphold your D'Evereau pride!"

Stop it! Rachel reined in her thoughts. What are you doing? Trying to kill yourself? It was a long time ago. Leave it there. Forget them. You don't need them! This is now, and you have to do something about Collins. You can't go on in this marriage.

Two days later she saw the divorce lawyer and instructed him to keep it simple. "I want nothing that belongs to Collins," she explained. "I simply want you to see to it that he gets nothing of mine."

"Are you sure, Rachel? Your husband is a very wealthy man," the lawyer argued.

"Only I know what my husband is worth," she responded coldly, "and I tell you he has nothing I want."

"Very well," the lawyer agreed reluctantly.

Rachel rose to go but turned back. "There is one other thing. I want this settled with all possible haste. I want the papers delivered to him immediately. Here is his current address." She handed him a piece of paper.

"Well, these things take time—"

"If you can't find the time," Rachel interrupted him, "just say so, and I will find someone who can."

The lawyer studied the granite woman in front of him, then asked, "Will, say, next Friday be soon enough?"

"Perfect."

# TWO

The next week was the final week of the semester for Rachel. She loved her job as a professor of education because it enabled her to spend so much time in elementary school classrooms. As she observed her own students teaching the children, she had many happy hours with the youngsters. Rachel loved children, but she had never been able to have her own.

The final week was always a frantic one with exams to be given, papers to be graded, forms to be filled in. It was all part of ending a semester's work. This particular semester the pace was welcomed by Rachel; it helped her keep her mind off her personal life.

Finally Saturday morning dawned, and with it came graduation ceremonies. Once again she donned her doctoral robe and mortar board, marched solemnly down the aisle of the auditorium with her colleagues, and helped another class of seniors start the transition from college to the world.

At the end of the morning's ceremonies, as she stood next to her car and slipped out of her robe, she felt a tremendous relief flood over her. Relief and pride. She had made it. Through the most difficult circumstances imaginable she had managed to do her job and do it well. In the face of her loss, this one triumph was her life preserver. It convinced her she could go on.

Colleagues waved and called out good wishes for the summer as she slipped into the car and started it up. A whole summer ahead! Three months to rest, to heal, to start over. Strange, she thought as she drove toward her house, I haven't even thought of how I should fill the next three months. Where do I start? She pondered various things she needed to do, decisions she had to make. When she saw her house, she chided herself aloud. "That can all wait until Monday, Rachel. At least until Monday! Right now you're going for a swim and get a start on a suntan. You're free, for heaven's sake!" The thought was so delightful she dashed across the lawn to the front porch.

Collins staggered up from a bench and confronted her. "I want to talk to you!" he growled as he swayed in front of her.

"We have nothing to talk about," Rachel turned cold the moment she saw him.

"I said I want to talk to you," Collins shouted as he grabbed her arm.

Rachel stared at him for a long moment. He was obviously drunk, too drunk to control his behavior, and she was in no mood for a public scene. "All right," she agreed, "but not here and keep it short and to the point."

She led the way into the house as Collins shuffled along behind. He reeks of alcohol, Rachel thought as fury once again mounted in her. He obviously shouldn't be driving. How on earth am I going to get him home? She threw her graduation robe on a chair as her anger escalated. Home? she demanded of herself. Home? What home? Shawna's? Is that his home? She resolved to march straight to the phone and call a taxi to take him to Shawna's, and she was on her way to do just that when Collins grabbed her arm and swung her around.

"There'll be no divorce!" he shouted. "No divorce! Do you hear me? No divorce!"

"I am not deaf, Collins! Quit shouting!" She shook her arm loose from his grip, and he staggered slightly. "There *will* be a divorce, and there's no way you can stop it."

"I said no divorce!" Collins yelled at her again.

"What difference does it make to you anyway?" Rachel demanded. "You have Shawna. I'm not taking one penny of your money. So what do you care?"

"I'll tell you why I care," he lunged at her, grabbed both her arms, and held her in a painful, steely grip.

"Let go of me! You're hurting me!" she yelled at him as she struggled to free herself, but his grip was firm. Slowly he pulled her closer as he stared down at her through hate-filled eyes.

"There will be no divorce, my darling Rachel," he snarled, "I won't allow it—no woman leaves me! Besides, I don't want my family upset. No one has ever been divorced in my family. I'm not going to be the first."

"You should have thought of that before you started your affair with Shawna. I didn't leave you. You left me when you took up with Shawna and all the others before her! I *am* divorcing you!"

Instead of arguing more, he shook her violently as he repeated, "No divorce! No divorce!"

Then suddenly he turned loose of her and staggered toward the door. She felt as limp as a wilted flower as her head reeled from the shaking. Even so, her brain was functioning enough to remember that he couldn't possibly drive in his condition.

"Wait, Collins! Stop!" she cried out. "You can't go! Not like this!" She forced her legs to scramble toward him until she stood in his path, blocking him from reaching the door.

"Get out of the way!" he snarled.

"No!" Rachel insisted sharply as she grabbed his arm.

Then she intentionally lowered her voice so he wouldn't bolt. "No, Collins, wait." Her mind was racing, I have to keep him out of the car. I have to stop him. I'll get him to sit down, and I'll call a taxi. "Come sit down—"

"I don't want to sit down!" He yelled as he wrestled to free himself from her grip.

"Collins! You can't go—not like this. You're too drunk to drive!"

"Too drunk!" he exploded. "Too drunk!" he wrenched himself free.

"Please!" Rachel begged as she grabbed him again.

"Drop dead, Rachel!" he yelled as he threw her across the room and staggered out.

Her body landed on the soft carpet, but her left temple struck the corner of the glass coffee table. Slowly her head also sank to the carpet, where it lay motionless as a pool of blood grew around it.

When Rachel regained consciousness, her neighbor Jean was leaning over her. "Don't try to move," she ordered gently. "We've called an ambulance."

Rachel felt herself swimming in and out of consciousness. When once again Jean's face appeared, she asked, "Who did this to you?"

Rachel tried to answer, but her lips wouldn't move. Finally she struggled one word out. "Accident."

"Accident?" Jean demanded quietly. "Are you sure it was an accident? I better call someone in your family."

"No! Don't call my family! It was just Collins, drunk," she murmured, as she slipped back into unconsciousness.

❧❧

When she next awoke, it was her father's face she saw. Surely I'm dreaming, she thought as her eyelids closed involuntarily and she slept again. However, when she opened her eyes again, her father, Jack D'Evereau, was still there, leaning over her bed.

"Hello, Baby," he whispered. "Everything's fine. You're going to be okay. You just had a nasty blow to your head, but the doctor says there's nothing to worry about."

"Daddy?" she whispered. "Is that really you?"

"Sure is," he took her hand. "That neighbor of yours called me, and I drove right up. Now don't worry. She's filled me in on all the details, so don't you try to talk. The doctor says you must lie still and sleep. Everything's being taken care of. Nothing to worry about."

"Collins?" she questioned weakly.

"Everything's taken care of, Baby. Just sleep."


When she stirred again, she felt someone jump to the side of the bed, and there was her father's face again. "How you feeling?" he questioned softly.

"Bit of a headache," she murmured. Then she smiled sheepishly, "And I'm hungry."

"Now that's what I call good news!" her father responded enthusiastically as he reached for the intercom button next to her bed.

She closed her eyes and rested as she listened to the nurse speak over the intercom and heard her father order some food. A doctor came in and looked her over and pronounced her much better, and then the food arrived. It was undoubtedly the worst tasting gruel imaginable, but it was warm and filling. And after another short nap she awoke with more strength. This time she found her father sitting by the side of the bed in a chair he had dragged across the room. He smiled, but there was a strange feebleness about it that she didn't understand.

"Daddy, what's wrong?" Rachel turned her head further to the side and winced from the pain.

"Does it hurt, Baby?" He jumped up and stood by the bed. "Do you want me to call the nurse?"

"No, no, it's fine. But you're not fine. What's wrong?"

"Nothing's wrong," he insisted lamely. "You're going to be fine and—"

Suddenly there was a loud, female voice intruding from the hall. "I insist on seeing Rachel!" the woman demanded. "Do you know who I am, young woman?" Rachel immediately recognized her mother-in-law's voice. "I will *not* be prevented from seeing her—not by anyone. Get out of my way this instant!"

Before her words had ceased, Rachel's father had dashed to the door and disappeared. An excruciating anxiety seized Rachel; she was certain something was horribly wrong. Helen Greyson's hysterical, insistent voice continued, only this time she was arguing with Jack D'Evereau. Rachel tried to lift her head, but the stabbing pain was agonizing, and she was forced to give up the effort and lie still. She strained to hear what was being said.

"Not now, Helen!"·she heard her father's voice raised above Helen's. "I won't allow it!" he insisted as his voice drifted away, and Rachel realized he was moving away from the door. Then there was silence again. Silence except for the pounding of Rachel's heart.

When he returned, he smiled with a false ease. "Nothing to worry about," he waved his hand as if to dismiss the whole affair. "You know how pushy Helen can be. I just didn't think you needed to see anyone—"

"Daddy!" Rachel interrupted him. "What's wrong? What's happened? Why are you here?"

"Well, Baby, I'm here because I'm your father," he began feebly, "so, of course, they called—"

"I want to sit up," she suddenly announced.

"Now, Rachel, there's no need to excite yourself—"

"Help me sit up! Where are the controls on this bed?" she tried to turn her head to the side to look for them, but pain exploded over her left eye and her hand instinctively went to the bandaged spot.

"It's not good for you to sit up, Rachel," her father pleaded with her. "Please. Just lie still."

"If you don't help me, I'll do it myself!" she shot back at him.

"You're a D'Evereau, all right, as stubborn as the rest of us," he sounded irritated. "I don't know why that should surprise me though," he added more gently, even proudly, "you always were!"

"Daddy! the controls!"

"Okay, okay. Let me figure this thing out." Slowly he fumbled with buttons until he found the right one. Then he put her hand on it. Resolutely she pushed it and manipulated the bed into a partial sitting position. Then she closed her eyes, gripped the blanket, and waited for the pain to subside. When she opened them again, she was able to look him directly in the face.

"Now, what is going on?" she demanded. "In the name of mercy just give it to me straight and quick."

He nodded and came and sat gently on the side of the bed. Picking up her hand, he squeezed it tightly and looked her straight in the eyes. "Collins is dead," he said quietly, but quickly. "He was killed in a car accident, apparently right after he left the house."

Rachel stared at him in stunned silence. Suddenly she sobbed out, "I tried to stop him! I tried! I tried to stop him! I knew he couldn't drive. He was too drunk. I tried to stop him!"

"I believe you, Baby, I'm sure you did!" Jack's voice cracked from his distress as Rachel continued sobbing. "Is that how you got hurt?" he finally managed to ask.

"Yes," she choked out. "I grabbed his arm—he was so

drunk, Daddy! I grabbed his arm, and he pushed me away, and I fell. I don't remember the rest. But I did try to stop him! I begged him not to go like that!"

"Okay, Baby, okay," Jack soothed her the best he could. "It's done. You did the best you could. This wasn't the first time he got drunk. You tried for years to get him to get help."

"He wouldn't let me help him!" Rachel clutched her father's hand with both of hers and sat up, her grief completely blocking her physical pain. "I tried and tried, but he wouldn't do anything about it!"

"I know, Baby. Don't think about it now," he tried to ease her back on the pillow. "You must lie still. Please lie still."

"But there's more, Daddy," she continued sobbing as she clutched his hands more frantically and refused to lie back. "There was a woman—Shawna."

"A woman?"

"I found out by accident. He was living with her—"

"Okay, now that's enough, Rachel!" Jack firmly forced her back on the pillow. "You can't afford to get any more upset. I insist you lie quietly and let me take care of—"

"But, Daddy, what about Collins? I have to do—"

"You don't have to do anything! I'll take care of—"

"I want to talk to you, Rachel!" Helen Greyson shouted from the doorway. "My son is dead because of you."

"Get out of here this instant, Helen!" Jack commanded as he bounded toward her.

"She killed my son!"

"That's not true!" Rachel tried to sit up again, but her pain overcame her, and she sank back helplessly.

Suddenly a nurse appeared. She took Helen by the arm and steered her outside the door while Jack rushed to Rachel's side and tried to calm her.

"I'll handle this, Rachel," Jack announced. "You are to rest. You know the truth. I know the truth. Helen will know the truth in a minute. And as far as I am concerned, you certainly have no further obligation to Collins Greyson. It is up to the Greysons to take care of him.

In the end the Greysons did a fine job of taking care of Collins. They managed to cover up his affair with Shawna and the fact that he was drunk when he died. The newspapers reported only an unfortunate accident that resulted from a blow-out of a tire on Collins' car and took the life of one of the city's most prominent citizens.

Much against Jack's will, Rachel attended the funeral, heavily veiled to conceal the bandage on her head. Jack stood at one elbow and Jean at another as they physically supported her. Everyone attributed the shakiness of her actions to her extreme grief.

As soon as it was all over, Jack took Rachel to her childhood home in Pineview, Texas, where she found a stack of condolence cards. The newspaper in Pineview had reprinted the account from the city paper, and the kind people of the small East Texas town were eager to support one of their own in her time of grief.

# THREE

Rachel's first week in her parents' home, her childhood home, was the longest week of her life. It was an endless agony of self-doubt and grief.

In spite of her years devoted to loving Collins regardless of his weaknesses for alcohol and other women, in the end he had devalued her totally. Losing her in a divorce meant no more to him than losing a possession. The thoughts whirled in her mind. Yes! Yes! I was often furious with him. I was no saint—I know that, but I did stand by him! I deserved more from our marriage. Now there is no remedy. I can never regain his love. I can never revenge my honor. He is dead. I hate him. I love him. And there is no remedy for either.

So she hurt. And she was confused. How *should* she feel about a dead husband whom she had loved, a dead husband who had betrayed her? Should she mourn him? Hate him?

She took the pills the doctor had given her, and she slept. Her life became a bizarre ritual. When she was awake, she sat on the windowseat in her childhood bedroom and agonized. When her father interrupted her, she stared at him while he talked and ate the food that Florence, the old, white-haired cook, brought in.

She said nothing. Nothing. He talked of her future. She was caught in her past. What could she say?

When he left, she took a pill to sleep, to escape. Sometimes she heard her mother, Patsy Longwood D'Evereau, fluttering outside the door whining, "What's going to become of us? What will people think if they find out?"

"Leave her alone, Patsy!" her father commanded. "She'll pull out of it. She's a D'Evereau!"

"But what will people think if they find out? What will they think?"

"I don't care what people think! She's my daughter! She's your daughter!"

And then her mother's tone would change to a resolute one, and Rachel's heart filled with love. "I must do something to help her! I must do something!" Then the confusion that over the years had slowly crept into Patsy's thinking would overcome her, and Rachel's heart grieved as her mother cried, "Oh! I can't think what I should do! I know I should do something, but I can't think!" Rachel could see her wringing her hands as clearly as if a heavy paneled door didn't stand between them.

"Stay away from her!" Jack ordered. "You're not good for her, Patsy. You're too upset."

"But I should do something! I should talk to her. I just know I should, but I don't know what to say!"

"I absolutely forbid you to bother her!"

"Oh! What will people think if they find out?" Their voices faded. Whether they had moved away from the door or Rachel was slipping into sleep, she never knew. Or cared.

Often, in a near-awake state, she heard two female voices close by the bed. Again it was her mother's voice, only these times the desperate whine in her mother's voice was whispered. "She simply can't stay here, Mammy Cassie! She just can't! Someone is sure to find out! Collins, a drunk all those years—another woman—this is a small town—they'll blame Rachel—if only she'd been a better wife—"

"Now don't you go making yourself sick again, Miz Patsy. She ain't gonna stay." Mammy Cassie's voice rose above the whine as she comforted the child she had raised from infancy, the fifty-eight-year-old child.

"How could she do such a thing to me?" Patsy suddenly demanded angrily. "I don't care what Jack says. She wasn't just some innocent bystander. She must have known what was going on. She must have driven Collins to another woman! How could my own daughter do such a thing to me?"

"She got the devil in her, just like I always told you," Mammy Cassie spoke with total authority. "She been trouble from the day she borned. And she always gonna be trouble." Even through her closed eyelids, Rachel could see the huge woman's fiery eyes and grim, angry face. Those furious eyes had flashed at her for as long as she could remember. A few pills could never block out that hatred.

"Oh whatever will I do!" Patsy worried aloud.

"Now don't you go getting all upset. You knows I's gonna take care of you. I always takes care of you. Ain't nothing changed. She ain't gonna stay. I gonna see to that!"

Then they too went away. And Rachel's only other conscious experience was of kindly old Florence sitting on the side of the bed and spooning warm liquids into Rachel's mouth. She always whispered the simplest, most heart-felt assurances, but she spoke as quietly as possible, and Rachel understood, even in her drugged state, that Florence had sneaked in with the broth. That was just like her. She had never had many words, so she lovingly made food to comfort with. And she had always managed to deliver it to Rachel one way or the other. No one would have ever guessed she was Mammy Cassie's sister. Or at least her half-sister. No one could be sure of more than that.

Naturally when Rachel emerged from her room for the first time, it was to Florence's kitchen that she took her shaky self one late afternoon. Florence was busy frying chicken for supper, but she took one took at Rachel, clapped her thick hands in delight and exclaimed, "My, my! Look at you! You's a sight for sore eyes!" Then she rushed to pull a chair out so Rachel could settle at the table, but Rachel took her hand and stopped her.

"I came to say thank you for all you've done, Florence."

The old woman's eyes dropped to the floor shyly. "It weren't nothing, Miz Rachel—"

"It was everything," Rachel cut her off emphatically, "it was love, and that's the best medicine of all. Thank you."

Florence's bent head gave the slightest nod of acceptance before her face bobbed up and she announced, "What you needs is a nice cup of tea!" Her heavy hand pulled out the kitchen chair and patted the seat. "You just sit a spell, and I's gonna make you a nice cup of tea!" She turned toward the stove, calling back over her shoulder delightedly, "And thank the Lord I just this minute pulled Mr. Jack's favorite pumpkin bread outta the oven. You gonna have a piece of that too. Why it still warm enough to melt butter!"

"Sounds wonderful!" Rachel responded happily. As soon as the words were out, she felt a strange movement in her face. For a moment it puzzled her. Then she recognized it. It's a smile, she thought, and it feels good. It's been a long time. She slowly surveyed the sunny, old-fashioned kitchen, remembering so many happy childhood and adolescent moments here, and her smile grew and deepened.

"I knowed Mr. Jack weren't in the house the minute I pulled this here pumpkin bread outta the oven," Florence announced. Then she turned to Rachel with a sparkle in her eyes and asked, "Guess how I knowed?"

"Because he didn't come running in for a piece," Rachel answered immediately. It was a long-standing joke between them that Jack could smell Florence's pumpkin bread a mile away.

"That's right!" Florence exclaimed as if they hadn't played this scene since Rachel was a tiny child, and they both dissolved into laughter. "Why he ain't even on the estate!" Florence chuckled while Rachel allowed her adult laughter to turn into her former girlish giggle. Oh it did feel good to laugh!

"Victoria Rachélle!" her mother burst through the swinging door from the dining room. "What have you done?" she demanded. "How dare you put me in such a position? How dare you?"

Rachel stared up at her mother's scarlet face and flashing eyes. "Mother—"

"Don't you 'mother' me! You're no child of mine! You don't care about me!"

"That's the truth if I ever heared it!" Mammy Cassie appeared behind Patsy and joined in. "She ain't never cared about nobody but herself."

"Well, what have you go to say for yourself?" Patsy demanded.

"I can't say anything until—"

"She can't say nothing cause they's nothing to say," Mammy Cassie stepped forward and glowered down at Rachel. "This just like her. She ain't changed a bit. Never gonna change. She borned a devil child and she gonna stay that way."

Rachel stood, turned her back on Mammy Cassie and demanded of her mother, "What are you talking about? What is going on?"

"I'll tell you what is going on, young lady! Thanks to you, I'm ruined in this town. I just received the most humiliating call of my life! Allison Clark, president of the Pineview Garden Club and one of the biggest gossips in town, called me up and asked me if my only daughter, my flesh and blood, had a drunk for a husband who was living with another woman."

"Mother, I did the best I could. Maybe I could have—"

"How could you do this to me? Your own mother? Everyone who is anyone in this town will know by nightfall. I'm disgraced. Utterly ruined!" Suddenly Patsy's face blanched, and she slumped into Mammy Cassie's arms. "Oh Mammy! I feel faint, and my head is simply pounding. It's one of my migraines. I just know it is. I must have the doctor!"

Mammy Cassie glared over Patsy's carefully coiffured curls at Rachel. "I hope you's finally happy. You ain't been home even one week but you's gone and made your mother sick again. Just like you always does. Just like you gonna do the rest of your life!"

Something clicked deep inside Rachel's mind. A buried memory, too bitterly painful to endure at the conscious level, signaled her most basic instinct—survival. As her mother held her head and moaned, Rachel bolted out the screen door. Without a pause, she sprinted across the back lawn and plunged into the woods.

She fled.

At the age of thirty-five she fled her mother's words and Mammy Cassie's indictment as desperately, as angrily as she had when she was a child. She sped through the trees, crushing pine needles and snapping twigs under her feet, until her stinging lungs and hammering heart forced her to stop. Collapsing onto the soft, moist bed of decaying pine needles, she turned onto her back, gasped for air and squeezed her eyelids shut to block out the whirling world her dizzy eyes perceived.

Finally she normalized her breathing, and when she opened her eyes, the ancient pines were standing still. Limply, her recently injured head pounding, she dragged herself to the base of one of the huge pines and propped herself up. She held her head in her hands until the throbbing ceased. Then she dropped her hands to the ground beside her. Her right hand felt the prickle of brittle pine needles, but her left hand landed on something billowy and soft. Slowly she looked down her left arm, and there they were.

Violets. Wood violets growing at the base of the pine. A shaft of afternoon sunlight illuminated them as she watched, and to her amazement and delight the blossoms turned to brilliant amethysts right before her eyes. She leaned over and cupped them in her hands as gently as she could and buried her face in them. They were the perfect healing balm for her soul. She lay there and held them and remembered.

❧❧

She remembered a day from her fifth year, a day of confusion, of anger, of deep hurt. A day much like today, a day she had forgotten until now, until she needed to remember it.

It had started out so badly and continued so painfully that by early afternoon she was a pressure cooker whose steam had been forced to rise beyond its capacity until finally the lid asserted its independence and blew completely off, bouncing violently off the ceiling and spewing boiling liquid everywhere. And so she ran away from home. She ran into the piney woods and recklessly threw herself on the thick bed of needles beneath the trees, and with all the strength in her five-year-old body she pounded the ground with her clenched fists, kicked furiously, and screamed, "I hate them! I hate them all!"

And she did! Oh, how she hated them! Finally though the force of her anger, as well as her tiny body, were exhausted, and she lay there quietly, weeping and hating herself for the tears she couldn't control. She felt totally helpless, absolutely vulnerable to those who had injured her.

Finally she stopped, all cried out, and rolling over and sitting up in the cloud of mahogany-colored pine dust she had created, she gazed down through swollen eyes at her pink organdy, lace-trimmed pinafore and white shoes and socks—the Sunday uniform of the affluent little girl of that day. A scowl of hatred reshaped her face as she recognized the link between her clothing and the despised adult world she intended to leave behind. Suddenly she jumped to her feet and began trying to tear off her dress, but there were endless buttons and sashes trapping her inside the despised clothes. Struggling more furiously, as if the clothes were suddenly on fire, she finally ripped free of the dainty ruffles. Next she forced off her shoes without bothering to unbuckle them, jerked off her socks and sent every piece of the hated uniform flying into the woods. Only one link of the chain remained; she ripped the pink taffeta ribbon out of her hair and viciously ground it into the pine needles with her bare foot.

There she stood in the dark coolness of the woods—a tiny girl clad in a simple white slip with her tangle of golden curls covering her shoulders. Her dark blue eyes were once again running over with tears, which she indignantly brushed away with her dust-covered hand, but her jaw was locked in a posture of determination. "I won't go back home—not ever!" she screamed at the towering trees, her arms rigidly locked at her sides, each one ending in a clenched fist. "I will go far, far away!" While she spit out her verbal defiance at the trees, she whirled around in a circle as if she were surrounded by enemies and determined to face them head-on as they attacked. "I will live in the woods and never talk to anyone again—never ever again!" In short, as she planned it, she would be free of them, safe from them.

Resolved in her plan, she chose the direction that would lead her farthest from home and began to march into the woods. Quickly the woods became more impenetrable; undaunted, she scrambled over moss-covered, fallen trees that felt to her hands like moist velvet and forced her way through imprisoning undergrowth with the determination of a foot soldier on manuveurs.

Although she was quickly distancing herself from her house, physical distance did not lessen the emotional impact the day had had on here. Her mind was assaulted by adult voices, a chaotic collage of voices, the confusing and destructive adult voices that reminded her of the day's events. They ran together in a painful jumble, humming around inside her head like a determined mosquito after blood: "That's Daddy's girl—don't you look pretty!" "You's a child of the devil—I knowed it the minute you's borned." "Jesus loves the little children." "Don't upset your mother!" "You must be washed in the blood of the lamb!"

Hounded by the haunting voices and confused by the conflicting messages, with renewed franticness Victoria Rachélle forced her way through the dense pine trees and undergrowth, oblivious to the briars that tore at her legs and to the branches of saplings slapping her face. Laboring to breathe now, she hurried through the humid warmth, but no amount of speed could silence the voices in her head. The faster she moved, the more fervent, the more demanding the voices became until finally they escalated into a shrill babble and became a maddening shorthand swimming in her head, commanding her attention. "A child of the devil—Daddy's girl—washed in the blood of the lamb—don't upset your mother—Jesus loves—child of the devil—upset your mother—blood of the lamb—devil child—mother—Jesus—Daddy—blood!" Maddened by the babble, Victoria Rachélle slammed her hands over her ears, screamed "No!" and desperately plunging forward, broke through the last of the undergrowth and fell forward on her knees.

When she stood again and gazed around, she was surprised by the openness of the terrain. She saw a wide creek in front of her—sparkling and inviting. Exhausted by her emotional torture as well as her physical journey, she stumbled into the shallow, rushing water, sat down on the creek bed and splashed the cool water all over herself. It felt wonderful! And happily the shock of the coolness against her feverish face chased all the voices away.

It was over—this time. The anguish, the frustration, the fury—all were gone. They had washed out of her and disappeared downstream with the moving water. Victoria Rachélle fell over on her right side, her right elbow burrowed into the fine sand on the creek bed, and she tiredly propped her head on her right hand and let the water run over her body, cooling, calming, cleansing her. Her mind was blank except for its recording of her sensory responses.

Time passed. Pine trees undulated in the breeze high over her golden head, wood ferns at the edge of the creek gently swayed with the water's movement, and the clear, healing water eddied around and over Victoria Rachélle's trance-like body, massaging her and then moving on downstream. Her breathing slowed; her expression lost its burden of pain; she was in control again. She sighed loudly and began to piece together and to try to understand the events of the day.

The day the five-year-old Victoria Rachélle was reliving as she sat in the creek was a Sunday, a day of enforced formality at the D'Evereau house. Thus, it was the most potentially disastrous day of the week for an exuberant little girl. It was a day of rigid decorum, a day when breaking the rules of conduct and dress was not merely a social disgrace; it was also an affront to Almighty God Himself.

Furthermore, in Patsy's belief system there was a non-debatable connection between the cost and elegance of one's Sunday dress and the degree to which one was worshipping God. For a rambunctious five-year-old like Victoria Rachélle, who was more energy and motion than physical form, the whole process of Sunday dressing was incalculably tedious.

However, she endured all the required primping as patiently as possible for its one bright spot—the moment she entered the living room and her daddy turned to her and said, "That's Daddy's girl—don't you look pretty!" He always said exactly the same thing in exactly the same way, but its predictability in no way lessened its impact on Victoria Rachélle. This weekly moment was the highlight of her life, for she craved her father's attention, and he only noticed her on two occasions—when she was dressed from head to toe in ruffles and when she had upset her mother again. Victoria Rachélle much preferred the first of these two possible occasions.

On this particular Sunday she had stood patiently—at least she thought so—in front of the full-length mirror in her room while Mammy Cassie jerked her around as she irritably decked her out with starched, pink, organdy ruffles and lace.

"Stand up straight and quit your jiggling, child! You

knows your mother's gonna have a hissy if this here sash ain't just right." Having finally tied the sash to her practiced eye's satisfacion, she reached for the hairbrush and began to untangle Victoria Rachélle's mane of golden curls. "Lordy! I ain't never seed so much hair in all my borned days—not even on a growed person. If you was mine, which you ain't, thank the Lord, I'd cut it all right off. Stand still—don't you go figgeting now. I knows your tricks, Missy. I knowed you since you was borned, and you's a bad one. Just let me get this here hair bow tied so's I can get rid of you and go help your mother. She ain't never dressed herself in her whole life without me a-helping her."

After what seemed an eternity to the child, she was finally dressed to Mammy Cassie's satisfaction and allowed to leave the room. She promptly bolted out the door with Mammy Cassie fussing after her in a rising voice, "Don't you go to getting messed up now, you hear?" But it was the standard warning, and Victoria Rachélle was too eager to join her father in the living room to listen.

As usual, her father, already immaculately groomed and very handsome, was standing in front of the living room mantel reading the Sunday paper when she skipped in so covered with pink ruffles that she looked like pink cotton candy come to life. "Hi, Daddy!" she sang out eagerly. He lowered the paper, eyed her at first critically and then approvingly and finally made his usual pronouncement, "That's Daddy's girl—don't you look pretty!" Victoria Rachélle beamed up at him, glorying in his attention and approval, while she turned daintily around, just as her mother had taught her to do, so he could admire her from all sides.

"That's a pretty dress," he declared, "where did you get such a pretty dress, Baby?"

Victoria Rachélle cocked her head to the side quizically.

"From you Daddy, for my birthday, don't you remember?" There was a tiny sadness sprouting in her.

He was silent for a very long moment, but soon he gaily answered, "Well, Baby, that dress looks a hundred times better with you in it than it did in the box—I almost didn't recognize it!" Victoria Rachélle beamed, happily accepting this explanation rather than concluding that he had forgotten her birthday dress.

Her smile, however, was not returned. Something obviously was troubling him. A crease was appearing between his eyebrows, and his thick, black moustache had swallowed up his smiling teeth. He looked down at her gravely.

"Now, Victoria Rachélle, I want you to be very careful not to upset your mother today. Don't do anything to make her unhappy—okay?" After further thought, he added more plaintively, "Will you do that for me, Baby?"

Thus, what had begun as a stern warning from a strong man to a little girl had turned into a plea for help in the face of a possible disaster. Instinctively Victoria Rachélle recognized the worry and need in her father's voice. She replied quietly, "Okay, Daddy," and walked over and slipped her hand into his. She wanted to express the comradeship she felt and her desire to help, but he was staring grimly out the window, and the crease between his brows had become a furrow. When he didn't look down at her again or take notice of her hand in his, she knew their weekly visit was over, and it was time for her to leave. "Can I go out on the porch and play till time for church?" she asked quietly, as she withdrew her hand.

Still he did not look at her. "Okay, Baby, but stay clean. And remember what I said about your mother." Victoria Rachélle reluctantly drifted out of the room, wistfully glancing back at him as she skimmed her hand along the shiny, polished surfaces of the tables on her way.

The front porch of the D'Evereau house was one of

Victoria Rachélle's favorite places to play; it was spacious and airy and full of wicker furniture. She had spent many a delighted hour fantasizing there and creating all the playmates she wanted. Today, however, all those starched, pink ruffles hindered her. At first she sat primly on one of the wicker chairs and swung her feet back and forth under the chair; however, this amusement lost its simple appeal quickly, and soon she sighed heavily. It seemed to her she spent her entire life waiting for her mother to get dressed.

To a five-year-old, any movement is preferable to the dreariness of waiting, and it quickly became obvious to Victoria Rachélle that she couldn't sit there any longer; her mind wanted stimulation, and her body demanded movement. Standing up and looking back over her shoulder through the screen door into the dark, empty hall, she determined that her mother was nowhere in sight and no one would notice if she slipped over to the kennels to see her Daddy's hunting dogs, those cheerful, barking friends of hers.

She scurried down the front steps, and furtively looking over her shoulder, she hurried around the side of the house and over to the stable area. There she encountered not only six joyous hounds but also a quagmire of red mud created by a recent East Texas thunderstorm. The result on Victoria Rachélle's carefully polished, white shoes was predictable and quickly manifested itself. When she heard her father's irritated call from the front porch and began racing to the house, her legs suddenly felt weighted with lead. She glanced down at her feet and halted in dismay. Her dainty white pumps were caked with thick, red clay; in fact, the mud had so thickened the soles of her shoes that Victoria Rachélle was suddenly two inches taller.

"Oh no! Daddy's gonna be mad—what am I gonna do?" She was panicky, it was true, but Victoria Rachélle could always be counted on to be resourceful. Today was no exception. Quickly she slipped out of her shoes, hid them under the shrubbery at the side of the house and raced to the front sidewalk wearing only her white socks. A quick glance up revealed her father standing on the porch, three feet off the ground, towering over her like a glowering, but well-dressed giant.

She dropped her gaze to her white socks; then slowly, cautiously she raised her eyes up the stairs one by one, pausing at the top of each. She stopped totally when her gaze reached his shoes. Swallowing hard, finally she summoned her courage and continued up the length of his body to his neck where once again her fear stopped her. At last she gathered the remainder of her strength and willed her eyes to slip upward again to his face. Tentatively, cautiously she tried to read his expression. His heavy black mustache was drooping at the ends, a sure and unsettling sign of his displeasure with her, but when her gaze finally reached his blue eyes, she knew he was only mildly annoyed.

"Where have you been? Are you ready to go? Get in the car! Your mother is dressed at last!" His words were piled on top of one another so quickly she knew she needn't respond. So she turned, scooted across the few feet of lawn between the house and the circular drive, and jumped into the back seat of the shiny black Cadillac. Saul, the driver and gardener, was waiting to drive them to church.

Immediately Patsy, followed by the hovering Mammy Cassie, made her grand entrance on the porch. She put her graceful, perfectly manicured hand around her husband's extended arm, paused at the top of the stairs like a perpetual debutant making perpetual entrances into perpetual presentation balls, smiled sweetly at the world, and elegantly descended the stairs. The debutant performance would have been perfect except she was visibly pregnant.

Jack placed his wife in the back seat with the care he would use in handling fine china, solicitously helping her settle in, and joined Saul in the front. Victoria Rachélle was carefully sitting on her feet, busily pretending to look out the opposite window.

They made it almost to the gates of the drive before Victoria Rachélle's feet began to tingle, then feel like needles and pins were sticking into them. Finally, in desperation, regardless of the cost, she had to stick them out straight in front of her.

## FOUR

The D'Evereaus continued their drive to church as Victoria-Rachélle studiously avoided looking down at her shoeless feet, fearful she would draw her mother's attention to them. However, there was no escape for Victoria Rachélle. A moment later, Patsy casually glanced down, and a cloud passed over her face. Her isn't-it-a-wonderful-world smile vanished as she shrilly demanded of her daughter, "Victoria Rachélle! Where in the name of heaven are your shoes?"

Victoria Rachélle looked down at her extended, offending feet and tried to express genuine surprise that they were shoeless. "Jack!" Patsy shouted in a tone that would have been perfect if she had suddenly found a snake in the backseat with her, "Victoria Rachélle has no shoes on!"

Certain his wife was overreacting as usual, Jack quietly sighed, assuming that he would once again have to assert his firm male authority to straighten out the females of his family. Without even turning his head, he quietly ordered, "Victoria Rachélle, put your shoes on!"

"I can't, Daddy," was the quiet reply from the heap of pink ruffles and golden hair that was his daughter.

"Of course you can," he answered, still looking out the front window, refusing absolutely to have a crisis on this peaceful Sunday morning. A shiver of fear shook Victoria Rachélle for she knew that nothing annoyed her father more than being late for a social engagement, and since he was himself a Catholic, attendance at the First Baptist Church of Pineview, Texas was merely a social occasion.

"Put your shoes on, Victoria Rachélle," he persisted authoritatively.

"No, Daddy, I can't. Really." There was a plea for understanding in his daughter's small voice that Jack must have missed.

"Why not?" he demanded harshly. "You've been putting your shoes on since you were two years old. Now put them on!" His neck stiffened as if he suspected himself to be the victim of a female plot to infuriate him. First, his wife had kept him waiting an unreasonable amount of time while she primped, and now his daughter had begun what appeared to be a premature, adolescent rebellion by refusing to put her shoes on.

"I can't, Daddy." Victoria Rachélle's voice was so meek it was barely more than a whisper.

Jack obviously gave up on the peaceful Sunday notion, turned his head just slightly, and exploded, "Why not? Why can't you?"

"I don't have any." There was total silence in the car as the adults grappled with this reality. A moment later Jack's military training surfaced, and he barked an order, "Stop the car, Saul!" The Cadillac came to a screeching halt in the gravel drive and was lost in a billowing cloud of red dust. There was an ominous silence, the danger of which Victoria Rachélle immediately recognized. Her father was perfectly still for a long, long moment. Everyone waited. Slowly he turned and looked at Victoria Rachélle, who was cowering in one corner of the back seat, her offending feet sticking straight out.

Suddenly Patsy broke the silence, "And you wanted another one—" she began to accuse him.

"Not now, Patsy! One crisis at a time," Jack was glaring

at Victoria Rachélle, and he refused to be diverted, much to her disappointment, for she knew that her father's boiling point, which was always close to explosion, had been reached. "Where on earth are your shoes, Victoria Rachélle?" he demanded.

"I lost them?" She ventured timidly, hopefully.

"Victoria Rachélle," he was speaking through dangerously clenched teeth now, "people do not lose shoes. Now, where are they?"

"Under the bushes, Daddy." Hiding them under the bushes had seemed like such a good idea under the stress of the moment when she had first thought of it, but now somehow it seemed like a dastardly deed.

"Under the bushes. . . . ." He appeared to be meditating on the profundity of her response. He exhaled deeply, forcefully, before commenting in a deceptively cool voice, "I know this is an asinine question, and no one in his right mind would even ask it, but *why* are they under the bushes?"

"I put them there." There was another silence, this one more ominous than before. Both parents glared at Victoria Rachélle while Saul kept his eyes riveted on the hood of the car and pretended he was deaf. He knew Jack D'Evereau, and he wasn't "gonna mess in."

"You know, Victoria Rachélle, somehow I suspected all along that they hadn't gotten there by themselves." Jack's sarcasm smothered the inhabitants of the car, for they knew it was the quiet oppressiveness before the storm broke.

Suddenly Jack turned back to the front of the car and demanded of Saul, "Did you think they'd gotten under the bushes by themselves?"

"No sir!" Saul continued to keep his eyes straight ahead, knowing full well that his employer's code of gentlemanly conduct would make it impossible for Jack to attack either of the females in the car, so he was the obvious scapegoat.

"Turn the car around!" Jack savagely commanded.

"Yes sir!" Saul quickly followed orders, whirled the big car around in a fog of red dust and raced back up the slope to the house.

Mammy Cassie had seen them coming, and fearful that her beloved Patsy was ill, she swarmed around the car. Ignoring her completely, Jack jumped out, thrust her aside, jerked open the back door, and ordered Victoria Rachélle out. She climbed clumsily over her mother's feet and lightly jumped to the ground; immediately her father jerked her up into his arms and demanded, "Show me where your shoes are!" Victoria Rachélle's face was inches away from her father's, and at that distance there was no doubting his anger. His blue eyes were fiery, his teeth were clenched so tightly that his mustache was perfectly still, and there were glistening beads of sweat on his tanned forehead.

Victoria Rachélle meekly pointed to the side of the house, and Jack marched resolutely off in that direction with her firmly gripped in one arm. Patsy set up a wail for Mammy Cassie's ears about the burdens of her life, with special emphasis on the worthlessness of her daughter. As her father turned the corner of the house, Victoria Rachélle looked furtively back over his broad shoulder and saw Mammy Cassie helping the whining Patsy up the stairs, onto the porch, and into a comfortable chair.

When Jack reached the shrub with the secret, damning cache, Victoria Rachélle pointed to it reluctantly, and Jack bent over and picked up the tiny shoes whose weight had now quadrupled from the mud on the soles. "No wonder you 'lost' them!" was her father's only bitter comment, but it was enough. He strode back around the house with Victoria Rachélle in one arm and the disgraceful shoes, the abhorrently visible symbol of her sinfulness, held in his other hand, which was outstretched as far away from his immaculate suit as he could get it. When he gained the porch, he thrust the mud-soled shoes at Mammy Cassie, who exclaimed in dismay, "Lord a-mercy!" Totally devoid of interest in her response, Jack ordered her, "Get these cleaned up and back on Victoria Rachélle at once!"

"I can't leave Miz Patsy; she gonna faint she so upset," she announced defiantly, glad for any excuse to avoid the mud on those shoes.

"She is *not* going to faint!" Jack shot back at her and then directed his dictatorial tone at his wife. "Patsy, don't you even think about fainting. I forbid it! Mammy Cassie, get these shoes clean, now!"

She half-heartedly tried to stand her ground, "But Mister Jack—"

"Now!" There was no mistaking the tone he used or the consequences if she argued with him. She was willing to risk almost anything to pamper and protect her beloved Patsy, but she knew that when Jack D'Evereau sounded like that, heaven itself could not move him, and she would simply be futilely sacrificing herself in the effort. So she grabbed Victoria Rachélle's hand, took the muddy shoes, and yanked the child through the screen door into the dark hall. Victoria Rachélle dragged her feet, curiously looking over her shoulder at her parents on the porch. She sensed that a formidable conflict was in the air. And sure enough, just as she passed over the threshold the volley of verbal gunfire began just as she had expected.

"And you just had to have another one—" Patsy angrily accused Jack, pointing to her swollen stomach.

"Not now, Patsy. Let's just try to get to church on time," Jack responded soothingly.

"Not now!" Patsy shouted back at him. "That's easy for you to say. You're not sitting here held captive by another brat growing inside of you. You haven't lost your entire life for nine months. It's not your body that's being distorted into ugliness."

"Patsy!" Jack was obviously struggling to control his temper now, and his carefully regulated tone indicated what an effort it was for him to do so. "A man is entitled to an heir, you know. I *do* give you everything you want. It seems that the least you could do is—"

"Well, I hope you know that this is the last one!" she yelled. "This is absolutely the last one! I didn't want the first one, and I don't want this one. I won't ruin what little health I have by having endless babies—"

"Calm down, for heaven's sake! You're going to make yourself sick—and all over a pair of shoes! If you won't think of yourself—think of the baby!"

"The baby!" Patsy's voice crescendoed shrilly with each word now. "The baby! That's all you think of, Jack, all you ever think of! All you care about is the precious son you think you're going to get. You don't care about me. All you care about is having your precious D'Evereau heir. Well let me tell you something," she laughed hysterically now. "There's a fifty-fifty chance this baby will be another girl. And then what will you have?"

Those were the last words Victoria Rachélle heard before Mammy Cassie pushed her through the door into the sunny, large kitchen at the end of the hall and forced her down into a chair. "You just can't stand for her to be happy, can you?" Mammy Cassie demanded. "You just gotta make her miserable. I never seed such a child in my life! You's suppose to love your mother, but no! You's a child of the devil, and you ain't gonna be happy till you makes your mother sick just like you always does. Yes mam, you's a child of the devil. I knowed it the minute you's borned."

"I didn't mean to make her unhappy—really! I just

wanted to see the dogs," Victoria Rachélle was vascillating between crying over her grief that she had hurt her mother and the alternative of defending herself against Mammy Cassie's excessive accusations.

"Just wanted to see the dogs, she says," Mammy Cassie snorted. "Well you done made your mother upset, and I figure you's gonna upset her a heap more before you's growed. Ain't no help for it with a devil child like you round." Mammy Cassie took advantage of the growing remorse Victoria Rachélle was feeling and eagerly moved her attack to another sin.

"Look at these here shoes! They's covered with mud. I's gonna have to take a knife to these here shoes to clean 'em they's so filthy. And you gonna go to church without no shoes! Don't you know you's a Longwood? Even if your name is D'Evereau—you's still a Longwood, and Longwoods don't go to no church without no shoes like some kind of poor white trash! I expect I ain't never gonna get these here shoes clean. Then what you gonna wear to church?"

"My other shoes?" Victoria Rachélle suggested.

"No mam! These here is your Sunday shoes, and you gotta wear them to the Lord's house. Ain't nothing else gonna do at all!"

"What difference does it make anyway?" Victoria Rachélle demanded belligerently. She was fast becoming tired of the way things were going.

"It make a heap of difference. I told you you's goin' to the Lord's house, and you gotta look your best to please Him." Mammy Cassie was absolutely confident on this theological point after her many years of dealing with "the Lord."

"Doesn't Jesus like you if you aren't dressed up?"

"He ain't gonna like you at all, seeing as you's a child of the devil." Mammy Cassie ignored the real question entirely. "Now come on! I got these here shoes as clean as they's gonna get. Put 'em on and let's go. And don't you make your mother upset no more, you hear?"

Victoria Rachélle put on her shoes, and ushered by Mammy Cassie's firm hand on her shoulder, she joined her parents, both encased in icy silence, for an uneventful ride to church. At the church Jack deposited his daughter at the door to her Sunday School class and warned her sternly, "Make that shoe mess this morning the end of it, Victoria Rachélle. I mean it! I've had enough! You've used up your quota of misbehavior for the day." And then he stalked off down the long, empty hall. Victoria Rachélle watched forlornly as he grew smaller and smaller in the distance. She felt abandoned and guilty.

She didn't know what "quota" was, but she surely knew what her father meant just the same. So, she was subdued for the hour, but as she sat in the circle of tiny chairs with the other beautifully dressed and perfectly groomed children and sang "Jesus loves the little children," she was very glad she had on her Sunday shoes, for she figured she had a better chance with Jesus if she had on her best clothes "in the Lord's house," as Mammy Cassie had said.

The actual worship service of the Baptist Church was often a painful experience for Victoria Rachélle, and this particular Sunday was no exception. The first half hour was always fine because she loved to sing, and she sang along joyously and loudly with the choir, even when the congregation was not supposed to join in, until her mother slapped her lightly on the knee and hissed "Sh-h-h!" at her. But even when she stopped voicing the words of the oft-repeated, beloved hymns, the lyrics and melodies still raced merrily in her head. After all, she had been to the Baptist Church three times a week for her entire life. Besides, even at home the Negroes sang hymns as they worked, and Victoria Rachélle had spent many happy hours harmonizing with Florence, the cook.

However, when the music stopped and the preacher, imposing and formidable with his bushy gray eyebrows and stern, steely eyes, rose from his chair, Victoria Rachélle's heart sank. Five years of experience had taught her that from this moment on in the service she was trapped in a nightmare. For what would seem like an eternity to the little girl, he was going to shout at her and make her feel awful, just awful. No matter how quietly she sat in the pew, all dressed up to please God, the preacher was going to shout at her and tell her she was bad. To her, his message always seemed to be the same, "You are a sinner! No matter how hard you try, you can't *stop* being a sinner! If you live to be a hundred, you will still be a sinner. God has prepared a place for sinners like you. It is the deepest, hottest fiery pit where you will burn forever. You are going to burn in hell! You deserve to burn in hell!"

Every Sunday as the sermon continued, Victoria Rachélle grew more and more depressed. She felt like a daisy she had seen in the garden. There had been too little rain, and the sun was blistering hot. Before the daisy could even open its petals, the sun had wilted its stem and the closed bud of the daisy, its head, had flopped over as if its neck were broken. Victoria Rachélle felt like that daisy looked. She wasn't sure what sin was, but she knew she had it, she had it bad, and she had it on purpose. After all, the preacher said she had chosen to be sinful.

This particular Sunday, just as she reached the depths of depression, the preacher paused for dramatic effect, seemed to be eyeing her particularly, leaned across the pulpit, and spoke in a confidential tone. "Folks, there is only one way out—one way to save yourself." A flood of relief washed over Victoria Rachélle; she relaxed in her seat as the tension drained out of her body. Oh thank heavens, she thought, there is a way out! There is a way out! She waited, eagerly leaning forward in the pew, for the answer to her dilemma.

Slowly the preacher began again, very quietly. Then his tone became more and more vehement; his voice increased slowly but dramatically in volume until finally he was shouting so loudly that Victoria Rachélle wondered why the roof didn't come crashing down. "You must be washed in the blood of the lamb! There is only one way to be saved from hell. You must be washed in the blood of the lamb! You will burn in hell *forever* if you are not washed in the blood of the lamb!"

Victoria Rachélle recoiled into the pew with horror as her heart sank! She could never do it, she thought hopelessly, not ever! She could never wash herself in blood—never! She couldn't even imagine such a thing. Then she remembered the gentle, white lambs on her Uncle Lloyd's farm, and she shuddered violently. Cautiously she looked up at her parents' faces and the faces of the other adults. Had they washed themselves in the blood of a lamb? Could they, she wondered? The very thought was making her sick to her stomach.

The preacher continued with the same theme, this time pleading with the congregation to save themselves by washing in the blood of the lamb. Nausea burned Victoria Rachélle's stomach and threatened to erupt as sweat broke out all over her tiny body. Finally the preacher called for everybody to stand and sing the invitation, the hymn that invited the damned to come forward and be saved. The choir and congregation began the hymn; dazed, Victoria Rachélle stood between her parents. She did not catch the words of the stanzas, but the refrain, repeated over and over, invaded her consciousness and intensified the horrible picture in her head. "Are you washed in the blood, in the soul-cleansing blood of the lamb? Are your garments spotless? Are they white as snow?" Victoria Rachélle thought of her white shoes caked with red mud because of her sinfulness, and she hung her head in grief and despair. At last the song finished by demanding one more time, "Are you washed in the blood of the lamb?" She perceived that she had never been in such trouble, and there was no acceptable way out.

After church her parents lingered in the sanctuary while Patsy floated around and greeted her friends with intense gaiety and seemed determined to talk endlessly. Jack spoke nothing but the barest civilities. Victoria Rachélle listlessly waited. Normally she would have been driven to verbalized impatience by her gnawing, noonday hunger, but today she felt dead inside.

In the car on the way home, her mother talked enthusiastically about what a wonderful sermon the preacher had given, occasionally throwing in remarks about one of the women's Sunday clothing. She even had that little, high-pitched, nervous laugh in her voice that told Victoria Rachélle that everything was okay—for the moment. Her father, however, seemed strangely quiet.

Sunday dinner at the D'Evereau house was the major family meal of the week. It was always early afternoon before the family ceremoniously sat down at the elegant table which was heavy-laden with tantalizing, steamy dishes. The D'Evereaus ate heartily at this early afternoon meal, for they took great pride in the fact that they generously gave the Negroes Sunday evening off to go to their own church, and thus only leftovers would be available for the family's supper.

On this particular Sunday, Jack suggested that Patsy ask the blessing. And even though Patsy's prayer was her usual lengthy and formal discourse with God, Victoria Rachélle did not fidget. She simply stared mournfully at her plate. Finally the family was served Victoria Rachélle's favorite, fried chicken, with mashed potatoes and gravy. Her father's genial mood returned as he began to eat, and Patsy was still in high spirits so they chatted lightly about various subjects. Normally Victoria Rachélle was talkative also, relating every incident of her Sunday School hour, but today she sat silent, sadly playing with the food on her plate. Toward the end of the meal her mother turned her gaze on her daughter, smiled and asked her usual question, "Well, Victoria Rachélle, what did you learn at church today?" The child avoided her mother's gaze and her question.

"Not much, Mother." She didn't like what she had learned, and she desperately wanted—needed—to forget it.

Her father stared at her curiously, but she quickly looked down at her plate and pushed her food around with her fork. It was obvious she had eaten nothing.

"You're awfully quiet," he commented. "Do you feel okay?"

"Yes, sir," she continued to stare at her plate gloomily. In fact, she felt sick again, and there was something in her throat keeping her food from going down.

"Well then, let's hear about church. What did you learn?" her mother persisted.

Victoria Rachélle recognized the tone in her mother's voice that demanded a command performance. What could she do? She didn't know enough to lie. Besides, she thought that her parents had approved the preacher's sermon and thus would approve her summary of it. What was there to fear? She was the only one distressed by what she had heard. Still she didn't want to talk about it. She began tentatively, "Well, we sang 'Jesus Loves the Little Children' in Sunday School, and we sang in church, too."

"That's nice, but what did you learn?" Patsy was beginning to sound impatient, and when Victoria Rachélle glanced up at her, she saw that her mother's eyes were riveted on her face like a pious confessor who has sensed guilt and is determined to ferret out the sin.

There was no hope, she realized, no escape from telling the horrible truth. If her mother wanted to know, she would have to tell her. Slowly she gathered her courage, raised her head proudly, looked her mother in the eye and blurted out, "I learned that Jesus loves little children when they are clean and dressed up, but you have to be cleaned special with the blood of a lamb, or He'll send you to hell to burn up."

There was absolute silence in the room.

Her mother's face seemed to have turned to stone. Finally her mouth opened, and she muttered ominously, "What did you say?"

Victoria Rachélle was frightened by the look on her face, but she was too far in to turn back, so she quietly said it again, "I learned that Jesus loves little children when they are clean and dressed up, but you have to be cleaned special with the blood of a lamb, or he'll send you to hell to burn up."

There was a loud gasp from her mother followed by a wail, "This is too much! Jack, for heaven's sake, do something with her!" She quickly raised her crumpled linen napkin to her red face and tried to fan herself with it.

"Victoria Rachélle," Jack's voice was conciliatory. "I'm sure you just misunderstood—didn't you?" He was nodding his head affirmatively and encouragingly as he spoke.

"No, Daddy, that's what they said at church today," Victoria Rachélle said quietly.

Patsy, breathing audibly and rapidly now as she frantically fanned herself with her napkin, altered Victoria Rachélle's alleged sin against religion and proper breeding into an attack against herself. "To think that it should come to this! To think of it! She's had everything a child could want. Everything! There's no end to the trouble I've had from her! From the minute she was conceived! I feel a headache coming on right this minute! Right this minute!"

"That's enough, Patsy!" Jack's own anger was rising now. "The child simply misunderstood. Calm down. I'll handle it."

"But Daddy," a strong sense of injustice and mistreatment was rising in Victoria Rachélle and fast replacing her distress that she had upset her mother again. "The preacher said—"

"That's enough, young lady!" her father shook his finger down the table at her, determined to defuse the looming crisis at any cost. "I'll hear no more about it. Now that's an end to it. Drink your milk and go outside and play."

"But, Daddy—" Victoria Rachélle protested weakly one more time.

"Stop this at once!" he commanded and slammed his fist on the table, shaking the silver serving pieces and rattling the china. "Can't you see you're making your mother sick?"

"I *am* sick!" Patsy whined from across the table as she burst into tears. "She never misses a chance to make me sick. She doesn't care any more about me than you do!" She angrily flung the accusation down the length of the table at him in an obvious attempt to widen the scope of the war to include previous battles.

"Why me? Why me?" he demanded of the ceiling. Then he glared down at Victoria Rachélle and barked, "Drink your milk!"

Victoria Rachélle understandably jumped at his violence-promising tone, and she shot her hand forward to grab the glass, but instead of grabbing it, she forcefully knocked it over in the direction of her weeping mother. Before anyone could respond, milk streamed quickly across the table, saturating the embroidered linen cloth, and finally ending in a puddle in her mother's lap. Patsy sprang up from her chair, screamed "Jack," looked down at the huge, dark circle on her favorite, green silk dress, and collapsed back into her chair holding her head in her hands. Shouting for Mammy Cassie, Jack grabbed a napkin, ran to the opposite end of the table and began dabbing at Patsy's dress, but Patsy slapped his hand away and screamed, "Don't touch me! This is all your fault! You don't care about me! All you want is the son you think I'm carrying!"

Mammy Cassie ran in and tried to pet and sooth Patsy, but Patsy's voice grew shriller and shriller, as Jack stood by helplessly watching her. No one remembered Victoria Rachélle, who was watching her mother in horror, until Mammy Cassie suddenly glared at her across the milk-soaked table and hissed with biting hatred, "I hope you's finally happy. You's done gone and made your Mother sick just like you always does." Patsy's sobs rose to a higher pitch with these words. Jack looked at Victoria Rachélle, who felt like she had been struck in the face, and then at the sobbing bundle that was his wife, and muttered in despair, "I am cursed! God has cursed me!"

Victoria Rachélle ran. Desperately she fled the elegant dining room. She tore through the kitchen so fast that the startled Florence dropped a pan, which clattered to the floor, as Victoria Rachélle disappeared out the back door, slamming the screen behind her. Racing wildly across the backyard, all she could think of was reaching the woods, the safe woods. The painful tightness of unshed tears in her throat invaded her whole chest as her heart pounded furiously. She would have gladly sobbed out her hurt, but her breath was completely taken by the running. Finally, she reached the haven of the woods, threw herself onto the pine needles and beat out her fury and hurt on the ground—at least some of it.

# FIVE

I was so angry, so incredibly angry, recalled thirty-five-year-old Rachel as she lay with her face in the violets. I was a helpless, vulnerable five-year-old caught in a situation I could neither endure nor escape.

She sat up slowly and glanced around the woods as she continued thinking. But that feeling of helplessness, as terrible as it was, wasn't the source of my pain—not really. Even then there was a great, gaping wound in me, a wound caused by injustice and denial. Injustice because I had tried so hard to be what they wanted, and it was like they had decided long before I was born that I would never make it. Denial because they never really looked at *me*, saw *me*. They always saw what they wanted—not what I was. Always what *they* wanted, and I wasn't it. And I'm still not.

But they had no right to decide I was bad! They had no right to define me themselves, rather than looking at me, trying to see my heart. They should have at least *tried* to see my heart! And I knew it. Even then, when I was only five, I knew it was unfair.

And so I didn't go home.

Rachel reached down, stroked the tiny, delicate petals of a single flower, and remembered why the presence of these violets now gave her such comfort. Again her mind returned to that Sunday thirty years earlier.

After sitting in the creek and remembering what had sent her flying into the woods for refuge on that horrible Sunday, the five-year-old Victoria Rachélle looked back into the woods in the direction of her parents' house. She looked down at the clear water skimming over her, dividing her past from her future, and she looked at the opposite side of the stream where she had never been. She would not, could not go back, she decided. She never wanted to see any of them again. Thus, her only choice seemed obvious to her; she would go and live in the woods on the other side of the stream. Having made her decision, she resolutely rose from the water and splashed across to the other side.

The foliage close to the water's edge on the opposite side was very dense, too dense to push her way through, but Victoria Rachélle, determined to go forward and away from her past, splashed her way up the edge of the creek for quite some distance before she reached a clearing and could leave the water. There on the edge of the creek was a huge weeping willow with half of its branches moving gently in the water and its remaining branches swaying like a sheer curtain just above the damp ground of the bank. Unable to see through the delicate branches, Victoria Rachélle had no idea what mysterious terrain lay behind them. She paused in the water, her fingers gently clasping one graceful willow branch which had floated to her on the current of the creek, inviting her to come forward. This was the unknown—both frightening and provocative. Once again she considered the past; it, by itself, was argument enough for going forward. And then, too, there was something intrepid about this five-year-old.

Slowly she parted the first branches and walked through; the ground was soggy and gave away under her feet, the mud oozing slightly between her toes. Undaunted, she parted another layer of branches and moved forward again to whatever destiny lay behind the curtain of the tree. The experience was like slowly unwrapping a surprise gift in an oversized box. Layer after layer of tissue paper must be pulled out before the recipient of the gift learns if the contents are truly a gift or only a practical joke. With every layer one must decide all over again whether to go forward until the contents are revealed to be whatever they are, or to go backward, close up the box and never know.

Slowly Victoria Rachélle moved forward, unwrapping the layers of branches cautiously, but steadily. When the last vestige of the veil was pushed aside, she confronted the base of a hill. The air was oppressively muggy with steam seeming to rise from the mud sucking at her feet, but she chose to push on. She stumbled hurriedly through the dark clearing until she reached the base of the hill and began to climb laboriously.

It was steep, and she was tired now and breathing heavily in the dense, moist atmosphere as she exerted herself, grabbing on to low-lying bushes and pulling herself forward with effort. Step by step she struggled upward, out of the wet darkness until finally she reached the summit and collapsed, exhausted and breathing painfully, under a single, enormous pine. Hanging her head as she gasped, she stared down at the ground, listening to her pulses pounding in her ears. On the outside, she was a sticky, disheveled heap with sore feet. On the inside, despair had caught up with her once again. She couldn't go back; there was no apparent reason to go forward. The promised surprise gift was a practical joke. She sat there in despondency.

High over her head, a whispering noise began—a message, a promise, an allurement. She began to listen, and finally looking straight up into the myriad branches of the large pine, she saw that its needles were swaying hypnotically. Slowly, the breeze that made the pine tree dance descended until it touched her feverish, sticky face. It was dry, cool—different from the air on the other side of the hill. It swirled around her body, embracing and invigorating her until she simply could resist no longer. She stood up, and holding out her arms in wing fashion, she swayed from side to side in the cool breeze and twirled in a circle like a dancer in slow motion, bathing herself in the breeze's cool stimulation. Her golden hair and the full skirt of her white slip floated weightlessly, gracefully as she moved, and soon the breeze was filled with her little-girl, delighted laughter. In time she was refreshed, she stood motionless again, and her attention was drawn forward to the other side of the summit. She took a few tentative steps to the edge and looked down on what was virgin territory for her; involuntarily, a slow "ah-h-h" of delight escaped her lips, and her face shone in a smile of pure delight.

Spread out below her was an enchanted valley, a vision of sensory delight. There was light here, a warm embracing light—a light guaranteed to produce peace, to gentle the soul through the senses. The fearful darkness, the oppressive moistness, the stagnant, warm air—all were contained on the other side of the summit. Here spread out invitingly in front of her lay a new experience. The sun, cheerfully yellow, dappled the ground below her and danced merrily from place to place under gigantic, ancient oaks that spread their enormous limbs protectively. Victoria Rachélle stood at the pinnacle of a steep slope which descended quickly into the valley and then gentled into an undulating plain before it once again became steep and climbed up the opposite hill. At the lowest point of the miniature valley spread before her, she could see a tiny, delicate stream flowing along and sparkling like a silver ribbon in the sunshine.

All this was beautiful, inviting beyond description to the stressed little girl, but there was more—there was one magical element of the scene that would change it for Victoria Rachélle from a delightful, inviting place into an ecstasy that could not be resisted. Spread out below her was a sea of purple tones, gently pulsating, appearing to breathe, begging for her company. Violets! Everywhere! She was entranced; in all her experiences, real and imaginary, she had never seen anything so magnificent, yet so comfortable. Here she belonged, and she knew it instantly. With joy flooding triumphantly through her tiny body, she ran down the steep slope, straight into the midst of the violets, and threw herself headlong into the sea of purple, burying her face in the multitude of flowers. Slowly she turned over on her side and began to roll over and over in the flowers, inhaling deeply their sweet earthy scent. Finally she lay with the side of her face on her extended right arm and looked at the violets at ground height. From that vantage point the whole world was a rich combination of dark green, gentle purple, delicate splashes of warm sunshine on her skin and a peace-inducing scent. It was glorious! And even more so because it was an unexpected gift that came at just the right moment. Victoria Rachélle extended her left arm and gently entwined her fingers in the flowers to assure herself that they were real, and surrounded by the beauty, she rested.

Perhaps an hour later, Victoria Rachélle sat up suddenly. She had fallen asleep, and for a disappointing moment she believed that she had dreamed about the miraculous valley of violets, but as she blinked her eyes repeatedly and looked around her, it was all there—the ancient oaks standing guard over her, the sunshine dancing around the meadow, the stream meandering through the grasses, and the sea of violets. "It's real!" she shouted with joy, jumped up eagerly and ran further down the slope to the edge of the stream. Even here there were violets everywhere, coming right to the edge of the water. She found a flat rock, and sitting down on it, she extended her tiny feet into the cool water. A wonderful exhiliration seized her; uninhibitively she stretched her body back in the sun, supporting herself on her arms extended behind her, and began to kick her feet vigorously in the water. The water foamed around her feet and splashed high and sparkling in the air. Victoria Rachélle kicked and laughed and kicked and laughed. It was even better than Christmas or Florence's chocolate cake.

In the midst of her joyous splashing, a bright shaft of sunlight suddenly fell over the right side of her face. Startled by its intensity, she stopped her energetic kicking and looked up to her right; however, the light was so intense she could not look into it. Even when she shaded her eyes, she could not look at its brightness, so she quickly returned her gaze to the water. Immediately a shadow fell over the water in front of her, and once again she looked up. There was a man standing there, gazing down at her with the kindliest smile imaginable.

Startled, Victoria Rachélle stared at him; she had seen many men like him before. He wore old, tattered clothes and had scraggly, long hair and a graying beard. Her father would have called him a poor, homeless tramp. Her mother would have called him a filthy bum. Really, the only remarkable thing about him was a beautiful white bird sitting on his shoulder. He walked slowly toward her and a sense of absolute, all-encompassing peace flowed through Victoria Rachélle. She could not take her eyes off the man who had stopped and was quietly standing opposite her, on the other side of the narrow stream. Suddenly the white bird flew off the man's shoulder and landed in

Victoria Rachélle's lap. Surprised, she looked down and watched with curious fascination as the bird made a nest of her lap, settled in and tucked its wings under.

"Don't be afraid, my child," the man smiled kindly, and his voice was soothing and warm, "he is the most loving of all the birds in the universe." Victoria Rachélle was still unsure, as she looked down apprehensively at the quiet bird in her lap. "You may pet him if you like," the man continued, "he likes you."

"Why?" Victoria Rachélle uttered the word quietly but with intense interest in the answer to her question. After the day's events, she was sure she was quite unlikable.

"Because you are good and full of love," he responded as if his answer were the most obvious thing in the world.

"No I'm not! I'm bad—the baddest little girl in the whole world! Mammy Cassie says I'm a devil child!"

"Dear me. . . . that sounds terrible." He was not the least bit perturbed by Victoria Rachélle's outburst, as she had assumed he would be. Instead he slowly settled on a rock across the narrow stream, opposite her. "Perhaps we best talk about that. But first, what is your name?"

"Victoria Rachélle D'Evereau," she slowly chanted as if it were a ponderously long name, and she was quite disgusted with it. "My mother wanted to name me Victoria because that's her mother's name, but my daddy wanted to name me Rachélle because that's his mother's name, and they had a big fight about it. So now I have to have both names!"

"That's a big name for such a little girl," he reflected thoughtfully.

"I know. I hate it!" Her whole body tightened as she spoke.

"I see." He said nothing more for awhile. In contrast to Victoria Rachélle's tensed body, he was a picture of ease, the definition of peace. Finally he questioned, "Why do you hate it?"

"Because it's not *my* name, and because Mother and Daddy gave it to me!" she shot back at him and began to kick her feet belligerently in the water, splashing as violently as possible.

He continued to sit quietly until she had finished. When her feet finally hung limp in the water, he asked the question that released her emotional flood again, "Don't you like your parents?"

"No! I hate them!" she shouted angrily. "They make me hurt in here." She pointed to her heart. "They don't like me."

"Ah. I see . . . why is it they don't like you, do you suppose?"

"Cause I'm bad," she announced defiantly. "I've always been bad. Mammy Cassie says I was born a devil child, I'm a devil child now, and there ain't no help for it." Her defiance was fast turning to visible grief as she continued hurriedly, trying not to cry, "I make my mother sick and she cries and Daddy gets mad. All cause of me. I'm bad." By the time of this final pronouncement, her whole body was a picture of despondency as she looked mournfully at the water.

The man's eyes filled with tears as she spoke. When she had finished, he silently watched her grieve for a few moments, and then he began to speak quietly but with intense conviction, with absolute certainty. "You are not bad, my child, and you are not a devil child. I know you better than they do. I have always known you, and I tell you that you are good. You are full of love, and that love makes you beautiful inside and outside."

Victoria Rachélle stared up at him in surprise, her desperate desire to believe him poignantly displayed on her face. "I am?" she asked in amazement. She so needed to believe him.

"Yes, you are. And because you are good and loving and beautiful, I shall give you a new name. I shall call you Rachel."

"Why Rachel?" Victoria Rachélle asked quietly, mystified by the meaning of this declaration. She had never heard this version of her name before.

"Because Rachel was very loved. She was worth waiting for. She was worth working for." He paused a moment before adding, "When you are older, you will understand more."

Victoria Rachélle made no comment, but the words miraculously affected her. She looked down at the dove sitting contentedly in her lap, and she began to pet it gingerly. Quietly she observed, "I think this bird likes me."

The old man smiled knowingly, "Of course he does; he loves everyone, but he is especially comfortable with people who are full of love like he is—like you are, Rachel."

Victoria Rachélle desperately wanted to believe the man, but it was hard to believe that all the adults in her life were wrong about her. Still, she *needed* to believe him. "But I got my white shoes muddy," she confessed sadly, "and I spilled my milk and said something bad about the church and made Mother sick, and Daddy got mad." Her lips quivered as she ended in a tone of despair, for the list of her badnesses seemed long and hopeless.

The old man waited for a few moments for her to calm down before he quietly said, "That may all be true, or perhaps only some of it is true. But even if you really did do all those things, those are only your deeds, only what you *did*—not what you *are*. You are loving and good, and I know it. That bird knows it too."

He paused, but she seemed doubtful, so he continued,

"I'll tell you, my child, you can't fool animals, and I've known them all, and this is the wisest bird I ever met. He even knows things people don't know. He sees inside of people, he sees their hearts, and *he* knows you are loving and good."

Victoria Rachélle pondered his words a few minutes, looked down at the miraculous bird who had chosen to sit in *her* lap, then said quietly, "Rachel. . . . Rachel. . . . Rachel D'Evereau. I like it!"

At that moment, much was decided.

Then looking him squarely in the face, she asked, "What's your name?"

"Oh . . . folks call me lots of things. You can call me whatever you'd like to call me." He paused as Rachel pondered what his name should be. "What's your favorite thing, Rachel?"

"Sunshine!" Rachel shouted with glee, her spirits completely restored.

"Well then, Sunshine I am . . . that's my name. And I make the flowers and the trees and the wild strawberries and all the animals grow. What do you think of my violets?" he waved his hand around at the field of purple.

"I love them! They're beautiful!" she gazed happily at the solid mass of blossoms. "But I've never seen so many."

"Yes, they are beautiful," he smiled contentedly as he surveyed them, and looking back at Rachel he explained, "They grow here in abundance because—like you, Rachel— they love the light." He paused as she looked at him with curiosity in her eyes.

She understood, although she didn't realize she did.

Then he questioned softly but seriously, "Have you ever looked deep inside of one of my violets, Rachel?" She shook her head. He encouraged her as he pointed to the flowers closest to her. "Pick one and look. There's a whole world inside of each flower."

Rachel eagerly picked a stem, raised it close to her face and stared deep into the bloom. "You're right, you're right! I see! Yes, I see!"

"Very few people ever see that world, Rachel, just as there are other worlds that very few people see. Only special people—like you, Rachel—people of light. Don't forget, Rachel, don't forget!"

Suddenly the dove took flight from Rachel's lap. Startled, she looked up and saw it fly straight into a blinding shaft of light. She quickly diverted her eyes down to the stream, for the light was too strong to bear, but a moment later she looked up again and the light, the old man and the bird were all gone. She was alone, but she felt wonderful!

Enjoying her sensation of rightness with the universe, she sat still for several moments with her feet dangling idly in the water and her eyes fixed on the violets next to her. Slowly she began to pick the violets one by one and stuff them into the top of her slip. Then she picked a bouquet to carry in her hand. Splashing her feet joyously in the stream one more time, she laughed aloud at the sun dancing on the water, ran her hand across the top of the violets as if she were carressing them, and stood up. She was happy with herself.

Turning her face toward home, she found her way back to the weeping willow by the stream, followed the stream down to the place she knew and set out through the pines to her house. All along the way she would pause and look down the front of her slip at the violets and smell the nosegay she carried and laugh. How she laughed!

When she had crossed the large backyard, she slipped into the kitchen where Florence was sitting at the work table in her Sunday clothes. Florence looked up from her Bible and exclaimed in horror, "Lord a mercy, child, look at you! Where's your clothes? Where you been?" Instead of answering, Rachel broke into peals of delighted laughter and held out her bouquet of violets for Florence to see. Florence could only think of the practical. "We's gotta get you cleaned up before anybody sees you, child. Quick, let's get you in the bathtub!" She hurriedly pushed Rachel ahead of her toward the bathroom and breathed a sigh of relief when they had closed the door behind them without being spotted. Quickly she turned on the water in the tub. When she pulled Rachel's slip over her head, the mass of violets fell in a shower of purple to the floor, and Rachel once again broke into a merry laugh. "This ain't no time for no foolishness," Florence warned sternly. "We gots to get you clean 'fore Mammy Cassie sees you. Now get in this here tub."

After her bath, Florence dressed Rachel in her night-gown and took her back into the kitchen to feed her. The child had eaten half a sandwich when Mammy Cassie came into the kitchen and saw her. Mammy Cassie drew herself up to her full size and indignantly began her usual assault on the child. "You's done a day's work today, you devil child! Your mother's head hurt her so much she can't hardly stand it. Your daddy, he want to call the doctor, but your poor mother, she so brave she won't let him. Yes mam, you's done a real day's work. You's a devil child Victoria Rachélle! You's borned a devil child and—"

Suddenly Rachel slammed her fist down on the table, as she had seen her father do. Jumping down from her chair, she defiantly confronted Mammy Cassie. With her clenched fists on her waist, she shouted authoritatively at the huge woman, "I am *not* a devil child! I am *good!* And I am *not* Victoria Rachélle. Don't you call me that anymore. I am good! I am Rachel!"

Mammy Cassie and Florence watched in amazement as Rachel, her head held high as a queen's, stood her ground. Mammy Cassie was so dumbfounded she turned and disappeared out the backdoor. Florence's face was covered with a happy smile as she asked, "Don't you want to finish your supper now, Miz Rachel?"

❧❧

Even thirty-five years later Rachel grinned as she remembered Mammy Cassie walking out the backdoor in total bewilderment, and her anguished, weary face was momentarily transformed by the memory of that victory so very long ago.

I may feel like a total failure now, Rachel thought, but that day really did turn out to be quite a victory. A gift from someone I never saw again. It was the first time I dared define myself as worthy and demand recognition of my worth. It was the first time I dared say what was in my heart all along. I loved them so—Mother and Daddy. I loved them, and I knew it. And deep inside of me—call it an instinct, a basic axiom of being—I knew that bad people didn't love the way I did. So there was no way I could be as bad as they said I was.

It was a turning point, a beginning of a new me—an assertive me, a me who was willing to defy my whole world to demand my just dignity. I was worth something, and that day I found the voice to say so because someone else said it first.

It was my epiphany.

Tenderly she touched the violets at the base of the old pine. I forgot, she thought. I forgot about the violets, I forgot about the valley and the stream. And I forgot about the man.

No, that's not really true, is it? I must have remembered, for the whole experience obviously became an indelible part of me. His words, his evaluation of me, his assurance. I suppose his words have always been there to battle the darkness. I never saw him again, yet his words were there, firmly planted in me like a seed buried too deep in moist ground to be blown away by the wind or washed away by the floods or even picked out of the ground and devoured by a ravenous crow.

So the seed was planted; the soil was moist and fertile. The seed needed only light and the warmth that light brings. And that was Grandmere's part. Soon she would come into my life, a feast of love for a starving child, a bright ray of light for a dormant seed.

"Oh Grandmere!" burning tears inundated Rachel's eyes and washed down her cheeks. "If only you were here now! I am still a little child, and I still need your light!" The adult in her, however, remembered too well the grave cut into the red soil at the D'Evereau plantation so many years earlier. And the white coffin, the pristine white coffin, lowered into that red ground as those who loved her, white and black alike, sobbed softly. Rachel had not cried then. All she had felt was fury that this white box should be covering up her Grandmere's beloved blue eyes. All she wanted to do was to take an axe and hack that horrid box open.

Her tears came in torrents now, and she buried her face in the clump of violets and sobbed. She cried for Grandmere, for her beloved brother Justin, killed in Viet Nam, and for herself. She even cried for Collins.

When she finally raised herself from the violets and wiped her face with her hands, the early summer sun had slipped below the horizon, and the woods were darkening. Still Rachel lingered, reluctant to move, unwilling to return to her parents' house, to confront once again the present with its pain. She sat a little longer, listening to the dusk sounds of the woods, and considered the pain of the present. She worried that perhaps the present pain had the ability to swallow her up, that perhaps she had finally been forced by life to confront a horror that would undo her, that would wither the plant that had sprung from that seed planted so long ago in these very woods.

However, when she finally rose to return to the house, to confront whatever her fate would be, she discovered that the memory of that day, that Sunday thirty years earlier, had created a strong glow, deep, deep inside of her. She recognized that there was a lantern in her soul, a lantern with an inviting, golden flame that called reassuringly, "Come home, child, come home," a lantern that had been there always. True, it had been covered up for years and had just taken the worst of beatings, a beating that nearly extinguished it, but it was still there burning brightly. And somehow, seeing the violets had pulled back the veil of years that had hidden it. And she could see it again, and she knew she had to follow it. But where? Where was it trying to lead her?

As she walked through her parents' house, her father met her in the dimly lit main hall. "I'm sorry your mother blew up like that. She hasn't been well since Justin—for years now. Emotional troubles, you know," he stumbled on, "the doctor says she does the best she can . . ."

"It's okay, Daddy. It's okay," she lied and struggled for words to comfort him, to reassure herself—and then she remembered the violets. The violets of thirty years before. Sparkling amethysts in a valley of light. An old man with a white bird. The violets of today, waiting for her. Waiting to remind her, to nurture her. Suddenly she suspected she would be whole again—someday—and her most immediate desire was to protect him. He had no violets, or perhaps he had forgotten his.

"I will be fine, Daddy," she spoke with such resounding firmness that he raised his head and looked her in the face once again.

"I will be okay."

He nodded his agreement, at first slowly and then more confidently. She could think of nothing more to say. He left her side and walked down the hall.

Suddenly he turned, his eyes gleaming fiercely. "You *will* be okay. You're a D'Evereau! Right?"

Rachel nodded as resolutely as she could. He was himself again, and she had one less burden to bear.

Although she had no appetite, Rachel headed for the kitchen for a light snack. There she was met by a worried Florence.

"Is you all right, Miz Rachel?" Florence left the sink full of soapy dishes to peer into Rachel's face. "I's been worried to death about you! When you didn't come home for supper, I didn't know what to think."

"I'm fine—"

"Well your mother ain't!" Mammy Cassie came booming through the door. "Put on some milk to heat up," she ordered Florence. "Miz Patsy got to take some more of that medicine for them awful headaches she get." These last words she delivered to Rachel, who ignored her and pulled out a chair to sit down.

"Florence," Rachel spoke quietly to the old cook, who was placing a pan of milk on the stove. "While you're at it, would you mind putting on the kettle for some tea? And I wonder if you've got something for a sandwich."

"Your mother is too sick to eat, thanks to you!" Mammy Cassie moved over in front of Rachel. "But of course you don't care nothing about that."

"Has the doctor been called?" Rachel demanded, breaking into the old woman's predictable tirade before she really got going.

"Course not!" Mammy Cassie snorted. "You think she gonna call the doctor and have her family disgraced all over this here town?"

"That will be enough, Mammy Cassie," Rachel warned through clenched teeth. "I am not five years old."

"Five years or thirty-five, it don't make no difference. You ain't never cared about nobody but yourself!"

Rachel sprang from her chair and sent it crashing over backwards against the wall. "Shut your hate-filled mouth this minute!" she commanded without raising her voice. "I will hear no more of this from you. You are the very embodiment of hate, and you are not my judge." She stared into the fury-filled eyes of Mammy Cassie and through sheer willpower forced herself not to crumple from fatigue and weakness. "Florence?" she asked without unlocking her eyes from Mammy Cassie's, "Is the milk ready?"

"Yes, Miz Rachel, I's pouring it up right this minute." Hurriedly Florence prepared a tray with the cup of warm milk on it and set it on the table between Mammy Cassie and Rachel, who were still staring at each other.

"Take it and get out!" Rachel ordered.

Mammy Cassie jerked up the tray and left. Once she was gone, Rachel clutched the table to support herself while Florence rushed to pick up her chair.

"I's shamed to say I's kin to her!" Florence exclaimed as she eased the shaking Rachel into the chair. "She always been so hateful, and she ain't—" Florence stopped herself in mid-sentence and started down another path. "Never you mind, Honey. Just rest your head on the table a minute; your tea's about ready, and I's gonna fix you some supper."

"Just a sandwich will do, Florence," Rachel murmured as she eased her throbbing head into her hands.

The kitchen was silent except for Florence's bustling as Rachel struggled to regain her composure. The whole world seemed to have gone mad. Desperately she searched her mind for one corner of peace to hide in, and as kindly

Florence placed a cup of tea in her hands, she remembered the violets. In all the world and in all her life, it seemed that they were the only oasis of comfort left for her.

Silently she drank her tea, nibbled at the sandwich Florence made, and thought of today's clump of violets. Petal by petal, cluster by cluster, leaf by leaf, she thought of their color and their shape until she had regained some composure. When she had finished her sandwich, she stood, went to Florence, and silently hugged her. Then she went to bed.

## SIX

Just after the sun was up, Rachel jerked awake in the middle of a nightmare. She had been dreaming about Collins lying in his coffin, but Mammy Cassie was there with her watching them lower the still-open coffin into the ground, and yelling at her that she had killed Collins because she was a devil child. The whole thing was a ludicrous mixture of her experiences, but it had shaken her thoroughly just the same. She hauled herself out of bed and stumbled to the bathroom. After stripping off her perspiration-soaked nightgown, she stepped into the shower and stood under cool water until her heartbeat returned to normal and she had convinced herself that she had only experienced a nightmare, a nightmare she must release immediately.

Resolved to forget the dream, she dressed as quickly as possible and surprised her father by joining him for breakfast in the dining room.

"Your mother's sleeping in," he added awkwardly after greeting her. "She's fine though. Just took one of her pills and went right off to sleep last night. Sorry about yesterday. You know how upset she can get and—well—she doesn't mean what she says when she's like that. She just says whatever—"

"It's all right, Daddy," Rachel interrupted him before he could blunder on. "Let's just let it go."

"Good idea! What we need to do is consider the future. I won't have you going back to that city."

"Daddy, I am grown—"

"Well, what I mean is, I hope you wouldn't even consider going back."

"I do have a job there."

"You could get another teaching job."

"Not this late in the year."

"Well then, take the year off. Do some traveling. How about a nice long stay in Europe? Yes, that's it. You just decide where you want to go—do something you've always wanted to do. Don't worry about money; I'll take care of that—"

"Daddy, wait a minute. I'm still reeling from all that's happened. I don't know what I want to do; I don't think I'm able to decide right now."

"You did take quite a bump on the head," he conceded, "but maybe by tomorrow you'll feel like coming down to the office, and we can start making some solid plans for you."

"Yes, that sounds good," Rachel agreed just to get him off the topic. "What happened to my car? Did you send Saul after it like you said you would?"

"Now you're talking!" he jumped to his feet, "I've been waiting for days for you to ask that question." Rachel stared up at him as he pulled her chair back from the table and tugged on her arm. "Come outside. Have I got something to show you!"

"Daddy!" He was pulling her out of the room and into the kitchen.

"Just come with me."

Finally she gave up resisting and allowed him to hurry her toward the garage. As they approached it, he yelled at Saul, "Bring it out, Saul." Then he positioned Rachel where he wanted her and watched her face as old Saul started a car engine and began to back an unfamilar car out of the garage. When the car was totally revealed, Rachel saw a new Cadillac.

"What do you think of it?" Jack demanded eagerly.

"It's beautiful, of course."

"It's yours!"

"Daddy, I don't need a new car," Rachel protested.

"Yes you do. You need to leave behind everything that's attached to the nightmare you've been through. You need to start over. How could you ever do that if you keep driving the same car?"

"Daddy—"

"Please accept it, Rachel. If you don't like the color or something, you can trade it for another one."

"Daddy—"

"Baby, I know it's just a car, but it's something I can do to help you, and it seems like there's so little I can do—"

"I love it!" Rachel announced the minute she understood his need. "It really is beautiful, and you know how much I love blue, and you're right about leaving things behind that bring up bad memories."

"Great! The keys are in it. As soon as you feel like it, take it for a drive." he suggested. Rachel was amazed at how excited he was. "I don't guess you would want to try it right now, would you?" She couldn't help herself; she started laughing.

"Are you kidding?" she demanded. "Somebody gives me a new car—of course, I want to drive it."

"I don't suppose you'd like some company?"

"Get in, Daddy!"

Rachel drove the car around the small town while her father talked non-stop about all the many special gadgets it possessed. When they returned home, he was a happy man.

As they walked back to the house, Rachel promised

to go by the Cadillac dealer later in the day and sign the necessary papers. When they reached the kitchen, Rachel said, "It really is beautiful, Daddy. Thank you." She hugged him for the first time in years. It was a strange, uncomfortable moment for both of them.

"Well, better get to work," he announced awkwardly.

"Right," Rachel agreed. "Thanks again." And he was gone for the day.

An hour later she fulfilled her promise and drove to the Cadillac dealer where she signed the necessary papers.

Unwilling to go back to her parents' house and needing time to think about the future, she drove around aimlessly. When sometime later she found herself parked in front of the Catholic Church, she wasn't at all surprised. She felt like the farmers of long ago who allowed their teams to choose their own direction, knowing they could trust them to find their way home. She offered no resistance when an invitation gently wafted through her brain. Come inside! Come inside!

It had been many years since Rachel had been inside this particular church. So many years, in fact, she couldn't remember the last time, but the first time, her first visit to this particular church had been with her Grandmere. She yielded to the invitation, and soon she was walking down the center aisle to the front of the church, all the time staring up at the enormous wooden cross bearing the crucified Christ. "I was holding Grandmere's hand the first time I saw that enormous cross," Rachel murmured as she slipped into a pew. "It was Justin's baptism, yes my new baby brother's baptism. His birth brought Grandmere into my life."

❧❧

In early spring when Rachel was six years old, a profound change occurred in her life. She was awakened in the middle of the night by great confusion in the house. When she sleepily appeared in the front hall, she discovered that her mother was being rushed to the hospital because it was time for the baby, the baby her parents had fought so much over, to be born. Rachel's understanding of this process and the nine month period that had preceded it was very limited. She had seen many babies, of course, and she knew that her mother's protruding stomach contained a baby. However, the dominant impression that she had received about this particular baby was that its coming was a problem, just as she knew that her own birth had been a problem. What she had heard repeatedly from her mother and Mammy Cassie strongly suggested to her that babies were not very cherished items.

Early the next morning she rushed eagerly into the kitchen to ask Florence if the baby was born, but Florence looked worried and said sadly, "Lord help us. This baby fighting for its life." Rachel was frightened. Immediately she thought of her father's excitement about the coming birth, how he had hoped for a son. Then she thought of her mother, and her fear increased to panic. "Is Mother going to be all right?" she demanded frantically. Florence saw the fear in the upturned, urgent little face, and she rushed to reassure her, "Your mother gonna be just fine, and that baby gonna most likely be fine too. It just having to work real hard to get borned, that's all." She hugged Rachel to her as she continued, "Ain't no need for you to worry yourself none. You just go on out and play or go see the dogs." Feeling helpless, Rachel left the kitchen and headed down to the kennels. Florence had given her some biscuits for the dogs, but today feeding them and watching their crazy antics didn't lighten her mood a bit.

Finally, looking for other distraction, she wandered down to the woods. Just after she had moved into the shade of the pines and her eyes had adjusted from the bright sun she had left, she saw a little flurry of movement over to her right. It was the tiniest quivering motion down on the bed of pine needles. At first Rachel was startled, but as the quivering motion continued, her curiosity led her to edge slowly toward the spot. Finally she came close enough to see the tiniest little bird with just a tinge of red to its feathers. It was caught in a piece of chicken wire that was lying crumpled on the ground. Overhead Rachel heard frantic, angry cries from several birds. She looked up and saw a geranium red bird challenging her presence with sharp tones. A further movement in the trees revealed another bird with a bright, marigold-colored beak. Over and over the baby bird fluttered at her feet, struggling to free itself, but its claws had become so entangled in the maze of wire that it was hopelessly imprisoned. Rachel watched it in its helplessness, and she was filled with pity for the tiny bird and grief that such things could happen.

Suddenly it dawned on her that *she* could make a difference, she could change things, she could free the bird. The bird need not be a helpless victim of circumstances if she intervened. Until this moment, her life had been a matter of seeking her own happiness, of defending herself from the onslaughts of her own environment, and of suffering the pangs of guilt that came when she upset her parents. Here, however, was her first chance to move outside herself, to have an undeniably positive impact on another creature's fate. Her young age and her small stature had always made her a recipient, and in some cases, a victim of life, but here was something smaller than she, more helpless than she, and *she* could change its fate.

Slowly she walked up to the baby bird and knelt on the pine needles. She saw the little bird's frantic heartbeat, and her eyes filled with tears. "It's okay, baby bird," she whispered, "It's okay. I won't hurt you." Carefully she began to untangle the wire until she could lift the bird from its imprisonment. For just a moment she held it in the palm of her hand; she was amazed at its tininess, its fragility. Carefully, she placed her own small forefinger on the bird's head. "You're so beautiful!" she breathed as her heart warmed with emotion. "I like you. Oh, I like you!" Gradually she opened her hand; the bird looked at her intently as it paused for just a moment and then flew to a low-lying shrub. Immediately the bright red bird joined it and escorted it as the tiny bird flew from bush to bush and finally onto a lower branch of a tree. There the other bird also joined the baby bird, high over Rachel's head, and then the three flew away together. In time they were entirely out of Rachel's sight, but they would always be in her memory.

Rachel felt good. For no reason that she could have explained she thought of violets, and she liked herself. She felt hopeful; she felt active instead of passive, and there was hope in activity. She had felt the pangs of helplessness often in her life, and it gave her a special joy to have liberated something.

By mid-afternoon the baby was safely born, and later Rachel's father returned home for supper and proudly told her all about her new baby brother. His excitement about his son caused Rachel to experience a confusion of feelings that included jealousy, a touch of her father's excitement, and a great relief that everything was okay.

A week later Rachel was pacing up and down the front porch and impatiently staring down at the gates of the estate. With her were an extremely anxious Mammy Cassie, who was furious that she had not been allowed to go to the hospital to care for her beloved Patsy, and an excited Florence, who saw the coming into the house of the new male heir as a festive occasion. Finally, a cloud of red dust was seen at the gate, and two vehicles emerged, a long, black ambulance and the family Cadillac. The small caravan made its way to the front porch with what seemed to Rachel to be interminable slowness. At last it stopped in front of the steps. Jack leapt out of the Cadillac, and the attendants emerged and opened the doors at the back of the ambulance. A stretcher was lifted out, and Rachel felt a clutching at her heart when she saw her mother and realized that she was so ill she had to be brought home lying on a bed. She darted to her side and felt only slight relief when her mother weakly smiled up at her. However, her mother's face lit up with joy when Mammy Cassie leaned over and began to pat her head, and as Mammy Cassie began to croon about how everything was going to be okay now that Patsy was home again, Rachel relaxed. She had confidence that Mammy Cassie could and would take care of her mother, no matter what.

Suddenly she was distracted by another movement at the back of the ambulance. The attendants were lifting something like an enormous white egg with four legs out of the back of the ambulance and setting it gingerly on the ground. Rachel was fascinated and mesmerized by the giant egg as she watched her father lean over it and smile at something inside it. Her father glanced at her and said, "This white thing is a bassinette for the baby to sleep in. Come meet your new baby brother, Rachel. This is Justin Alexander D'Evereau."

Immediately she heard her mother's angry voice coming from the stretcher, "Not yet, he's not! And if I have anything to say about it, he never will be!"

Jack ignored the comment, took Rachel by the hand, and pulled her to the edge of the bassinette. With great expectation and a little apprehension, she gazed down and saw a diminutive human being with dark hair sleeping soundly on his stomach. She looked up at her father, who winked at her, and she decided that somehow she must learn to like this baby because he obviously made her Daddy happy.

That evening after supper Rachel waited and watched until the new baby's nurse had gone to the kitchen for her supper. Quietly sneaking into the softly lighted room, she tiptoed over to the bassinette and peeked in. All afternoon she had wanted to see the baby up-close and to touch him, but Mammy Cassie and her mother had kept her at a distance, with threatening words, "Don't touch the baby! You'll hurt him!" As she leaned over the bassinette and peered at the infant, he opened his eyes and made a gurgling noise with his mouth. Rachel knew nothing about infants, so she assumed the baby was looking at her for the first time and trying to talk to her. She put her finger forward with great care and gentleness and touched his hand. His little clasped fist suddenly opened and closed around her finger, a simple gesture that caused Rachel to release her heart to the child. She was overwhelmed with a desire to protect this tiny person who was holding on to her so tightly. He was little and weak and reminded her of the baby bird caught in the wire in the woods. She felt the same strong instinct to intervene in behalf of a weaker being and the same exhilaration at the thought that her actions could make a difference. From that moment she commissioned herself to protect him.

Suddenly she heard the sound of heavy footsteps coming down the hall, the unmistakable tread of her father. She dashed to the closet and hid herself, leaving the door slightly open so she could peek out the crack. Her father approached the bassinette and leaned way over and seemed to kiss the baby. Then he placed a chair at the side of the bassinette, sat down and began to speak quietly to the baby.

"Hello, Justin Alexander. How you doing, son? You

sure are tiny, but you're a D'Evereau all the way, and the D'Evereaus are the finest family in all of Louisiana. And when you get a little bigger, you and I will make the D'Evereaus the finest family in all of Texas." He paused and looked down at his son as if he were seeing the future. "Yes, there's a lot we're going to do together, you and me, but first I want to tell you all about your Grandfather D'Evereau. You were named for him, you know. Justinien Alexandre, that was his name. And I just anglicized it a bit to pacify your mother. You know how she is—well, I guess you don't yet, but you will!" He stopped and stroked the baby's head for a long time. Then suddenly he blurted out, "If I have anything to say about it—and I will!—you're going to grow up and be just like your Grandfather D'Evereau. He was the finest man I ever knew, and you're going to be just like him—strong, assertive, and successful. You're even going to look like him; he was the handsomest man in Louisiana." Jack sighed and stared into space for a moment, "How I wish he were here now—to see you! He would really be proud, son, just like I am. But wait till your grandmother sees you! She'll take one look at you and be a captive for life." Again he was silent. "You know, Justin, this foolishness has got to stop. I've been separated from my family, from my roots long enough. Your coming is going to be a turning point. I want you to know all about the D'Evereau family history, and I want you to know the D'Evereaus, and I want you to grow up like a D'Evereau. You're the D'Evereau heir! You're not a Longwood—you're a D'Evereau, and the world's going to know it! And the first thing we're going to do is bring your grandmother here from Louisiana and baptize you."

Rachel had heard every word of this soliloquy, and if she had ever doubted the importance of this new baby to her father, her doubts were eliminated. A strange sadness settled on her.

She had never heard her father speak so fervently about his family. Even though she was only six, she had been aware for years of an underlying tension between the Longwoods and the D'Evereaus, and since she was living here in Texas, she had known only the Longwoods and had mostly heard their side of the feud. She had heard her mother, as well as her mother's family, speak openly against her father's family. She had determined from their comments that the D'Evereaus were rich and powerful in Louisiana, but they were "different."

"They're not like us," was the frequent comment of her mother, and Rachel had discerned in a vague way that this difference, which appeared to be too horrible to discuss, was the result of the D'Evereaus being French and Catholic. Hearing her father's comments now, she recognized that the baby was immensely important to him for a reason she had never suspected and did not even now fully understand. Because he was a boy baby, he was uniquely connected to her father's family in a way she had not been, could never be. She felt a pang of jealousy, but that jealousy was tempered by her new understanding that the coming of Justin meant that a whole new, exciting world, peopled with strange but fascinating beings, was about to open up for her. And her mysterious and intriguing grandmother, whom she had never known, was coming!

After another week had passed, Patsy was up and around the house. Jack took action on the vows Rachel had overheard him make to his son. At breakfast he announced that Justin would be baptized in the Catholic Church as soon as Jack could arrange things and as soon as his mother could come from Louisiana. Patsy stared at him in disbelief, and for a few painfully tense moments Rachel looked back and forth from her mother's astonished face, which was rapidly turning furious, to her father's face, which was a picture of quiet resolve.

"You are absolutely out of your mind!" Patsy threw her napkin on the table and rose to leave, "and I have no intention of staying here and discussing such an absurdity!"

"That's fine with me, Patsy," Jack eyed her coolly, "I have no desire to discuss the situation either. I have made up my mind that our son is going to know his heritage."

"You mean you're going to make him a Catholic!" Patsy snapped back at him, and an ugly sneer covered her face as she continued. "I thought you had outgrown all that pagan superstition since you came to Texas and began to associate with rational people. No son of mine is going to be baptized in the Catholic Church; I'd rather die first!"

"Patsy!" Jack stood up suddenly. "Justin Alexander is a D'Evereau, and he's going to know what that means!" He raised his voice as he continued, "For years I have buckled under to your wishes and your family's pressure to deny my heritage. You and your family of bigots have disparaged everything French, and you have vilified everything Catholic, and I am ashamed to say that in the name of family peace I have kept my mouth shut. I've allowed you to manipulate me into turning my back on my family, my former friends, and my church. I know that I'm a lousy Catholic, but what sickens me is that I'm an even lousier son. My daughter is six years old and doesn't even know her grandmother. My mother hasn't been in my house for four years, and why? Because you threw such a tantrum the last time she came. Her concern for me and what I have to endure when you are angry has kept her from returning, and I've taken the coward's way out and sold my soul to keep the peace."

"You've seen your mother plenty of times," Patsy challenged. "In fact you're always sneaking off to Louisiana to see your precious mother and leaving me here by myself."

"Oh, I've *seen* Mother—at least I've done that much, but she hasn't been a part of my life or her granddaughter's life. And why? Why, Patsy? You tell me!" he was shouting at her now.

"Because I don't want her around my daughter." Patsy shouted back. "I hate everything about her. She's foreign! She's Catholic! She's—she's never liked me!"

"I wonder why," Jack responded sarcastically. Then there was a deadly silence. Her parents had forgotten Rachel entirely, but she was caught in their anger, her body perspiring with tension, her eyes darting from one speaker to the other. She had never heard them fight like this. They fought often enough, but there was a viciousness this time she had never seen before.

"You will hear from my family about this—and before the day is out!" Patsy threatened.

"Don't waste your time, Patsy. I've buckled under to Longwood pressure as long as I'm going to. This is my house, you're my wife, and this is my son we're talking about. Now listen carefully, My Dear, this is the way it's going to be. Justin will be baptized in the Catholic Church. He will be taught about his D'Evereau heritage. He will know his grandmother D'Evereau both here in this house *and* in Louisiana. He will be given Catholic instruction, but he may attend the Baptist Church with you if he wants to. When he is old enough, he can make his own choice. As for me, I will continue to play my duplicitous role by attending church with you on Sunday and privately going to mass during the week."

"You're not going to get away with this!" Patsy insisted. "This is *not* decided—don't you think it is!"

"Oh it's decided, My Dear. You can scream as loud as

you like or get as sick as you choose or bring your whole family in to argue, but it will make no difference. Justin is a D'Evereau. He may be the only son I ever have, and if he is, he'll inherit Belle St. Marie and all the Louisiana holdings. But more importantly he'll inherit the traditions of my father and grandfather. They were great men, and he's going to be just like them. I may have previously shamed my name and reneged on my heritage, but that's all over. I have a son now!'' With that final proclamation he stormed out the door.

Rachel looked at her mother, who was so angry she was crying, and she knew that Patsy would not give in easily. But Rachel also knew that in the end her father would win and that her own life was about to change.

The house seethed with hostility for the remainder of the day. Rachel, Florence, Saul—everyone who could—stayed out of Patsy's way. Instead of taking to her sickbed, which was her usual manipulative device, Patsy stalked through the house spewing venomous comments against Jack and his family. Mammy Cassie followed behind her voicing a sympathetic rage.

Rachel wisely took to the woods with her favorite dolls and teddy bear under her arm. Florence had strongly suggested she go and had even made her a lunch to encourage her to stay a while. Rachel busied herself through the morning in the dusky shadows of the cool woods building *her* version of a home. She picked out an enormous pine tree which had a thick bed of needles under it and set to work. With a large piece of bark she began to scrap the pine needles into mounds until she had uncovered the hard-packed, slightly damp soil underneath. This area, which radiated out in a half-circle from the base of the pine tree for about six feet, she claimed as her house. Quickly she set about moving the mounds of pine needles into appropriate places for the walls. She divided the interior into three rooms—the living room nearest the base of the tree, the dining room opening to the left, and the bedroom to the right. Next she skipped back and forth through the woods gathering leaves to mound up to represent furniture.

Now she was ready. She moved the family in. The teddy bear was the father because he was the biggest; her walking doll was the mother, and the baby doll in diapers was, of course, the baby girl. For the rest of the day she played God, ordering the lives of these three "people" to her liking. There was no Mammy Cassie; in Rachel's ideal world the mother took care of the baby herself. There were no fights; everyone went to the same church and came from the same place. Most importantly, the mother and the father spent most of their time with the baby and told her over and over how much they loved her.

Hours passed as Rachel sat on the ground under the enormous pine and fantasized a world to her liking. At the same time she was God, ordering the events, she was also the baby receiving all the loving attention. Significantly, this world contained no Justin and no in-laws on either side. It was a world of three, except by mid-afternoon she had added a large pine cone as a dog. Rachel was happy in this gentle world; she played and ate her lunch, and when she was tired, she put her dolls to bed and fell asleep herself under the sheltering pine, which stood as sentinel over the little girl. She was still asleep when she heard Florence'a voice calling her from the edge of the woods to come home and get ready for supper.

Rachel and her father ate alone at the large dining room table. At first he seemed unwilling to talk and only politely asked her what she had been doing that day. She quickly replied, "Playing with my dolls, Daddy." He responded with, "That's nice, Baby" and ended the conversation with his preoccupied look.

As the meal progressed and finally reached the dessert course, Rachel gathered her courage and asked the question that had been on her mind all day. "Daddy, is my Grandmother D'Evereau really coming from Louisiana?"

Startled, he looked up and then smiled at the excitement in her voice. "You'd like to meet your grandmother, wouldn't you, Baby?" he asked. Rachel nodded enthusiastically, and her father's smile broadened. "She's coming next week to see Justin, and she's very eager to get to know you. You don't remember, I'm sure, but she was here when you were two. Every time she sat down somewhere, you would try to climb in her lap, and you cried when she went home."

"Did she like me, Daddy?" There was a poignant hopefulness in the question.

"Of course she liked you, Baby." He laughed, but then grew quiet and thoughtful before continuing. "You know, you are her only granddaughter. I want you to really get to know her, Baby. In many ways you are a lot like her."

A thrill of pleasure shot through Rachel's body at the thought of a new person in her life, a person who liked her. There was silence between them as they both thought their private thoughts, but finally Rachel voiced the question that had been on her mind since she had hidden in the closet and heard her father speaking to Justin. "Daddy, am I a D'Evereau like Justin even though I'm not a boy?"

She was stunned by the look on his face and frightened that she had angered him. Then she saw tears gather in his eyes, and her fear became guilt that she had hurt him somehow. He cleared his throat and looked away from her.

When he faced her again, the tears were gone. There was a new tenderness toward her in his voice. "You are definitely a D'Evereau, Baby, and nothing will ever change that. Nothing can."

## SEVEN

Justin was born twenty-nine years ago, Rachel reflected as she sat in the stillness of Pineview's Catholic Church, and my life was changed forever. Changed for the worse and changed for the better. The worse came in the form of an open war between my parents. All the small battles about religious and ethnic differences, which I had lived with all my life, now escalated into war. And that war wounded us all—forever, I suppose.

On the other hand, my life was changed for the better too because the very person Mother had fought so hard to isolate me from, Grandmere, became my best role model. I shudder to think what kind of adult I would have become without Grandmere's influence. Also, she was the only island of peace I could go to when the war around me grew too ferocious.

I wonder if I would have ever known Grandmere if Justin had not been born. But Justin was born, and Grandmere came to Pineview.

One week after Jack's announcement that the infant Justin would be baptized, Rachel was sitting on the top step of the front porch anxiously peering down the drive. She was awaiting the arrival of her grandmother. She was dressed in blue at her own insistence because her father had told her that blue was her grandmother's favorite color. Carefully she spread her skirts out on the step to keep them unwrinkled, and every few minutes she reached her hand around to her back to see that her sash was still properly tied in its bow. This was one day that no one needed to tell her to stay clean; she desperately wanted to make a good impression.

Looking back over her shoulder, she saw her father standing in the hall; he smiled broadly and leaned out the screen door to encourage her, "She's coming, Baby. It won't be too much longer." Rachel gave him a look that plainly indicated that she was not so sure; then without saying a word, because she didn't want to break her concentration on the driveway, she turned her back on him and re-dedicated herself to wishing for the magic cloud of dust that would signal the approach of a car.

A few moments later it was Mammy Cassie who interrupted her vigil. "Lord a mercy! I ain't never seed you set so still. Is you sick or something?" Rachel ignored her. Mammy Cassie stood in the doorway with the screen door pushed open; she had her cumbersome arms out to the sides with her thick hands perched on her abundant hips. She was determined to command Rachel's attention, so she tried again. "What you doing anyway? You waiting on your grandmother? She ain't gonna be here for hours and with a little luck she won't come at all!" Rachel continued to ignore her; today Mammy Cassie's sniping was simply not important enough to fool with. Besides, she knew she was driving Mammy Cassie crazy by refusing to become angry. Frustrated by her inability to rile Rachel, Mammy Cassie tried another tactic. "What you doing setting on the floor? You's gonna get just filthy setting on them steps. Why can't you set on a chair like the lady you's supposed to be?" She would have continued in this particular vein for some time, but suddenly Patsy appeared behind her.

"Oh there you are, Mammy! I *cannot* make Florence understand one single thing about the way dinner has to be served, and Jack's mother will be here any minute. Mammy, for heaven's sake, go into the kitchen and try to make Florence understand that I want dinner served in courses while Mrs. D'Evereau is here. I won't have her looking down her Creole nose at us just because we don't do things the French way." Patsy's face was flushed, her features set in an angry scowl, and she wrung her hands in frustration. When Mammy didn't move immediately, Patsy's voice rose angrily, "Mammy! Do something! I thought I could at least depend on you!"

"I's going right now," Mammy Cassie promised as she turned back into the hall. "But you's got to settle down, Miz Patsy. You's too riled up."

"Riled up? I feel like I'm under a sentence of death with that woman coming here to stay! She's never approved of me; I can see it in her face every time she looks at me. And those frigid blue eyes! They could freeze you right out of the county. And, of course, Jack had to go and inherit them and give them to Rachel!" She turned to Rachel and glared down at her. "What in the name of heaven are you doing sitting there? The Queen of England isn't coming—it's just your grandmother, heaven help us! Go on off and play somewhere. You can meet her at dinner." She turned to go back into the house, but she stopped and added an afterthought in her severest tone, "And Rachel, I *do not* want you to bother your grandmother while she is here. She's coming to see Justin; thank God he's just an infant and won't remember a thing. But there's absolutely no reason for you to be exposed to her. Just be polite and stay away from her!" With that final command she left in a flurry of nervous activity, and

Mammy Cassie followed her, sympathizing with her every complaint.

Rachel stubbornly returned to her vigil. Another fifteen minutes passed, but still she sat there like a statue. She leaned forward with her elbows propped on her knees and her chin propped on her upturned hands. Forlornly she stared at the gate. She wasn't simply waiting for the arrival of her grandmother; she was nurturing a hope. She wanted to be loved, to be special to someone.

Suddenly she saw some movement, then a cloud of red dust, and finally a large black car emerged through the gate and started the ascent to the house. Rachel jumped to her feet and began to clap her hands excitedly. She ran to the front door and shouted for her father, "Daddy! Daddy! She's here! She's here!" He appeared immediately and hugged her as they watched the car approach the house. "Is it Grandmother, Daddy? Is it Grandmother?" Rachel demanded urgently.

"Yes, Baby. Here she comes at last!" He bounded down the stairs and the walk to stand at the edge of the drive. However, Rachel didn't follow him; she was suddenly overcome with shyness and could move no closer to her hope than the bottom step. There she waited, barely breathing, as the car slowly came to a stop.

Rachel watched, her eyes bright with anticipation, her heart full of both hope and apprehension, while the chauffeur walked around the car to open the back door. Her father had rushed forward to assist her grandmother from the back seat and had thus blocked Rachel's view. Finally he moved aside, and she saw a tiny woman embracing her father. From this distance Rachel perceived her grandmother as an exquisite, fragile, porcelain doll. She had not yet seen her grandmother's face, but she was already aware of great delicacy, of grace, of refinement. And then she heard her grandmother question eagerly in a soft, lilting voice, "But where's Rachélle?" Rachel's heart beat wildly when she heard her grandmother ask for her, and all her belligerent insistence that her name be pronounced "Rachel" dissipated. Her father turned and motioned to Rachel on the steps, "Here she is, Mother, but I'd best warn you. She insists on being called Rachel."

Her grandmother turned to face her for the first time, and as their eyes met, Rachel drew in her breath, and when she released the air in her lungs, all of her fear was expelled with it. She was bathed in the light from her grandmother's eyes. Mesmerizing love shone from her blue eyes, and extraordinary peace radiated from her grandmother's face, a peace that gentled Rachel's entire being.

"Hello, Rachel," her voice was little more than a whisper at first but gained in intensity and volume as she continued, "How I've longed to see you—to know you! We must spend every moment together!" She walked over to Rachel as she spoke, and when she reached her, she gently stroked her golden head. Rachel's spirit opened to this loving affirmation as a blossom opens and reveals its beauty under a warm, sustaining sun. Eagerly she gazed at her grandmother's face, but she couldn't seem to speak.

"Say hello to your Grandmere, Rachel," Jack laughingly prodded. "'Grandmere' is French for grandmother."

"Hello, Grandmere," Rachel shyly tried the new word. Her Grandmere smiled down at her, put her arm around Rachel's shoulders, drew her close, and together they started up the steps.

Patsy awaited them in the living room, and to Rachel's stunned surprise, she greeted her mother-in-law effusively. She hugged her and babbled on about how delighted she was to see her and how it had simply been too long since her last visit. Grandmere received Patsy's effusions graciously and made complimentary remarks about the decorations of the room and Patsy's appearance. Jack stood by nervously, waiting to jump into the conversation should there be a lag. Finally, a dangerous pause occurred, and he quickly suggested a visit to the nursery. Patsy responded enthusiastically, "Oh yes! You must see our adorable Justin at once. Jack says he looks just like his Grandfather D'Evereau; I can't tell you how pleased I was to hear it! And of course I just insisted that he be named after his grandfather. I mean, what other name could possibly do? He must be named Justin Alexander; after all, he's the D'Evereau heir!"

Rachel stared at her mother as if she had never seen her before. Patsy, chattering enthusiastically, began ushering Grandmere out of the room and down the hall toward the nursery. Jack followed silently. Uninvited, but eager to stay with her Grandmere, Rachel trailed behind her father. Suddenly Mammy Cassie grabbed her from behind and demanded, "Where you thinks you's going? Your mother don't want you in the way. You got to get washed up for dinner." Taking Rachel by the arm, she roughly hauled her in the opposite direction.

Dinner was amazing to Rachel. Her mother seemed to be buoyant with gaiety; to hear her talk, she was the luckiest woman in the world. Furthermore, her happiness was doubled by the presence of Grandmere. Rachel was mystified by what was happening around the table. For the preceding two weeks, since Jack had named the baby Justin Alexander, meals at the D'Evereau house had been unpleasant. Her parents' hostilities sometimes rumbled beneath the surface of their superficial comments to each other and often times erupted into full-scale battles. But all was pleasant now, and Rachel began to wish that her Grandmere would never leave.

To Rachel, everything about her Grandmere was shiny. Her glistening black hair was highlighted with streaks of silver. And one of those streaks seemed to have broken lose and partially encircled her Grandmere's delicate neck in the form of a dainty silver chain. It sparkled as it caught the light, and then it disappeared into the bodice of her dress. For a moment Rachel wondered what was at the end of that chain, but soon her gaze was brought back to her Grandmere's face. She smiled so lovingly at Rachel, and her eyes gleamed so happily at the sight of the little girl that Rachel was instantly and eternally hers.

By mid-afternoon Rachel was pacing around her room, fingering her different possessions. She was actually biding her time until she could slip out of her room, where she was supposed to be napping, and go see her Grandmere in the room across the hall. Her Grandmere was resting, and Rachel had been told by Patsy to leave her alone, so Rachel was trying to decide how much rest grandmothers need and trying to calculate when it would be safe to interrupt her. Thirty whole minutes had passed thus far, an eternity to a six-year-old. She's got to be all rested by now, Rachel thought. I'm not a bit tired. But she wasn't quite sure, so she waited another five long, drawn-out minutes. Then she stealthily slipped out of her door, looking both ways in the hall for Mammy Cassie, and hurried across to her Grandmere's door, where she quietly knocked.

"Come in, Rachel," her Grandmere called through the door. Rachel was surprised to hear her name and amazed that Grandmere was expecting her.

She opened the door and peeked around its edge. "Are you through resting yet, Grandmere?" she asked hopefully. Not waiting for a reply, lest it be negative, Rachel entered the room and turned back to face the door as she quietly closed it. When she once again turned toward the room, she was startled by what she saw.

Sitting gracefully on the velvet-covered window seat was

the dark outline of her Grandmere's tiny form. The room itself was dusky and shadowed, but a bright, pale yellow afternoon light burst through the window behind her Grandmere. This combination produced a perfect silhouette of Grandmere, and the light radiated around her like a body-sized halo. Rachel stopped and held her breath as she gazed at this apparently supernatural spectacle.

"Come in, Darling. Come sit by me." A graceful hand, silhouetted by the radiant light behind it, reached out and patted the windowseat. Rachel was intrigued by this mysterious, hidden figure that sounded like Grandmere, but she was still hesitant, apprehensive. The beckoning figure rose, and as it moved out of that mysterious halo of light and into the dusky room, Rachel saw her Grandmere's warm, loving eyes looking down at her. Crinkles appeared at their corners, and an inviting smile began to cover her face. For Rachel, Grandmere's smile felt like the first spring-time sun bursting forth on her winter-laden face. Her smile brought with it a feeling of profound well-being and an all-encompassing acceptance. Most significantly for Rachel, it brought promises, hopes for the future.

Drawing Rachel over to sit by her on the windowseat, Grandmere made Rachel feel that she had brought a priceless joy into her life simply by coming to visit her. "At last we're alone!" she rejoiced. "Now we can finally get to know each other. I am so eager to learn all about you. Now where shall we begin?" Rachel gazed up at the vivid sapphires of her Grandmere's eyes, and she knew that she—little Rachel, just as she was—had stimulated the vibrancy there. The soul-hungry child was intoxicated with happiness.

"You have eyes just like mine!" she blurted out, then fell silent for a moment before adding, "but I don't think mine look as shiny as yours, and yours are always smiling."

Grandmere paused before suggesting, "Well, perhaps you aren't seeing the world in the same way as I am, Darling." She pulled Rachel closer, pressing her against her side, holding her tight. The shiny crystal and brass clock on the mantel piece ticked away methodically, but despite the lack of verbal communication, Rachel was content. She was pleased to sit there quietly with the soft velvet under her bare legs and her Grandmere's warm arm firmly, but gently encircling her. She felt safe in a way she had never experienced, as if she had been miraculously encased in a cozy cocoon.

In time she gazed up into her Grandmere's face, and when she did, she noticed once again the delicate silver chain around Grandmere's neck. It was so fragile that once more, for just a moment, Rachel imagined that it might be one of Grandmere's silver hairs escaped from its hairpin and loosely encircling her neck. Rachel's youthful curiousity was piqued by that chain which disappeared into her Grandmere's dress, but fearful of offending her new-found love and perhaps losing the warmth of her cocoon, she hesitated to ask. The clock continued its patient ticking until finally Grandmere seemed to be coming out of her reverie, for she began to stroke Rachel's shoulder.

Still plagued by her curiosity, Rachel decided to risk a question. "Grandmere, what's on that chain around your neck? Is it a secret?" She had lowered her voice to a whisper on the last question, just in case it was indeed a secret.

Grandmere smiled immediately and leaned over very close to Rachel's face and whispered back. "It's not exactly a secret, Darling, but very—few—people—know—about—it." She dragged out the last part of the sentence and winked down at Rachel as she spoke.

Rachel was intrigued! "Can I know the secret?" she whispered excitedly, "Will you tell me? I promise not to tell anyone!"

"You're sure you won't tell?" Grandmere inquired very solemnly as her eyes twinkled.

"Oh, I'm good at keeping secrets, really! I didn't tell anyone at Sunday School that Santa Claus isn't real—not even when I knew for sure!" Rachel assured her earnestly.

"Well, I think I can trust you," Grandmere began cautiously as Rachel started beaming. "What I have on this chain is my most precious possession because your grandfather gave it to me on the day we were married. It is the most meaningful gift I have ever received." Slowly she began to draw the end of the chain up out of her dress while Rachel leaned forward and held her breath in anticipation. Finally the secret emerged.

"It's Jesus!" Rachel whispered, awed by what she saw.

"It's a *reminder* of Jesus, Rachel," Grandmere corrected her. "It reminds me that God is here, right this minute."

"But why did Grandfather give you Jesus on your wedding day?" Rachel queried, ignoring Grandmere's comment about God's presence. She was more concerned with the fact that she saw no connection between God and weddings.

"He gave it to me to assure me that I could wear a reminder of Jesus next to my heart at the same time I wore a reminder of him, my wedding ring, on my finger. He wanted to say he was not taking me away from Jesus."

Rachel was troubled with thoughts she could not quite formulate, but Grandmere said no more. Once again the clock was the only sound in the room as Rachel sat holding the crucifix in her small hand and staring at the figure of the crucified Christ.

Suddenly belligerent words spilled from Rachel's lips. "I don't like this Jesus! I like baby Jesus, but I don't like this Jesus!"

Grandmere waited a moment before inquiring softly, "Why not, Rachel? Why don't you like this Jesus?"

"Because He's the one who sends you to hell to burn up. He's not nice unless you're perfect, and I just can't be perfect no matter how hard I try!" Rachel dropped the crucifix as she plopped despondently back on the window seat.

"Oh no, Darling! This Jesus is the one who saves you from hell. This Jesus loves you," Grandmere's tone was definite and ardently reassuring. Rachel said nothing. Her head was down as she watched her hands repeatedly smoothing the short skirt of her dress. Grandmere waited in silence until Rachel chose to speak.

Are you sure, Grandmere?" Rachel inquired cautiously, for she enjoyed her Grandmere's love and was not willing to alienate her, but at the same time she was too honest to agree with her simply from expediency.

"I am positive, Rachel, absolutely positive," Grandmere's tone was quietly firm.

"That's not what they said at church, Grandmere," Rachel warned, jerking her head up and staring Grandmere right in the eyes.

"I am *still* positive, Darling, and some day you will be too." Rachel continued to stare up at her, and she did indeed seem to be very sure.

Suddenly there was a soft knock on the door, and Patsy's voice sang out, "Mother D'Evereau! Tea is ready to be served in the living room. Won't you join me?"

At the first sound of her mother's voice Rachel jumped down from the windowseat, raced to the bed, and crawled under it.

"Mother D'Evereau!" Patsy opened the door. "Didn't you hear me? I've had the servants prepare us a lovely tea."

Grandmere ignored Patsy's question and responded instead to the idea of tea. "What a wonderful idea, Patsy!" Rachel peeped out under the bedspread and watched her Grandmere, a portrait of composure, rise from the windowseat and glide toward Patsy. "A cup of tea sounds delicious." Gracefully she shepherded Patsy from the room, closing the door behind them.

"Whew!" Rachel gasped as she wiggled out from under the bed. "That was close!" She hurried to the door, listened for a minute, and than darted back across the hall to her room.

That night Jack had a large, elegant dinner party in honor of his mother's visit. Rachel ate in the kitchen where she watched Florence and Mammy Cassie fretting over every detail. When she was finished, Mammy Cassie decreed that she looked tired and took her to bed early, warning her to stay in her room. Rachel lay on top of the sheets, surrounded by her collection of stuffed animals and listened to the loud laughter from the living room. She couldn't go to sleep no matter how she tried, so she finally got up, collected her favorite storybooks, brought them to bed, and began to look at the pictures.

At some point she must have fallen asleep, for she was awakened when someone sat lightly on the edge of the bed. She opened her eyes to find her Grandmere smiling down at her.

"I thought I dreamed you," Rachel confessed sleepily. "I thought you weren't even real." Her eyes were so heavy she had to fight to keep them open.

"I'm here, Darling, I'm here," Grandmere whispered, and she raised her hand to smooth Rachel's hair. "Close your eyes now and go to sleep. Tomorrow is a big day." Rachel smiled, too sleepy now to speak, but she heard Grandmere's gentle voice as she drifted into rest, "I've waited so long to know you, Darling, but you are worth the wait."

Rachel was brought back to the present by the sound of a side door of the church being opened. She watched as an elderly lady slipped into a pew, knelt, and began fingering rosary beads.

As Rachel looked away from the woman, her eyes settled on one of the stained glass windows, particularly on the brilliant blue of the Virgin's robe. Grandmere's eyes were just about that color, Rachel thought. Looking into them was like looking into deep, deep water. There was a peace, an unexplainable, extraordinary serenity with life that shone from her eyes. I always felt certain that she was seeing something beautiful all around her—something that I could not see directly; I could only hope to glimpse a reflection of this beauty as I watched her react to it.

It was that quality that called out to me as I sat across the dining table from her; it was that quality that would draw me to her side for many years to come. Of course, I didn't understand any of that then; I just felt it. And that special feeling I had for her made it possible for me to survive Justin's baptism the next day.

At eleven o'clock the next morning six-year-old Rachel was standing outside the Catholic Church in the bright, golden sunshine excitedly waiting for everyone to assemble for Justin's baptism. She had never seen a Catholic Church before, but in spite of the six years of damning comments about Catholics she had heard from the Longwoods, she was predisposed to like it. After all, it was the church of her beloved Grandmere, and in addition to that important fact, Mammy Cassie had spent the entire morning telling her it was "wicked just like you is." Rachel already felt at home.

Finally the whole group had arrived. Patsy stood defiantly to one side, holding baby Justin, and as soon as the Longwoods had coldly greeted Jack and his mother, they surrounded her. They were openly hostile, announcing to Jack that they were there "merely to support dear Patsy through this abomination." Jack stood halfway between his wife and his mother, who stood serenely holding Rachel's hand a few paces away. The only neutrals present were the Barclays, Robert and Carol, who were to be Justin's godparents. Rachel had never seen them before, but she knew Mr. Barclay worked for her father and that he and his wife were Catholics.

The parish priest, a man whose face was brightened by a sunny smile, came hurrying around the corner from the rectory, saw Jack and rushed forward to shake his hand and slap him on the back as he congratulated him. Jack introduced everyone, and although Father Deering was himself cordial with all present, he was greeted with icy silence from the Longwoods. Rachel stared up at him, but she jerked her head down when he turned suddenly and winked at her. Honestly she didn't know what to think about him; he was friendly and gregarious, but he wore funny clothes, and he sounded strange, and besides he said such crazy things like, "Oh, it's such a beautiful day, such a glorious day! To be sure the angels are laughing in heaven!" Rachel wasn't sure what she thought of him, but she was definitely interested in finding out if he had actually seen an angel—a real angel, not just a Christmas, pretend angel with aluminum foil wings.

"Well, let's get the boy baptized before the millennium comes!" Father Deering urged cheerfully, as he began to direct the silent, stiff-necked Patsy through the doors. The Longwoods marched resolutely ahead of the others with one brother supporting Patsy and the other practically carrying Grandmother Longwood. They were all dressed in unremitting black. Grandmere, Jack and Rachel were left to enter together. Jack sighed as he held the door for his mother, and Rachel watched as her Grandmere paused just long enough to pat her son reassuringly on the shoulder. Inside the door they paused again in the foyer while Jack and Grandmere put their fingers into a bowl of water and made a movement with one hand across their chests. Then they hastened to the next set of doors. Once again Jack opened the door, stood back, and waited for Grandmere and Rachel to enter, but this time, rather than walking in front of him, Grandmere reached for his free hand with her free hand, and the three of them—Rachel, Grandmere, and Jack—walked hand in hand down the center aisle of the large church.

Rachel was glad someone was holding her hand! It was the biggest place she had ever seen; the vaulted ceiling seemed to rise for miles above her head. But oh! it was so beautiful! Everywhere she looked, as she walked down the long aisle, she saw vivid, jewel-like colors—rubies, sapphires, emeralds, topazes, amethysts. The windows were full of jewels. She turned her head from side to side, the excitement racing through her whole body as she tried to take in all the living colors of the stained glass windows.

The life-sized figures depicting the familiar Bible stories seemed ready to spring forth from the window casements, step down and touch Rachel. They were more alive to her than her father and Grandmere holding her hands. To Rachel, they were breathing miracles of color and light. The bright sun shone through them creating dancing, vibrant reflections everywhere she looked. The shiny walnut of the pews joyfully reflected the dancing lights, and the marble she walked on changed color foot by foot, an ever-changing, freshly created collage reflected from the windows.

The reflections so mesmerized Rachel that she noticed nothing else until her Grandmere stopped suddenly. Then Rachel looked straight ahead, and as she saw her Grandmere's eyes lift, she too looked up. There He was—the same Jesus that Grandmere wore around her neck. There He was, hanging from the ceiling—enormous, commanding her attention. Before Rachel had time to think, both her Grandmere and her father quickly knelt on one knee and moved their hands across their chests. Rachel's attention darted from the height of the cross down to the floor where her father knelt and up to her mother's face. Quickly she cast her eyes down again to her feet, for she was afraid of the hate she saw in her mother's eyes.

"Now, Mrs. Barclay, if you will kindly hold little Justin, and you and Mr. Barclay move forward here, we'll get started." As the priest spoke, Carol moved toward Patsy, smiling, and reached out her arms to receive the baby. Patsy stared at her coldly and made no move to hand over Justin. There was silence in the enormous church, a sterile void, a suspension of time as everyone waited for Patsy to respond in some way, any way. She made no move to cooperate. She had found her way to dominate the situation. Finally, her older brother Lloyd leaned over her shoulder and said, "Let's get this over with, Patsy. If we've got to do it, let's do it."

Still she did not move; she simply turned her defiant eyes on Jack. Clearly her message to him was, "Now what are you going to do, powerful man?" Once again Lloyd tried, "Patsy, let's get this over with. It's just a meaningless gesture anyway. Let's get through with it." Patsy still made no move to hand over Justin, but she stopped staring at Jack and blankly looked at Carol. The would-be godmother gently reached forward and took Justin from his mother's arms.

The church walls seemed to sigh with relief as Robert and Carol, with Justin cradled in Carol's arms, moved forward to stand in front of the priest. Father Deering cleared his throat and began the ritual.

"Dear parents and godparents: You have come here to present this child for baptism. By water and the Holy Spirit he is to receive the gift of new life from God"—the priest paused momentarily, as he looked at Patsy on one side surrounded by Longwoods and Jack on the other with Grandmere and Rachel, and finally continued emphatically—*"who is love."*

As the priest continued, Rachel stared around her, first up at the waists of the Barclays who were almost covering the priest from her view. They weren't even people anymore to Rachel; they were just impersonal backs, and they had Justin and were doing something to him her mother didn't like. Maybe they were going to hurt him!

Rachel couldn't see Justin at all; she could only see her father standing in a rigid military fashion to her left and her mother crossing her arms across her chest and staring in fury at Jack, who refused to divert his eyes from the priest.

Suddenly Rachel felt hot; she couldn't breathe. It was like the giant adult bodies were blocking all the air from reaching her, or with their hatreds they had burned up all the oxygen in the church! Rachel's breath started coming in jerks as beads of perspiration broke out on her face. Rachel furtively looked up at the enormous cross overhead. He was still there. Pale and thin, He looked so sad, and He was stuck on that horrible brown cross with the splinters sticking out of it.

A shudder ran down Rachel's spine, and she held on more tightly to Grandmere and looked up into her peaceful face. Gentle blue eyes smiled lovingly down at her, and Rachel felt like Grandmere had read her mind, had known and understood her joy at the beauty of the colors and her oppression from the adults' hatreds. Rachel sighed with relief; everything was okay now. She was at peace.

Grandmere took Rachel by the shoulders and guided her up to the front of the group, placing her between Robert and Carol where she could plainly see Justin being placed in Father Deering's arms by Carol. Rachel watched, filled with wonder.

"I baptize you, Justin Alexander, in the name of the Father . . ." He poured water over the back of Justin's head. ". . . and of the Son . . ." Again he poured the water over the back of Justin's head. ". . . and of the Holy Spirit." The third time Rachel saw the water trickle over the back of her brother's head. Justin opened his eyes briefly and looked into the priest's face, but he was perfectly peaceful. Rachel was happy. Soon there was a resounding "Amen!" from the Catholics present, and Rachel knew that the baptism was over.

With a broad smile on his face, Father Deering walked over to Patsy and handed her Justin. "He's a fine lad, Mrs. D'Evereau, a fine lad indeed! You must be very proud of him."

Patsy made no response; although she took Justin from his arms, she acted as if the priest did not exist. She walked past him, followed by the Longwoods. The building was silent except for the sharp, staccato sounds of Patsy's high heels as she stalked out of the church.

"He *is* a fine lad, Jack," Father Deering walked over and patted Jack on the shoulder, "and the Lord *will* provide."

"Thank you, Father." Jack looked defeated. Rachel had never seen him look so sad; she started crying silently. He walked away slowly, paused and turned back, "Father, I think we had best cancel the celebration lunch."

"No problem, son," the priest assured him. "I'll walk you out." He turned and genuflected, and Jack did the same. Then Father Deering put his big hand on the back of Jack's neck and started walking with him down the long aisle.

"There's no hurry, Father. She'll already be gone with her family—and with my son."

Rachel was heartbroken at the sight of her father's slumped shoulders and shuffling feet as he walked away from her and Grandmere. Enormous tears began to fall down her tiny face as she turned and stared up at Grandmere for help.

"It will be all right, Darling. I know it hurts very much now, but it will be all right in time." Grandmere drew Rachel to her side and enclosed her in her arms. "Your daddy is a strong man. He'll be okay, and he'll make things better." Rachel said nothing. "Before we leave, let's say a special prayer to Jesus to help your daddy." She lead Rachel over to the altar rail where she herself knelt and clasped her hands in front of her. Rachel stood next to her Grandmere and listened as her Grandmere whispered prayers. Slowly Rachel raised her eyes to the cross. He was still there. He was still suffering and sad. She thought of Justin. They hadn't hurt him at all. He didn't even cry once. Why was everyone so upset?

Grandmere rose from her knees and assured Rachel, "God will take care of everything, Rachel. He always does. You must believe that. He loves you; He loves us all, and He will take care of everything." As Rachel struggled to believe what Grandmere had said instead of what she had just experienced, Grandmere took her hand and slowly began to walk down the long aisle. The beautiful, vibrant lights flashed on Rachel as she walked through the various reflections from the windows. Grandmere genuflected when she reached the end of the aisle, and Rachel turned back to look at the cross. The vibrant, dancing colors were reflected on Jesus' face. He doesn't exactly look happy, Rachel thought, He just doesn't look so sad. He looks peaceful. Maybe Grandmere is right; maybe everything will be okay.

Mid-day dinner that day at the D'Evereau house was a somber affair rather than the festive celebration that Jack had planned. By the time he, Grandmere, and Rachel had returned home, Patsy had already taken to her bed in a fit of nervous prostration brought on by her anger. Jack made no attempt to see her; he simply left her to the care of Mammy Cassie. Instead he ordered that dinner for his mother, Rachel and himself be served out on the porch.

A cooling breeze flitted across the porch as Grandmere and Jack talked quietly throughout dinner, never mentioning the baptism in any way. Apparently there was an unspoken agreement to speak only of pleasant things, and that agreement naturally led them to the past, to Louisiana, to Jack's beloved father, to his childhood. Rachel listened intently, her curiousity about Louisiana growing minute by minute. Peace settled over the table, and Rachel noticed with great relief and joy the happiness that settled over her father.

After dinner her Grandmere went off to her room to rest. Since there was no Mammy Cassie to order Rachel to take a nap, she wandered back out on the porch and sat down on the top step to think. But her thoughts kept returning to the morning, and she felt tense and confused. She didn't want to think about all that hatred; she wanted to be happy like they had been at dinner. She grew sad and lonely until finally a super idea came to her. She walked back through the house to her Grandmere's room, quietly entered, walked over to the side of the bed, and stood there. Without even opening her eyes, Grandmere reached out both of her arms for Rachel, and Rachel crawled up on the bed, snuggled up next to Grandmere's side and fell asleep with Grandmere's arms around her.

When Rachel awakened several hours later, her Grandmere wasn't there. Rachel jerked herself up and scanned the room hurriedly. When her anxious eyes reached the windowseat, there was Grandmere, holding a cup of tea and smiling back at her. Rachel bounced out of bed and ran over to her.

"Well hello, sleepyhead!" Grandmere was laughing as she spoke, "I thought you were going to sleep the rest of the day."

Rachel stretched and yawned and climbed up on the windowseat. Then she spotted the goodies on the tea table. Her eyes widened with delight, but before she could say a word, her Grandmere read her mind. "Yes, you may have some. Florence has brought us all kinds of delights. She even remembered to bring you a glass of milk—" Rachel's face fell with disappointment, but Grandmere quickly laughed and added, "—and an extra cup just in case you preferred a cup of tea."

"Are we going to have a real tea party, Grandmere?" Rachel demanded excitedly. "A real tea party with real tea and everything?"

"Real tea and everything!" Grandmere laughed as she reached for the extra cup and began to pour Rachel's cup of tea. Gracefully she stirred the steaming, light brown liquid, adding milk and sugar. Then she placed the cup and saucer right in front of Rachel. "There you are, Darling; I hope you enjoy it. But be careful—don't burn your tongue."

Slowly Rachel lifted the delicate cup to her lips and gingerly sipped her first cup of tea ever. It tasted funny, but she was determined to like it no matter what because all the grown-up ladies drank tea, and she was going to be grown-up too.

As her Grandmere handed her a plate with cookies and sandwiches on it, she suggested, "Let's take a walk in the woods after our tea. I've been cooped up in buildings ever since I got here, and spring is popping out all over outside. Let's go see what's happening in the woods."

"Oh yes!" Rachel agreed enthusiastically, "I'll show you the house I built!"

"A house? You built a house? Oh my goodness, I absolutely must see that," Grandmere agreed. "How's your tea, Darling? Do you like it?"

"Oh, I love it, Grandmere!" Rachel responded enthusiastically while she assured herself that she wasn't really lying because she intended to learn to love it—she really did!

Half an hour later Rachel was happily skipping ahead of Grandmere as they entered the edge of the woods. Occasionally she would look back and urge her partner on, "Come on, Grandmere, come on! We're almost there! We're almost to my house!" Finally she turned the last corner, and there was the giant pine tree with her house still intact under it. Grandmere walked up behind her.

"Oh my, this is impressive!" Grandmere began, but Rachel enthusiastically broke in.

"This is the front door, and this is the living room, and this is the dining room, and this is the bedroom. Of course, all the people are gone right now because I left all my dolls at home—oh wait! Here's the dog." She picked up the giant pine cone she had used as a dog and shoved it in Grandmere's hands.

"And a fine dog, she is, too!" Grandmere laughed heartily at Rachel's excitement.

"And over here's where I found the baby bird, Grandmere. It was over here on the ground." She dragged her Grandmere to the spot where she had untangled the tiny bird.

"What baby bird, Darling?" Grandmere questioned as she allowed herself to be pulled toward the special spot.

"It was all tangled in a piece of chicken wire, and its parents were all upset, and it couldn't get loose at all, and I saved it!" Rachel was jumping up and down with excitement now as she told about her experience.

"You saved it? Oh my! How on earth did you do that?" Grandmere leaned over to catch every word that Rachel would say.

"I was very careful, Grandmere, so I wouldn't hurt it." Rachel lowered her voice and spoke with intense seriousnesss. "I reached down and took it out of the wire, and I held it in my hand for just a minute. It was so tiny, and it had sorta red feathers, and its heart was beating real fast."

"Oh my, Rachel, that's wonderful! Then what happened?" Grandmere peered intently down at Rachel.

"I opened my hand, and it flew away, and its parents took care of it!" Rachel raised her voice again in her excitement and flung her arms into the air; she was pleased with herself. "It was so beautiful, Grandmere, and one of its parents was bright, bright red."

"What a wonderful experience!" Grandmere took Rachel's hand, "why don't we go sit down over there in your house and talk about it."

Slowly they returned to Rachel's house and settled down in her outdoor living room, comfortably leaning their backs against the large pine. "It sounds to me like you saved a baby cardinal, Darling."

"A cardinal," Rachel practiced pronouncing the new word. "How do you know?"

"Because the male cardinal is bright red like the bird you

described in the trees, and the babies often have reddish feathers."

"A cardinal, I saved a cardinal." Rachel smiled happily.

"I'm very proud of you," Grandmere patted Rachel's knee. Both gazed back at the spot where Rachel had found the bird. Rachel's memory carried her back to that day. Once again she was holding that quivering little ball of reddish fluff, that baby cardinal, in her hand. Once again she saw its frantic little heart beating wildly. And once again she experienced the flood of love she had felt for the tiny—but oh so precious!—being.

And everything was peace for Rachel.

Slowly the light changed, creating new shadows and mellowing the shapes of the woods, and the earthy smell of dusk settled around them. They sat for a few more minutes before they began to amble back to the edge of the woods, and when they reached the last tree before the clearing, they discovered that the sky had been miraculously painted by a master hand. Grandmere was holding Rachel's right hand firmly in her own, but Rachel kept looking down at her upturned left hand where she felt the quivering softness of the baby bird.

When Grandmere was ready to leave the next morning to return to Louisiana, a bereft Rachel stood on the front porch. She put her arms around Grandmere's neck for a final hug.

"I love you, Rachel," Grandmere assured her, "and I will see you soon, I promise."

"I love you too, Grandmere," Rachel whispered in her ear for she could hardly speak for the lump in her throat, "but I don't want you to go."

"Remember how you loved the baby bird, Darling?" Grandmere whispered back. Rachel nodded. "That's how I love you. Remember the baby bird!"

Then she was in the car, and the car was quickly disappearing out the gate, but Grandmere's words echoed in Rachel's ears, "Remember the baby bird!"

Somehow—somehow Grandmere was still there.

❧❧

"How I wish Grandmere were sitting here right now!" Rachel whispered. "She could help me sort out my feelings about Collins. I love him, but I hate him and I just don't know how to go on! But Grandmere would know. How I wish—what's the point?" She sighed, took one last look at the church, and left.

When she arrived back at her parents' house, there was only one place she could endure the thought of going. She joined Florence in the kitchen.

"How you like your new car, Honey?" Florence asked excitedly. "I's been just about to bust trying to keep Mr. Jack's secret!"

"It's wonderful, of course," Rachel answered quietly. "I just wish I could work up more enthusiasm for Daddy's sake. I'm just so tired—"

"Course you is, Honey. You been through too much and your nerves is just all wore out. But you gonna come around. I bet you ain't even eat nothing since breakfast, has you?"

"No, but I'm not really hungry."

"You gots to eat; that be the only way you's gonna get your strength back. Now we ain't having no dinner seeing as Mr. Jack ain't coming home, but I fixed up some stew for anybody that want some."

"I think what I really need is a nap, Florence. I'll eat something—"

"Florence! Fix Miz Patsy a tray—" Mammy Cassie burst through the kitchen door in her usual fashion, but she stopped short when she saw Rachel. Her eyes filled with fury, and she opened her mouth to spout her usual condemnation of Rachel, but Rachel straightened up to her full height, raised her chin in the air, and stared coolly into Mammy Cassie's angry eyes.

"Florence," Rachel called the cook to her side without taking her eyes from Mammy Cassie's. "Fix a tray for Mother, please. Mammy Cassie, go set a place in the dining room. I shall eat my dinner in there."

"That ain't my work!" Mammy Cassie protested.

"It is now." Rachel replied calmly.

Mammy Cassie hesitated, obviously debating with herself how to handle this new adult Rachel. Rachel continued staring at her until Mammy Cassie stalked off into the dining room. When she returned a few minutes later, Florence handed her Patsy's tray, and she left without a word.

As soon as Mammy Cassie was out of hearing, Rachel said, "Just dish me up a bowl of stew, Florence. I'll eat it here." Florence chuckled as Rachel sat down at the kitchen table.

Rachel ate in silence, lost in her own thoughts, but when she stood to leave, she realized that Florence was preparing some food at her work table. She was shaking chicken in a brown bag full of flour. Undoubtedly it would be left overnight in the flour-filled bag in the refrigerator and then fried for tomorrow's dinner.

"Thank you, Florence," Rachel murmured "You're a lifesaver." Then she turned to go, but Florence stopped her, "I wants you to promise me something, Miz Rachel." Rachel turned back and nodded her assent. "When you starts thinking on Mammy Cassie's ugly words, I wants you to remember this." She held up a large drumstick.

For a moment Rachel was bewildered by Florence's action. Then a flash of memory streaked across her mind, and a smile lit up her whole face.

"You wasn't no more than seven years old!" Florence chuckled.

Rachel's smile brightened. "Yes, it was toward the end of first grade."

Suddenly Florence burst out laughing, apologizing as she did, "I's sorry, Miz Rachel, this ain't no proper time for no laughing, but that was one of the happiest days of my life!"

"On the contrary, Florence," Rachel was beginning to laugh herself, "this may be the best time of all to laugh. Thank you! Thank you for the memory!"

# EIGHT

In spite of Rachel's emotional and physical exhaustion she could not help smiling as she settled back on a stack of pillows on her bed. That flour-covered drumstick Florence had waved at her had sparked just the right memory in her, a memory of who she had been at seven—a spunky, indomitable child. It was a memory she needed now in the midst of her defeats, a memory she could cling to, a piece of her true self before it had been so adulterated by life.

"And could I ever really lose my true self?" anxiously she questioned the room around her. "Isn't that little girl still in me somewhere?" she demanded urgently as she sat up straight, her muscles automatically tensing. She thought of confronting Mammy Cassie just moments before in the kitchen, of reaching down into what seemed like the empty well of herself and finding just enough water, just enough strength to maintain her dignity. By sheer force of will she had found it. She had found the will of that indomitable child of so long ago.

Then Florence waved that drumstick at me, Rachel laughed softly as she remembered, and reminded me of my most glorious triumph over Mammy Cassie. I was only a child then, a child doing battle with an adult. I was David fighting Goliath with a slingshot. And what a slingshot!

I was seven years old and adored animals. They were

nicer than the human beings I knew. They were always glad to see me coming, didn't care what I looked like, were great listeners, and were always grieved when I had to part from them. What more could I ask? So I adopted every hunting dog Daddy ever bought, and several times a day I visited the kennels to have long chats with them. I was crazy about those hounds, but Mammy Cassie certainly wasn't!

Mother was caught up in her usual social whirl, so Mammy Cassie was in charge of me, and we fought constantly about my visits to the kennels. Mammy Cassie *said* she wanted me to stay away from the dogs because I always got dirty at the kennels, which was true, and because the dogs might hurt me, which was not true. But even at the age of seven I knew the truth; Mammy Cassie was terrified of those hounds.

And I guess she had good reason. Very good reason if all those stories she repeatedly told me were true or even half true. Her stories were basically all the same and were obviously the product of her childhood when she had come to associate dogs, especially big hunting dogs, with white owners of the land who only showed up at the workers' cabins on their property when they were angry. At such times there would undoubtedly be verbal violence, even physical violence on occasion. How many times did she tell me about being a small child cowering behind her mother's skirts in the open doorway of their rickety shanty when a furious white owner had come to deal with her shiftless father (or one of her mother's string of resident boyfriends) who had stolen something or had simply not done his assigned work?

And she told me all the stories she had heard when she was little, stories about the Reconstruction days after the Civil War, about white men with dogs who arrived in the middle of the night. Mammy Cassie's mother had told her children these stories, and she always ended them with a prophecy that chilled Mammy Cassie's blood. "There's men of the devil gonna come take your Pa away and we ain't ever gonna see him no more." And finally her mother's prophecy seemed to come true. In the middle of one dark, moonless night when the wind was shaking the cabin in its paws, a mass of white men came with their pack of hounds swirling underfoot, tied Cassie's father's hands behind his back and marched him off with the hounds barking at his feet and tearing at his flesh. To little Cassie it seemed that the hounds—not the men—had dragged her pa to hell, for she knew he had been a bad man and she never saw him again.

When Mammy Cassie told me all those stories, even though she was middle-aged then, she still believed the devil used hounds, and she still had nightmares about dogs dragging her to hell if she wasn't good enough. I guess it was only natural that she would try to scare me into behaving. I remember the first night she tried it.

❄❄

One evening when she put Rachel to bed, Mammy Cassie began her campaign. Rachel was clean and tucked in under the covers when Mammy Cassie did something she had never done before. She sat down on the edge of the bed and began to speak in a soft, soothing voice. Rachel was immediately suspicious as Mammy Cassie lovingly smoothed her golden hair back off her forehead and said, "I's been worried about you, honey, worried you's gonna get yourself hurt by them dogs. Them dogs is too big and mean for you to handle; it take a man to handle them dogs. If one of them dogs ever get loose down there, he'd eat you up sure in one bite—no trouble at all."

"But Mammy Cassie, the dogs like me. They do! We're

friends. They wouldn't even bite me if I stuck my whole head in the kennel," Rachel protested. She didn't like having "her" dogs maligned, especially by Mammy Cassie. "You're just afraid of them, that's all. Well, I'm not! I'm not afraid at all!" she defiantly shook her head out from under Mammy Cassie's hand.

"Now, Miz Rachel, I's just trying to do what's best for you and for Miz Patsy. What if something happen to you down at them kennels? Them dogs might get loose and kill you. I want you to promise me you'll stay away from there, you hear me?" Mammy Cassie had dropped the caressing tone from her voice and taken up something closer to her usual dictatorial manner.

"No, I won't!" Rachel belligerently folded her arms across her chest. "They are my best friends. They won't hurt me, and I won't stay away from them."

"Now you listen to me, Miz Rachel!" Mammy Cassie sounded totally normal now. "Them dogs will hurt you. They's servants of the devil, and they do whatever he tell them to. When he want you in hell, he send them dogs to drag you off."

"I don't believe you, Mammy Cassie! Yeller Girl wouldn't drag anybody anywhere. Even Cotton wouldn't. Besides, I like them!"

"I knows what I's talking about." Mammy Cassie's temper was rising. "When I's a little girl, the devil he send a big black dog to drag me to hell. He send him right there in the woods."

"Really?" Rachel's curiousity, tempered with suspicion, was aroused even though nothing could make her afraid of her dogs.

"Yes mam! He done just that. I's walking in the woods, minding my own business when this dog come running through the brush and start chasing after me."

"What did you do then?" Rachel quickly sat up in the bed. "Did you climb a tree?"

"No, I's too little to get a leg up on a tree, so I run and run till I couldn't run no more and I falled on the grass and started bawling." Mammy Cassie was remembering her terror and had forgotten Rachel.

"Then what did the hound do?" Rachel demanded impatiently.

"He just come and stood over me and panted real loud and showed me his sharp teeth and slobbered all over me."

"Yuk!" Rachel responded with a typical little girl judgment. Then she remembered the devil part. "Did he drag you to hell?" She was all attention again. "What's it like?"

"Course he didn't drag me to hell! I wouldn't be here if'n he had. He let me go." Mammy Cassie's attention was snapped back to her original purpose.

"Oh," Rachel said despondently and plopped back on her pillow. It's going to be hard to forgive the devil for this one, Rachel thought to herself. When he had his hands on a mean one like Mammy Cassie, why on earth did he let her go? "Why did he let you go?" she demanded indignantly.

"It was a warning," Mammy Cassie leaned forward in Rachel's face and said ominously. "He done warn me I better be good or he gonna come back and get me. It just like the dream I had just last night. I dreamed a gigantic, black dog come through the kitchen and into my bedroom, and he jump on my bed and grab me by the hair and drag me outa the room and outa the kitchen and cross the yard and into a big black hole in the woods and down to hell."

"What was it like?" Rachel popped back up off her pillow.

"It was hot! Hotter then Texas, and everything was on fire—the ground, the trees, the bushes, even the chairs you sits on. And when you fans yourself, it don't do no good cause the air is on fire and when you drinks a glass of water, the water, it's on fire. It's hot!"

"Oh." Rachel was again disappointed, for she had heard all of that before in Sunday School and had been hoping that an eye-witness account might be more interesting.

"Now, I wants you to promise me to stay away from them dogs or one of them is gonna drag you off to hell," Mammy Cassie warned, shaking her finger at Rachel. "What's more, I wants you to be very good and not give me no more trouble or that big, black dog of Satan's that I dreamed about will come and get you by the hair and you be gone for sure." With that comforting thought, she tucked Rachel's arms back under the sheets, stood up, towering over Rachel, and before she turned off the light, she warned one more time, "Remember what I told you—you better be good!" Then the light was off, and she was gone.

Rachel immediately wiggled out from under the sheet and ran to the open window. Many times before she had climbed out of the low window and wandered around as she pleased, but this time she simply stuck her head out and whispered in the direction of the kennels. "Don't worry, Yeller Girl and Mischief and Snoozy. Don't worry, Cotton and Molasses and Honey. I'd rather go to hell with you than go to heaven with Mammy Cassie any old day."

The very next morning Rachel was sitting on a wicker settee on the front porch all dressed up for church when a delapidated, disreputable-looking pickup truck appeared at the entrance to the circular drive and cautiously began to wind its way to the front of the house. When it finally neared, Rachel saw two people in the cab, a man and a boy. However, what really took Rachel's eye was the dog tied in the back of the truck. He was enormous, with thick, broad shoulders and powerful upper legs. As she gazed at him in wonder, Rachel calculated that her whole body must surely fit into his mouth. And he was the blackest thing she had ever seen! He was shiny coal black in the sun, a beautiful hound, but there was something strange about his mouth. Rachel stepped cautiously forward and stared up at the panting animal. Suddenly she realized what it was that was so unusual, even frightening about his mouth. Except for his sharp teeth, it was *all* black! His gums, the lining of his mouth, even his enormous tongue—everything was jet black. There was not one speck of the animal that was not a glistening black shade except his teeth.

"Stay away from that there animal, little girl, he's a vicious one, he is," drawled the man. When the man spoke, he moved menacingly toward the dog with his hand upraised as if to strike him and made the dog growl and lurch against the rope restraining him. "Yes mam, your Daddy wanted a big, mean dog, and I sure enough got one for him."

Rachel said nothing but looked at the man and the boy. They were what the Negroes on the place disdainfully called "po white trash." Such people were dirty, diseased, and drunken. Out of sheer laziness they refused every and any opportunity to better themselves. The men, if one could rightly call them by that name without slandering the other members of their gender, were content to do no more than raise a hunting dog occasionally and sell it to one of the gentry like her father and make just enough money to get dead drunk and stay drunk for a month, and forget about their wives and families. This man had absolute, visible proof of his shiftlessness accompanying him in the form of his son who stood beside him in filthy, patched clothes, no shoes, sores on his legs from infected mosquito bites, yellow skin and rotten teeth. There was a look of deadly hopelessness on the boy's face and with good reason, for there was nothing out there in the future for him. Rachel gazed from the boy imprisoned by his upbringing to the dog imprisoned by the chain, and she felt sorrow. Then she looked at the man, who was spitting tobacco juice on the lawn, and she felt hatred.

Behind her she heard her father coming out the screen door and across the wide porch. "Where in tarnation have you been, Slugg? I told you to be here at dawn before my wife was up and around."

"I guess my prayers lasted too long this morning, Cap'n," Slugg said grinning and showing his few remaining teeth, which were oozing with tobacco juice.

"Prayers! When I tell you—" then he remembered Rachel. "Go see if your mother is about ready, Baby. This is no place for you." He turned back to the truck and the semi-human figures standing in front of it, but before he could speak, Mammy Cassie came out the screen door, saw the enormous, black dog standing in the back of the truck and started screaming, "Lord, have mercy! It's Satan hisself. This time he come for sure. Oh Lordy, what we gonna do! Mr. Jack, you gotta do something!"

Jack wheeled around at her first scream and stared at her in amazement as her giant body shook with fear. Soon he began to laugh at her. "Oh, Mammy Cassie, it's just a dog. Calm down." His laughter initiated laughter in the man and the boy, and all the bedlam frightened the dog who started barking wildly, snapping at the air, and straining ferociously at his rope. The more violent the dog became, the more hysterical Mammy Cassie became, and the more the men laughed. Rachel couldn't take her eyes off the magnificent dog; she was filled with compassion for his plight. He was simply too magnificent to be at the end of anyone's rope.

"I done had the warning years ago," Mammy Cassie screamed. "A big black dog gonna come and drag us off to hell. This is the one! This is Satan's dog!"

"Now, Mammy Cassie, stop this foolishness," Jack's voice was taking on a sterner tone as he was tiring of the joke. "You'll frighten Rachel and have Patsy out here screaming before long."

"I'm telling the truth, Mister Jack. Satan have a big, black dog. I's seen him in a dream of prophecy. He gonna drag us all to hell if we ain't good as the Lord want. And here he is!" Mammy Cassie pointed accusingly and fearfully at the dog who had barked so vigorously he was now frothing at the mouth. Frantically she whisked around and ran back into the security of the house. The dog immediately quit barking.

Rachel spoke for the first time. "Can we keep him, Daddy? I like him—he has a wonderful black tongue."

"Well we certainly are not going to let a little Negro superstition stop us from getting the best hunting dog in the county. Here's the money I owe you, Slugg," he handed the man a roll of bills, which Slugg had the good sense not to count in front of him. Instead he just smiled broadly, and Rachel stared in disbelief at the brown tobacco juice spilling out of the man's mouth and dribbling down his stubbled chin.

Jack was disgusted and eager to get him off his property. "Pull your truck around back to the stables—if it'll go that far—and put the dog in the kennel with the others," he turned to leave but changed his mind abruptly. "No, wait a minute. He's a mean one—better put him in that empty kennel off to the side of the stable till I see how he behaves."

Slugg lazily nodded his assent, stood as if in a stupor with only his jaw working on the tobacco, and finally ambled off with the boy behind him. He never said a word of farewell, nor did her father say anything approaching a cordial word.

As Slugg's car crept around the corner of the house toward the stable, Jack turned to his daughter who had stars in her eyes, as she did about every creature on the place. "What shall we name him, Daddy? Can I name him? Can I?" She was jumping up and down with excitement.

"Okay, Baby. What's his name?" He knew her well enough to know she had already decided; she named every living creature.

She shot him a wicked glance, laughed gleefully, and feeling very satisfied with herself for her choice, she shouted, "His name is Satan!" Her father burst out laughing at her mischievous wit. His mustache wiggled all over his mouth, he slapped his knees, and when he turned back to the house to check on Patsy's preparations for church, she saw that he had been laughing so hard there were tears in his eyes.

"Satan, Satan, Satan," she whispered softly as she thought of the huge, black dog. "You and I are going to be good friends. I like you, and you are going to like me."

Four weeks after the arrival of Satan it was Sunday again, and it was Patsy's thirtieth birthday. Rachel jumped out of bed as soon as the sunlight peeped through the window and touched her face. Many hours of her life in the last week had been spent at the kitchen table making a special birthday card for her mother, and she was eager to deliver it. Florence had showed her how to press flowers and paste them onto construction paper with ribbons and lace. But it was Rachel's idea to write pretty words on the card, so she had made up a poem and carefully printed it in big, block letters inside and then signed her name.

Finally the big day had arrived. After dressing and impatiently eating breakfast in the kitchen, Rachel persuaded her father that it was time to take in her mother's breakfast tray and give her her presents. Florence prepared the tray, and Rachel carefully placed her card on the tray where her mother would see it first. She and her father paused outside Patsy's door, she carefully carrying the tray and he laden with presents, and they agreed to sing "Happy Birthday" as they went into the room. Her father opened the door with two free fingers, and they marched in singing at the top of their voices. They sang enthusiastically as they moved over to the chaise lounge where Patsy was reclining, and when they finished with a loud flourish, they were both beaming from ear to ear. Rachel's eyes eagerly watched her mother's face, waiting for the anticipated smile of pleasure, for Patsy always enjoyed being the center of attention. Suddenly a low sob escaped from her mother's throat, and she began to cry hysterically into a lace hankie. Mammy Cassie bent over her saying soothing things, but nothing could stop Patsy's waterfall of self-pity.

"I simply cannot bear it! I can't bear it!" she repeated over and over. Rachel was confused; in fact, she felt guilty, although she didn't know why. She had been told repeatedly by Mammy Cassie that it was she who made her mother unhappy and eventually sick. Her father had cautioned her many times to be good to keep from upsetting her mother. Still, this situation was bewildering and frustrating. She had been good, very good, better than ever before, and seemingly she had made her mother cry anyway. She felt hopeless, defeated. Slowly she withdrew from the room and waited in the hall while her father took control. "This is ridiculous, Patsy. Everyone gets older. Everyone has to be thirty someday."

"I'd rather be dead and buried in my grave than be thirty!" wailed Patsy. "You just don't understand, Jack.

It's different for a woman; it's over—all over—oh! I can't stand it!"

Jack stood over his weeping wife for a moment longer, then turned angrily to leave. He found Rachel in the doorway. She had put the heavy tray down on the floor and was standing there clutching the card she had made to her bosom as if it were a life preserver. He took a long look down at her, wheeled around and returned to the whining Patsy. With a voice the dead would have obeyed, he coldly commanded between clenched teeth, "Stop this nonsense at once! Get up and go wash your face in cold water and compose yourself. Rachel and I will return in a few minutes, and you *will* receive us graciously, Patsy." He stalked to the door and picked up Rachel, who watched her mother as long as she could while he carried her out to the porch.

He seated Rachel on the wicker settee next to him and said nothing. Rachel sat dejectedly by his side and glanced up at his face occasionally. She was afraid to speak to him for she could see the muscles moving in his jaw, his mustache jerked around spasmodically, and his eyes could have started a fire. In her uneasiness, she felt a vague sense of responsibility for what had happened. She waited. And waited. In time Jack took out a cigarette, lit it and began to take long drags on it. Rachel watched him furtively. His jaw had loosened, and his mustache was moving normally again; only his eyes were still angry. She waited. Suddenly Jack burst out with a completely unrelated question, "How many more days of school do you have left before summer vacation?"

Rachel jumped, for her father's voice had been so powerful and had had such a sharp edge, it could have been heard at the stables. Meekly she answered, "Just five more days, Daddy. But we get to have ice cream on Friday because it's the last day."

"That's nice." He didn't sound to Rachel like anything would ever be nice again. He leaned forward stiffly and began to grind the butt of the cigarette in an ashtray. Rachel watched apprehensively as he methodically pulverized the butt into totally unrecognizable pieces. "Rachel!" Again his voice was sharp and made her jump. "Do you understand what's wrong with your mother today?"

"No, Daddy." Although he had never touched her in violence, she felt that he was about to explain why he was going to pulverize her just as he had done the cigarette butt. Since punishment seemed inevitable to her confused mind, she just wished he'd hurry and get it over with.

"Your mother is upset because she's thirty years old today. She thinks she's old now, she's got one foot in the grave—of all the asinine things women can think of, this takes the cake!" His anger was rising again as he reviewed the situation.

"Is she going to die, Daddy?" Rachel inquired cautiously, trying to understand. Thirty did seem like an advanced age to Rachel, and he had mentioned a grave.

"No," he said bitterly, "she's going to be around to drive me crazy for the rest of my life." Then turning to Rachel, he said harshly, "Let's go open those presents." And as he rose from the seat, in the severest of tones he added "I want you to remember to be as good as you can today so you won't upset your mother. Do everything you can to make her enjoy her birthday, Rachel. Do it for me!" With this last remark his tone had lost its threat and become pleading.

Rachel glumly nodded her assent. As they passed through the front door, her father paused, looked down at her and said cryptically, "Remember, Rachel, your sins always find you out. You always pay in the end for your pleasures. Remember what I'm saying, Rachel. You can't get away with anything!'' Rachel assumed he was talking about her.

When Jack and Rachel returned to Patsy's room, she was waiting for them with a face which expressed a veneer of patient endurance covering intolerable and undeserved pain. She received her birthday gifts on the second attempt with sweet, long-suffering smiles and proclaimed, "You shouldn't have! Oh, I am so unworthy of such attention!" In a saccharine voice she pronounced Rachel's card "Quite lovely," and when Rachel emphasized that she had made the card herself, her mother responded resignedly, "Yes, dear, I see that. Really you are too kind," and she gave Rachel a limp hug as if she were at that very moment succumbing to a fatal disease.

❧❧

All through the Sunday School hour that morning Rachel pondered ways to make her mother enjoy the day. She felt responsible for her mother's happiness and health, especially today. Hadn't her father given her the commission? So it followed that he thought she had the power to mold her mother's moods and health. Mammy Cassie had told her for years that she made her mother sick. Now her father said she could make her happy and well. But how? Rachel felt frantic. Although her mother had ceased crying aloud, Rachel was very aware of the pain in her eyes, and she was afraid the tears would come again, so she feverishly cast around for ideas to please her mother.

Rachel's Sunday School teacher had had a birthday that week, and she was telling the children about it. She said that one of the nicest presents she got was a telephone call from the pastor of the church to wish her a happy birthday. Rachel was barely listening until she heard about the joy the pastor's recognition had given the teacher.

When all the children left the general assembly and went to their respective classes, Rachel slipped unnoticed out the door. She had to search and ask directions from many people, but finally she found Brother Stone, her pastor, in his study thinking over his sermon. He knew Rachel on sight, for her mother was a very prominent member of the church. Rachel excitedly asked him for a special favor, and he gladly acquiesced.

Some time later when Rachel joined her parents for the worship service, she was so excited about her secret she couldn't sit still. She waited for what seemed like time enough for Christmas to roll around, and finally Brother Stone got up to make the announcements. Rachel sat up on the edge of the pew expectantly. Brother Stone talked about choir practice, cub scout meetings, Thursday visitation night—it seemed like he talked about everything in the world except what she was waiting for. Then he paused and changed his tone.

"Today is a very special day, folks, for a beautiful, Christian lady here in our congregation today. I am happy to announce that today is Patsy Longwood D'Evereau's thirtieth birthday, and I know you will want to join with me in wishing Mrs. D'Evereau the happiest of days and in lifting up her name in prayer on this special day."

Rachel felt her mother go stiff beside her and draw her breath in quickly. Nervously, Rachel looked into Patsy's face, and there she saw a battle. For just an instant Patsy shot Jack an accusatory, murderous look. Almost immediately, however, as several people leaned over to congratulate her, she covered her face with a gay smile and formed "thank you's" with her lips for all the people who were waving and nodding at her from across the congregation.

"Let me just add," the pastor continued enthusiastically but disastrously, "that we also want to thank the Lord for little Rachel D'Evereau. She is a special blessing for her mother today. Rachel was the one who asked that her mother be recognized today." He smiled broadly, approvingly down at Rachel who felt successful at last.

Rachel beamed, for by this time her mother was busily receiving congratulations from people who had even stepped across the aisle to speak to her. As the whole congregation rose to sing the Doxology, Rachel glanced up at her father's face. He was white—but he feebly smiled down at Rachel and patted her on the head. She took the pat as a sign of approval. This is one church service I'm going to enjoy, she told herself. I won't even mind if the sermon is long—as long as it's not too long, she added as an afterthought, for no joy could make a long sermon tolerable to a seven-year-old.

After the service it was a long time before they reached the car, for many more people came up to congratulate Patsy on her birthday and to say how adorable Rachel was and how sweet to think of her mother that way. Strangely, Jack seated Rachel in the front seat with him and Saul, the driver, and left Patsy alone in the back. Patsy waved gaily and called good-byes to wellwishers as they drove off, but when they were out of sight of the church, a deathly pall descended on the car. Rachel nervously squirmed around to look at her mother's face. There she saw the strangest smile she had ever seen. It was dead, petrified on her mother's face. A shiver ran down Rachel's spine.

No one said anything—not one word—all the way home. When they reached the front door, Patsy spoke for the first time, "Jack, I want to see you and Rachel in the living room—now!" She turned her back on them, walked through the screen door Mammy Cassie was holding open, brushed Mammy Cassie off with a "Stay out of the way, Mammy. I'll call you when I need you," and regally entered the living room.

When Jack and Rachel entered the room, she ordered Jack, "Close the door!" Nothing happened.

Jack stared at her coldly for a full minute before he said, "Rachel, go somewhere and play and close the door *after you* when you leave." Rachel, who was totally baffled but fearful she was responsible for this strange state of affairs, made a move to follow his orders, but her mother's hysterically rising voice stopped her in her tracks, "Oh no! She's not leaving. She's the very one I want to talk to." And losing control, she raced forward and grabbed Rachel by the shoulders and began to shake her, "You have ruined my life! It's not enough that because of you I had to leave my home and marry a crazy Creole with all his stupid Catholic superstition. On no—that's not enough for you. You have to continue to make me miserable for seven years. Seven years of my life wasted!" Patsy's voice was clearly hysterical now. Rachel stared at her, too startled to be frightened. "And now—now you have humiliated me in front of everyone I know. I can never face that church again—never see any of my friends!"

"That's enough!" shouted Jack. He wrenched her hands from Rachel's shoulders. "You're making yourself sick over nothing, Patsy! Stop it!"

Suddenly her hand shot out, and she slapped him, "It's you—it's you, Jack D'Evereau—you ruined my life. You gave me her!" she pointed accusingly at Rachel. "I never wanted to marry you! I certainly did not want to go through childbirth—and for what?—for what?—a child who would turn on me in my weakest hour—my hour of greatest need!" Rachel watched, cowering behind the camel-backed sofa, while her mother screamed her anger until finally Jack gave up trying to reason with her, walked over and slapped her soundly on the face.

There was instant quiet. Rachel was horrified! Her parents had yelled at each other until they had come to blows, and somehow she was the cause. How had it happened? How had this day, the day she had looked forward to so excitedly, come to this? Patsy was quietly sobbing in Jack's arms; he was petting her head, saying soothing things to her, but she became increasingly overwrought, and finally he picked her up in his arms and carried her out the door. Rachel, not knowing what to do, followed.

Mammy Cassie was standing in the hall waiting, listening, "Oh, Lord, help us!" she cried aloud, and then as Jack walked past her toward the master bedroom, she turned on Rachel, "This time you's killed her. That's what you done!"

"But Mammy Cassie, I just wanted—"

"Don't you give me no just. You don't care 'bout nobody but yourself. I knows you backwards and forwards, Miz Rachel, and you's the devil's child. You's ruined your mother's life, that's what you's done."

"I just wanted to make her happy like the teacher at Sunday School—like Daddy said to—" Rachel choked out between her own sobs.

"Happy!" Mammy Cassie snorted derisively, "She ain't been happy since the day she knowed you's coming into this here world, and she ain't never gonna be happy again. You's conceived in sin, and you comes from the devil, and someday he gonna come take you with him, and it ain't gonna come too soon for me and Miz Patsy. The sooner we gets rid of you, the better. Miz Patsy be better off if you never been borned!" Having flung her final venom at Rachel, Mammy Cassie quickly followed her mistress, who could be heard wailing from the bedroom.

Rachel stood in the main hall alone. Her grief and anger overwhelmed her, and she threw herself on the polished floor and wept until a tiny puddle had formed under her cheek. Finally she had cried herself out. She became quiet, lying still, exhausted. There were no sounds now from her mother's room.

In time she stood up and wandered into the kitchen where Florence was trying to keep Sunday dinner warm. "I guess your parents don't want no dinner right now," Florence wisely observed, for she had heard the fight all the way into the kitchen. She looked kindly at Rachel, "But I can fix you up a plate right here in the kitchen."

"No thanks, Florence," Rachel sat glumly at the kitchen table. "I'm not hungry."

"Sure you is. Hearing all that preaching make a body mighty hungry. You just sit yourself down, and I's gonna fix you some of this here chicken. It's your favorite—all fried crispy like you likes it." She bustled around, and soon she put a plate of fried chicken, potatoes and gravy, and green beans down in front of Rachel. "Try some of this, Honey, it'll make you feel real good. Go on, now, try it." Rachel picked up her fork and began to play with the mashed potatoes. "You just ignore that Mammy Cassie," Florence advised while Rachel stared at the drumstick in front of her. "She don't always know what's right. Sometime she don't know enough to come in outa the rain. I's knowed Mammy Cassie all my life—" Florence drawled on, but something had happened in Rachel's brain—something significant—something that would change her life. Her thoughts of Mammy Cassie and fried chicken had joined in an unholy alliance. Rachel had a plan.

Rachel was caught in the grief of being unwanted by her mother, it was true. There was nothing she could do about that but cry, but there was no need to endure Mammy Cassie's abuse without avenging herself. Suddenly she smiled broadly at Florence and asked, "Can I have some more of this fried chicken, Florence? It sure is good!"

"You ain't eaten what you got—you ain't even touched it," Florence pointed at the plate in confusion.

"Oh I know it's good—it's always good when you cook it, and suddenly I'm starving!" Florence shrugged her shoulders and turned to the stove for more, just grateful Rachel was feeling happier.

Rachel looked down at the chicken and muttered," If I'm bad, I'm gonna be the baddest there is!"

Rachel kept a low profile all afternoon and through the early evening, but when Mammy Cassie put her to bed that night, she was still blaming Rachel for Patsy's hysteria, so she dumped her usual poisonous accusations on Rachel. This time, however, Rachel listened to her with immunity for she knew that retribution for Mammy Cassie was around the corner, and she would be there to watch it.

Finally Mammy Cassie turned out the light and left the room. "Now," whispered Rachel, "all I have to do is wait," and she propped herself up on her pillows, crossed her arms on her chest and smiled serenely into the darkness.

She must have fallen asleep, for when she awoke with a start, the house was dark and completely still. She bounded out of her bed and crept into the kitchen to look at the big clock on the kitchen wall. It was two o'clock. Rachel had no idea how much longer it would be dark, so she put her plan into action immediately. She tiptoed back to her bedroom and took a plate of fried chicken out of her closet where she had hidden it all day. During the afternoon while the household's attention was on Patsy, Rachel had been sneaking into the kitchen, when Florence's back was turned, and stealing one piece of chicken at a time from the covered platter on the table. There was plenty available, for with all the confusion from Patsy's fit, the adults had never eaten dinner.

With the plate of stolen chicken in her hands, Rachel

crept to the back of the house to Mammy Cassie's door. She bent her ear to the wooden door and heard the huge woman's loud, rhythmic snoring. Cautiously she turned the door knob, opened the door and slid silently across the room toward the bed. For just a moment she gave herself the special treat of standing right by Mammy Cassie's head and staring into her face while she held the fried chicken in her hands and grinned.

Suddenly Mammy Cassie snorted and rolled over! Rachel's pulse started jerking in her throat as she jumped down to the end of the bed and hid. She waited out of sight until Mammy Cassie was again soundly asleep, and then, realizing that she had no time to waste, she stealthily crept around the bed placing pieces of chicken all over the cover. Finally, holding her breath, she tiptoed right up by Mammy Cassie's head and placed a big drumstick on her pillow. The first step of her plan executed, Rachel quietly scooted out of the room.

After slipping out of the back door of the kitchen, she raced across the yard to the kennels. She went straight to Satan's kennel, sweet-talked him a few minutes, as she had been doing every day since he arrived, and then opened the gate. Holding out her chicken-smelling hands to him, she began to back off toward the house, enticing him to follow. Slowly, methodically she lured Satan across the backyard toward the kitchen door. Using this method, the tiny Rachel completely controlled the 100 pound dog. Although he had never been in a house before, he followed her through the kitchen because the smell of chicken was an overwhelming temptation to him. Soon they had both reached Mammy Cassie's closed door.

Satan stopped, cocking his head in wonder for just a moment; then his keen nose picked up the smell of all that chicken behind the door. He became so frantic that Rachel barely managed to get the door open in time. Satan stampeded across the room, barking joyously, and jumped right in the middle of the bed with one powerful leap. Landing squarely in the middle of Mammy Cassie, he proceeded to root around for the chicken and grind chicken bones between his powerful jaws. Chaos greater than anything Rachel had ever imagined erupted! Mammy Cassie let loose with blood-curdling screams that could have been heard in the next county, and she began flailing so frantically with her arms that the extra weight of the dog and the violent movement caused the bed to come crashing to the floor. The first sounds out of her mouth were totally unintelligible gibberish. As the dog continued to pounce on the pieces of chicken, an unbreakable tangle of leaping dog, flailing woman, and twisting sheets developed. Mammy Cassie's screaming began to take on the form of phrases.

"Oh Lord! Lord! Help me! It's the devil dog come to get me. Sweet Jesus! I ain't a-going—don't let him take me, Jesus! I been good. Help! Help!" The more she screamed, the more excited the huge dog became. He actually wasn't much more than an overgrown puppy, and since Rachel had been treating him with kindness, his gentle character had emerged, but after all, there was chicken all over the bed! And every time Mammy Cassie rolled one way to get away from Satan, she rolled over on another piece of chicken, and squeezed its aroma into the air. Satan quite naturally pounced on her or started digging under her trying to unearth the tasty treasure whose scent was driving him wild.

"I's sorry, Lord! Sorry for all my sins. Oh! Don't let him take me! Sweet Jesus—have mercy on old Cassie!" the hysterical woman's voice rose to a screeching pitch as Satan realized that the chicken was all gone except for that tantalizing smell on Mammy Cassie's gown. The dog began to tear at her clothes, growling with the joy of the experience.

"Oh Lord, I's gone! He gonna drag me off. He got me now for sure. Oh Jesus, I'll be good—just don't let him drag me to them hell fires! Help! Somebody help!"

By this time the commotion had awakened the rest of the house, and Jack came pounding down the hall ready to do battle. Rachel heard him coming and ran to hide behind the curtain. When Jack flipped on the lights of Mammy Cassie's room, everything was over. The bed looked like a battlefield which urgently needed recycling, and the victor of the battle was unmistakable, for Satan was sitting on top of Mammy Cassie's huge middle section happily crunching a drumstick. Mammy Cassie had lapsed into incoherent moanings about the devil. When Satan saw Jack, he happily wagged his tail for here was his master apparently ready to go for a run. Jack stood just inside the door frozen in a posture of amazement with his mouth hanging open in disbelief. Suddenly he came to life, "What in tarnation is going on here? Mammy Cassie! Satan! I don't believe this! Mammy Cassie, why on earth did you bring Satan in here?"

Mammy Cassie slowly recognized Jack's voice. She opened her eyes and slightly raised her head, "Oh, Mr. Jack, it's you. Praise the Lord!"

"Of course, it's me, you batty old woman, and you'd better have a good explanation for why you woke up the whole darn household!" He turned and pointed to the door which contained Patsy in the front with Florence, Saul and several Negro children wedged in between. All were staring in disbelief. Mammy's exhaustion had forced her to close her eyes again, but she tried to explain.

The devil sent his big, black dog to drag me off to hell, but you done come and saved me," she breathlessly explained, then added "I can't breathe, Mr. Jack."

"Of course you can't, you superstitious witch! You've got a hundred pound dog sitting on your chest!"

Mammy Cassie's eyes flashed open, and she let out a last blood-curdling scream, this time so loud she scared Satan, who dashed from the bed and forced his way through the crowd at the door, throwing Patsy to one side and running over one of Florence's children. "Praise the Lord!" shouted Mammy Cassie. "The devil he done quit. He ain't a-gonna get me! I's safe!"

"That's what you think, you crazy witch!" shouted Jack. "You've never been in more danger in your life than you are right now—bringing a dog in here and waking me up in the middle of the night. What time is it anyway?"

No one answered. "Mammy! I want some answers, and if you don't want to go packing before sunrise, you'd better start talking. What is my prize hound doing in bed with you?" Jack demanded.

"Mr. Jack, Mr. Jack! It ain't my fault. The devil he send his dog to claim me—to drag me to hell. I's just sleeping like a baby and this big black dog suddenly jump right in the middle of me and start trying to drag me off by my nightgown."

"Oh really!" Jack's tone was pure sarcasm. "And did this dog bring his own supply of fried chicken, or did you supply his midnight snack from yesterday's dinner?"

"Fried chicken! What fried chicken? I ain't got no fried chicken for no devil dog," Mammy was outraged at the thought. "He just jumped me."

"Mammy! Don't you lie to me. The bed—what's left of it—is covered with chicken grease and bones and—" suddenly Jack stopped. "Where's Rachel?" he demanded. No one answered. He looked around the room, marched straight to the curtain hiding Rachel, and jerked it aside.

The game was up.

No one got any more sleep that night. Mammy Cassie was moved in with Florence's family over the garage, and Patsy and Jack spent the remainder of the night fighting over Rachel's future. Patsy announced that Rachel had to go; she had to be sent away to a boarding school. Jack adamantly refused; no seven-year-old child of his, he said, was being shipped off to a boarding school. Finally they agreed that she would go to spend the summer with relatives. Patsy insisted that she stay with the Longwoods, but Jack announced with a touch of pride, "My dear, you might as well face it. What we have here is a D'Evereau. And a D'Evereau belongs at Belle St. Marie."

Rachel, who had been standing in the living room door throughout her parents' battle, jumped with joy.

"Not so fast, young lady!" Patsy turned toward her and directed her words to Rachel for the first time. "I absolutely refuse to have a child of mine living in Louisiana in the midst of that pagan Catholic voodoo."

"She either goes to Louisiana, my dear, or she stays here with us," Jack announced calmly. "Your choice."

"Do anything you want with her," Patsy shouted as she strode to the living room door and past Rachel. "Just so you get her out of my sight!"

Once she was gone, Jack sat down on the couch and sighed. Rachel approached him cautiously, but when he saw her coming, his frown turned to a grin.

"You've given us quite a night, young lady," he observed.

"Yes sir," was all Rachel ventured. Jack fell silent, but he stared down at her thoughtfully, a smile still playing across his lips.

"I ought to give you a spanking," he noted as firmly as he could, and Rachel nodded her assent. "But it wouldn't change a thing, would it?"

Rachel quickly shook her head. Then Jack burst out laughing and exclaimed, "I swear Rachel, as long as I live, I will *never* forget the sight of Mammy Cassie in that broken bed with Satan sitting on top of her chewing a drumstick!"

Rachel's long pent-up giggles escaped even though she clamped her hands over her mouth.

"Oh I give up!" her father said as he started laughing, picked her up and sat her in his lap. When they had both quieted down, he gave her a long, serious look and announced, "You're a D'Evereau all right, and God help us all, Rachel, for better or worse you're just like your Grandfather!"

"Does that mean I'm going to Belle St. Marie? Am I going to stay with Grandmere?" Rachel demanded eagerly.

"Yes, Baby, you're going to Louisiana to spend the summer with your Grandmere," he answered and then added quietly, "you're going home. And how I envy you!"

❦❧

Still laughing at the memory of Mammy Cassie and Satan in the chicken-laden bed, the adult Rachel murmured, "God bless Florence for reminding me." Then she snuggled further down in the bed and slept peacefully right through the supper hour and into the night.

When she awoke, it was about midnight. She could remember no specifics of her dreams; all she remembered was that they contained her Grandmere. Nevertheless, she felt comforted, stabilized. "If only you were here, Grandmere," she sighed. "If only—no point in wishing for the impossible." She climbed out of bed, wrapped her robe around her shoulders and settled herself on the windowseat to watch a full moon lighting the yard and the woods beyond.

Suddenly a voice popped into her head. It was singing a song she hadn't heard in years, and the voice was strangely familiar.

"Take my hand, precious Lord, lead me on through the night. I'm tired, I'm weak, I'm worn. Through the storm, through the night, lead me on to the Light. Take my hand, Precious Lord, lead me on."

How strange, she thought, how very strange. But who? Who is it?

The face of her Grandmere's beloved housekeeper flashed before her eyes. "Lovey! It's Lovey! Grandmere is gone, but Lovey is still there. Belle St. Marie is still there. Home! Belle St. Marie! Grandmere's home." An image of the gracious old plantation house sitting serenely in the early morning light filled Rachel's mind. "I must go there! It's the only place I could possibly heal. It's home. I must go home! I must go now!"

## NINE

By two o'clock Rachel was on her way to Louisiana, to her Grandmere's plantation, Belle St. Marie. A few minutes earlier she had placed a note on the dining room table at her father's place, telling him that after considering her options, she had decided that there was really only one place that she could go and have the quietness and peace that she needed to pull herself together, and that place was Belle St. Marie. She expressed her appreciation for his offers of help; however, she assured him, it was necessary for her to make her own way, and in her opinion her best chance for future success lay in returning to a familiar place, a place where she had known a special contentment. She encouraged him and her mother not to worry about her. She intended, she wrote, to take a year off from teaching in order to sort out the things that had happened to her, to figure out how to make a new beginning and to decide what that new beginning should be.

So by two o'clock she was driving through the night alone on a road that wound and curved up and down the endless hills. The valleys were filled with ground fog, and always close by the side of the narrow, two-laned, decaying road were the pine trees shooting straight up to the sky. Rachel had a sense of profound isolation driving in the dark, alone in the car, surrounded on two sides by the walls of pine tress. Slow mile after slow mile she drove. At times the road heaved up under her bringing her to the crest of a hill, freeing her from the dank fog and presenting her with the gift of the moon and the bright stars in the black sky. Then suddenly the road plunged her back down into the ground fog and the creeping anxiety that came with the sense of isolation the fog produced. Always, always she felt herself winding as the road pushed her out of the fog and pulled her back into it.

It was inevitable that she would think about the past, the very distant past, the past of her childhood. Only that afternoon she had sat in the church and remembered two days of her life in her sixth year when she had first met the woman who was her grandmother, the woman who owned Belle St. Marie and had made it a haven for Rachel when she was a distressed child. Grandmere had been, as Rachel had understood only a few hours earlier, a light in her life, a light that had fought the darkness.

Yes, it was inevitable that she would think of the summers of her childhood at Belle St. Marie, but it was also inevitable as she faced the darkness alone, that she would compare this night with others when she had been alone and felt isolated. She remembered nights of waiting up for Collins or else going to bed in anger, determined not to worry, determined not to care. But she cared—yes, far too much for anger to scorch it out of her. Even when she knew he wasn't out drinking alone. Even when she knew there was another woman. Yes, she had felt the same isolation she felt now because she could talk to no one. The neighbors must never know! Certainly not the family! She had felt isolated, fighting her battle alone, telling herself those women didn't count. Just quick affairs. But he had actually set up house with Shawna! Shame washed through her, shame and grief. And memories of dark waitings, nights when she had mentally abused herself with the repeated questions. What did you do wrong this time,

Rachel? Why can't you ever get it right? Why can't you fix him? What's wrong with you? And, of course, those thoughts led her inevitably to think of another darkness, a darkness very different indeed. The darkness of a rectangular hole in the ground, a hole that now held Collins, the remains of Collins.

For at least the first hour of her three-hour journey her mind seemed to be stuck on the events she had endured in the city, the helplessness, the confusion, the fear, the insanity of it all, a puzzle that would not fit together. And here she was driving in the darkness with the pine trees, which she normally loved so, shooting up at the side of the roads and closing her in in the dark, much like a hole in the ground. "The only difference is, I am alive. I don't get to just lie down in this hole in the ground that has been created around me. I don't get to just lie down and give up. I will go on breathing, and I must choose to do more than breathe. I must choose to live, and I must figure out how to do that, how to go on. I don't have the option of stopping."

As she reconsidered all that had happened, it was inevitable that she also questioned her own behavior and held herself to a ruthless standard of responsibility. "Has this hole been dug around me, or did I have a part—at least a part—in digging the hole myself?" she asked herself. Having been raised the way she had been raised, she inevitably took responsibility when bad things happened. Her church experiences, as well as her social indoctrination, had taught her that bad things don't happen to good people. So if bad things happen to a woman, then that woman is not good, not good enough. She thought back over her years with Collins, not just the last months, but all the years of her marriage, and she wondered where she had failed, where she had failed him. Was I too caught up in my career? Did I somehow not show him how much I loved him? Did I jump in and take care of him when I should have stopped and looked at the difficulties he was having, the weaknesses he was feeling? She was haunted by such questions. Phrases came to her mind, phrases connected with angry looks from Collins, phrases about her being eternally competent or something like that. Was I competent enough? Was I too competent? Surely I must have been able to do better. I'm strong, intelligent. I must not have tried hard enough.

As the miles passed, up the hills to the stars and down into the ground fogs of the valleys, she tried to remember what she knew about Collins' childhood, his adolescence, all the things that happened to him before she knew him at all. It was not a pretty picture. It was not an environment that would produce a healthy ego, a person ready to stand on his own. "How could I have controlled that?" Rachel demanded out loud. "Why should I feel so guilty? Why should I beat myself continually because I didn't somehow sense the trouble he was in and fix it? Why should I feel so guilty? I had no control over his early years, and how on earth could I have countered them? What could I have done? Still, maybe I didn't give him enough time. Maybe if I hadn't been a professional woman, if I hadn't been pushing so hard to finish my degree and start my career, maybe if I had been home more, maybe if I hadn't lost those babies." Tears sprang to Rachel's eyes at the thought of her miscarriages, at the thought of her inability to carry a child. This was the wound that would never heal, the wound so agonizingly painful she had to flee from it even now, especially now. "If only I had done more!"

"Done what?" she demanded of herself. "What could I have done? What could I possibly have done?"

"I could have gotten him to a counselor or something! There must have been something I could have done. I tried so hard, but maybe I didn't try hard enough. I mean, he's dead! This horrible, catastrophic thing has happened. Surely there was something I could have done!"

Rachel's flood of self-argument and self-accusation was dammed up by the sudden appearance of the Louisiana state line sign. When the headlights of her car flashed on the rusting sign, she slowed, stopped and stared at it for a long moment. She released a loud sigh and felt the choking tightness in her chest relax. It wasn't the sign alone that had released her; it was an image that had flashed through her mind, an image that rose from her memory, a picture of herself the first time she had seen the sign. Thanks to her revenge on Mammy Cassie, the marvelously creative revenge she had engineered with the help of her father's new dog, Satan, and Florence's fried chicken, she had finally managed to get herself exiled to the place she most wanted to be—with her Grandmere. Rachel drove on in the night past the sign as she remembered her first sight of it.

❧❧

When at the age of seven she heard Saul call back from the front seat of her father's black Cadillac, "There she is! There's Lusiana!" she pressed her face to the backseat window and stared out into the dense woods. It looked just like East Texas to her except the trees seemed bigger; she was disappointed.

"Where?" she demanded, "Where's Lusiana?"

"We's coming to it just up ahead here. See, there's the sign right there!"

"I don't see Grandmere's house anywhere," Rachel sighed. The 100 miles of the trip seemed like an eternity to her. "We're never gonna get there!"

"Yes we is, Honey! Now don't you go losing heart. It's

just about another half hour; won't be long now, Honey."

Rachel threw herself back against the padded seat; it was worse than waiting for church to be over, she thought tiredly. What on earth would she do for a whole half hour? Then she remembered the money her father had given her. Excitedly she opened the little white purse that matched her perfectly polished white pumps and stared in. "There it is!" she breathed, "it's still there!" She took out the wad of bills Jack had thrust at her after she had climbed into the car. Slowly she counted the green pieces of paper, stringing out the process as long as she could to make the time pass, as well as to enjoy her new wealth. "Fifty dollars! Daddy gave me fifty dollars!" She had never had so much money in her hands before. But her excitement dissipated as she remembered how sad he had looked when he leaned into the backseat of the car and said quietly, "Have a good time, Baby. I want you to have a good time." Then he had fallen quiet and looked down at the seat for a moment. She had stared at the top of his head until he spoke again; his voice sounded funny. "Uh, listen Baby, I know things haven't been too good for you lately, but I want you to know that I—" he stopped. When he raised his head and looked her in the face again, he added, "Here take some money. I want you to have a good time." Then he left and slammed the door and yelled angrily at Saul to get going.

Rachel looked out the window at the trees whipping by, but she mostly saw her daddy's sad face.

"We's at the turn off, Honey. Just a few more minutes!" Saul called excitedly from the front seat.

"Are you sure, Saul?" Rachel demanded. She was in no mood for false hopes.

"Look here, Honey, here's the sign just like Mr. Jack spelled it out on this here piece of paper." Saul had brought the car to a complete stop and was staring in amazement at the wrought iron gate to the plantation. Rachel jumped up on her knees and leaned out the window. There she saw an iron gate, wide open to welcome them, and over the gate was an iron arc that contained large letters that spelled out "Belle Saint Marie." Under the name in smaller letters Rachel spelled out "Enter in peace."

❦

Rachel drove on in darkness, a weak smile in her eyes at the memory of her excitement almost thirty years ago. When she reached the same antique, wrought-iron gate this time, she found it closed. Certain that it wasn't locked, she shifted the car to "park" and climbed out to open it. When she had pushed it back and moved back to the car door, she paused for a moment and stared at the words, now illuminated only by the moonlight and the headlights of her car, "Enter in peace."

"If only I could," she sighed, "if only I could." Then she climbed back into the car and continued up the long drive as she once again remembered her first trip.

❦

When little Rachel had seen the gate the first time, she had shouted with glee, "We're here! We're here!" but then she noticed that there was no house. "Where's the house?" she demanded. "Where's the house, Saul?"

"It be down the road a bit, Honey, don't you worry, it be down the road. The D'Evereaus owns lots of land, and they ain't gonna build their house where no common folk can see it, no mam!" He started up the car and began winding it down the long drive.

Rachel stayed up on her knees as they wound around

giant oak trees for what seemed like miles; finally they made the last curve, and she caught in her breath suddenly and let out a delighted, elongated "Oh-h-h-h!"

Saul was more verbal, "Holy cow! I ain't never seed nothing that big before in all my borned days!"

"Let's go, Saul, let's go!" Rachel shouted at him, for in his amazement he had brought the car to a halt. "I can't wait any longer!"

Saul stomped on the accelerator, and the car surged forward as Rachel continued staring at the enormous white mansion and exclaimed, "It's beautiful, oh it's the most beautiful thing I've ever seen!"

The noonday sun was showering the spacious, elegant house with streams of light, and it looked so large and so bright that it seemed supernaturally infused with a happy spirit that was shining forth from every inch. Rachel was mesmerized and was still hanging out the window by the time Saul had stopped the car in front of the mansion and had hurried around to let Rachel out. She could see nothing but the brightness and especially the enormous pillars seemingly rising straight to heaven. "We's here, Miz Rachel, you got to get out of the car," Saul gently tried to stir Rachel for he had seen Grandmere coming out the front door to greet her. "Here's your grandmother."

He had said the magic word! Rachel leapt out of the car at the sound of her Grandmere's name and eagerly looked up at the porch just as Grandmere came hurrying down the stairs, "Darling! Oh Darling! I'm so glad to see you at last!" Suddenly all Rachel could see was her Grandmere's hyacinth blue eyes beaming out at her, and just as she shouted "Grandmere!" her Grandmere's arms had encircled her and hugged her so hard she raised her slightly off the ground. As Rachel's feet once again touched the ground, her Grandmere knelt in front of her repeating her joy at Rachel's presence. Rachel's eyes passed over her

Grandmere's shoulder and focused on one giant pillar
which surely, it seemed to her, ascended all the way to
heaven. When her eyes had traced back down the height
of the pillar almost to the porch, she found a new face
with cinnamon skin, the warmest brown eyes she had ever
seen, and an excited, happy smile. Grandmere saw Rachel's
glance, stood up, and turned to the Negro woman on the
porch, "This is Lovey, Rachel. Lovey is one of God's best
creations." '

❦ ❦

There will be no Grandmere waiting for me tonight, Rachel reminded herself as she neared the house, she is long,
long gone. And I can't be sure where Lovey is, but probably in her same rooms behind the kitchen. I can't imagine
that anything could get her to leave Grandmere's house
unattended. But of course she must be sound asleep now.

When she drove her car around the last bend of the
drive and first saw the house again, she stopped breathing
for a moment as she was flooded with sheer joy. The
shuttered, closed-up mansion glowed in the moonlight
and projected a serene, comforting, welcoming spirit to
Rachel. It was not the gleaming, vibrant house, shining
in the sunlight, that she remembered from her childhood,
but it was still there, still graciously waiting for Rachel,
waiting in the mellow moonlight to welcome her home.
She stopped her car and parked it a hundred feet or so from
the house and got out to walk the remaining distance.
She walked slowly, never noticing where she put her feet
because she could not take her eyes off the smiling house.
When she reached the stairs to the front verandah, she
stared up the length of the closest pillar and once again

gloried in its height and breadth. Then she climbed the steps, and when she reached the top of them, she sank down on the last step, happily leaned her head on the massive pillar, and slept. Rachel was home at last.

## TEN

"Lord a mercy! It be Miz Rachel! Quick, child, run get Alice to help me get her in the house!" Rachel heard the shocked, worried words as if they came from the entrance to a deep cave she had crawled into to rest. The words had only a shadow of substance to her. Even the brown face leaning so close to her face and the gentle hand caressing her hair seemed dreamlike. More words wafted in from the distant entrance to that cave where she imagined herself curled against the back wall, and another brown face was added.

"You gonna be all right, Miz Rachel. Quick Alice! Help me get her in the house. She too weak to stand. Everything gonna be all right, Miz Rachel, don't you worry none."

"What's wrong with her? Are you sure that be Miz Rachel, Lovey?"

"Don't you think I knows my Rachel, don't you think old Lovey know her little Miz Rachel?"

Lovey! Rachel's exhausted mind came racing back to the present and tried to fight its way to the cave entrance. Lovey! It's Lovey! And then she thought no more.

When she awoke, she was propped up in her childhood bed in the large, front, upstairs bedroom. A bright sun outside was filtered through organdy curtains at the open french doors and through the organdy bed hangings. She moved her head and felt once again the lingering pain of her concussion. That slightest movement brought an old brown face into her view and a brown hand began stroking her forehead with a cool cloth. "Lovey!"

"That right, Honey. It be old Lovey. Now you just lie still; I's gonna take care of you just like I always done."

"I made it!" Rachel whispered weakly, "To Belle St. Marie! I made it home!"

"You's home, Honey. After all these years you's finally home."

"Oh Lovey! Horrible things—"

"I knows all about it," Lovey quickly stopped her, "ain't no need for you to say nothing at all. You just rest yourself now."

"But you can't know!" Rachel struggled to sit up, but her head swam so she allowed Lovey to press her back on her pillow. "How? How could you know?"

"Mister Jack tell me on the telephone."

"Daddy?"

"I call Mr. Jack the minute I got you into this here bed. He say call the doctor, and I did."

"Doctor? I don't remember—"

"Old Dr. Brevard. You remembers him; he always take care of your Grandmere. When the doctor come, he say you's all wore out. That be what he tell *me*. But I hears him talking to Mr. Jack and he say your head ain't healed proper. But to *me* he just say, 'ain't nothing wrong with her excepting she's all wore out.' I says to myself, 'she didn't get wore out like this over no teaching, and it weren't teaching that hurt her head neither. I knows it ain't my place, but I's gonna call Mr. Jack back and he gonna tell me what's wrong with my baby.' And that's what I done."

"You did?"

"I sure did, and he told me everything, and there ain't no need for you to bother about it now. You's only gonna upset yourself and make yourself sicker. Later on be soon enough if you still wants to talk."

"Yes, not now," Rachel fought with herself, fought to be rational and stay calm, but the black memories of Collins' betrayal and his death and—the whole disaster was overwhelming her like a tidal wave. It was crashing over the small boat of self-control she was trying to survive in, ruthlessly dashing it until she felt the boat splintering apart under her. "Lovey!" she cried out, "Lovey! I can't stand it! I thought I could if I could just get back here, but I can't!"

Lovey cradled her face in her brown hands and stared straight into Rachel's panicked eyes. "Ain't nothing you can't stand, Miz Rachel, cause you ain't standing alone. You's God's child."

"No, Lovey! No, it's been too long—"

"God don't count *time*," Lovey raised her voice and forced Rachel to look into her eyes, "He count *desire*, and if you wants His help, He right here beside you. If you done forgot how to depend on Him, I know you ain't forgot how your Grandmere depended on Him. You think on *her* faith. Don't you think on nothing else. Every time you start to think on something else, you close your eyes and remember your Grandmere kneeling in the church. For right now you borrow some of *her* faith. It plenty strong enough to pull you through. You understand?" Rachel nodded weakly. "Now I's gonna get you some soup off the stove and you's gonna eat it and take your medicine and sleep some more."

The first two weeks of June were much like those first moments of Rachel's return to consciousness. She panicked over and over as fear, shame and guilt surfaced. At times she thought she would lose her mind, but Lovey calmed her by holding Rachel's face in her hands and suggesting that Rachel picture Grandmere's faith and cling to it. When Rachel had quieted down once again, Lovey cajoled her into eating something, gave her her medicine, and Rachel slept. The doctor came and went, but there was little he could do. At Rachel's insistence Jack stayed away. She knew she could only handle the trauma she had endured that spring. She couldn't also handle her confused feelings about her parents. With Lovey there was no confusion; she had never received anything but unequivocal acceptance and affection from Lovey. Lovey was the only steadfast relationship she had left in the world. Rachel was in the right place with the right person; recovery was merely a matter of time.

During the second half of June, Rachel's major need was to talk her pain away. She relived every detail of the spring, constantly repeating herself in an obsessive, circular fashion. And she wept. Lovey, her brown eyes reflecting her own pain as she watched her beloved Rachel suffer, listened patiently to whatever Rachel needed to say. And when Rachel burst into tears again and again, Lovey said, "That's right, Honey, you cry good and hard. Those is cleaning tears, and they's gonna free you." She was right. Slowly the nightmare began to recede.

One night in early July Rachel fell asleep at dusk from the sheer exhaustion of one of her crying spells. The last thing she heard as she slipped into sleep was Lovey saying, "You's home now. Everything's gonna be all right cause you's home."

As Rachel slept, her mind, triggered by Lovey's words, wandered far back into the past, and she dreamed about the first evening she had spent at Belle St. Marie when she was seven.

❄❄

It had been the most exhilirating day of her young life as she made her first trip away from her parents and finally saw Belle St. Marie for the first time. She had been awestruck by the mansion but even more so by Grandmere's total delight in her presence. And she had met Lovey for the first time, quiet, sweet Lovey—so aptly named. After supper that night, as her Grandmere entertained two guests on the verandah, Rachel slipped away to wander around the gardens.

The sun had set, but faint rays of pink light illuminated the gardens as Rachel restlessly explored. Something was bothering her, something she could only bring to the surface of her mind by continually moving. She had had the most wonderful day of her life, she felt, and she didn't want it to end. She believed she could never have such a day again, and even though her Grandmere had said she was going to stay for three months and that they were going to have a wonderful time, Rachel had her doubts. Her mother's mercurial moods had taught her that nothing good lasts long. The more she thought about the inevitablity of losing her present happiness, the more Mammy Cassie's hateful parting words rang in her ears, "Don't you get no hopes up! They ain't gonna let you stay there long. You's a devil child, and they's gonna find it out and send you home. It just a matter of time. You's a devil child! You can't be good no matter how hard you tries. Your grandmother won't keep you no more than three days!"

Rachel's spirits sank lower and lower as the light disappeared from the landscape, and finally the tears brimmed over her bottom eyelid and ran down her cheeks. She was in the bottom of a pit dug for her by the adults of her Texas world. Her depression added a jerky breath and then quiet sobs to the tears. Suddenly a voice spoke from behind a darkened bush, "There you is! I bet you's getting real sleepy and—" Lovey stopped in mid-sentence, came forward, and put her hands under Rachel's chin to raise it. "What you crying for, Honey?" she asked quietly, her eyes filled with concern, "you ain't homesick already, is you?"

"No! I don't ever want to go home!" Rachel crashed her wet face against Lovey's waist.

"Don't you like Belle St. Marie?" Confused, Lovey grasped at the only thing she could think of.

"I love it!" Rachel sobbed out, "I don't ever want to go home!"

Lovey held her tight for a moment while Rachel sobbed, then she raised Rachel's chin again and asked quietly, "Then, why you crying? You can tell Lovey."

"I can't stay here," Rachel choked out as she tried to control her voice, "I'm gonna be sent back to Texas!"

"Who gonna send you back?" Lovey demanded, incensed at the very idea. "Ain't nobody gonna send you away from Belle St. Marie! Miz Elinore ain't gonna let nobody send you away! Why you think they is?"

"Cause I'm bad," Rachel confessed.

"Who say that?" Lovey demanded, her fury mounting. "Who say that? I'll just take care of them right here and now!" Lovey held Rachel tighter as if she were defending her against an approaching enemy.

"Mammy Cassie said I was a devil child," Rachel blurted out as she began to sob again between words. "She said I was born with the devil in me and that I can't be good no matter how hard I try—" Rachel broke down for a moment before she was able to go on, "and that Grandmere wouldn't keep me three days. She'd send me home." Rachel was grieved beyond hope, but Lovey was ready for a fight!

"Mammy Cassie say that?" she demanded. "She gotta be the meanest woman in the world. Miz Elinore told me some about her when she come back from Texas, but you knows Miz Elinore. She ain't gonna say much bad about nobody, but I ain't no fool. I seen how upset Miz Elinore was about that Mammy Cassie, and I sees the proof now right here in my arms. That Mammy Cassie oughta be horsewhipped, and I's just the one who can do it too. It just real lucky for her she be in Texas and I be here or I take me a horsewhip to her, and even if she beg me to stop, I wouldn't never stop till I beat all the meanness out of her if it take a hundred years! And it probably would!" she added as an afterthought. Then she looked down at Rachel, who had quieted and was thoroughly enjoying the idea of Lovey whipping Mammy Cassie. "Honey, you ain't no devil child," Lovey assured her, "you ain't bad. You's good. I sees it already."

Lovey knelt down on the ground in front of Rachel and softened her voice, "You's just a sweet little Jesus child, Honey. And your Grandmere ain't gonna ever let you go. You's gonna be here all summer, and we's gonna have the best time you ever seen." She stopped her earnest words and peered at Rachel. Slowly a smile was born on Rachel's face. "That's better, Honey, that's better," Lovey encouraged the smile to grow. "Let's you and me go sneak in the kitchen and get us some more of that pecan pie before bed."

After Rachel and Lovey had raided the kitchen, Lovey took Rachel upstairs and helped her pull her clothes off, slip into her nightie and crawl into the huge bed. Rachel was so tired she could hardly stay awake, and yet so much had happened she was too excited to sleep. Lovey must have sensed her condition because she drew a chair to the side of the bed and announced, "I's just gonna sit here a spell and keep you company till you goes on off to sleep."

Rachel lay contentedly, watching the gossamer curtains hanging from the bed. They were barely swaying in the breeze in a hypnotic way, and soon she drifted off to sleep.

It may have been a short or a long time later, Rachel

didn't know, that she heard the piano in the music room below being played. Sleepily she turned her face toward Lovey. "What's that, Lovey?" she whispered.

"That your Grandmere playing the piano for your Grandpere, Honey," Lovey replied peacefully. "She do that every night before bed."

"But Grandpere's dead, Lovey. Grandpere's dead."

"He still here, just the same, Honey, he still here."

Lovey's tone increased Rachel's peace, and she turned her cheek into the softness of the down pillow, and the breeze from the French door floated her conscious mind away. She slept so soundly, so securely that she remembered nothing of the night except just the slightest impression that after the music downstairs had stopped, her Grandmere had appeared by the side of the huge bed, leaned over, and kissed her.

When Rachel awoke the next morning, the sun was streaming through the French doors as if it were a lonely playmate eagerly standing by, waiting for her to wake up and come outside and play. And she was ready to play! She scrambled over to the edge of the big bed and slid down its side to the floor. In an instant she had dashed over to the organdy curtains dancing in the early morning breeze, thrown them apart and run through them onto the upper front verandah. Quickly she crossed over to the railing, stood up on tiptoes and hung as far over the side as she could. She couldn't have been happier to be alive as she waved her arms over the railing, jumped down and twirled in the bright sunshine flooding the verandah. Round and round she danced, her feet taking joy each time they touched the warm boards of the sunny floor. When she was too dizzy to go on, she collapsed into a convenient wicker chair and giggled with the lack of inhibition that only childhood possesses.

When her head quit spinning, she glanced through the

spindles of the railing and saw a dainty figure emerging from the garden in front of the mansion. Rachel knew instantly from the blue tones of the woman's clothing that it was her Grandmere. She raced to the edge and hung as far over the railing as possible.

"Grandmere! Grandmere!" she called loudly, "look at me! Look at me, Grandmere! I'm way up high!"

Grandmere shaded her eyes with one hand as she looked up at the bright house and laughed as she saw Rachel's excitement. "Good morning, Darling! Look what I found!" She held up an enormous white flower for Rachel to see. "I believe this is the biggest magnolia blossom I've ever seen! Stay there, and I'll come up and help you dress, and we'll have breakfast up there on the verandah."

She disappeared under the place where Rachel was standing and soon reappeared behind her. "Lovey's going to bring a tray up here in a few minutes," she announced as she grabbed Rachel and held her close. "I'm so glad to wake up and find you here at Belle St. Marie!" Rachel snuggled for a moment before she broke loose, ran to the railing again and exclaimed, "You can see forever from here! I like being this tall!"

"Yes, I like it up here, too." Grandmere moved to the railing with her. "Many, many times since I came to Belle St. Marie I've come out on this upper verandah early in the morning and searched the landscape looking for your Grandpere. He was always such an early riser, and rather than awaken me, he would slip out by himself and look over the land." Grandmere paused as she remembered.

"Lovey says Grandpere's still here," Rachel blurted out. "Even though he's dead!"

"Yes, I think he is, Darling," Grandmere agreed quietly as she stared out at the horizon. Then she snapped her attention back to the present. "Well, let's get washed up for breakfast, Darling."

After they had finished the breakfast tray Lovey brought, Rachel began at one end of the enormous verandah that circled three sides of the house, and sliding her small hand on the top of the railing, she walked the entire length of the verandah, staring out at the horizon. Grandmere walked beside her, holding her other hand, and only once did they speak when Rachel asked, "Do you and Grandpere own all this land?"

"Yes, Darling, we do—as far as you can see," Grandmere responded. "God has been very good to us—very, very good."

❧❧

Gentled by her dream, Rachel awoke. She opened her eyes and glanced down in surprise at her adult body. The dream about her childhood had been so real that she felt confused to find herself grown. She sat up and slipped out of the bed. She glanced around the beloved old room and found little changed from the room of her dream. The breeze was blowing the curtains at the French door, inviting her to walk through onto the sunny verandah, and she accepted the invitation. As her bare feet touched the sun-warmed boards of the verandah floor, she stopped to enjoy the sensation. Then she moved to the railing, wrapped one arm as far as possible around a massive column and stared out at Belle St. Marie. She knew she had experienced a dream; she knew she was now grown and had endured much pain; she knew Grandmere would not come walking out of the woods, but she was just as certain that in the course of her sleep, she had somehow reached a different plateau of experience. She was at peace for the first time in months. She had won a major battle and set herself on the road to freedom from her sufferings. She and Lovey and Grandmere's ever-present spirit had won.

Intentionally Rachel went to the end of the verandah and lightly touching the top of the railing, she walked the entire distance of all three sides. It was a ritual she chose to perform to link her with the good in her past. Then she went down to the kitchen and surprised Lovey. Lovey hugged her with all her might and fixed her a breakfast tray, which Rachel carried back upstairs to the verandah. There she sat and stared at the beautiful morning light as she ate and rejoiced that she had finally taken a step forward.

Rachel was wise enough to know that winning one battle was not winning the war and that there were undoubtedly other battles ahead. She knew that one step was not the whole journey. She also knew that she was very tired; even so, she was no longer going to spend her days in bed. So for the remainder of July she spent most of her time on one of the lower verandahs or in the kitchen with Lovey. Her head was healed, and she could read again. So she began a three-volume, nineteenth century novel hoping that the heroine would overcome all her troubles and be victorious in the end. Even if the heroine didn't succeed, Rachel reasoned, she needed to bury herself in some fictitious, distant troubles for a few days. The few days lengthened into a month as Rachel finished that novel and found others in the mahogany, glass-doored bookcases in the parlor.

By the end of July the humid heat was taking its predictable toll on the plantation. By noon each day the trees were wilting, the birds had taken refuge in the shade where they quietly awaited the coming of dusk, and even the verandahs were stifling. Only the old house with its thick walls offered any relief, but Rachel had steadfastly refused to allow Lovey to open any of the downstairs rooms. They remained shrouded in their dust cloths—large, grand rooms darkened by closed shutters and filled with odd lumps of dust cloth that Rachel knew contained furniture and decorative items.

Her father called often, and each time he insisted she open up the entire house and use it, but each time she refused. He simply couldn't understand her reluctance, he said repeatedly. It was hard for Rachel to explain even to herself. All she understood was that she couldn't deal with any more losses. She had said all she could say about Collins, and she had cried herself dry, but there were other losses. Belle St. Marie was her best refuge, but it held griefs too. They were out there in the D'Evereau cemetery. Oh, it was so confusing! If Grandmere and Justin were buried out there, it should be sufficient that she had not gone near the graveyard. Somehow it wasn't enough though; it wasn't just that they were buried out there, it was that they were absent here in the house. Rachel was afraid that if she opened the rooms, the absence of her beloved Grandmere and her little brother would overpower her and send her reeling back into more grief.

Rachel's other problem was her father's insistence on coming to see her. She begged him to stay away, to believe that isolation was her best medicine. She knew that seeing him meant dealing with another piece of her painful past. She was grateful for his help, of course, but before that, after Justin's death, she had intentionally broken off contact with him. She had been angry with him for so long, yet she did not understand her own anger. She blamed her father for the loss of her brother; she knew that much, but there were things that went back much farther in time, things that had caused deep resentments in her, things she had never allowed herself to look at squarely. Some of them had reared their ugly heads the short time she was in Pineview when her father had taken her there. It was those things that had forced her to flee here. Oh! It was all just too much for her right now.

While Rachel fretted, Lovey acted. Rachel awoke in early August to unusual bustling noises. She threw on her robe and hurried down the elegant staircase. In the wide entry hall, which ran from the front to the back of the house, she found a jumble of furniture and other objects from the music room. She also found Lovey presiding over a team of house cleaners. When Lovey saw Rachel, she hurried over to her to exclaim, "Oh Miz Rachel, my rheumatism was so bad this past spring I's afraid I didn't get no spring cleaning done. It come to me in the middle of the night last night, 'What must Miz Elinore be saying when she look down and see the way I's taking care of her piano? I ain't got no rheumatism now. I's clean out of excuses!' I couldn't hardly wait for daylight to get started!" Suddenly Lovey saw something she disapproved of, and she scurried off, calling out orders to the women.

Left alone, a bewildered Rachel went back upstairs to dress. Before she had finished, Alice appeared at her door with a breakfast tray. "Lovey got such a ruckus going downstairs, Miz Rachel, she say you be happier eating up here. I's gonna put this here tray out on the verandah."

By noon the noise downstairs had ceased. Rachel ventured back down the staircase and found the entry returned to its normal state. The tall, wide doors to the music room were open, so Rachel stuck her head in hoping to find Lovey. She was stunned by what she saw. The lumps of dust cloth had been transformed into a gleaming array of mahogany antiques set on a shining floor that reflected their magnificence. However, it was the focal point of the room, Grandmere's beautifully carved Steinway grand piano, that took Rachel's breath away. It was opened up and had music waiting on its music stand just as if Grandmere had left the room for a moment and intended to return to play more. Rachel could not stop herself; she was drawn to the piano as if she were rushing to throw herself into her Grandmere's arms for a reunion hug.

"Fourteen years!" she spoke the words aloud as she caressed the beautiful wood. "She's been gone for fourteen years, but right now she doesn't seem gone at all." Rachel pressed one of the sacred ivory keys and was startled by a discordant note. She struck the note again, this time louder. "Oh no! This won't do, this won't do at all!" Rachel scooted onto the bench and played several octaves. Half the notes were flat, and many wouldn't play at all. "Lovey!" Rachel called. "Lovey!" Once again she placed her hands on the keys and tried to play. "Merciful heavens! This is an abomination. Lovey!"

"Yes, Miz Rachel," Lovey rushed in from the hall.

"Lovey, I don't want you to think for a minute that you've fooled me. I know exactly why you cleaned this room this morning. And I want everything re-covered with dust cloths as soon as possible, but *not* before this piano is in perfect order."

"Yes, Miz Rachel."

"Listen to this!" Once again she played the octaves. "How could Daddy let this happen? It's disgraceful!"

"Yes, Miz Rachel."

"I'm going to telephone for a piano tuner right this minute," Rachel jumped up from the piano bench.

"It gotta be somebody what know about old pianos."

"That's true. Not just anybody could work on it." Rachel paused and sighed irritably. "Do you remember the tuner's name, the man Grandmere preferred?"

"Course I does! As long as Miz Elinore alive ain't nobody gonna work on her piano but Mr. Simone. He was an old friend of hers. Last time he be here be right before Miz Elinore died."

"That was more than fourteen years ago! I hope he's

still alive! Well, there's only one way to find out. Where's the phone book, Lovey?"

"Out in the hall, Miz Rachel, with the phone, but he ain't gonna be listed in that phone book."

"Why not?"

"He be from New Orleans."

"New Orleans? He was from New Orleans?"

"Yes mam. Don't you remember hearing all them stories about Mr. Alex fussing cause Miz Elinore always sent to New Orleans for a piano tuner? He fussed and fussed, but he always gave in. I think he just teasing with her. He knowed she brought this piano with her when she come from New Orleans as a bride cause it was her grandmother's piano, and she wasn't gonna let just anybody work on it cause it be so old and so precious to her."

"Yes, I'm starting to remember," Rachel sighed, then gave Lovey a stern look, "and I'm starting to realize that I've been outwitted. You knew perfectly well I couldn't stand to leave Grandmere's piano in a mess, and you knew perfectly well how long it would take to get the right man up here from New Orleans, didn't you?"

"Why, Miz Rachel, I ain't done nothing but clean the music room."

"And you just happen to remember this Mr. Simone's name?"

"Well-l-l. It didn't hurt none that I looked through Miz Elinore's address book."

"God is going to get you for this, Lovey!"

"I's willing to take my chances," Lovey was trying hard to stifle a grin.

Rachel sank down on the piano bench and ran her hand lightly over the keys. "I *could* just tell you to cover everything else up and leave the piano uncovered until it's fixed."

"It gonna be days before them dust cloths is washed and dried."

"I *could* just walk out and close the doors behind me and in a few days you could re-cover things, everything but the piano."

"Or you could sit yourself down right over there and let me bring your dinner to you. Then you could eat and look at Miz Elinore's piano and dream about playing it again, just like she taught you to."

Rachel said nothing. She turned away from Lovey and carressed the keys as she thought.

"There be more joy in this room than pain, Miz Rachel," Lovey's voice was firm. "And whatever pain be here you gotta lay to rest so's you can be strengthened by the joy and go on with your life."

Rachel remained turned away from Lovey as she stared at the piano. Its deep patina reflected Rachel's face, and she communed with herself for several moments as the silence between them lengthened. I've survived what surely must be the greatest losses and the worst pains of my life, she reflected. I've come through it all. I'm still alive; I'm still sane. I need a clean sweep of the past so I can move into the future. Suddenly she made her decision. "What's for dinner?" she demanded.

## ELEVEN

Lovey's plan worked; by the time Rachel had finished her dinner, she was determined to have the piano restored at any cost or any amount of trouble. The problems in her recent life had drawn her away from the music she loved just as Grandmere's death had separated her from this cherished piano. The simple act of touching those keys and thus producing sound, however discordant, had reopened a room of her being, an essential part of her identity that she had temporarily lost. For the first time in months there was something to do other than survive. There was something she desperately *wanted* to do; she wanted to make music.

By suppertime she had found Mr. Simone in New Orleans. At first he insisted that he had retired and turned his business over to his son, but when he realized that Rachel was calling about Elinore D'Evereau's piano, he denounced the idea that anyone else should touch it. He spoke of Grandmere's piano as if he were remembering a long-lost love, and he made Rachel swear that she would protect his love until he could reach the plantation. Rachel's spirits soared as she listened to the man's enthusiasm and to his promise to come as soon as possible and to accept Rachel's invitation to stay a few days.

After Rachel had finished the supper tray Lovey had

brought to the music room, a beaming Lovey appeared to take it away.

"Which bedroom we gonna open up for Mr. Simone?" she demanded. And before Rachel could answer, she chattered on. "And what's we gonna serve him? We got's to get a plan and get everything ready. Why this old house ain't had no company since Miz Elinore been gone! Maybe I fix a turkey. And where we gonna serve him his dinner? You can't expect company to eat off of no trays. Miz Elinore already turning over in her grave cause you's eating off a tray all this time. If she's here, she send me packing, letting you eat off a tray like some kind of—some kind of—I don't know what! Like you ain't even a member of the family!"

"Lovey! Have mercy! Slow down!" Rachel insisted good-naturedly. "Let's take one thing at a time. It's hard enough for me to believe I'm sitting in Grandmere's music room and that we're going to have company."

"I gotta strike while my iron's hot! I knows you, Miz Rachel. You can be the most downright stubborn body on this here earth. I gotta strike while my iron's hot!"

Rachel burst out laughing at Lovey's vehemence.

"Now look at you! You's laughing! I done won the war!" Lovey boasted as she picked up Rachel's tray. "We ain't gonna take no more steps backwards now cause you's laughing."

"Okay, okay! I surrender!" Rachel laughed on. "I don't know why I ever tried to argue with you in the first place. I should have known I was outgunned from the beginning, but could we *please* discuss the details tomorrow? I think I've had enough change for one day."

"Whatever you says, Miz Rachel," Lovey said, grinning. "You's the mistress of this house, not me."

"I wonder."

After Lovey was gone, Rachel stretched her legs by walking the length of the verandah several times, but it was too muggy to settle outside. She returned to the comfort of the music room and began to browse around it, looking at various photographs and other treasures of her Grandmere's. Very quickly she found a picture of her brother Justin taken when he was in junior high. She tried to pass it by, but soon she returned to it, took it in her hands and settled in a comfortable chair. There she sat for a long time staring into his handsome, gentle face. She had not seen a photograph of him for months.

As she stared at his picture, a succession of feelings overwhelmed her. First, she felt happiness at seeing his face again and remembering his loving personality. "He was just like Grandmere," she murmured, "much more than I ever was." Then she missed him terribly, and she discovered that the grief she was afraid she would find in this room was indeed here. And then she felt anger, the same anger with her father she had felt for years, the anger that had cooled only to an entrenched bitterness after Justin's death.

Poor Justin, she thought, he never had a chance. From the moment he was born, he was the battleground on which Mother and Daddy fought. He was the country they battled to control. Only the weapons used were different from those of an armed conflict. Instead of bullets, tanks, and bombs, they fought with manipulations, sarcasms, and raised voices. And like all battlegrounds Justin was ravaged by the fight. They took no notice of the landscape they destroyed—Justin's unique being. Their only thought was to win. And winning meant re-creating Justin in the D'Evereau or the Longwood image or at least in their fantasy images of their families. Both images were never more than myths from the distant past. Both families had had their problems. Nevertheless, Mother marshalled the Longwood forces to make Justin an Anglo, Protestant Longwood. Daddy had to fight alone to make him a

French, Catholic D'Evereau because Grandmere would not fight. Instead, she pleaded with Daddy to bring Justin—and me—up in peace, to let us both be the unique individuals God made us to be.

Though I think she must have known Daddy would never listen to her. On other subjects, yes, but not on this one. She must have known because she knew her son, but most of all because she knew her husband, Daddy's beloved role model, and she knew the South and the role it taught its men to play.

Neither one of them, Mother or Daddy, wasted any time beginning the war. The moment Daddy knew he had a son, probably while Mother was still under sedation, he executed a pre-emptive strike. He named his new son for his own father. The world now had an Alexandre Justinien D'Evereau the IV. Then while Mother and her brothers were stunned on that front, Daddy struck again. He planned Justin's baptism. I will never forget that day as long as I live.

So many new experiences all at once—meeting Grandmere for the first time and being introduced to Catholicism. I had never seen such an ornate church. Its stained glass windows, the statues of Mary, that special light—so many things came together to give me my first experience of mysticism. And that crucifix! That gigantic crucifix. I had never seen Christ crucified; I had only heard about it. Suddenly it was so overwhelmingly real. That day I had my first glimpse of Daddy's true identity, of where he came from, of what his life had been like before Mother, before me.

Something else became overwhelmingly real. I had seen dislike between my parents, and I knew that that dislike was there because they came from different worlds. Until then, however, I had never seen them hate each other.

That day was a confusing combination of beauty and ugliness.

Rachel glanced up at the portrait of Grandmere's beloved Alex, Alexandre Justinien D'Evereau III, over the mantle. *I never knew him. I know only what I have been told about him. Everyone always describes him as bigger than life.* She thought about that a moment. *No, not everyone, come to think of it, not Grandmere. Everyone else, but not Grandmere. She only talked of how much she loved him, but to Daddy, Grandpere was a man among men, the best role model for any boy. So Daddy was determined that Justin would be a reincarnation of his father. But whatever Grandpere was in reality, Justin was cut from a totally different cloth. So naturally he wasn't like Daddy either. He was so quiet, so pensive, so gentle. And he had an appetite for peace that made it possible for him to bend himself into any shape necessary to keep the peace. Not like me. I would fight with anyone who encroached on my identity. Justin would just withdraw into himself and externally conform to others' wishes.*

*Except here, here at Belle St. Marie. Here his forbidden sketch pad could reappear, and he could bury himself in a book for hours and no one would reprimand him. I think that's the way I remember him most—curled up on one of the verandahs with a book or with his hand moving rapidly across his sketch pad, recreating something he had seen. My playmates and I dashed everywhere—doing, always doing—but Justin watched. He didn't do; he watched. He was the artist.*

*But not at home, not if Daddy was around. Then he was coaxed to do, cajoled to do, bribed to do, even forced to do. And this was the one part of Justin's life that Mother and Daddy agreed on; they had the same definition of masculinity, and they both wanted him to fit that definition. Daddy was determined he would be a sports-*

man, but Justin failed at every sport. He tried, he endured, but he failed. It wasn't that he wasn't robust and strong. He grew to be bigger than Daddy, but he was a gentle giant.

When Justin failed on the sports fields, Daddy decided to make him a hunter, to initiate him into the joys of killing for sport. I remember he presented Justin with a rifle at his tenth birthday supper and announced their first hunting trip. Justin panicked and ran. When I found him in the woods, he was too sick to stand up. I was sixteen, and I had figured out the adults in my life. I knew there was only one person in the world who could stop Daddy. I hid Justin in the garage, went back to the house and lied. "I can't find him anywhere. He's disappeared off the face of the earth, and it's pitch dark." I knew what to expect next. Mother would burst into tears and run to the phone to call her brothers. Daddy would stop her. "I don't need your brothers to find my own son!" he would snap. Then he would promptly order every adult on the property to light a lantern and comb the woods for Justin. He would lead the search himself, of course, and Mother would naturally collapse into Mammy Cassie's arms. I was sixteen, and I had them all figured out; this time I was dead right.

It was no problem at all to take the keys to one of the Cadillacs, sneak out to the garage, and leave with Justin. Naturally we were headed for Belle St. Marie.

When we arrived, Grandmere called Mother immediately to say we were safe; then she suggested I wait in the music room while she tucked Justin into bed. I figured I was in for quite a scolding, but I didn't care. When she returned, the phone rang, and it was Daddy. I could only guess at what he said; whatever it was, it didn't please her. Suddenly she announced in her most gracious tone, "Dinner will be served at 1:00 tomorrow, Dear. It will be such a pleasure to see you." And she hung up the phone! I wanted to laugh as I imagined Daddy hearing the click and staring at the receiver dumbfoundedly. However, I hurriedly wiped the smile off my face as she entered the room.

"Now, Grandmere," I prepared to defend myself. "I hope—"

"Lovey is bringing us some hot chocolate," she interrupted me as she indicated I should be seated on the loveseat and then she joined me. "Ah! Here she is now! Thank you, Lovey." She poured a cup of steamy liquid and handed it to me. "Now, tell me all about this play you want to be in. Are the auditions over? Did you get the part you wanted?"

I was stunned into silence, an unusual state for me at the age of sixteen. Her response to my actions was the last thing I expected.

"Rachel?" She sipped her chocolate peacefully. "Did you get the part you wanted?"

"Yes mam," I managed to stammer. "I'm going to play Joan of Arc."

Her laughter filled the room. "How very appropriate, Darling! Simply perfect!"

I grinned, but I dared not laugh. I felt a strange sympathy for my father who, I figured, was feeling as confused as I.

Grandmere continued laughing, "Now if we can just keep you from being burned at the stake when your father arrives tomorrow!"

I felt confident she could and would.

And she did.

When Daddy came storming into the house the next morning, he saw me and immediately started making all the predictable demands, "How could you do such a thing? What in the world possessed you? Don't you know we have been worried out of our minds?"

He would have undoubtedly gone on in that same tone for quite some time, without ever allowing me to get a word in, but suddenly Grandmere appeared in the hall and commented in a tone of such gentility that God Himself would not have dared disagree, "My dear Jack, desperate situations require desperate solutions. Let's you and I take a stroll in the woods and have a little talk. I feel confident that after we talk *you* will not create this particular desperate situation again."

That was the end of the whole affair. Since it was Friday, we spent the weekend with Grandmere and drove home Sunday night. When we arrived, the rifle had been removed and never reappeared.

Rachel studied Justin's photograph again. He must have been about fourteen, she decided. Grandmere was killed when he was fifteen, so she wasn't there when Daddy decided Justin should be a soldier, should carry on his family's tradition by attending a military boarding school. And, of course, I was in college, so I only saw him on holidays. He was so miserable! Oh how I begged him to defy Daddy, to refuse to go back! But he never did. Not then, when he was in high school and not later after he had begun college and the fighting was so fierce in Viet Nam and Daddy saw it as such a wonderful opportunity for Justin.

"A wonderful opportunity!" Rachel jumped up and paced around the room. "How that makes my blood boil, even now, even after all these years! I will *never* understand how Daddy could have even suggested Justin give up his student deferment and march off to glory in a rice paddy! But he did! He did!"

Rachel burst out of the music room and slammed out the front door onto the verandah. "He pressured a 19-year-old boy who couldn't shoot a rabbit into going off to shoot his fellow human beings. With Mother and me both fighting him every inch of the way, he forced Justin into the ultimate enactment of the male D'Evereau mold. In spite of everything he knew about Justin's personality, he refused to acknowledge Justin's identity. He killed my brother! Any fool could see that Justin would just stand there and be shot before he would hurt anyone. And that's just what he did!

Rachel ran to the west verandah, the verandah that faced in the direction of the D'Evereau cemetery, and shouted, "Why didn't you defy him, Justin? Why did you go?"

Then she stared at the heavens and shouted, "And where were You, God? Where were You when You let him be shot? Where were You when You let Grandmere be killed? She was the only one who could have saved Justin. She could have stopped this insanity!"

When she was silent again, there was no sound except the sighing of the pines as the night breeze swept through them.

Rachel collapsed against a pillar and demanded of herself, "Why do I keep asking the same useless questions?"

# TWELVE

Andre Simone turned out to be more than a piano technician. When he stepped out of his car at Belle St. Marie the fourth week of August, Rachel almost wished she were sixty-five or seventy herself. He was a handsome figure of a man, with bushy white hair and beautiful blue-green eyes. Rachel greeted him on the front verandah, and when she held out her hand to welcome him, he took it in his, and much to her surprise, he raised it to his lips and kissed it.

"It is with indescribable pleasure that I return to this home that was hallowed by the presence of my beloved Elinore," he announced with grand dignity. "And now that her hand is forever gone from me, I gladly kiss her granddaughter's, knowing that she is alive in you."

Rachel was struck speechless by the man's words and the old-fashioned, but delightful courtliness of his manner. For a long moment she stood there while he continued to hold her hand. Finally, he broke the silence, "Thanks be to God," he said solemnly, "you have Elinore's sapphire eyes."

Rachel snapped her attention back to her duties as a hostess, welcomed him to Belle St. Marie as she had watched Grandmere welcome so many others, and reintroduced him to Lovey, who had been standing to one side. Then she escorted him inside for a cool drink in the music room.

He glanced in the direction of the piano and whispered to Rachel, "I dare not look at it now for *she* is not seated there. It will take me a little time to adjust to realities. You will forgive me a little emotion?" He removed an elegantly monogrammed, linen handkerchief from his coat pocket and dabbed at his eyes.

Rachel seated him where he could not see the piano, and Lovey served him a cool punch. Rachel was very careful to speak only of his trip up from New Orleans in the interval before she showed him to his room to rest before dinner.

When she returned downstairs, she found Lovey in the dining room checking the table setting for the fiftieth time.

"I can see why Grandpere fussed about bringing Mr. Simone up from New Orleans, Lovey." Rachel grinned mischievously.

"It sure wasn't the money, was it, Miz Rachel?" Lovey laughed quietly.

"He absolutely must have been in love with Grandmere!"

"Oh, he was, Honey! But there wasn't nothing uncommon about that. I don't guess there was ever a man who visited here who didn't take one look at Miz Elinore and worship her on the spot, but that Mr. Simone he was one of the worst."

"Poor Grandpere!"

"Poor Grandpere! Don't you poor Grandpere me! When Mr. Simone come, Miz Elinore get double her money's worth. She get her piano fixed, and she get Mr. Alex to behave hisself for at least a month after Mr. Simone gone home."

"What on earth do you mean, Lovey?"

"Ain't proper to speak ill of the dead—but—well—Mr. Alex he wasn't no angel. He could be good and tempersome when he took a mind to. But if'n somebody like Mr. Simone just been here, then Mr. Alex could see how special Miz Elinore was."

"I see."

"Anyhow, I's glad to see he still hisself cause you's gonna have a good time."

"It's like meeting someone from the nineteenth century. I mean, his manners and his speech and everything."

Lovey chuckled. "You keeps forgetting where you is. Belle St. Marie ain't never changed no matter what century the rest of the world say it is."

Lovey was right about Rachel's enjoying Mr. Simone's company. At supper that evening he proved to be a charming conversationalist whose favorite topics were music and books. Best of all, he was a born storyteller. No matter what he talked about the subject came out woven into a fascinating, often humorous tale. That evening Rachel laughed away years of stress.

After saying good night to Mr. Simone at the bottom of the staircase, Rachel sought out Lovey in the kitchen. She gave the old woman a long hug. "Lovey, tricking me into opening the music room was one of the best things you've ever done for me. I think you've forced me to take a few steps back into life. It feels good."

"Course it does. You *is* alive. And I bet you's glad we opened the dining room."

"Yes! You were right. Grandmere would have turned over in her grave if we'd served Mr. Simone off a tray." Rachel fell silent a moment before commenting softly, "I'm going to hate to see that man go. He's only been here one day, but he's made so much difference. I hate to think of going back to where I was."

"You won't, Honey. Once you takes a few steps toward life, you can't choose anything else again. Oh, you may get the blues and take a step or two backwards, but once you seen the glory of the life God given us, you can't walk away from it."

"You know, Lovey, sometimes it seems like I've never lived except when I was here. Everywhere else I've only existed or lived some kind of false life. What's the difference? Is there some sort of magic here?"

"I don't knows as I can say, Miz Rachel. I ain't never lived nowhere else. But Mr. Simone, he has, you ask him."

"I think I will. Thank you, Lovey, and promise me you'll let Alice and the other help do the work. You supervise. Promise me?"

"I promise I won't do nothing I don't enjoy!"

When Rachel was ready for bed, she slipped out onto the verandah and wrapped her arm as far as it would reach around one of the huge pillars. She listened to the breeze in the pines and felt its moist touch on her checks. There was a moon that was almost full lighting the plantation. Suddenly it came to her that the same moon had shone on this verandah all the years that Grandmere had lived here with her beloved Alex, all the years Mr. Simone had come and re-opened her grandpere's eyes to the beauty of his wife. The moon lacked just a few nights before it would be full. Rachel sighed happily at the thought of the coming days of Mr. Simone's visit; she sensed that as the moon rounded out, her understanding would round out, not as completely as the moon, for there was never full understanding in this world. Still, she would learn more of life, the life of the past and perhaps some idea of how to live life as it should be lived.

The next morning she was awakened early by Lovey. "Mr. Simone, he already up, Miz Rachel, and gone for a walk in the woods. He say he want you to go with him, but I told him you don't take walks. He say he want to get an early start on Miz Elinore's piano."

"Then I better get a move on, Lovey. I'll be down as soon as possible," Rachel slid out of the bed and reached for her robe as Lovey turned to go.

"I's gonna be sure Alice making breakfast right. I still don't see no need for you to bring in more help."

"Now Lovey, what would Mr. Simone say if you were the only one working here?"

"He say we done gone to the poor house for sure."

"And what would Grandmere say?"

"She always say 'give your company your best.'"

"Right!"

"Okay, I ain't gonna grumble no more long as you knows I could've done it by myself."

"I know, I know," Rachel hugged Lovey and watched her disappear into the hall.

When Rachel came down for breakfast, she found Mr. Simone on the west verandah staring off in the direction of the cemetery. She had no doubt where he'd been.

"Good morning, Mr. Simone, I hope you had a pleasant walk."

"Good morning, My Dear," his voice was quiet, solemn, and when he turned to face her, Rachel saw sadness in his face. She assumed he was thinking of Grandmere. "Yes, the woods are quite pleasant early in the morning. It is a refreshing change from New Orleans."

"Yes, I'm sure."

Lovey called them for breakfast before she could say more. Once they were seated and eating, it was obvious that Mr. Simone was not his usual self. She worried that his walk had upset him too much; he was not a young man. He talked only of the piano, so she assumed he would go right to work.

"Well, I shall leave you alone with Grandmere's piano," she commented as she stood up after the meal was finished. "Just call me if you need anything."

"I won't hesitate, My Dear, to find any excuse to bring your lovely presence to me," he struggled to return to his usual manner as they walked into the music room, "and I promise you as I promised Elinore this morning that I shall not leave until her magnificent piano is in perfect condition; until, My Dear, you can sit before it and play your husband's favorite piece. And after seeing you, I realize I best hasten with my task for no husband could stay away from so beautiful a wife for long. Indeed he may appear this very day!" With a grand flourish he seated himself before the piano and opened it.

Rachel was speechless for a moment; this charming man had unknowingly brought the pain of Collins' death and all that came before it back like an angry fist slugging into her diaphragm.

She sank on to a loveseat while her mind whirled in time and space, uncertain of what part of her life she was living.

When she became aware of the room again, Mr. Simone was sitting beside her, and Lovey was leaning over her pressing a cold cloth to her head.

"Forgive me, My Dear, I did not know. I had no idea," Mr. Simone was pleading with her. Apparently Lovey had told him of Collins' death. "I felt so close to you the moment we met. I thought it must be dear Elinore's blood flowing in your veins, but now I know there is another bond. You have lost your beloved Collins just as I have lost my beloved Elinore."

"There is really not as much similarity as you imagine," Rachel murmured as she sat up. "My husband died because he was a drunk, a drunk who drove."

"But you loved him?"

"Yes."

"And now he is gone."

"Yes."

Mr. Simone silently put his arm around her, pulled her to his side, and held her close for a moment. When he spoke, he said simply, "My Dear, I am over twice your age, but I have no special wisdom to offer you. Loss is loss. There is only one thing you can do; after you have shed your tears, reach for life."

"Mr. Simone's right," Lovey encouraged. "You gotta listen to him."

"I tried that after Grandmere died, Lovey, and after Justin died."

"No, Miz Rachel. You reached for anger. You reached for action. You didn't live."

"We all take that route the first time we experience death," Mr. Simone reassured her, "our first response is anger followed by meaningless action, and every time we lose another loved one, we do the same for a little while. But if we are fortunate, we learn to let our anger go and reach for the best of life—its beauty. It's all around us—in people, in music, in nature, everywhere—but we can't see it through angry eyes. And it is easily buried under empty action."

Rachel looked into the eyes of first Lovey and then Mr. Simone. She found beauty in both places. "Do you think it's still cool enough for a short walk, Mr. Simone?" she asked quietly.

"There's a lovely breeze."

"Then I would like to see the woods again."

"Do you want company?"

"Thank you, but no, not today. How about to-morrow?"

"I look forward to it."

Rachel did not walk far into the woods on her first

outing because the heat was beginning to build, but even at the end of August when the heat seemed to be overwhelming nature itself, she found some of the beauty Mr. Simone spoke of. In the dimness of the woods she watched the birds and squirrels flit and jump through the trees in the course of their morning tasks. Even the sunbeams that found their way through the pines, the beams that would soon become scorching, cast enchanting light.

It's so strange, she thought, how quickly things change. A piano causes me to meet a man, and I learn to laugh again, only to find myself thrust back into the hole of grief. And now here I am, just a few minutes later, in the woods enjoying the sounds, the movements of these creatures. Even as I stand reveling in the magic light of a sunbeam, I know it will later intensify and cause uncomfortable heat. But in time it will also decrease in intensity and become once again an enchanting sunbeam.

When Rachel returned to the house, she found it punctuated with the discordant sounds of Mr. Simone's work on Grandmere's piano, sounds that had always been torturous to her ears. She closed herself away with a book and gritted her teeth, bolstering herself with the thought of the happy results of the present noise. Mr. Simone worked throughout the day, taking only an hour off for dinner with Rachel, and by evening Grandmere's piano was repaired. After supper, at Mr. Simone's insistence, Rachel gave the inaugural concert.

"Bravo! Bravo!" Mr. Simone applauded wildly when she had played the last note. "My dear Elinore would have been proud. The tradition of great music at Belle St. Marie lives on!"

"Thank you," Rachel tried to brush away his compliment, "but you really are too generous."

"No indeed! You make that marvelous old instrument sing just as Elinore did."

"Now I *know* you're either just being kind or you've completely lost your senses. No one could match Grandmere's playing."

"True, true, My Dear," Mr. Simone conceded quietly. "She was an extraordinary musician, one of a kind. She had such a unique touch, especially for any piece with an air of poignancy."

"Poignancy? What do you mean?"

"Oh, it's hard to put into words." Mr. Simone paused as he thought about it. "Those passages that are so mesmerizing because they make one reach down into the depths of life; they make one feel its beauty, but they also make one aware of the illusiveness of that beauty."

"Yes, yes, I know what you mean. Music that moves one to tears because it is so beautiful. I've never understood the paradox of beauty producing tears. Perhaps you are right. We cry because beauty is so illusive. We see it, but the sight is fleeting, and we know it."

"That's it, My Dear. I think you've come as close as you can to saying it. I am amazed you know of such things; young people seem to have decided long ago to rush past such things."

"I'm sure I learned about beauty here," Rachel answered. A comfortable quietness filled the room as they were both lost in their own thoughts.

"I wish I had been born seventy-five years ago," Rachel suddenly announced.

"You do? Why?"

"I would like to have lived as Grandmere lived. I would like to have lived a life of graciousness, of happiness and peace."

"Is that the way you see her life?" Mr. Simone asked quietly.

"Yes, of course. It was that way, wasn't it?"

"Well, it was, and it wasn't."

"What do you mean?" Rachel was surprised by his words as well as by the cautiousness of his tone.

"My Dear, the externals of her life were often anything but happy. As for the graciousness and peace, she produced those herself."

"Are you sure?"

"I'm positive."

Rachel was bewildered by his response, so she said nothing for a few minutes. "How long did you know Grandmere?" she finally asked.

"From the day she was born. You see, our families were close even though the Simones were tradesmen and the Chretiens were landed. Our mothers were in school together, best friends. I was born only a few months before Elinore, and when she came into the world, her mother, my mother's best friend, died. It was only natural that my mother would take an active role in her upbringing."

"I know she lost her mother, but other than that she had everything," Rachel insisted. "Her father's love, education, music, society. And then Grandpere. She really loved him. And Belle St. Marie. She always had everything she needed or wanted, and she was so adored by everyone. Later, of course, she lost Grandpere. I know that losing him must have been awful for her, but other than that, she never had to suffer much. It's no wonder she was always at peace, no wonder she could have such strong faith in God."

"No, My Dear! I can see this myth you have created is very important to you, but you are wrong. You have it backwards. Her life was often painful. It was the pain that brought her to God, to that peace you speak of."

"But she never spoke of any pain," Rachel countered.

"My Dear, you were a small child when you first met her. I remember, she was so excited. She told me all about you in a letter. You were what—about five or so?"

"Six."

"And then you came here for that first summer. How old were you then?"

"Seven."

"Would your Grandmere have told such a little child about her troubles of the past? No, My Dear, you saw the *end product*. You saw the reward of long years of struggle—struggle coupled with great faith. How old were you when she died?"

"Twenty-one."

"Ah-h-h. You saw the best."

"But no one ever told me. Daddy never told me."

"He wouldn't in some cases because he was the problem. In other cases he probably couldn't because he didn't know."

"You tell me, Mr. Simone. I need to know."

"I don't know that it's for me to tell you these things, My Dear. I am not a member of your family."

"But you must! I am here at Belle St. Marie because I cannot go on until I find a better way to live, and Grandmere had a better way. No matter how she got it, she had what I need. But she is gone; she can't tell me. *You* must tell me!"

"I can only tell you some of it. Perhaps Lovey can tell you more, but none of us can tell you what Elinore did with her tragedies, how she used her tragedies to produce such peace in herself, to produce that special light we all saw."

"Why can't you tell me?"

"I don't know. I would have taken the same path if I could have found it. Don't you think I would have chosen to live with that light she had during the last half of her life, if I could have?"

"Someone must know."

"Lovey surely understands it more than anybody else."

"Yes, of course, Lovey."

"And you, My Dear. I believe you know more than you realize."

"Why? Why do you think that?"

"You are so like her, especially when she was your age. Seeking. Seeking in faith. Unshakable faith. Refusing to settle for less than the peace she believed God had chosen for her."

"You mistake me, I'm afraid. I long ago lost whatever faith I had."

"I cannot judge your faith or lack of it, but I doubt very much you could have lost the faith you undoubtedly learned from Elinore. It's in you somewhere. And I have no doubt you are a seeker because here you are. You could have gone anywhere, if all you desired was a retreat, but you came here. Why?"

"Because Grandmere had what I need. Peace."

"Yes, she had peace, but not because she led some kind of charmed life, free of trouble."

"You knew her from the day she was born. Please tell me what you know."

"Well, let's see. Her mother was very religious, and when she died, Elinore's father was so distraught that he adopted his wife's habit of attending daily mass. He never married again; instead he devoted his life to raising his daughter. He was absolutely crazy about Elinore. She was very precocious, especially in music. And she was very religious. When we were children, I thought she was crazy to *want* to go to mass, but she loved it. I loved her as soon as I had any notion that girls were nice, but she didn't have the same kind of feelings for me. She was determined to be a nun. Her father had mixed feelings about that. He loved the Church, but he knew he would lose her if she did become a nun. And she came from a class where a fine marriage and children were expected of her. Indeed, she was her father's only heir. On the other hand, he did not want to lose her to a husband either, and he didn't want to risk her life in childbirth. He didn't know what to do, but when Elinore was seventeen, she insisted on joining a religious order in New Orleans. Her father sent her up here to the Cane River country to visit her newly married cousin for several months. She obeyed her father although she was certain that God wanted her to be a nun. It was here that she met Alex D'Evereau. He worshipped her the minute he saw her and set about winning her hand. Much to her amazement she found that she loved him, but it was some time before she was certain that God's will for her was marriage.

"Her father was delighted with the match. I was not. I wanted her to marry me, but I wasn't even in the running. It wasn't easy for her to leave New Orleans and her father and come live in the country, but she soon grew to love it here because she loved Alex. He was impatient for children, especially for a male heir; after all, he was a thirty-eight-year-old bachelor when they married. It took two years, however, and when the baby was born, it was a girl. That fact was disappointing to Alex, but the heartbreaking thing for everyone was that the child was retarded. Alex behaved very badly. He refused to see the baby or to let others see her. When he even refused to baptize the child in public at the church, Elinore's iron will asserted itself. Normally she would have allowed Alex to rule in anything; she was of that generation and that disposition, but for Elinore there were definite lines of integrity and morality, and when anyone stepped over them, he had to confront her. And she was immovable. It was their first fight, I'm sure. If you could call it a fight. Elinore never raised her voice in her life. She could win a war with a single gracious sentence."

"Yes," Rachel interrupted him for a moment, "I know exactly what you mean."

"Well, the little girl was baptized with Alex in attendance. He was there, and so was I, but he wasn't happy about it."

"What was her name?" Rachel asked.

"Marie Therese, for Elinore's mother. You see Elinore had every intention of giving that child the best she had."

"But I've never even heard of her!" Rachel exclaimed.

"The little girl died a week later."

"Oh dear God! Poor Grandmere!"

"Yes, it nearly broke Elinore's heart. Alex was relieved, I would guess. And when Elinore conceived again about a year later, he was jubilant. This child proved to be a son."

"Daddy!"

"No, My Dear. This child was stillborn."

"Oh dear God!"

"Yes. Alex was distraught. He was consumed with guilt. Elinore had little time for her own grief she was so worried about him. He began to drink excessively, and Elinore spent more and more time on her knees in the church. I think Lovey would know more than I about this time of Elinore's life. I do know that she conceived another child and gave birth to it. When Alex saw that he had a healthy son, your father, he begged Elinore's forgiveness and immediately went to the church. From the day your father was born to the day Alex had his heart attack, Alex never missed mass. Elinore had always gone daily; now the two of them went together."

"How long were they married before Daddy was born?" Rachel asked.

"About six years, I suppose."

"Plenty of time for Grandmere to wonder if she should have been a nun!"

"Yes, I suppose she must have wondered. Still, she loved Alex a great deal."

"And Lovey said he was no angel."

"That he was not!"

"And there were no more children?"

"None that lived."

"But some that didn't?"

"Yes. I don't know how many."

"I can't think of anything more heartbreaking for Grandmere. She loved children so much! And to have given up her religious vocation for them. And at the same time to know how disappointed Grandpere was."

"And then her father died when your daddy was about five years old. He had been her only parent, her mainstay for thirty years."

"It sounds absolutely overwhelming to me!"

"It wasn't for Elinore. It was those pains that brought her to that peace you experienced in her. Don't ask me how. I saw it happen from the outside. All I can tell you is it was a slow transformation, and each sorrow moved her a step closer."

"Thank you, Mr. Simone. I don't exactly understand how this information will help me, but I sense it will. And thank you for giving me back Grandmere's piano. It makes me happy just to touch it."

"Well, My Dear, my work is finished, and I must go."

"Oh no! Who will discuss books with me at dinner? Surely you can stay a little longer. I won't let you go!"

"Thank you, My Dear, it does this ancient heart good to excite a lady's attention, even if it is over books! However, I have promised to be back in New Orleans for an appointment on the first of the month, which is Tuesday. So after mass in the morning I must bid you adieu."

Rachel sighed her acceptance of the situation and took his hand in hers and squeezed it.

"We shall attend mass together before I leave," he announced as he held her hand. "It is an old custom of Elinore's. She used to say that after two people had received communion together, they could never really be parted."

Uncomfortable with his suggestion, Rachel shifted her position and said quietly, "I haven't been to mass in years."

"No! You can't mean it! Here at Belle St. Marie all these months, in Elinore's house, and no mass?"

"What can I say?" Rachel shrugged her shoulders.

"Say you will be ready at 7:30 in the morning. I can see there *is* one other thing I can do for Elinore."

"I'll think about it."

"No! You won't think; you will go! You say you seek Elinore's peace. You know best where to find it."

Rachel nodded, and Mr. Simone rose from the couch.

"Good night, My Dear," he leaned over and kissed the top of her head, "sweet dreams."

"Good night." She watched him as he left the room. I always knew I would go to mass eventually, when the time was right, she conceded to herself. I suppose the right time has arrived.

The next morning Rachel drove to mass with Mr. Simone and experienced an apprehension similar to the kind she had experienced almost thirty years before when she had come to mass with Grandmere for the first time. When they arrived, Mr. Simone took her hand, placed it in the crook of his elbow, and escorted her into the church. As soon as she had knelt and mechanically said a prayer, she sat down and began to survey the interior of the church. It had changed little since she was seven. As she remembered her first experience here, she began to realize she had not changed much, if at all, in her relationship to God.

❧❧

Seven-year-old Rachel nervously sat down in the pew next to her Grandmere. Grandmere leaned over and whispered "Now Darling, we've come here to pray and worship God. There will be many things in this mass that you've never seen before, but I shall whisper very quietly in your ear and tell you what is happening." Rachel nodded her understanding. The fact that Grandmere was already whispering indicated to Rachel the need for quiet. She wasn't sure what was going to happen, but the quiet suggested to her that it was very important, whatever it was, and she planned to be on her best behavior. Grandmere continued whispering, "Darling, you can simply sit quietly in the pew and watch what happens or you can participate as much as you want."

"What if I do the wrong thing, Grandmere?" Rachel's apprehension was mounting into fear.

Grandmere pulled her closer to her as she spoke, "There is nothing to worry about, Darling, you can't do anything wrong. God is interested in your intentions. He knows what is in your heart, and He knows that you came here today to worship Him."

"I don't think I came here to worship God, Grandmere," Rachel confessed in a whisper and then looked hurriedly over her shoulder, "I think I just came here to be with you." She was genuinely concerned about angering God, whom she believed was somewhere in the church but hopefully not where He could hear her whispers. Her religious instruction thus far had taught her about God's anger and its painful results for humans. She was terrified she might offend Him and He would take the summer away from her and send her back to Mammy Cassie.

Grandmere reassured her, "Darling, that's okay. You came to mass to be with me because you love me, and loving one of God's creations, whether it's a person or an animal or a tree is one of the best ways to worship Him." She paused before asking, "do you understand, Darling?"

Rachel peered at her Grandmere's face a moment more before her lips turned up in a smile, and she questioned eagerly "like loving the cardinal, Grandmere?"

"Just like that, Darling, just like that," Grandmere reassured. Rachel relaxed.

Grandmere knelt in prayer after they were seated, and Rachel sat on the pew looking around. Rachel's eyes were caught by the large golden crucifix sitting on the altar surrounded by candles. It was much more inviting to her than the enormous wooden cross of the Texas church, with its graphic depiction of the suffering Jesus and all those sharp splinters. With this cross, which was a very refined work of art, it was almost possible for Rachel to ignore the figure of Jesus on it altogether.

Finally Rachel got lonely sitting in the pew by herself, and she joined her Grandmere on the kneeling bench. It was the first time in her life that she had ever knelt. She knew everybody around her was praying, but the only prayer she could think of was the one she had learned in Sunday School and which she said every night as Mammy Cassie impatiently glared down at her, waiting to turn off the light. It didn't seem the least bit appropriate to Rachel, but it *was* the only prayer she knew, and she had no idea she could just talk to God. Besides, Grandmere had said that God was interested in her intentions, and she intended to pray to Him like everybody else was doing. She decided to risk it!

"Now I lay me down to sleep," she barely whispered the words and stopped after the first phrase to see if anyone was staring at her. No one was, so she continued, "I pray the Lord my soul to keep." She stopped again, glanced at Grandmere's hands, and noticed that she was running some beads through her fingers as she prayed. Rachel was concerned. She had no beads, and she was afraid that maybe God required them or something, but then she remembered that nobody had beads at the Baptist Church and they still could pray, so she felt better. "Remember I'm a Baptist, God," she whispered as she started the prayer up again, "If I should die before I wake, I pray the Lord my soul to take."

She was finished, but it was too short! Everybody else was still praying, and her knees were starting to hurt. There was nothing else to do, she decided, but to start the prayer all over again and repeat it. This time she said the words very slowly, trying to make the prayer last. But it didn't. "It just isn't long enough!" Rachel whispered desperately as she began the prayer for the third time and made a solemn vow to herself that she would learn another prayer before the day was out.

Rachel was the happiest person in the room when the choir started singing, and her Grandmere rose to her feet and joined in the hymn. She had said her prayer seven or eight times—she had lost count, and her knees were killing her. Boy! she thought, it's hard to be a Catholic!

The mass was mostly incomprehensible to Rachel, not only because she didn't know what was going on, but because it was conducted mostly in Latin. However, the music spoke directly to her soul. With the greatest of ease it circumvented her mind and communicated directly with her spirit. She had never heard such music before!

Rachel snapped her attention back to the present as Mr. Simone and the congregation rose all around her. Grandmere receded into memory. The choir was singing a beautiful Gregorian chant, and Rachel was once again moved by the music. But life at thirty-five is a good deal more complicated than it was at seven, she thought, and I will not find peace simply by listening to beautiful music. To gain the peace I want, I am going to have to work for it.

Mr. Simone shared a late breakfast with her after mass, and then he left for New Orleans. The house seemed very empty again, and for the remainder of the day Rachel wandered around the open rooms restlessly thinking about the things she had learned from his visit.

As the sun was setting that evening, she slipped onto the piano bench, opened some music she had found that afternoon, and began playing her favorite pieces, some of Chopin's "Nocturnes." I'm really too rusty to tackle something this difficult, she acknowledged to herself, but they are so beautiful and feel so right for the moment. I suppose because it's dusk. Or maybe it's more than that. She listened carefully to the passages she was playing and felt a yearning rise in her. They're like the music Mr. Simone and I spoke of. Poignant. They tell of the great beauties of life—so fleeting, just glimpsed, then gone.

These last three days have been a great gift. In fact, this month has been remarkable. Tomorrow is the first of September, and a month ago I would never have believed I could be sitting here at this piano in this room. I would never have believed I could entertain anyone, much less enjoy a guest so much.

Rachel stopped playing and stared straight ahead. And

to learn so much about Grandmere, about her early years. I had no idea! Mr. Simone is right; I saw the finished product. It wasn't all sweetness and light for her. How happy she must have been when Daddy was born healthy and male! How excited Grandpere must have been! Rachel walked over to the mantel and looked up at the portrait of Alex. Grandpere was a handsome man. Daddy looks just like him except for his eyes. Daddy has Grandmere's blue eyes.

"I's off to bed, Miz Rachel, if you's fixed up for the night," Lovey interrupted Rachel's thoughts. "Mr. Alex was right handsome, wasn't he?"

"Yes, he was. I wonder how old he was when this was painted. Were you here? Do you remember?"

"Sure I remembers. He was about forty-five."

"About the time Daddy was born. I wish I'd known him."

"He was a fine man."

"But used to getting his own way?"

"Yes mam!"

"Mr. Simone told me some things about the early years of Grandmere's marriage I can hardly believe. I didn't know Grandmere had such a hard time having children. I had never even heard of Marie Therese!"

"They was hard, hard times for Miz Elinore. I's just a teenager, but I worked here in the house, and Miz Elinore always watch over me with special care. I hurt and hurt for her. And I gots to tell the truth, Miz Rachel, they was lots of times I didn't much like Mr. Alex at all in them days."

"No, I don't blame you."

"They's so happy when they first come after the wedding in New Orleans, and we had lots of company, and everything was all joyful like, but when Marie Therese be born and she not just right, well Mr. Alex he just act shameful. Poor Miz Elinore she had to say she gonna leave him forever if'n he don't come to the baptism. She gonna go back to New Orleans with her baby girl. She'd a-done it too."

"And the son Grandpere wanted was born dead."

"Yes'm. And Mr. Alex he went on a rampage like you never seen the likes of. Drinking. Lord, Lord, how that man drank!"

"How could he treat Grandmere that way? I thought he was supposed to be in love with her."

"I guess he just so disappointed. He didn't blame Miz Elinore. He was furious with God Almighty. Swore he'd never darken a church door again. Nearly broke Miz Elinore's heart the way he roamed this plantation, drinking and cursing God."

"He cursed God in front of Grandmere?"

"Oh no, Miz Rachel! She wouldn't a-stayed a minute more in this house if he ever done that, and he knowed it. When the anger boil up in Mr. Alex, he just bolt out of the house and not come back. Sometimes he be gone for days."

"Would Grandmere send someone after him?"

"No mam! She say 'He's a grown man. He's responsible for himself. When he comes to his senses, he'll come home where he belongs.'"

"I don't see how she stood it. What about her own grief?"

"One day I took her tea up to their room. I wasn't sure if I should take it cause Mr. Alex had just stomped out of the house, but the cook say Miz Elinore need it special. The door to their room was sorta open, and I heard her crying. It make me so mad I could've killed Mr. Alex, but I just walked on in with the tray. There was Miz Elinore on her knees in front of the crucifix on the wall. She was taking turns praying and crying. I couldn't understand why God let such a sweet lady that believe in Him so much be hurting so. I had to know, so I went over to her. When she saw me, she held out her hand to me just like she always did when I was near her. I knelt down beside her, and I asked, 'Miz Elinore, why do the Lord let you suffer so much pain? It ain't your fault about the baby.' She say, 'I don't know, Lovey, but there is a reason. And in time I will know.' I asked, 'But how you gonna go on till then?' And she say, 'I am going to hold on to the hand of Jesus and continue to pray for peace.' I asked, 'But what if He let you get hurt again?' And she answer, 'I will hold on tighter.' I was so young and didn't understand much of anything about God, so I up and demanded, 'How can you?'"

Lovey stopped, lost in her memory, until Rachel pressed her, "What did she say, Lovey?"

"She say, 'I choose to. I choose to because I know that God loves me. He won't let me down.' I said, 'You looks awful down to me, Miz Elinore,' and she say 'You wait, Lovey. Things will come right. God will provide.'"

"And then Daddy was born."

"That's right. It was less than a year after I talked to her that Mr. Jack was born."

"And Grandpere straightened up."

"He sure did!"

"So I suppose she believed God had answered her prayer."

"Of course she did!"

"But maybe God didn't, Lovey. Maybe it was just an accident that she had another baby who happened to be a boy."

"She wasn't praying for no baby, Miz Rachel! Ain't you been listening to me? She was praying for peace, and she got it! She got it long before your daddy was born. Your daddy was a special gift."

"Was she at peace when she lost the babies after Daddy was born?"

"She was the woman you knew, Honey."

"Then she *was* at peace." Rachel glanced back at Alex's face and then moved her eyes down to the photograph of Justin. "So Grandpere really changed after he knew he had a son?"

"He was a different man."

"Daddy changed too after Justin was born. He just came to life, especially about his past, about Louisiana and this plantation and being a Southern gentleman. Even about Catholicism. I never heard much about any of it until Justin came."

"I think maybe all mens wants their sons to be just like them."

"Was Grandpere that way?"

"He sure was. He did everything he could think of to make your daddy into a Southern gentleman. Even before Mr. Jack could understand a word he say, Mr. Alex always sitting him on his knee and telling him about his D'Evereau ancestors and what all they done and how Mr. Jack gotta keep up the tradition."

"And did Daddy keep up the tradition?"

"He sure did. He learned to ride almost before he could walk. And when he got old enough he learn to hunt. He spent half his time in the woods with Mr. Alex, and Mr. Alex took your daddy with him everywhere. Sometimes Miz Elinore didn't like it, especially when Mr. Alex send your daddy off to military school. He was a teenager by then, but Miz Elinore didn't want him to leave home. Mr. Alex say he got to have a proper education and learn to be a gentleman, and he couldn't do it here at the Catholic school. So off he went! Nearly broke Miz Elinore's heart the first time, but he's soon enough back home for Thanksgiving. When he's grown, he went on off to

Charleston, South Carolina to The Citadel, just like all the D'Evereau mens had, and he graduate and gonna come home and help run the plantation, but the war broke out. So he become an officer in the army right after he graduate. Miz Elinore was just heartbroke he couldn't stay home, but Mr. Alex was proud as could be."

"That Daddy was going off to war?"

"Yes Mam! He say all the D'Evereaus fights for their country as long back as anybody can remember. He went down to New Orleans hisself and volunteered, and they put him to work."

"But Grandpere must have been sixty-five or more!"

"He was! But that didn't stop him. Course Miz Elinore always say it was doing all that war work that gave him the heart attack that eventually killed him."

"Where was Daddy when Grandpere died?"

"Right here, praise the Lord!"

"But I thought he was off fighting Nazis."

"They already done that landing on Normandy, and Mr. Jack was wounded in that, and they sent him back to New York. When he was healing pretty good, Miz Elinore and Mr. Alex was making plans to fetch him back to the closest army hospital, the one down in Baton Rouge. But Mister Alex, he had this heart attack, and Miz Elinore and I went down to New Orleans to bring him home. The doctors say he wasn't gonna do no recovering so Miz Elinore wrote to Mr. Jack. Next thing we knowed he showed up on the doorstep. Weak as a kitten, but he was here. And it sure was a blessing! Mr. Jack had a medal for bravery, and Mr. Alex was so proud you'd thought he was the one hisself that got it. Anyways they got to be together a couple of weeks before Mr. Alex died."

"That must have been a terrible time for Grandmere."

"Well, she was just glad they's all three here in the house. She knowed Mr. Alex gonna die, but he wasn't suffering. And she had her boy home safe from the war, which was more than lots of mothers around here had. You know Miz Elinore. She always count her blessings, not her troubles."

"Yes. I wish I were like her."

"You coming round to it, Honey. I sees more of Miz Elinore in you everyday."

"I hope so," Rachel sighed and raised her eyes to the portrait of Alex D'Evereau. Then she looked at the photograph of her father in his military uniform and finally at the picture of Justin. "Thank you, Lovey. You've done more than just tell me my family history. You've given me the beginnings of understanding, I think."

"Understanding be real important, Miz Rachel, cause it lead to forgiveness, and forgiveness is the road to peace."

Rachel nodded as she picked up the photographs of her father and her brother and looked down at them.

"Do you understand what I's saying, Honey?"

"I understand what I need to *do,* Lovey, but understanding and doing are two different things."

"Everything got its time and place, Honey. That be God's way of dealing with us cause we can't handle too much too fast. You's in the right place, and the time be coming round. God's time. There ain't no other time, so you just as well wait for it."

"Is that all I have to do is wait?"

"Wait and want it and believe it gonna happen. That be enough. Good night, Honey."

# THIRTEEN

Rachel was playing the piano about 4:00 in the afternoon on a late September day when suddenly she became aware of a presence in the music room. Her glance darted from the music to the figure who stood just inside the door from the entry hall.

"Daddy!" she exclaimed as she jumped up from the piano bench.

"Don't stop, Baby, hearing that old piano is the most beautiful sound I can imagine. I had no idea you could play like that."

"Well, you paid for enough lessons. You ought to know." Shyly Rachel walked over to him and gave him a tentative hug. "Why on earth didn't you tell me you were coming?"

"You would have said '*no*.'" He leaned over and kissed her forehead, and Rachel did her best not to stiffen.

"I couldn't stay away any longer," he admitted. "For heaven's sake, I haven't seen you in four months!"

"I know," Rachel glanced at the floor, "it's just—"

"You don't have to explain. I know you've needed time, but I got selfish. That's about the truth of it; I just had to see if you're okay."

"Well, what do you think?" she looked him in the face and smiled.

"Outside looks great. What about the inside?"

"It's coming along," Rachel murmured hurriedly and quickly changed the subject. "You must be ready for something cool to drink. I'll call Lovey."

"No, don't bother her. I just had a Coke, and I've got to go see a couple of planters who are leasing some of the fields. Just dropped by to say I'm here and I'll be back for supper," he kissed her on the forehead again before he turned to go, "I'll see you in a couple of hours, and we'll have a chat over some of Lovey's cooking." He turned and strode out of the room so fast Rachel stood there for a moment wondering if she had imagined the whole incident. Then she went to tell Lovey who exclaimed, "I just knew this gonna be a good day! And here Mr. Jack done come home."

Rachel wasn't so sure it was a good day.

After supper that evening Rachel hastily left the dining room thinking that she would escape upstairs to be alone. Through the entire meal she had made superficial, socially acceptable conversation with her father. It had been such a bizarre experience for she had spent so little time with him these last eight years he was like a stranger to her and yet he was as familiar as her own face. Confused feelings had welled up in her as she sat there graciously passing dishes to her father and talking about his business and family and friends they had in Texas, talking about everything that was unimportant to her. It was her way of escaping the storm that had been brewing inside of her for as long as she could remember.

So as soon as the formality of supper had been endured, she said good night to her father and walked through the music room with the idea of going upstairs to bury herself in a book. She wanted to escape herself, to escape this relationship that hurt so much because it had gone awry so long ago. She had no idea how it had become such a mess or imagine how to repair it.

Just as she set foot in the hall, she heard her father's voice behind her, "Rachel!" She turned and looked at him and looked away.

"Yes, Daddy."

"Are you terribly tired, Baby?"

She wanted to lie; she wanted to do whatever it took not to open the doors between them. So many years had passed; it seemed so hopeless to try. However, when she looked into his eyes and saw his pain, she could not be heartless enough to run away.

"No, Daddy, I'm not particularly tired. I just thought you might like some time alone."

"Well, actually I would like some time with you, Rachel. That's why I came."

"Of course. It's just that we've talked so much—"

"We haven't talked at all," he insisted. "We've made a lot of noise, but we haven't talked."

"Is there something in particular you came to tell me?"

"No, Baby, I didn't come to tell you anything. I came to listen to you."

"To listen to me?" she asked. "What is it that you think I'm going to say?"

"I don't know. Actually tonight is one of the few times in my life that I've felt afraid," he admitted. "I guess I'm afraid of what you might say."

"I can't imagine what you're talking about."

"Rachel, we have had some strong disagreements—"

Hastily Rachel interrupted, "Those things happened a long time ago. I see no point in bringing them up now. What would be the point?"

"Communication. Renewed communication with my daughter. That would be the point, and it's important to me beyond any words I have to explain." Rachel looked at the floor and said nothing. "Look, Baby, could you please just come back and sit down for awhile? I know you've been through horrible things, and I don't want to add to your pain. I know you've stayed here at Belle St. Marie in seclusion to give yourself time to heal, but I can't help myself. I've been so concerned about you all summer long. I've stayed away because you asked me to, but you've never been off my mind. I want you to know that."

"I do know that. You've called—often—and I know you would have come. I'm grateful for your concern."

"That sounds like a line from a perfect thank you note from a perfect lady."

"What do you expect me to say?" Rachel raised her voice. "Until Collins died, I had hardly seen you since Justin was buried."

"That's more like it! You're losing your temper."

"That's what you want?" she demanded, "for me to lose my temper?"

"I'll take anything. Just come back in here and talk to me, *really* talk to me."

Reluctantly Rachel returned to the music room and sat on a loveseat while her father settled himself in a chair.

"Baby, it's just that I want to know how you really are. I know how you look. You're looking pretty well. I know what you say, but I want to know how you really are, what you're thinking."

"Well, Daddy, I've had time to come to grips with what happened in Dallas and to do a lot of grieving and a lot of crying away of the pain, and I guess I've just been so exhausted since that process I've mostly not allowed myself to feel anything. I've just buried myself in reading because I'm so tired—tired of feeling, tired of thinking. So I guess I don't really feel or think anything right now."

"I guess that makes sense. I'm grateful you've had Lovey here."

"Oh yes," Rachel agreed. "She's been the key to speeding this process along, and she has a lot of wisdom that I suppose only comes with age and experience. She's really helped me to grieve, and she's helped me to release some of the anger that I felt about what Collins did. And also I've had to think a lot about the part I might have played in all of it."

"I can't see that you played any part in it at all!" he insisted.

"There are all kinds of parts a person can play. I think my part was more a matter of omission rather than commission. I do feel a certain responsibility that perhaps I should have been more aware of the trouble Collins was in and should have been able to help him more. I think perhaps I was too self-absorbed, too interested in only seeing the world through my personal tunnel vision." Rachel paused before adding, "I really can't talk about it yet. I guess I just need more time to sort it out. And you wouldn't understand it anyway, Daddy."

"I do understand, Rachel. Who else could understand better? I know it's a sore subject, but don't you realize I've had years of those thoughts, those self-recriminations since Justin was killed?"

Rachel stiffened at the mention of Justin's name.

"Rachel, must your brother's death be an unbridgeable chasm between us? I know you blame me—"

Rachel raised her voice to stop him. "Daddy, I really can't see any point in getting into this. It was a long time ago now, and nothing is going to change. Justin is dead; what's done is done. Nothing can undo it. All we're going to do is cause ourselves pain."

"Don't you think it's possible that we might release some of the pain?" he asked. "After all, we've suffered separately for years to no avail. Perhaps we *need* to talk about it."

"I just can't imagine what difference it would make," she replied stiffly. "The facts are the facts."

"What are the facts, Rachel?"

"Do you really want me to say this again?" she demanded, her temper rising.

"Yes, I do."

"Very well. The facts are very simple and straightforward." Rachel struggled to keep her voice even. "You never accepted Justin for what he was. You always wanted him to be some super Southern hero. You never even took a look at how wonderful he was. You always pressed him into a mold where he did *not* fit, and finally you pressed him into a mold where he got killed. He got killed trying to be what you wanted him to be."

"Yes, you made it very plain at his funeral, that he was dead because of me. Obviously you haven't changed your mind."

"I'm sorry, Daddy. How could I change my mind? Nothing has changed. The facts are still there. You insisted on making him into a super D'Evereau. You forced him into the army. He died in Viet Nam. What can change about any of that?"

"A lot of men died in Viet Nam, Rachel."

"*Not like Justin!*" Rachel leapt up and glared down at her father. "He said he would never kill another human being, and you wouldn't listen to him! I came to you, and I begged you to listen to him, not to press him into taking the road to glory and honor that all the D'Evereau men had taken, the road you yourself had taken, the road you felt he had to take. I begged you to see that he was not like that, that if someone pointed a gun at him, there was no D'Evereau killer instinct in him to rise up to save himself, that he truly preferred to die rather than kill. But you pressed him anyway. Why? Why did you do that? Because you were so concerned about your own reputation, about your family name, about D'Evereau honor, D'Evereau tradition. Now my brother is dead, and I don't want to talk about it any more!"

"Don't you think I've given myself that same lecture every day since he died?" Jack demanded as he stood to glare back at her.

"No, I don't think so!" Rachel retorted.

"Why not?"

"I don't think you ever understood what you did."

"I didn't understand at first," Jack admitted, "but like what you're doing with your relationship with Collins, I went through a long period of grieving, of sorting out. Inevitably I came to the conclusions you say you are coming to now. I began looking at *my* responsibility, how I fit into Justin's death. And I swear to you, Rachel, if it had not been for your mother's need of me and the need of me I thought you might have some day, I would have put a bullet through my skull when I realized the part I had played!"

Rachel picked up a needlepoint pillow and stared at it while she ran her finger along its design. Silently she warned herself, I don't need this now. I don't need it! I've been through enough. But she made no effort to stop her father because she wasn't sure she was telling herself the truth. Maybe she did need it. Maybe Lovey was right; she would have no peace until she released her anger.

"Rachel! Can't you see that we're alike? Can't you see that that tunnel vision you had with Collins, that insistence on seeing him the way you wanted him, is exactly what I did with Justin? Can't you see that?"

Rachel threw down the pillow and stared straight into Jack's eyes, "Yes! I see it! And I hate myself for it!"

Jack sighed and was silent a moment. When he spoke again, his tone was sad, resigned. "Don't hate yourself for long, Baby. You inherited it, I'm afraid, and probably learned it from me too. It's a D'Evereau trait, another one of those D'Evereau traditions. Your Grandpere was like that and probably his father too."

"I don't want to be like Grandpere! I want to be like Grandmere!" Rachel was still angry, unmoved by the change in his tone.

"I'm praying you will be, believe me. Because she would have found room for forgiveness, and I need your forgiveness." He paused and seemed unable to go on. Rachel was stunned by the tears that appeared in his eyes, but she was still boiling mad. "As you go through this process of forgiving Collins for what he did and, I hope, forgiving yourself for your part in it, can you not find room in your heart for forgiveness for me? I would lay down my life if I could bring Justin back to life for you. If killing myself would make Justin appear in this room, I would do it this instant."

"I have nothing to say, Daddy."

"Well, I do." he spoke quietly now. "I should have said it years ago. When I understood what I had done to your brother, the way I had denied him and tried to make him into someone else, I should have come to you and asked you to forgive me."

"Why didn't you?" she demanded.

"Pride. I didn't want to say I was wrong."

"Well, what made you suddenly able to lay down that famous D'Evereau pride?" she demanded sarcastically.

"A single telephone call. A call that informed me that you were hurt. As sorry as I am that you have been through this terrible pain, I am glad it has given me the chance to be a part of your life again, to help you. It has opened a door between us, and as God is my witness, I am not going to lose my daughter again! Even if you reject me for the rest of my life, I am going to keep my foot in that door!"

"Spoken like a true D'Evereau!" Rachel jumped up and stalked toward the door.

"It takes one to know one, Rachel!" her father called after her. She wheeled around to retort and found that he was approaching her. "What is that D'Evereau pride of yours covering up, Rachel? God knows you have every right to be furious with me about your brother, but that's not the whole story, is it? What else is there? I said I won't lose you, and I mean it! Forget your mother taught you to be a lady and your Grandmere taught you to be a saint and tell me the truth!"

"All right! Just remember you asked for it," she warned. "Where have you been all my life?"

"What?"

"Where were you? Why did you stand by and leave me in the clutches of Mammy Cassie?"

"I left you in the care of your mother," Jack insisted. "How was I supposed to know how to raise a child?"

"You sure jumped in and raised Justin!" Rachel retorted.

"Justin was a boy! You were a girl. What was I supposed to know about raising a girl? I never saw a girl raised. I didn't even have a sister. Raising you was your mother's job."

"You knew very well that Mother turned me over to Mammy Cassie. You knew Mother was controlled by that hate-filled woman. You sat by and let Mammy Cassie raise me, knowing full well what she was, how she hated me. I was a baby, a little child! Why did you leave me in that mess? Why did I have to spend my entire youth battling for my worth, my self-esteem, my identity? Why did I have to fight Mammy Cassie all my life in *your* house? Why didn't you step in and do something? I'll tell you why! You ignored me because I was a girl. And once Justin came, you acted as if I didn't exist."

Jack's shoulders slumped, and he walked over to the fireplace, put his elbows on the mantle and lowered his head into his hands. He said nothing for several minutes.

Suddenly Rachel felt exhausted and sick. She said quietly, "Well, Daddy, if you have nothing to say, I'm going to bed."

"I *do* have something to say, Rachel," Jack stood up straight, turned to face her, and spoke in an even, firm voice. "I learned a lot the first twenty-five years of my life, but nowhere did I learn how to face war on the beach at Normandy, nowhere did I learn how to face the death of my father, nowhere did I learn that death can make a young man fall into the arms of the wrong woman and marry her, and most important, nowhere did I learn how to be a parent. What you have said is true. I was twenty-five years old when you were born, and I failed, but not because I didn't love you. I failed because I was ignorant. Good night!" He walked slowly past her and headed toward the verandah.

Rachel slowly crossed the hall and started up the stairs. She was in a daze as she pondered what he had said. The war, his father's death, falling into the arms of the wrong woman—her mother obviously. When she reached her room, she crossed to the upper verandah, went outside and leaned against the pillar. Her pulse raced as she remembered their heated argument. They had never fought, not once in her whole life. They had never really talked. Until now she had never even seen him as a human being, a person who was once young and confused. To her, he had always been the strong-willed giant she had known when she was a child.

Suddenly she saw him start walking across the yard. It was a humid night, and there was a ground fog. In no time he was swallowed up by it, and she could see him no more. Her heartbeat increased, and the tears flooded her eyes. "Someday I will lose him too," she whispered. She dragged herself back into her darkened room and sat down and stared into the darkness. She did not stir until she heard him return, walk up the stairs and enter his own room. Then she made herself a vow, "I will live with this anger and hurt no more. I know it will take time, but I *will* understand what it was like for Daddy when I was born. If I understand, I will be able to forgive him and learn to relate to him. And I intend to relate to my father, not avoid him!"

She slept little that night. Her mind replayed the argument she had had with her father and recalled the years of hurt and anger that had preceded it. She also thought of Collins. In particular she kept remembering arguments she had had with him over the years. He had insisted she had never accepted him, never found him worthy, and she had been totally surprised by that accusation. At the time she had easily denied what he said because the specifics of his accusations were always wrong. He had said he had never made enough money for her, that he had never been as financially successful as her father. However, as she lay in the dark and the clock ticked away the minutes of the night, she finally allowed herself to see that she had not accepted Collins as he was. It wasn't a matter of money; it was a matter of personality. Collins had never been as dynamic, as strong-willed as she had wanted him to be. She had always considered him weak and ineffective and had made no special effort to hide her evaluation of him and had, in fact, even demanded he change.

"Dear God!" she whispered as she sat up abruptly in bed. "I did the same thing to Collins that Daddy did to Justin! I married him and set about trying to remake him in my own image!" The thought made her nauseous, and she climbed out of bed and slumped in a chair. "The only difference is that I started out with a twenty-five-year-old man, and Daddy started out with an infant."

She left her bed and walked out on the verandah with the hope of catching a night breeze to blow over her and somehow cleanse her of the guilt she felt. But there was no breeze. The ground fog had intensified so much she found herself staring into a murky white wall.

She turned back into the bedroom and looked at the clock. "Five o'clock," she sighed. "There's no use in trying to go to sleep now." She sat down again and stared straight ahead for a long time trying to decide what to do. "I could ask the same question of Collins that I asked of Justin a few weeks ago. 'Why didn't you fight back?'" she told herself. "But unfortunately I know the answer. You don't fight back when you've been raised with a certain view of yourself and of life. Or if you do live long enough to know you need to fight back, you don't know how. By then, you're too weak to do anything but drink."

"I could ask myself why I didn't see what I was doing. After all, I've been demanding that Daddy have that kind of insight about Justin. Why didn't I demand the same of myself? I don't have an answer for that one." She stood up and walked to the desk and sat down and wrote that question on a piece of stationery.

"And I could ask myself how I dare go on being so furious with Daddy after tonight. Obviously I can't, but I'm not sure how to change my attitude; it's become such a habit. And I certainly don't know what to do with my feelings about the way he allowed me to be raised. The things he said, about the war and his father's death and unwisely marrying Mother have opened my eyes, but I need to understand more. I want to understand more!"

She pulled the piece of paper closer to her and began to write down the thoughts she was having, the things she wanted to resolve. When she had finished, she pulled another piece of paper out.

"I only know two things for sure at this moment. I did the same thing to Collins that Daddy did to Justin, and I have to tell Daddy what I've done and how knowing about it changes my feelings about him. And there's another thing I have to tell him. I have to say I'm going to try to understand what life was like for him when he married and I was born. Dear God! The last months have been hell on earth, but maybe some good *can* come out of them."

She began to write a lengthy note to her father.

By the time she had finished, she heard him moving around in the hall. She dressed quickly, but by the time she got downstairs, he had gone outside. His overnight bag was in the hall, and his suit coat was draped across the back of a chair. She slipped the note into the pocket of his coat and headed for the kitchen.

Lovey was by herself, happily mixing up biscuits for Mr. Jack. "I don't know why he gotta go back so soon," Lovey greeted Rachel, "but he ain't gonna go without some of my buttermilk biscuits."

"You'll get no argument from me," Jack walked in the back door with a forced smile on his face.

Rachel smiled back awkwardly; then before she could think about it and talk herself out of it, she walked over to him and gave him a hug. She didn't look up into his face because she wanted to hide her own tears.

"I don't know why you gotta rush off, Mister Jack," Lovey hadn't noticed the awkward moment. "And while I's on the subject, I wish you'd tell this daughter of yours that she don't have to worry about staying here too long."

"Are you worried about that?" Jack asked Rachel, who had walked over to the work table. "Why on earth would you worry about that?"

Rachel intentionally chose a light tone, "Well, it does cost you a lot for me to be here, especially since I've opened up some of the house. Just the same, I have to confess I'd like to stay a while, through this school year if that's okay, so I hope you're not planning to evict me any time soon."

Jack laughed much more heartily than her comment warranted. "No chance of that, Victoria-Rachélle D'Evereau, alias Rachel. No chance in the world!" Much to Rachel's amazement he continued laughing as he walked to the dining room door. When he reached the door, he stopped, turned and looked her square in the eyes. "You see, Baby," he paused a long moment, "nobody can evict the owner of Belle St. Marie from her own property." Then he opened the door ánd sauntered through it.

Dumbfounded, Rachel stared after him. "What on earth does he mean?" she demanded of Lovey who was heaping biscuits onto a platter.

"You best ask your daddy," Lovey said knowingly.

"I will!" she exclaimed and walked into the dining room with Lovey close behind her. "What do you mean?" she demanded of her father.

"Mean by what?" he asked nonchalantly as he picked his plate up off the table and headed for the buffet where Lovey had addded her biscuits to the breakfast she had prepared.

"You know good and well what I'm talking about. What do you mean 'nobody can evict the owner of Belle St. Marie from her own property'?"

"Just what I said," he turned and winked at Lovey who was grinning broadly.

When Rachel saw that wink, she was sure she had figured out what her father was up to. "Daddy, I appreciate it beyond description, but you are not going to give me

Belle St. Marie and that's final. I understand what you're trying to do—"

"No, you don't understand, Baby. I couldn't give you Belle St. Marie if I wanted to. It's not mine to give."

Jack's eyes twinkled brightly, and Rachel was reminded of the way he had looked when she was a child, long before so much trouble had extinguished that light in his eyes. Lovey was chuckling softly.

"Okay, you two, what's up?" Rachel demanded. "Give it to me straight before I die of curiosity."

Jack stood and looked down at her solemnly. "I don't own Belle St. Marie, Rachel. I never have. You own it. Your Grandmere deeded it to you three years before she died."

Rachel was stunned into silence, so he continued. "You were a minor, so she made me the trustee of the plantation until you were twenty-one. We were going to tell you at that time, but, of course, she was killed when you were nineteen. And you were so upset by her death that you wanted nothing to do with this place. So I've just managed it myself until you were ready."

"I can't believe it! I can't believe she didn't leave it to you!"

"That would have been the normal course of things, as you know. When she died, I would have naturally have inherited it as her closest heir and after me—"

"Justin," Rachel finished his sentence.

"Yes, Justin, since he was my closest male descendant. And your Grandmere knew that. She knew the plantation would come to me and then to Justin. But she knew more than any of us. It's uncanny, Rachel, what she knew. When you were sixteen, you remember you celebrated your birthday here?"

"Yes, of course I remember."

"Well, that evening she called me out on the verandah

and had me sit down by her. She took my hand and she said, 'Jacques, I don't want to hurt you, so I'm trusting you to understand. I know Rachel is going to need Belle St. Marie in the future, not just as an investment, but as a home. I know it, Jacques. I also know that Justin will never need it. I am absolutely certain. You will never again live here as your home. Justin will never live here. Rachel will live here, sometime in her future life, sometime after I'm gone. She is going to need Belle St. Marie as a home. I am positive beyond a shadow of a doubt. That is why I am deeding it to her now, so it won't have to go through the court system when I am gone."

"What did you say?" Rachel asked.

"I knew and trusted your Grandmere, my mother, so I knew to trust what she was saying. I knew I wasn't trusting merely her judgment; I knew I was trusting her closeness to God. I knew that God had shown her this path. So I said, 'Okay, Mother, we'll go take care of it tomorrow.'"

"And you did?"

"No," Jack started laughing again, "you know your Grandmere, Rachel! She pulled some papers out of her prayer book and handed them to me. She had already done the legal work. You see, she trusted God to make it right with me too."

"Yes sir, she did," Lovey added softly. "She came back from one of her long walks in the woods one day and told me about the same thing she told you. And she told me God would see to it that you would understand and not be hurt."

"And were you, Daddy? Were you hurt?"

"No, not at all. And that surprised me because what she had done was a real break with the family tradition and I had always dreamed of owning this place."

"And how do you feel now?" Rachel asked.

"Just great, Baby, just great. Everything she foresaw has

come true. I love this old place, but I'll never live here again." He lowered his voice, "I guess Justin has as much of it as he needs out there in the family cemetery." Tears sprang to Rachel's eyes, but Jack recovered himself and added, "And you, you need a home. And what better one for you?"

"There's no place in the world I'd rather be," she fought to steady her voice. "Thank you, Daddy."

"Thank your Grandmere. She was quite a lady! Imagine seeing into the future the way she did."

"You know what she'd say to that," Rachel said.

"I sure do. She'd say, 'now, Jacques, all I do is pray; anybody can do that.'"

"But not with the same results," Rachel commented.

Lovey added quietly, "not with the same faith." Jack and Rachel looked at her, nodded and smiled.

"Well, the only question I have is, do you want to run your plantation, Rachel, or are you going to keep your old daddy as an unpaid overseer? And now that I think of it, I have another question. Are we ever going to eat breakfast?"

"Yes sir, you is!" Lovey answered, "cause my biscuits is getting cold."

After they had settled at the table, Rachel asked, "Daddy, do you think I really can run Belle St. Marie?"

"Of course you can! And some day you'll have to or else hire somebody to do it for you because you know what would happen to you if you ever tried to sell Belle St. Marie."

"Every D'Evereau who has ever loved this land would rise from the grave in mass and strangle me," Rachel responded.

"Oh, I think they'd think of something far more painful than that. The question is, though, do you want to run it? After all, you are a professor and have worked mighty hard to make your place in that world."

"I know," Rachel paused thoughtfully, "but I really don't want the pressure of teaching right now."

"Then why don't you just learn about running the plantation? It's all in place and running smoothly right now; most of the land is leased out to other planters. You don't have to make any big decisions at the moment. Just take this time to learn."

"This all takes my breath away! I haven't had time to assimilate it."

"Exactly," he agreed. "So I'll show you the books, and you can look them over, and when I come back, we'll discuss them. How's that?"

"Sounds like a good idea." Rachel sipped her cup of tea and ate one of Lovey's biscuits. Then she amazed herself by asking, "Can't you stay longer now?"

Jack looked up in surprise and stared at her a moment before answering softly, "No, Baby, I can't, but I sure am glad you want me to."

Rachel just nodded.

Before her father left about ten, he took her to the plantation office behind the house and showed her how to open the safe where he kept the books. "Do as much as you want with these," he said. "It would be good if you at least know what's going on, but the main thing right now is that you do what's good for you."

"I want to know," Rachel agreed as they closed up the safe and walked back through the house.

"I'll be back soon," Jack began as he picked up his bag and coat in the entry hall, "that is, if the owner will let me on her property."

"I'll think about it," Rachel responded mischievously.

"You do that, but I'm not worried. After you try to

sort through those books, you'll be glad to see your old daddy!"

"No doubt!" Rachel laughed.

"And do one other thing, Rachel."

"What's that?"

"Open up this house," he insisted. "Live in it the way your Grandmere would have wanted you to, the way I want you to. If you're going to stay here this year, stay here like a D'Evereau. There's plenty of money. Do whatever you want with the place. It's yours. The main thing is—live!"

Rachel was torn between smiling happily and bursting into tears, and she didn't understand why. She forced herself to choose the smile for his sake, and he hugged her and walked away to his car.

After his car had disappeared into the pines, she turned back to the music room and sat down. Lovey was dusting the piano with great care.

"How can things change so fast, Lovey?" Rachel asked.

"They just does, Honey."

"But it's been less than twenty-four hours since he came."

"That's just the way of things, Honey. They drags along for what seem like an eternity and then suddenly they's all up and changed."

"Yes, well I hope *I'm* up to this change."

"You is, Honey, else the Lord wouldn't have give it to you."

# FOURTEEN

Rachel slowly awakened to the sound of rain falling outside. She turned over on the crisp cotton sheets, buried her face in the goose down pillow, and murmured contentedly, "Ah. The first autumn rain; it's about time. October felt just like summer. Oh well. . . . autumn in November. . . . crisp days ahead at last." She began slipping back into sleep as she thought of leaves turning color. The sweet gum trees with their golden tones, the red oaks, the sumac with its deep scarlet, fern-like foliage. For a few moments more she slept.

Then another sound awakened her again. It wasn't the soothing, gentle sound of falling rain; it was more of a thump, thump. Just like a child's toy drum softly being struck. She shook herself a bit, raised her head from the pillow, and tried to push the remaining sleep from her mind. "What on earth is that?" she asked aloud. Thump. Thump. Thump. Then she recognized the sound. "Oh no! It's a leak. It sounds like a leak. The roof is leaking somewhere!" She pulled back the covers, slipped off the high edge of the antique bed, walked to the doorway, and turned on the overhead light. And there it was, a puddle accumulating right outside her bedroom door in the hallway. On the beautiful old pine floors, there it was, a small lake, growing as the rain came in too fast to seep through the many layers of wax that had been applied for a century and a half.

"Oh good grief!" She tousled her hair. "What time is it? It's so dark outside." She went back and looked at the clock on her dressing table. "2:14 in the morning! Well, I can't let that keep dripping on the floor, and heaven knows what it's doing to the ceiling below." She thought of the music room, her Grandmere's prized room, and the exquisite, ornate plaster on that ceiling. The thought of the plaster medallions and garlands on the ceiling below pressed her into instant action. She ran to her bureau, seized a large porcelain pitcher, removed it from its matching bowl, dashed back across the room, and stuck the bowl under the drip. "That won't hold it long," she told herself. She ran down the hall to the bathroom, grabbed the thickest towels, and came back and mopped up the standing water. Then she paused to consider what container she could carry up the stairs that would hold whatever amount of water might fall during the remainder of the night.

As she stood there watching the water continue to fall into the porcelain basin, she forced her sleepy mind to inventory the large containers in the house, and finally she remembered the tin wash tubs that were in the wash house, the laundry room attached to one end of the kitchen. Having made her decision, she hurried down the stairs, turning on a few lights as she went, and walked through the large central hallway of the house back to the kitchen. She felt the cool old tiles on her feet. It was a welcoming place to be; of all the rooms on earth, this kitchen was the one that most exuded a sense of home to Rachel.

She pushed open the old washroom door, a room that had long since been replaced by a modern washer and dryer in the kitchen, and smelled its mustiness. It was pitch dark. Holding one hand protectively out in front of her, she slowly edged into the middle of the room as she reached up, searching for the cord that would turn on the single light bulb. Finally her hand found it, and she jerked it. Fortunately there was a working bulb in the outlet, and the room was flooded with light. Even though the washroom had not been used in years, it was in perfect order, and Rachel quickly spotted the tin tubs against one wall, the type that were used with the old wringer washing machines. She dragged them into the middle of the floor to inspect them. They were a little rusted, but they were lightweight and large.

Rachel grabbed a tub and headed toward the door. By manuvering adroitly, she managed to get the huge tub to the second floor. She wasn't a minute too soon; the bowl was overflowing onto the towels. Carefully she edged the bowl over, replaced it with the tub, and cautiously carried the full bowl to the bathtub.

Just as she was beginning to feel quite satisfied with her solution, the storm increased and began to drive water against the house. The drip falling into the tub turned into a slow stream, and Rachel's satisfaction turned to frustration. She crossed her arms in disgust as she stared down at the fast-filling tub. Then she thought of the ceiling over her head. Jerking her head back, she glared at the ceiling, and her worst fears were confirmed. An ugly stain had spread across the overhead plaster and was widening.

"Oh no! I'm gonna have to have this whole ceiling ripped out if I don't stop that leak in the attic. It shouldn't be too hard to find, but if the rain doesn't let up soon, I'll run out of tubs!" She ran downstairs for another tub, and when she returned, she headed for the door that hid the steep flight of stairs that led to the attic. When she opened the door, the hall light only illuminated about five steps of the staircase, and above that short distance she saw only inky darkness. "Heaven only knows what's in that attic," she paused as she stared warily up into the darkness. "If I don't break my neck falling over something, I'm sure to have some hideous encounter with spiders and—" she shuddered as she stopped her own imagination. "Better not think about that."

"One thing's for sure—I'm not going up there in that darkness. I better get the light on. There must be a light switch somewhere here." She began feeling around the door frame inside the door. All she found was cobwebs, handfuls of cobwebs that sent shivers up her spine. Then suddenly she remembered, the attic had never been electrified. "Oh no!" she collapsed on the first step in dismay. "I am *not* going up there in the dark! I'll have to think of something." She sat there brushing cobwebs off her hands and considered the possibility of candles, but she soon dismissed that thought as being too dangerous and too spooky. "There's probably a good draft up there. The blasted things could just blow out and leave me in the dark, or, worse, I could catch something on fire. What I need is a lantern. Surely in a house this old there's a lantern. Besides these storms are pretty common here, they must have lanterns around. Probably in the kitchen."

She hauled herself up and resolutely marched back down to the kitchen. There, high on a shelf she found some old kerosene lamps with glass hurricane shades to protect the flame. "Perfect! Now, if they just have some kerosene in them, and knowing Lovey, they probably do."

Sure enough the lamps were full, and Rachel was soon back upstairs holding the lamp she had lit high over her head as she started up the stairs. "I'll find the leak first," she planned aloud to bolster her confidence, "and then I'll come back for the tub. I just hope all I find is a leak!" Her imagination ran wild as she considered what creatures could be nesting midst the centuries of D'Evereau relics she knew the attic contained. "I bet no one's been up here for years. I know Grandmere kept that door locked to keep us kids out of here."

Finally she reached the top of the stairs and was stunned by the enormity of the attic. Even with just the kerosene lamp to light her view, she could see that she was entering a veritable cavern of a room. In every direction as far as the light permitted her to see, she saw draped forms she assumed to be furniture and trunks and boxes beyond count. "Didn't anybody who lived here ever throw anything away?" she wondered aloud.

Then she heard the leak. She couldn't see it, so she held the lantern as high as she could, and zigzagging around various objects, she followed the sound until she found the spot where the water was hitting the attic floor. She sighed with relief when she saw that she wasn't going to have to move much around to get the tub in place. Quickly she headed back down the stairs and began her slow ascent with the cumbersome tub. Finally it was in place, and she heard the tinny sound of the first drops hitting the tin tub. "Finally!" she exclaimed as she collapsed back on what looked like an old settee of some kind. "Now," she set the lamp on a nearby crate, "I'd better look around and see if there is anything more I need to do up here tonight. A lot of water has gotten in. These dust covers are damp, but I guess they're okay for now, but those trunks have water standing on them. I wonder what's in those things." She walked over and inspected them more closely. "Better not take any chances," she picked up the lantern and headed back downstairs for more towels.

When she returned, she dried the tops of several trunks and then moved to the container closest to the leak. She placed the lantern where she could see and discovered that what she had assumed to be another trunk was in fact a sealed wooden crate with a small, wooden, carved box sitting on top of it. She wiped up the water in the area and began to examine the small box. "It looks like a document chest of some kind, probably made of cypress to keep the moisture and bugs out of it." This one looks like it's been sitting right here for a hundred years. I wonder what's in it."

After all her trips up and down stairs, Rachel was wide awake, and her curiousity about the contents of the chest had driven away her fears of the darkened attic. Eagerly she pulled the lantern closer and opened the latch of the chest. Inside she found bundles of old papers, letters and an old book. "This attic must be full of things like this," she chided herself. "What are you so excited about? It's ridiculous to stay here in the middle of the night."

Still, she stayed. She stayed and stared down into the chest and listened to the storm, which was quieting down.

As the last of the rain ran off of the roof, there was a delicate trickling sound like the soothing flow of water in a tiny garden stream. The wind murmured in the pines outside and embraced the eaves of the house with its gentlest touch. Rachel felt unaccountably snug and at home.

Finally she reached into the chest for the first bundle, placed it in her lap, and untied the ribbon that held it together. The attic was filled with a strange contentment, a serenity that comes rarely because it comes only when the right thing is happening at the right moment. The lamp cast a warm, golden arc around the tiny area that included Rachel sitting in front of the open chest. Rachel felt completely unhurried as she opened the bundle. "I feel like I am embracing some kind of turning point," she murmured. "I know that turning points can be quite abrupt, quite recognizable, a rash intrusion into one's life, like Collins' death." She grew silent as she thought also of the staggering news of Grandmere's death and the loss of Justin.

"Turning points are not always that way though," she whispered to herself, "some turnings are so gentle they are not recognizable for a very long time. Like my first morning here at Belle St. Marie, that first morning when I awoke to find myself in a gigantic bed with sunlight streaming through the French doors." She smiled as she remembered sliding off that bed, running to the verandah and dancing in the sunbeams. "That was one of the gentle turnings," she whispered. And here before her, she was certain, was another turning, a revelation, an epiphany, and its time had come. It could have come no sooner, for she would not have been ready. She would not have been able to receive it. And it could not have come later, for it was appointed for now.

When she raised the contents of the bundle up into the light of the lamp, she found only a slim, faded volume. Its binding had long ago collapsed, and only the ribbon had held it together. She carefully opened the front cover and found that the volume contained only a few pages covered with an elaborate, graceful handwriting in an ink that had turned light brown. The first page threatened to crumble as she lifted it closer to the light to read it. In the middle of the first page she found the words "Journal of Marie DuBois D'Evereau."

Slowly Rachel turned to the next page which was dated April 4, 1852. She began to read. "This is my wedding day. I cannot describe the multitude of feelings that I have on this day, but I am determined to begin my journal on this most blessed of days. It seems to me that the whole world is nothing but beauty, and I can hardly believe that God could love me so much that He could have given me all this joy. Everywhere I turn there are flowers. The house is full of flowers, even the magnolias have bloomed early for my wedding day. I am about to marry the most wonderful man on earth. His name is Jacques Eduard D'Evereau. He is a tall, dark-haired, immensely handsome man. And to-day I shall look into his eyes and promise to be his wife until death parts us. Then he will take me home to his family's plantation up north of here in the Cane River country, and I shall live in his house, and we shall have a family. And someday I shall be mistress of that plantation, and we shall live out our days in the golden surroundings of those thousands of acres he calls Belle St. Marie. But oh! I must not think of all that at once; it seems more than I could ever do. And it seems so far from home. I shall just think of how handsome Jacques is and how much I love him and how we shall do everything together.

"Soon now I shall don my wedding dress—my Mama's wedding dress—and descend the stairs on my Uncle's arm, and I shall become Jacques'. I do not know how I could be any happier! Unless, of course, my beloved Papa were here to give me away. It is the only flaw in a perfect day. I saw the tears in Mama's eyes this morning as we said our prayers. Every morning we do the same, and every morning tears come to her eyes for she misses Papa so even though it has been two years now, but this morning I think she wept because she believes she is losing her elder daughter too. But I won't allow that to be true! There will be many miles between us, but I shall see to it that she and Chyrisse spend much of the year with us. Already we have planned their first visit. They are to come to us in two months. We shall not be parted! I will not allow it!

"I shall think of that no more! I shall think of the magnolias blooming and of my handsome Jacques awaiting me and of how good God is to give me—"

Rachel turned the page and discovered that she would never know how the sentence ended. The next page and others that followed were missing. She peered at the binding. The threads that had held the pages together were broken, and great sections of the book had fallen out and been lost somehow. Laying the journal back in her lap, she tried to remember the D'Evereau family history. "If this Marie DuBois became Jacques' wife in 1852," she reasoned aloud, "let's see, that would make her—now, my father's father was Alexandre, and his father was Jacques. Yes, yes that's right. In 1852 she was marrying my great grandfather. So this must be my great grandmother's journal."

Eagerly Rachel settled more comfortably on the floor beside the chest. She felt like a child on a treasure hunt, a child who was eager to gather together all the required items and win the prize. She examined the next fragment of the journal that had survived all these years. It was also dated in April.

"April 20, 1852. Belle St. Marie is more beautiful than I could ever have imagined! When we arrived at the plantation house yesterday, I could hardly believe my eyes! Of course, Jacques has talked of nothing except Belle St. Marie for months. I felt as if I already knew every inch, but when I saw the house for the first time, I was overwhelmed! It was so large and so beautiful. I cannot describe the splendor of it as it stood there in a flash of sunshine. The light was so dazzling that it seemed that God Himself must have sent a special beam down to welcome me to my new home. And there on the front verandah stood Mama D'Evereau and Papa D'Evereau and a whole line of house servants.

"They came rushing forth to greet me as if I were their daughter! And of course I am, I am their new daughter. We had a sumptuous dinner and then a short rest. Soon I was downstairs again, and we chatted and chatted, and there was so much excitement in the house, so much gaiety as Mama D'Evereau talked on and on about all the D'Evereau relations and neighbors and all the receptions and teas planned in my honor. Finally toward dusk Jacques and I slipped out onto the side verandah where we could sit quietly and watch the dark descend. It was so incredibly beautiful! The shadows of the enormous oaks deepened, and I began to hear the night birds calling to each other. And Jacques sat there with one arm around my shoulders as he held my left hand and turned the golden wedding band he had placed on my finger only a few weeks ago. He talked of the future. I said very little. I could not bear to break the sound of his voice by inserting my own. He was dreaming aloud, that is what he called it, dreaming aloud, and the dream was so beautiful I just wanted to hear more and more of it. All of his plans, all of his thoughts about the future. And now they are my plans, my thoughts, I cannot exaggerate the generosity of God. I am only sixteen years of age, and I am so very happily married, and the future is a panaroma of happy possibilities. I shall have to say a special prayer of thanksgiving.

"Jacques was talking about sitting here a year from tonight and how much closer we would be then, how our love would have deepened. Suddenly it occurred to me that there might be three of us sitting here. I could almost see it: Jacques and I sitting here on the verandah and a baby in my arms. Oh, it seems impossible! And yet it could happen."

Rachel stopped reading and leaned back on the settee and considered the strangeness of it all. It is *this* house she is writing about. Just this morning I sat on the very verandah she writes about. The whole thing is almost impossible to take in. Sixteen years old, more than a hundred years ago, sitting on the verandah downstairs, full of such joy and hopefulness and thankfulness. As Rachel considered the difference between Marie's life and her own, the heaviness of depression weighed Rachel down.

"Why?" she demanded loudly, "why has my life turned

out like this? Am I such a bad person? Am I so much worse than Marie DuBois?" The unspoken questions which had haunted her for years were flung now at the darkened attic. "And what about Grandmere? She was the most loving person who ever drew breath on this earth. Why should she be killed? And Justin. Justin never hurt a living soul, yet he died. They killed him because he would not kill them first. No matter how good any of us are, we suffer! And this Marie. Poor sixteen-year-old Marie! She thinks her world will be beautiful, but it won't. She doesn't know it, but I do. There's a war coming! This place will be ravaged. What will she think of God's blessings then?" Rachel shouted. "Will she go say a special prayer of thanksgiving then?"

She sat there in silence for a moment. She wasn't listening for an answer, for she had decided long ago that there wasn't one. Finally she picked up the journal once again, turned the page and found that some more pages were missing.

"May 28, 1852. This is the first day that I have been able to bring myself to get out of bed and place my thoughts on paper."

"Oh no!" Rachel moaned, "what's happened? Not so soon!" Hurriedly she returned to the journal.

"Mama D'Evereau assures me that I must get up, that a week of lying in bed and crying will change nothing, and I know she is right. I have been down this road before. Perhaps writing my thoughts will help. I received word a week ago of the death of my dear Mama."

Rachel felt her shoulders tightening as anger engulfed her. It was anger for Marie, anger for herself, anger for all humanity. "Is this the famous love of God?" she demanded. But then she immediately felt ashamed of herself. "You're not supposed to say things like that!" she reprimanded herself. "You're not supposed to even think them!'' She tried to push the forbidden thoughts back down where she normally hid them, but they refused to go. ''But I do think them!'' she shouted at the dark attic again. ''Up here in the darkness, in the midst of the relics of my family—up here with the dead past that was full of suffering—can't I say it here? Can't we all just get together and demand, '*what . . . is . . . going . . . on?*' ''

Rachel jumped to her feet and began ''lecturing'' the trunks, boxes, and discarded furniture of the dark attic as if she were emphasizing a major point to one of her classes at the university. ''Life is a roller coaster ride, up and down, up and down. The great struggles up, the tremendous hopefulness that this time we will get it right and things will be good. Then comes the nauseating plummeting to the bottom into a quagmire of despair and worthlessness. And we feel worthless. We follow all the approved plans for a successful life, but we fail. And, of course, inevitably somebody's going to come along and reinforce our lousy opinions of ourselves by explaining to us that it was our fault somehow, that if we had only done this or not done that. So we believe them. Why? Because we are desperate for a formula for success, for a sense of worthiness, because *not* believing them means we have to stay in that swamp of failure, of worthlessness. We believe them and try to do it right one more time.'' She paused, just as she did when she taught, waiting for her students to absorb what she had said.

''Look at Marie's life already.'' She added the specific example she always used to reinforce her general point. ''She's only sixteen years old, yet in these three pages of her journal, it's all revealed. She's full of joy and hopefulness on her wedding day, even though she's obviously grieved over her father's death. And then, wham! She finds herself whizzing down the other side of that roller coaster, and she ends up flattened in bed. Joy and hopefulness, belief in the future—all shattered by loss, by death." Rachel halted and stared at the unresponsive, dark shapes of her "students" in the attic. She sighed as she acknowledged to herself that she was the only student present. She was teaching herself what she had been feeling for years, dark thoughts she had refused to acknowledge.

She sat down and turned back to the journal expecting to find her own anger mirrored in it. Squinting to read every word, she continued Marie's text.

"I confess that for this last week as I have cried and cried into my pillow I have been very angry with God. In my own thoughts I have shouted at Him, I have hated Him. And while I cannot say that all of those thoughts and feeling are past, I can say this much: I do take consolation in the news that Mama did not suffer at all. She was killed instantly when her carriage overturned on the way to Belle St. Marie. Mercifully, God spared Chyrisse, and by now Jacques is with her, caring for her, and will soon bring her here.

"Tears stream down my face as I think that Mama would have been here at Belle St. Marie this week, but I must gain control of myself. I must believe that God in His wisdom has done what is best. I cannot see it, but I must have faith. And now I must concentrate on caring for Chyrisse, my little sister."

"She is only sixteen," Rachel commented cynically to the attic, "she will learn soon enough that such consolations do not last." She turned back to the journal and once again found some pages missing. The next page was dated July 1st.

"The doctor has confirmed my suspicions. I am to have a child! Jacques' excitement is beyond description. When he returned from the fields at dusk, I asked him to stroll out onto the front lawn with me, and I told him my news. At first he simply stood and stared down at me. Then suddenly he swept me into his arms and began running back toward the house, yelling for the family. Papa and Mama D'Evereau raced onto the verandah in alarm as they saw him carrying me across the lawn, but when they saw the excitement in his face, they knew it could not be bad news. I'm sure Mama D'Evereau must have suspected all along since she knew the doctor had been to see me. One of the servants ran for Chyrisse. When she joined us, we both burst into tears. Neither of us could think of the joy of the baby. Instead we held each other and wept that Mama was not here to share in the news.

"The others stood around in quiet understanding. After we had exhausted our tears, Papa D'Evereau surrounded both of us with his arms and held us close and gently encouraged us to look to the future just a little, to recognize that life does go on, to remind ourselves that even though we had a right to our sorrow over our loss, we also had the blessing of expectation of new life to comfort us.

"I am so grateful to have my dear Chyrisse with me at this time, and I am so grateful to God for the support of all the D'Evereaus. But especially, of course, my wonderful Jacques. Constantly, but gently, he exhorts me to discipline myself to think of these blessings instead of my losses. I am so confused about life. Sometimes it seems so good, and sometimes it hurts so. I only hope I have enough discipline to—"

Rachel turned the page, but the remainder of that entry was lost. "Confused about life," she repeated the phrase. "Yes, that's well said. It *is* so confusing! You try to do the right thing, but—" She turned back to the journal rather than dwell on her own thoughts.

"January 1, 1853. It is New Year's Day. I am both glad and sad to see 1852 end. It was the year of my marriage, the year of the beginning of my child, and the end of

Mama's life here on earth. But I must look forward. The doctor says another month and my child will be in my arms. And just today, as a special New Year's present Jacques has promised me that the child will be named after either Papa or Mama. This is an especially loving gift he has given me because it is the tradition of his family that the first son of his family should be named for the child's grandfather.

"Thank God that Chyrisse is with me. We pray together twice a day. I feel sure that God will not desert me, and though I fear the pain and danger of childbirth, I am positive that my child and I shall come through safely."

Quickly Rachel grabbed the next crumbling page, eager to find out about the birth, hoping that the few pages she had would tell her how Marie had fared, dreading that they wouldn't.

"February 2, 1853. Chyrisse holds my journal as I write. My child is here, lying cradled in my left arm, a handsome boy. Jean-Paul DuBois D'Evereau is here! The doctor says he is perfect, and although I am very, very tired, he says that I am perfect too. Chyrisse and I are alone here with my son, for Papa and Mama D'Evereau and my beloved Jacques are at the church where a special mass of thanksgiving for my safe delivery is being said at this very moment. I know I should be thinking of the sacred words that are being spoken there, but I cannot think of anything but the delight I hold in my arm. He is enchanting! I think I shall just enjoy. Surely God understands new mothers and—"

The journal entry became unreadable; the ink had faded to match the paper. The next entry she could read was dated December 16, 1853. Eagerly Rachel read the legible parts. She found herself cheering for Marie, hoping that against the tremendous odds that Rachel knew she faced that Marie would make it.

"December 16, 1853. Jean-Paul thrives! And so does everyone around him. He has started walking a bit and gets into more mischief everyday. The house is full of laughter as everyone enjoys watching him discover his new world. We are all looking forward to Christmas so much! I can hardly believe the difference between Christmas this year and last year. Last year I was filled with apprehension about whether or not I would survive the birth of my first child. This year I simply look down into his angelic face and cannot keep from smiling. Neither can his father, nor his Aunt Chyrisse, nor his grandparents. They are all perfectly dreadful about spoiling him.

Chyrisse, Mama D'Evereau and I continue our daily prayers—"

The remainder of the page had crumbled away, so Rachel paused and considered aloud the words of this woman who lived so very long ago, who lived in this very house. "She sounds so buoyant, so jubilant, and indeed why not? Her life is full of happy surroundings and growth, but then she is well on her way up the ascending side of life's roller coaster. Inevitably she will reach the top and then? Will she keep saying prayers when the war comes? Will it do any good if she does?" Rachel wanted to believe that it would, that there was some way to make life work out well, and if it was prayers that were needed, Rachel wanted to say prayers. She wanted to know how to earn her happiness, how to earn the feeling that she was good. "But if bad things keep happening to me no matter what I do, than how can I ever feel good about myself?" Rachel anxiously asked the dark attic. "How can I even go on? How will Marie be able to go on? It's 1853. The war is only eight years off. That means that by the time she's twenty-five her world will be in chaos, and I suppose her beloved Jacques will be gone off to war. Will she be able to go on believing in anything then?" At that thought Rachel eagerly picked up the next fragment to see what would come next.

"April 2, 1855. She is the most beautiful being I have ever seen! I cannot believe the blessings that God bestows on me. To think that not only do I have Jean-Paul, but now I have a daughter too. And my wonderfully generous husband agrees that she is to be named for my dear Mama, Madelaine Marie. When I told Chyrisse, the tears sprang to our eyes, tears of joy as well as tears of grief that Mama was not here to see her namesake. Oh how she would have loved this little baby girl! How she would set about sewing and embroidering delicate little dresses. Oh, I must not think about it anymore! I cannot bring Mama back, but I feel I have a piece of her now, a new Madelaine in my life. God has placed her in my care, and I shall do my utmost to raise her to be the woman that my mother was, the most generous spirit I have ever known. She is the most beautiful being I have ever seen."

"Another baby!" Rachel smiled as she made the happy announcement to the attic. "And a girl this time. Think what it must have been like right here in one of the bedrooms of this house when the little girl was born." She picked up the next brittle page and groaned when she saw the date. "Oh! I wish so much of this wasn't missing!"

"January 1, 1857. It is very early in the morning of this first day of this new year 1857. I am awake much earlier than usual because not only is it New Year's Day, it is the wedding day of my beloved Chyrisse. I can hardly bear to think of letting her go; she's been here with me for five years. I don't know how we shall survive without her. And yet I know it is time. She is almost twenty, and she has been so fortunate to meet Louis. He is the first cousin of our nearest neighbors, so we know his background well. I only wish he were not taking her so far away; New

Orleans seems like the other end of the earth. I shall miss having her in the house, being able to see her constantly. Oh! I mustn't be selfish. She loves him so. Chyrisse will have a new life, a new life full of all the things a young girl dreams of. She will be Mrs. Louis Laballiere, and I shall have a new brother. And goodness! Who knows, in another year I could be an aunt!

"I must cease this musing, get myself dressed and see to it that every last detail is perfect for the wedding and the celebration that will follow. And then I must prepare myself to stand next to my sister as Jacques gives her away in marriage to Louis. Oh God, grant that she shall be happy and grant that she shall be safe! I must release her into your hands, Lord."

When Rachel turned to the next crumbling page and saw the shakiness of the handwriting, she knew instantly that something horrible had happened to Marie. "What on earth has happened?" she demanded as she struggled to read the handwriting. She bent over, peering urgently at the faded scribbling.

"December 17, 1857. I cannot let this day pass without recording in my journal the news I have received. I feel that a blow has been struck directly to my heart, and I cannot possibly survive. This whole year since Chyrisse married in January has been so full of hope, so full of happiness. To have her and her beloved Louis come north here to Belle St. Marie for so long this summer, to know then that she was expecting this child, to watch the contentment, the quiet, serene joy in her face as she waited and prepared for the coming baby, to sit on the verandah and sew and embroider with her for the baby. Oh I can't bear to remember! And now she's gone! Gone! And the baby too. When I saw the rider racing up the lane toward the house, I knew his news had to be dreadful. I hurried out to meet him just as Jacques rode in from the nearest field. The man threw himself to the ground and thrust the note into Jacques' hand. It had been hastily scribbled by Louis' father. 'Chyrisse has died in childbirth. The child did not survive. Louis is insane with grief. God help us all!' And then the poor man had signed it.

"I crumpled into the nearest chair on the verandah and shredded the piece of paper Jacques had handed me. I don't know what happened after that. I am told that I became hysterical, and the doctor was called. I only know it is dark now, and I see my faithful Nancy asleep over there in the corner, obviously directed to watch over me. And I have crept out of my bed, for I must not let this day pass totally without recording the passing of my sister. Dear God, there are not enough hours in the day for prayers for all my dead. I beg You to protect my little family here. I will do anything to keep them safe. Show me my sins, and I shall confess and do my penance thrice over. I cannot bear to lose any more."

Rachel stared at the last words of the sentence, "any more" where Marie, in her grief and exhaustion, had obviously just allowed her pen to fall over on the paper. There was a large stain of brown ink, a stain that suggested to Rachel's imagination the loss of at least some of Marie's lifeblood. How Rachel empathized with her! Wearily she picked up the next page, determined to read to the end.

"July 14, 1858. War, war, war! There is talk of war all around me, but I can do nothing but laugh, for here in my arms the most precious gift of all—life—lies once again. Another daughter! And so soon after the loss of my beloved Chyrisse. God is so good to me, so merciful. He has taken pity on my grief and brought me a new baby girl. She is to be named Chyrisse for my sister and Roseanne for Mama D'Evereau, but little Jean-Paul has already named her Rosy. Such a happy baby is little Rosy, just like my dear sister. So now our little family consists of three—

our delightful Jean-Paul, our beautiful Madelaine Marie, and now our little Rosy. May God protect them!"

"December 28, 1860. There has been nothing but talk of war for months, and now we have heard the news that South Carolina has seceded from the Union as of December 20th. Poor Jacques is in a state of great distress as he considers his options and obligations as a Southerner. He talks about the political problems constantly with everyone who visits the house, members of the family and with me. He is quite torn between his loyalties to the Union and his loyalties to Louisiana. He tosses throughout the night and sits up in the bed in the middle of the night to explain to me one more time that although he hates war, he is first and foremost a citizen of Louisiana. He says that for him the major issue is the issue of states' rights. If South Carolina chooses not to be a member of the Union, Jacques says it should be allowed to go. So I wait fearfully, as we all do, to discover whether or not Louisiana will make the same choice that South Carolina has made, for I know that should Louisiana join the Confederacy, that Jacques will go to fight for his state.

"I feel in my heart that the future is inevitable and obvious. There are so many around us who want a war. They are frustrated with years and years of tariffs; they want independence from the Union. I find it hard to believe that the state convention will have any choice other than secession. And so I know that we have just celebrated the last peaceful, normal Christmas for several years. Even though it was permeated with talk of war, at least we were able to pause on Christmas Day and have a mass for peace, to have a Christmas feast, to gather together friends and neighbors. At least we had that day of normalcy. And now we wait."

"February 10, 1861. Louisiana has seceded from the Union and joined the Confederate States. Jacques' mind is settled; he will go and fight for his native soil. I think that is exactly what he is fighting for—his plantation, his land, to go on living the life that he has chosen to live. I think that Jacques himself would gladly free the slaves or perhaps keep them and pay them if there were any way to do so. Papa D'Evereau does not agree with him, and I know there have been many heated discussions about the matter, but it really comes down to having no choice anyway. Jacques could never do what he would like; he could never free the slaves or pay them—not because of his father, but because of his neighbors. So he prepares for the possibility that he will have to go off to war to kill other white men so that he will be allowed to live his life the way he chooses, the way he has always lived it. As for us, he assures me that we are safe here, far from any conflict if war should come. I pray to God every hour, as I am sure women all over this country are doing, that we will be spared any kind of war. I beg Him to stop these political problems that I hardly understand, these things that threaten the lives of our men and perhaps even the lives of our children, these absurd events that are leading us so quickly into bloodshed, into horrors I cannot even imagine. God must intervene and bring a settlement. Surely there must be a way to settle these issues short of killing!

"April 17, 1861. Bad news travels fastest. It seems that we are at war with the Union. As I understand it, as the newspaper printed it, the first shots have been fired in the harbor of Charleston, South Carolina. The papers say that Confederate forces fired on a fort called Fort Sumter. I don't quite understand how all of this came about, and I am stunned at the effect it is having all around me. I feel our lives will never be the same. I have never even been to Charleston, South Carolina, much less seen this Fort Sumter, and yet now my husband moves with the fastest possible speed to prepare his provisions, and in a matter of days he will leave us. How is it that something that happened so far away, decisions that were made by people I never heard of—how can these things affect my life so horribly? Jacques keeps reassuring me that things will go on as normal here, but there can be no normal without Jacques. No normal whatsoever if I must worry about him continuously. Dear God! What path have these men taken us down? I know longer care whether I am behaving like a lady. I shall speak my mind. This war is insanity!

"April 22, 1861. I can hardly bear to write these words: Jacques left for the war this morning. He held me as long as possible, while I fought back oceans of tears. Then he kissed the children and his mother, and mounted his horse. Papa D'Evereau excitedly waited astride his own horse, waited to accompany Jacques to the edge of the plantation, to see his son off to what he considers the glorious war. He complains bitterly that he is too old to go and fight.

"I stood on the front verandah and watched them disappear into the morning mist while the children ran upstairs to the second-floor verandah to see their father for as long as possible. Mama D'Evereau and I said nothing while the men rode away and finally disappeared into the pines. Then we turned to each other, still silent, and embraced. What words could express our grief? I must be strong for the children. I must not let my fear show, and only my pillow can know of my tears.

"August 30, 1862. We have just returned from burying Papa D'Evereau. He did not die because of the war, not directly, but I think this hateful war hastened his death. He has worried far too much and worked far too hard in the last year and a half since Jacques has been gone. I have seen him turn into an old man. I thank God that he died so easily. Mama D'Evereau woke me up in the middle of the night crying for help. Papa D'Evereau was clutching his chest and struggling for breath. Mama D'Evereau kept begging for a doctor, but of course there are no more doctors in Lousiana now. They've all gone to the war too. It was just as well; there was little a doctor could have done. Papa D'Evereau had only a few moments. He gasped out his last words, telling his wife how he loved her, then he was gone.

"Now we have buried him, and I do not think that Mama D'Evereau can live without him. Papa D'Evereau was her life's blood, and since Jacques has been gone, she has been steadily declining. His few letters have been so long coming. She has been often depressed and sickly, and this latest blow will probably take her too. Dear God! What shall I do? I shall be alone here with my children.

"I shall try to get word to Jacques though I doubt that my letter can reach him. Papa D'Evereau is at peace now. Pray God we shall all be at peace soon. We have suffered enough!

"September 3, 1863. Will it never end? Will the killing never end? Will the dying never end? Every three or four days we go out to bury another. One of the old, one of the young, too young to go to war. And on the way to the gravesite we are met with the latest news of another man—another neighbor, another son, another father, another cousin, another brother—who has died far, far away. And we go and we put another pine coffin into the ground, but we don't bury the man we've heard of. We don't bury the dead soldier, for we cannot. His body has been dropped into clay faraway. Into the red clay of Georgia, into the clay of Virginia, not here. Oh, we bury, we bury, but we don't bury our men. They are buried by others, buried by strangers, buried in strange places, unmarked places, unmarked graves. We shall never know where. Those we bury die of age, but mostly of the fever. They die of malnutrition, but mostly of the fever. They die of fatigue and loss of heart, but mostly of the fever. Papa D'Evereau is gone. The servants are all dead or run away, all but old Isaac and Mathilde. I buried Mama D'Evereau this morning. That leaves only me and my children, and they are sick. And I have no word from Jacques for two years. What color is the clay that he is buried in? When I have buried my children, who will bury me?"

When Rachel had read the last word of the journal, she blew out the lantern. Only darkness seemed appropriate. "In these few pages the story of humanity is recorded," she whispered, "despite what theologians say." Rachel sat and grieved in the dark.

## FIFTEEN

"When I have buried my children, who will bury me?" That question and all that it summed up about Marie D'Evereau's life lingered in Rachel's mind. Dawn had come, and Lovey had found her in the attic and coaxed her down to the kitchen. However, in spite of Lovey's cheerful words and the warmth of the steaming grits and the crisp bacon she had pressed on Rachel, Rachel's thoughts about Marie's tragic life still encased her in anger and gloom.

After breakfast she carried the small chest out on the front verandah, where she placed it on a wicker coffee table in front of the wicker couch where she settled herself. She needed the right place to reconsider what she had read during the dawn hours and to determine what she thought about it. She wrapped her sweater around herself and stared out across the chest containing the words of Marie, through the huge white pillars, across the yard, and down the lane to the point where the woods closed the plantation off from the outside world. The air was cool and damp as it touched Rachel's cheeks, yet she felt scorched.

No doubt this was the spot, she thought, where Marie would have stood over and over and over again, looking down this lane hoping to see Jacques returning, hoping to see a neighbor coming to help, to comfort, to console, and eventually hoping to see *anyone* who could possibly help her save her children or perhaps bury them. A shudder ran down Rachel's spine as she asked herself, how many times during those short years that turned out to be eternities did Marie stand on this verandah and scan as far as her eyes could see, hoping against all odds, praying—no *begging* God to send help. And yet apparently help did not come from man or from God.

Rachel's mind was a chaos of conflicting thoughts, and warring emotions were the natural result. First, she had a sense of shame about herself. There was part of Rachel that wanted to turn herself over her own knees and give herself a good spanking. When she considered the hardships, the incredible sufferings of Marie—this Marie who had experienced such horrors before the age of thirty and had apparently buried her own children and died alone without ever knowing for sure whether her husband lived—when she considered Marie's sufferings, she was ashamed that her problems had brought her so low.

She was also angry, angry for Marie. From the fragments that she had read, she had come to know Marie as a loving person and a woman of great faith. It made Rachel furious that a good person should come to such a horrible end. Even as she felt the anger, her intellect reminded her of the naivete of such an attitude. Surely her own thirty-five years had taught her that the myth of the good being rewarded and the evil being punished was simply that—a myth. Nice for Sunday School lessons, but irrelevant in the world. And yet, she was intensely angry about Marie's fate. There were erupting geysers of contemptuous questions spewing in her mind. She wanted to demand of God, how can You call Yourself Love and yet treat such a good person so horribly? She wanted to demand of Marie, what good were all your prayers? Where was God when you needed Him? Don't you see that He rewarded your faith with His faithlessness?

The more the geysers erupted, the more she realized she was not simply angry for Marie; she was angry for herself. She really wanted to scream her questions at Grandmere and her youth's long line of Baptist Sunday School teachers and eleven years of schoolteacher nuns. The question she wanted to scream the most was "what good does it do to be good, to be faithful if God just lets you down in the end anyway?" She felt a compulsion to find the first faithful believer of any denomination and snatch that person close to her and demand, "How good do I have to be before I'm good enough for God? Just how much must I believe and do before He will take care of me?" But there was no one there to snatch up, and Rachel knew that even if she asked the questions, no one had answers to them. And no one had the answer to the question that haunted her most, had haunted her longest. If God doesn't value me enough to take care of me, how can I ever value myself?

Suddenly she thought of her Grandmere. She was the only person who could ever answer those questions for me, Rachel reflected, and she is gone before I'm angry enough to ask them. It always mystified me to see how Grandmere was able to accept whatever difficulties she had in life and yet she was able to assert insistently, constantly that God loved her, that she was separate from those difficulties that life brought her way. How *did* she do it? Why can't I?

I have always felt like a first grader, and there's a large poster on the wall. When one is good, one gets a gold star, and when one is bad, one gets a black star. When one finally gets enough gold stars, then one is labeled good, one feels good, one feels worthy. And when one finally achieves goodness, then things go well. That's how you know you made it. Things go well for you. That's how you know you're worth something. That's how you know God loves you.

"But how can that be right?" Rachel demanded aloud. "Marie obviously had plenty of gold stars and look what she had to endure! She was as good as you can be! If she wasn't good enough, what chance have I got? Oh, I can't figure it out!"

She jerked open the chest and grabbed another bundle—this time a large, blue-grey book. The faded ink on the front identified it as a ledger for Belle St. Marie. As she thumbed through the book, she found that it was a record of the accounts for the plantation, a record that began January 1, 1855. The book had endured quite a bit of abuse. There were torn pages, stains that clearly indicated water damage, and even the insects had feasted on it. "I wonder why this book is preserved here if it's simply an accounts book," she murmured.

Hastily she thumbed through the first pages; it was obvious that the plantation had prospered. There were accounts of good crops, many new slaves born, and various items purchased for the house and its inhabitants. It looked like nothing more than a book of figures; however, Rachel patiently turned the pages. The whole volume seemed to be intact; the binding had not broken. She continued following the dates, noting that beginning in 1861 the plantation began a severe decline. Suddenly in August, 1862 the record broke off. This, Rachel remembered, was the time of Papa D'Evereau's death.

When Rachel turned to the next page, she found a new handwriting, and the date was January 12, 1866. What followed was an inventory of the plantation after the war. Rachel held her breath, wondering if it could be Jacques' handwriting she read, until finally she reached the end of the pitiful inventory of what was left on the plantation and found a first person narrative.

"Two weeks ago I dragged my exhausted body back onto my own land after walking home from Virginia. The minute I knew I had touched my own soil I wanted to fall down on it and cry like a babe, but I was driven on by the mania that had pressed me every inch of my journey. I had to get to the house and find out if any of my family was left. I staggered through pine forests and across overgrown fields until I finally broke through the woods around the house and saw Belle St. Marie for the first time in five years. I stood and stared at it, the grandest house in the area, now totally dilapidated. But it was life I was looking for, a sign of any life. I reached down inside of myself for my last bit of hope and limped closer, believing any minute one of my family would surely appear. Then the wind caught the front door, and it banged open. It was then I knew they had been gone a long time; the door wasn't even latched, just blowing in the wind. When I reached the front verandah, I sat down on the top step and leaned against the pillar. I shivered, but not from the January cold. An icy fist had gripped my heart with the premonition that they had not merely taken refuge elsewhere.

"I wrapped my threadbare jacket around me and waited for strength to return. I planned to search the house as soon as I was able and then to make the journey I had been dreading for the last three years, the three years since I had last heard from Marie, the journey to the family cemetery to count the unfamilar graves.

"I must have dozed off and slept soundly, for when I regained consciousness, a servant was shaking me and calling me by name. It was old Isaac, one of the house slaves, and he was overjoyed to see me. I don't remember the details of the next few days. I know that his wife Mathilde was there ladling soup into my mouth, and I know I slept a great deal.

"When I finally awoke with my mind clear, I realized

that I was in a shack. Isaac came to my pallet and explained to me that they had fled the house when groups of raiders started coming through and stealing everything they could find and killing anyone in their way. Isaac and Mathilde had hidden in this shack in the woods.

"The first words out of my mouth were questions about my family. My words produced total silence in the cabin. When I demanded to know and started to rise from the pallet, Isaac knelt by me, gently pushed me back and said they were all dead.

"I didn't ask for details. What difference did it make? I just stared up at the ramshackle roof and hated God.

"In a few days Isaac helped me go down to the family cemetery and explained to me how they had died of the fever, how Marie was the last to go. When I looked down at those mounds that were all that was left of my parents, my wife, and my three children, I sank to the ground and wept. I am not ashamed to record it. I wept. Old Isaac waited by my side, and when my grief had quieted a bit, he talked about the last three months of Marie's life. He said she didn't suffer as much as I was thinking because she was touched in the head; he meant she was crazy. He said when the children started dying, Marie began to wander out into her garden in the middle of the night and plant rose cuttings she had made. He said that at first he would go after her, but then Mathilde told him to let her be. Somehow it must have helped her to plant those roses when everyone she loved was dying.

"I know he meant to comfort me, but I am haunted by the idea of my beloved wife wandering around in the dark planting rose bushes. My beautiful, serene Marie. Oh God! It is worse to me than anything I saw in the war! And there is nothing I can do. As far as I can tell from old Isaac's account, they died more than two years ago.

"So tonight I sit in what used to be our parlor with

only the fire in the fireplace for a light, and I record the end of my family, as best I know it, and what little is left of the plantation. I record this information in this ledger because it is the only paper I can find. I found it flung into a corner of the plantation office. Isaac provided the quill I use and Mathilde made the ink."

Rachel let the ledger drop into her lap. The handwriting was Jacques', of course, and although he had suffered this agony over a century ago, she wept for him. And she wondered if he found the strength to go on. That thought made her pick up the ledger once again, turn a few pages of figures, and through her own tear-filled eyes begin to read the next narrative she found.

"February 1, 1867. They've tried to take the plantation, but Marie has saved it! Even as I write these words here in the dark by the light of the fire, I can hardly believe what has happened. It is a miracle—no less than a miracle! But it is a miracle of Marie's doing, not God's. For the last year since I returned I have labored side by side with the few old men left here to put the plantation back into some kind of production. There was no hope of a crop, of course, for a long time, but we were able to keep ourselves fed and start clearing the fields again. I thought we had a good chance of succeeding until the tax collector showed up. It seems that the absurd excuse for a state legislature we now have, made up of freemen who can't even sign their own names and the looting Yankee trash who manipulate them, have passed new property taxes that are so high that all the plantations will have to be put on the auction block. And, of course, it will be the northern trash who made their fortunes off the war, who will have the money to buy them.

"The taxes that were levied against Belle St. Marie are beyond belief. Even in the good times before the war they would have been difficult to tolerate. Now with the economy devastated, they are impossible to pay. But, of course, that is the point. They have no plans to collect the taxes, only to steal the land.

"All I could think to do was to cut the timber and try to get it to the city where they are rebuilding, but I had only the old men to help me. It seemed impossible. Then Isaac spread the word that there would soon be Yankee owners at Belle St. Marie if I couldn't pay the taxes. Strong Negro men, ex-slaves who had refused my earlier requests to help me work the land until the plantation could afford to pay them, began to appear out of my woods. They had decided that they preferred me to a Yankee owner. *I* hadn't thrown them off my land when they refused to work but had no place to go. So we set about cutting timber and constructing the first barges to take down river. My hopes were high; I had a buyer for the timber, and the money from the first barges would barely be enough to pay the taxes. And just in time. It was a gamble, but my only hope.

"But in the middle of last night someone came and cut the logs loose, and I awoke to find my timber scattered from here to heaven knows where, wherever the river currents carried it. I thought I had lost all that my forefathers had built. Somehow I had not been strong enough. I had not been worthy of the trust they had placed in me. I had not even been worthy of the trust God had placed in me, for I had allowed my wife and children to die while I went on living.

"In a state of total despair, I went to the cemetery and sat by Marie's grave.

"As I sat there looking at the mounds of clay and the wooden crosses that were the only signs my wife and children had lived, I began to realize that soon I would not be allowed access to my own land, and these graves would be forgotten and lost. I had tended them the best I could, but I had not been able to buy a proper marker. Suddenly I jumped to my feet. There was one thing I could still do! I could not save my land, but I could mark my family's graves. I spent the whole day finding the right stone, moving it to their gravesite and chiseling their names on it. Marie, Jean-Paul, Madelaine, and Chyrisse. As the day passed, I relived those golden years of our marriage and the comings of our children. And I thought of their deaths, especially I thought of Marie suffering so as she watched the children dying. I wept every time I thought of her planting her rose cuttings in the middle of the night. She was such a strong woman; only unbearable grief could have made her so very confused. I could find no consolation anywhere.

"When dusk began to fall, I had finished my work, and I stood up to examine the monument I had made. It was a crude tribute indeed. Too crude for such a magnificent woman and our children, but it was the best I could do. I had no money, and I had used what little skill I have.

"I refused the supper Mathilde had prepared and sat on the east verandah looking at the remnants of Marie's rose garden.

"As the dusk began to turn to dark, it occurred to me to decorate the stone I had made with Marie's roses. Yes, I thought. She would like that. I wandered through the garden. Most of the larger bushes were dead from lack of care, but there were some younger ones coming along, and I judged they would probably bloom this spring for the first time. Also, they would have the best chance of surviving a transplant. I went for my spade, and by the time I had loosened the root ball of the first bush, the sky had darkened and I found I was working by the light of a full moon.

"I reached down into the soil to lift the plant onto a piece of burlap, and my hands struck something metal. I was amazed and even wondered if I had lost my mind. I paused in confusion, and then driven on by curiousity, I lifted the bush free of the surrounding soil. I stuck my hand back down into the dark hole and felt the metal again. Slowly I grasped whatever it was and lifted it into the moonlight. It was a small, plain metal box. I opened the lid, and there were Marie's jewels! Suddenly the whole truth overwhelmed me. I had dug up one of the bushes Marie had planted while the children were dying. Marie had not gone mad! She had only pretended insanity in order to escape suspicion while she buried her jewels.

"And what else? I gazed down the row of young rose bushes. She must have planted them all during those last months!

"I clutched the box to my chest and wept in awe. She had believed in the future, in the grace of God, even then! She had no reason to think I was alive, yet she did not know for certain I was dead either. Her children were still breathing, and so was she. She knew there was danger all around and probably more to come. Yet she had faith that God would save at least one of us, and she provided for our future. Her love—and her faith—had reached out from the grave and saved me.

"I tucked the box into my coat, wrapped the rosebush in the burlap and came in to eat my supper, as she would have wanted. If we were worth so much to her, if I was worth so much to her, how could I have ever thought of giving up?

"Tomorrow I shall plant the rosebush at her grave, and eventually I shall transplant more of them. I don't know how much or what is hidden under those remaining bushes, but it doesn't matter. Whatever is there is obviously safe.

"In time I shall redesign Marie's rose garden as a memorial to her, or so everyone will think. I can take my time.

For now, I have enough. I shall take the jewels to New Orleans tomorrow, sell some of them, and pay the taxes. Then I shall buy what we need to plant a crop this spring.

"No one but a D'Evereau will ever own Belle St. Marie! And that fact is the real tribute to Marie DuBois D'Evereau!"

"What a story!" Rachel blurted out. "I've heard a lot of fascinating tales of Southern women and their courage and cunning, but none more amazing than this!"

"What's that you say, Miz Rachel?" Lovey spoke from the doorway and startled Rachel.

"Oh Lovey, I was just reading part of this old account book, back after the Civil War. You wouldn't believe how close we came to losing this plantation and who saved it and how she did it!"

"I believes you's gonna catch cold if'n you don't come in this house, that's what I believes."

"Oh Lovey!" Rachel exclaimed, still too caught up in the story to think of anything else, "you've just got to hear this story!"

"Well, I believes I do. It sure brighten you up, but I ain't gonna hear no story till you comes in this house and gets yourself warm. I done put on the kettle for some tea."

"That's a bribe and you know it."

"I knows it always work, that's what I knows."

"I'm on my way," Rachel laughed as she rose and picked up the ledger and the chest, "but you've still got to hear this story."

"Miz Rachel, I gonna listen to any story that make you smile like that." Lovey turned and headed back toward the kitchen, and as Rachel followed, she was also struck by the change in her mood. There's something so triumphant about Marie, she mused. I don't really understand it, how I could think such a thing. I mean, she and her children are still dead, but—but—I don't know! Even so, she had something I wish I had. I don't know what it is, but I wish I had it.

She settled herself at Lovey's kitchen table. "It does feel good in here," she admitted. "It was colder outside than I thought."

"This tea gonna warm you up in a hurry, Honey," Lovey poured the steaming liquid into Rachel's cup, then poured her own and settled into a chair. "Now what on earth's this story you's so all fire worked up about?"

Rachel sipped her tea slowly and began telling Lovey everything she had read in Marie's journal as well as Jacques' occasional journal entries in the old ledger. As she unfolded the story of Marie's tragedy, Lovey occasionally shook her head up and down solemnly. Tears glazed her old eyes when she heard of Jacques' return and the certainty of Marie's death.

"That poor man," Lovey murmured, "that Miz Marie, she must've been a store of treasure."

"Just wait, Lovey, wait till you hear what she did," Rachel opened the old ledger, leaned forward eagerly and read Jacques' account of nearly losing the plantation until he found that Marie had planted her valuables beneath the roses.

"Lord a mercy!" Lovey exclaimed. "She wasn't crazy at all. She knowed all the time what she doing. Think of it! And with the fever already in the house."

"Lovey, she had—she had something special. I know she loved them all very much, but there was more to it. There had to be, otherwise she couldn't have withstood all those horrors and still—still. I just don't understand it!"

Lovey nodded knowingly.

"*You* know, don't you?" Rachel reached across the table and grabbed Lovey's old arm. "Tell me, Lovey! Tell me. I *need* to know!"

"She believe in herself, Miz Rachel. She know she worth something. She know she gonna triumph somehow someday."

"But how could she think that, Lovey? How on earth could she think that? Look at all she endured, not just at the last, but from the time she was fourteen. And in the end she must have known she would lose the children and die herself. That's the way the fever was."

"She still know what she worth, even when she dying she know."

"But how? How could she know when things kept going bad."

"Them bad things—even the worst—they couldn't touch her idea of herself. She know those bad things didn't have nothing to do with what she was. She was just fine, she was good, and she know it, no matter what."

Rachel relaxed into her chair and remained silent, wrestling to take in what Lovey had said. Finally she questioned in her most earnest voice, "How do you know? How do you know that, Lovey?"

"Cause I seen it before," Lovey's kind, dark eyes shone with an intense certainty that matched the tone of her voice. "Your Grandmere be that way too. Couldn't nothing make Miz Elinore stop believing that God loved her and she was fine."

Still mystified, Rachel hesitated, then gentled her voice and asked, "And what about you, Lovey?"

"I felt like dirt till your Grandmere pick me up out of the dirt and bring me here."

"And then?"

"Then I done what you's always done. If things was going good, I thought I was fine, but if somebody be ugly to me or something bad happen, I think I's no good all over again. I never could be like Miz Elinore. Time and again she tell me 'God didn't make any trash, Lovey. Just keep telling yourself that, whenever you feel worthless. Tell yourself and choose to believe it.' "

"And did you?"

"I sure did. I'd a jumped off a roof if Miz Elinore say to. Over and over when things got bad, I'd tell myself, 'God don't make no trash, Lovey. God don't make no trash.' "

"Did it help?"

"Sure did. Still does. It help a lot, but I never could be like Miz Elinore."

Rachel needed time to think about Lovey's evaluation of Marie and Grandmere, so she placed the chest in the parlor and busied herself with arrangements to repair the roof and plaster ceiling until late in the afternoon. By then the sun had burned off the fog and had been warming the west verandah for several hours, so Rachel took the ledger from the chest, carried it outside, sat down and began to thumb through it. After the story of the roses she found only page after page of accounting for the plantation. She studied the figures closely enough to see that Jacques was doing what he had said he would do; he was restoring Belle St. Marie, and the foundation for that restoration was Marie's faith.

As she turned the pages, she was acutely aware of the fact that each entry represented a piece of Jacques' life, perhaps a day, no more than a week, for Jacques kept very specific accounts. Rachel kept wondering what those days were like for him, how he had coped with his loss. From the information she had, she could only surmise that he had buried himself in his work. He made no more statements about his feelings. Finally she decided that personal loss was personal loss, and disappointment and anger and grief probably felt pretty much the same for everyone. And she remembered burying herself in her own work. She had no problem identifying with Jacques.

As the last rays of sunlight hit the porch, she ran across a narrative account again. It was New Year's Day 1876, about ten years after Jacques had returned to Belle St. Marie and learned of Marie's death. "I have asked Cecelia DuBois Benet to marry me, and she has agreed. I have known Cecelia since she was a child growing up on the next plantation. She is Marie's first cousin and was her best friend during the years that Marie and I lived here together at Belle St. Marie. Her husband and I marched off to war together, but he lived only long enough to fight heroically in the first major battle our regiment participated in. After his death Cecelia and her parents took up residence in their townhouse in New Orleans. There they stayed until 1871, at which time her father died. She and her mother brought him home to bury him, and they decided to stay.

"In the last five years since the death of her father, I have done what I could to help Cecelia and her mother put their plantation back into running order. Indeed, many of our old neighbors, or I should say the remnants of our old neighbors, for so many are dead, have managed to hold on to their land and return. At first, I helped Cecelia because she was my neighbor and my cousin by marriage, but as the years have passed, I have become more and more aware of the specialness of Cecelia, especially the gentleness of her nature. I have grown to love her. Perhaps it is because she is a perfect foil for my not-so-gentle nature. Perhaps it is simply that we have suffered through so much together and such similar things. Our love for each other has been slow in developing, but it is sure. I am forty-eight now, not a young man anymore with the great passions of youth pressing me. She is thirty-six, still very beautiful.

"I am grateful to have a second chance for love, especially the strong, steady love that, I think, youth cannot even understand. Cecelia says she is grateful to God. I am simply grateful. Somehow my stubbornness seems to have won me another chance. I love her dearly, and I have no doubt that Marie smiles down on us with her approval."

The ledger became a book of figures again, and Jacques' feelings were once again closed to Rachel, but she felt she did not need his own words to understand what he was thinking. Things are going well again for him, she thought, and he is just as confused about that as he is about the hideously long years of his suffering. Cecelia praises God for this good turning in their lives; he does not. He wonders what he has done to deserve it. Just as I would, just as I shall if things ever go well again.

Listlessly she turned the next pages of the ledger, once again finding only figures. Finally in the February 14, 1876 entry she found the simple statements. "I leave soon for the church where at noon I shall marry the second great love of my life. I feel alive again."

Rachel could not help smiling happily. She lay the ledger in her lap and stared out at the sunlight just beginning to wane. The sky showed great promise of the coming of a magnificent sunset, and for awhile she watched it forming. Then, certain it would be years before Jacques opened his heart again in this old ledger, she lifted it, and hurriedly thumbed through the next pages. She was no longer interested in the growth of the plantation; obviously Jacques had managed it well. She was hurrying through Jacques' accounts so quickly that she literally raced past the pages of a journal entry before she realized it. "Something important has happened!" she exclaimed aloud as she turned back to the beginning of the entry. "Otherwise he wouldn't be writing. It's been less than a year. I bet it's a baby! Cecelia was only 36 when they married."

She leaned eagerly over the ledger and read in the fading light. "I have a son, Justinien Alexandre—"

"My grandfather! Grandmere's Alex!" Rachel exclaimed.

"—and no wife."

"What? What? Oh dear God! No!"

"My gentle Cecelia lived only long enough to see her son baptized by the priest who had been called for her. She insisted he be baptized before she would take last rites. Then she held her son in one arm and me in the other. Her last words were breathed into my ear. 'Take care of our son, my dearest. I thank God that in His mercy He does not leave you alone.' Then she was gone.

"For weeks now I have hovered around her grave, but always I am drawn back to stare down at my infant son. I ride across my fields planning improvements to be made during the winter months, but always I am drawn back to stare down at this eight pounds of my flesh, this Justinien Alexandre, my son. I receive visitors, condolence calls from the neighbors, and pleas from the priest who begs me to return to mass, but when they are gone, I go upstairs and stare down at my son. I cannot sort it out. Where is God in all this? The violence of the war, the deaths of my loved ones, the destruction of my land, the rebuilding of my land, the wonderful promise that my marriage to Cecelia brought, her death, and now this son, this healthy, robust son. It all seems so random. Is there anyone in charge? Did I somehow bring this loss and destruction on myself or have I done something to earn this gift of a son? Is God insane, sadistic? Is this son simply another lure, another hope held in front of my face to keep me striving? For what? To give this boy all the material advantages with the hope that someday he will figure out what is going on in the world, that someday he will know what his father can't know?

"I don't have a single answer. All I know is that God refuses to let me die, that working hard keeps me sane, and that I am filled with unspeakable joy when I gaze down at my son. I know that if I were capable of reason anymore I should view the coming of a child into this confused, difficult world as a tragedy, but when my son clasps his tiny, perfect hand around my forefinger, I can hold no negative thought. I am filled with a completely unreasonable hope and a determination to work day and night for this eight-pound bundle, and if necessary, to stand between him and God Almighty Himself."

Rachel's heart was racing as she finished the entry. She was Jacques' descendant for certain and not just by blood. "Did I somehow bring this loss and destruction on myself or have I done something to earn this gift of a son?" He had done more than express her thoughts, he had described her perception of life. His question was the question that flamed through Rachel now as surely as the brilliant orange sunset was flaming across the sky. That was the question that had haunted her since Collins' death. "No, no!" she thought aloud. "Longer than that, much longer. Back to Justin's death. Back to Grandmere's death. Back, back, back into my childhood, into my relationship with Mother and Daddy. Back to every time I felt I failed or every time I felt I succeeded. It's just like Lovey said. I don't feel good about myself unless someone or something outside of me tells me I'm good. And if someone disapproves or things go bad, then I feel bad about myself. I'm just like my Great Grandfather Jacques; we both let external things tell us whether we are worthy. And they—those events, those people—never say we are good for long. And we don't have the ability to believe in ourselves without those props. Or we don't think we do. So most of the time we don't feel good about ourselves. But *why* don't we? How did we get caught in such a web?

How did Lovey get caught? And why didn't Marie? Why didn't Grandmere? I must know! I will know! Jacques had his son to return to, to stare down at, to work for. I have no child; I have only me, so I must be enough. I must be enough to motivate me to understand this and conquer it because I can't go on until I understand, until I gain control of my sense of my worth. I will understand!

## SIXTEEN

Rachel woke up the next morning with a case of emotional jetlag. She had been on a long journey of discovery about the human condition and had learned much, but she knew it was mostly an intellectual learning. It would take time for her to assimilate what she had learned into her daily patterns of thinking. *I feel like I've taken a forty-eight hour, round trip to India,* she thought, stopping only long enough to fill ten rolls of film with new images. *Now I need time to develop the film and pour over the photos until I understand what I've seen and can figure out what to do with it.*

She was throwing cold water on her face, trying to reduce her weariness, when she heard Lovey coming up the stairs. "I's got a hot pot of tea for you, Miz Rachel," Lovey called through the door.

"I'll be right there," Rachel called back as she dried her face and resolved once again to persuade Lovey to stop carrying heavy trays up the stairs.

Out on the upper verandah she found Lovey arranging the tray on a low table, and she was just about to give her a scolding, when Lovey looked up, and her face was covered with a jubilant smile.

"Guess who's coming," Lovey demanded, "that is, if you say it be all right with you."

"Who?"

"Aimee!" Lovey clapped her hands with delight as she pronounced the name of her granddaughter.

"Aimee? That's fantastic! That's the best news I've heard in years! When? When is she coming?"

"She call this morning and want to know if they can all come down for Thanksgiving."

"Of course they can! Now, Lovey—I really mean this— you must bring in Alice to help you."

"Now, Miz Rachel—"

"No arguments, Lovey. I've studied the account books, and we have plenty of money, and we're going to start fixing up the place and doing some living around here again."

"Now you's talking like a D'Evereau! I's gonna go get Alice right after breakfast. We's got to open up the parlor!"

Rachel sighed as she watched the old woman hurry off. "Well, if opening up the parlor is the only way to get Alice in here permanently, we'll open up the parlor." Then she hurriedly drank a cup of tea and went to dress.

When Rachel went into the kitchen, she found Lovey just turning two eggs in the skillet to lay along side of the ham she had already fried and put on Rachel's plate.

"Mercy, Lovey! I can't eat all that!"

"Yes, you can and you is," Lovey announced. "We's got to put a little more meat on you if you's gonna start entertaining." Then before Rachel could protest again, Lovey hurried over to the work table, exclaiming on the way, "Look what I found while you's dressing! It was in my memory book." She pushed an old photograph into Rachel's hands.

"It's Aimee and me! Look how little we are!"

"That be taken the first summer you was here. My! How you two tore round this old plantation. I never gonna forget it!"

"I was seven, and Aimee was six. What happy days those were!"

"They sure was. Now you take that picture into the dining room, and I'll bring your breakfast in."

"Oh, I'll just eat here, Lovey."

"No you won't! You's gonna eat in the dining room like a lady, like the owner of Belle St. Marie, like your Grandmere."

"I don't suppose there's any use in mentioning that times have changed?"

"No use in the world, Honey. They ain't changed here."

Rachel went into the dining room, sat down, and examined the picture. Looking back at a record of those days filled her with a nostalgic sadness, but her attention was soon diverted by Lovey's bustling in with her breakfast.

"Aimee she gonna be here in no time at all," Lovey smiled widely. "I be in the kitchen if you needs me."

After she left, Rachel ate her breakfast slowly as she stared down at the old, black-and-white photograph. The two girls were posed on the front verandah, both wearing pinafores. I don't remember this particular picture being taken, Rachel thought, but I vividly remember the first time I ever saw Aimee. Grandmere and I were having breakfast here in the dining room when Lovey came in.

❧❦

"She here, Miz Elinore, I told her to wait on the front verandah."

"We'll be right out, Lovey," Grandmere smiled mysteriously as she spoke. "Why don't you take that last sip of milk, Rachel, and we'll go out on the verandah and meet someone very special."

Rachel was buoyant and ready for anything her

Grandmere suggested, so she gulped down her milk and jumped down from her chair. Together they walked through the wide arch, into the center hall, and out the front door. Near the right side of the door Rachel saw a tiny girl. She was smaller than Rachel in stature, but her features were less delicate than Rachel's. She had warm brown skin and large black eyes, and someone had obviously dressed her very carefully. She wore a sparkling white pinafore with red rickrack. Her black hair was tied up in little knots all over her head and decorated with tiny, red yarn bows. The only thing missing that a white girl would have inevitably worn was a pair of carefully polished white pumps and white socks. Instead, this child stood before Rachel barefooted, her brown legs appearing out of the skirt of her white dress and ending in two tiny brown feet.

It was obvious that the child was nervous even though Grandmere smiled at her and spoke softly as she said, "Rachel, I would like to introduce Aimee to you. This is Lovey's granddaughter, and she is visiting Lovey for a while this summer." Rachel smiled at the little girl, who quickly jerked her head down and stared at the floor. Lovey stepped forward and put her hand on Aimee's shoulder to give her courage as Grandmere finished the introduction. "Aimee, this is Rachel, my granddaughter, and I hope that you two will have many happy hours playing together this summer." Aimee still could not bring her eyes up to look at anyone, so Grandmere continued, turning to Rachel, "I know that you'll make Aimee feel welcome, Rachel. Lovey and I will leave you girls alone and let you get acquainted." With that comment she turned toward the front door, and Lovey gave Aimee one last encouraging pat before she followed her mistress.

When Rachel was left alone with the little brown girl, the unusualness of the situation washed over her. She had never been allowed to play with a Negro child before, and suddenly her Grandmere was actually inviting her to play with this little girl. In silent amazement at this strange turn of events, she stood there staring at Aimee while the other girl continued to look at the floor. Suddenly Rachel saw a large tear fall from Aimee's bent head and splash onto her bare foot. That tear shocked Rachel into a sudden perception of the other child's pain. She rushed forward and exclaimed, "Don't cry! Why are you crying?"

Slowly a whisper answered her from the hidden face, "You don't got to play with me if you don't want to, Miz Rachel."

Once again Rachel's heart wrenched and she exclaimed, "But I do, Aimee, I do want to play with you! I like you!" Shuffling nervously from one foot to the other, she waited, but no answer came from the bent head, only more tears. Frantic with grief for the child, Rachel begged, "Please tell me why you're crying! I don't want you to cry!"

"I's scared!" the child finally blurted out, "I ain't never been in such a big place before." That was all she could manage to say, but it was enough for Rachel. She was needed.

"Don't you worry, Aimee, I'll take care of you!" Rachel announced boldly. "I'm not afraid of anything!"

Startled by Rachel's response, Aimee raised her head and stared. Slowly Aimee's lips turned upward. It was the beginning of a close friendship. The two girls were together all day long every day, and by the end of June Rachel had decided that she wanted to take Aimee home with her to live in Texas and to go to school with her. Grandmere, however, explained that Rachel's plan was impossible because Aimee was colored and was not allowed to go to a white school. Rachel was miserable until she remembered what she had learned in Sunday School— that God could do anything, and that He would answer prayers. She wasn't on very close terms with God, however. She had only asked Him for two things in her whole life, to make her mother well and to get rid of Mammy Cassie. So she decided that she had better "butter up" God before asking Him to make Aimee white.

She asked Grandmere how to make God happy, and she said He was happy with people if they helped the unfortunates around them. So Rachel decided she would spend the rest of the summer helping everybody and everything she could find to get in good with God. *Then* she would ask Him to make Aimee white.

To start off her campaign to please God, she was especially attentive at mass the next morning and smiled broadly at all the nuns. She made a quick survey of the people in the church, looking for unfortunates she could help, but everyone there seemed to be in pretty good condition. She wasn't the least bit discouraged, however, and after she had returned home and finished breakfast, she hurried out onto the front verandah to meet Aimee at their usual appointed time. As soon as Aimee appeared, Rachel grabbed her arm.

"I gotta talk to you fast!" Rachel whispered urgently. They both raced to the west verandah, to their secret hiding place and dove under a table that was draped to the floor.

"Aimee! Guess what? I'm gonna ask God—" suddenly Rachel dropped her voice to a conspiratorial whisper and looked suspiciously over her shoulder and then back at Aimee's eager face, "I'm gonna ask God to make you white!" Rachel sat back, beaming proudly at her friend.

"You is?" Understandably, Aimee was stunned by Rachel's words. "You's gonna ask God to make me white?" Rachel nodded eagerly. Aimee struggled for a long, silent moment to take in what Rachel had said. Finally in a tiny, hesitant voice she asked, "Is He gonna do it? Do you think He gonna make me white?"

"Of course He is!" Rachel retorted with total confidence.

"But why He gonna do that?" Aimee's eyes were full of the insecurity she was obviously feeling.

Rachel responded, "Oh Aimee, you just gotta be white 'cause if you're not, you'll be poor all your life, and they won't let you go to the white school, and we won't ever see each other again!"

Aimee's eyes turned mournful at that thought, and she whispered, "Never again?"

"Never again." Rachel's face settled into a pose of tragic despair for a long moment. But then she brightened and proclaimed confidently, "Don't you worry, Aimee. God's gonna do it—He's gonna make you white. I just know He is!"

"How you know that?" Aimee questioned with intense interest.

"Grandmere says God will answer our prayers if we work real hard to do our part to make God happy."

"How we gonna make God happy?" Aimee clearly thought it was impossible.

"Well, Grandmere says God is happy when we help 'unfortunates,' so that's what we got to do."

"What's 'unfortunates?'" Aimee pronounced the new word laboriously.

"The best I can figure from what Grandmere said is it's someone who is poorer than you," Rachel advised her in her wisest tone.

"I don't know no unfortunates," Aimee immediately insisted, "I's the poorest person I knows!"

"Yeah," Rachel agreed sympathetically, "it's gonna be tough for you. I got plenty of unfortunates 'cause I got you and all the other colored folks. But we gotta make

God happy so He'll make you white and you can come to live with me."

"I gotta find me an unfortunate fast!" Aimee concluded desperately.

Just as Aimee made her last pronouncement, one of the French doors opened, and Lovey appeared on the verandah and commented aloud to herself, "This sure is a beautiful day, just a beautiful day! Well sakes alive! Look at that poor, unfortunate dog comin' out of the woods."

Simultaneously both girls' hearts leapt with joy! Here was Aimee's chance! Here was a creature even poorer than she was. "I knew it!" Rachel shouted with joy, startling Lovey half to death as she raced out from under the table, dashed across the verandah, and down the steps toward the pathetic dog, with Aimee close at her heels.

"Don't you touch that dog," Lovey yelled after them, "it might be sick!" But it was too late, for both girls had reached the filthy, limping, starved dog and had thrown their arms around its neck as if it were their only hope for salvation. By the time Lovey got to them, they were cooing sweet endearments into the grateful dog's ears and were trying to decide whether it was a girl or a boy so they could name it. Lovey had no problem guessing the dog's gender. She took one look at the animal's protruding belly and informed the girls that in her judgment they'd best come up with six or seven names. Naturally squeals of joy greeted her announcement.

That starving dog and her puppies were the successful beginning of Rachel's campaign to make God happy—a campaign that she and Aimee continued throughout the month of July. Their imagination was unbounded as they searched the plantation looking for unfortunates to aid. At one time or another they gravely concluded that almost every person and animal on the plantation was an unfortunate, and they eagerly hatched a scheme to save him or her. Working diligently, the girls made a success of every one of their cases, turning every unfortunate into a fortunate. Every time they succeeded, they looked heavenward, and then glanced at each other and shook their heads in agreement. As Rachel put it, "He's up there, alright, and He saw it."

August was passing quickly, and every morning now Rachel and Aimee woke up happy but immediately experienced a kind of dread as they realized that another day had dawned that brought Rachel closer to leaving Belle St. Marie. Foremost on her mind was choosing the right time to make a formal petition to God to make Aimee white so she could take her home with her. She waited as long as she dared, adding more and more unfortunates to her list, making every possible effort to please God.

Finally she chose the Friday before her Daddy was to arrive. She didn't know much about formalizing this kind of situation, but she felt that God would be quite a bit more pleased if she and Aimee had some kind of service before they asked for a favor. All that week Rachel agonized over what should be included in the service. She was particularly concerned as to whether it should be like the Protestant or the Catholic services that she had attended. Finally she decided to take no chance on which kind God preferred, so she worked up a combination of the two.

On the appointed Friday Rachel and Aimee met in the stable after supper. All day they had organized and practiced the solemn ceremony that was now to take place. Then after supper they began their final campaign to please God. They ran upstairs to Rachel's room and dressed up in Rachel's best clothes. Rachel had carefully chosen a white dress for each of them from her own closet because she had noticed that white was always worn at solemn occasions in the church. The girls even made the supreme sacrifice of wearing shoes.

When they arrived in the stable, there was still plenty of light, but it was a soft light because of the time of day, a softness that Rachel considered appropriate for this solemn occasion. As she whispered to Aimee, "It's like the inside of the church—not too bright and kind of foggy looking." Aimee nodded her agreement.

Rachel had chosen to begin with a processional, so she and Aimee had arranged an orange crate "altar" in one end of the stable with a single pew in front of it. Rachel carefully covered Aimee's head with one of her Grandmere's lace handkerchiefs just as a Catholic would do, but she left her own head bare in case God was a Protestant. Then as Rachel walked solemnly down the "aisle," Aimee followed several paces behind, doing her best to imitate Rachel's demeanor. They both sang "Onward Christian Soldiers" at the top of their lungs, a song that seemed particularly Protestant to Rachel, who was trying desperately to create an ecumenical effect by balancing the Catholic processional with a Protestant hymn.

When they arrived at the "altar," Aimee genuflected slowly and dramatically in front of the crossless orange crate while Rachel stood rigidly tall, just in case God didn't like genuflecting. Then Aimee took her seat with the other members of the "congregation" while Rachel went and stood behind the orange crate and gave the "sermon," which consisted of explaining to the "congregation" that they were gathered there for a very solemn occasion.

"We are here to ask God to make Aimee white," Rachel explained very gravely, "but before we ask Him, we will have a special musical selection."

Aimee immediately jumped up and went over to the side where the "organ" was. Standing very straight and looking directly out into the "congregation," she sang

"Jesus Loves Me" at the top of her lungs. Rachel never blinked or moved during the entire selection, but when Aimee had finished and had taken her seat, Rachel suddenly stood and chanted in a voice designed to wake the dead, "In the name of the Father, the Son and the Holy Ghost," as she slowly made the sign of the cross as large as she possibly could in the air in front of her.

Now they were ready for the big moment. Rachel had decided on a baptismal pattern. She came around to the front of the altar, where Aimee joined her. With the deepest voice she could muster she loudly prayed, "Dear God, we are gathered here today to ask You to make Aimee white." She paused for a long moment because she knew it would be such a surprise to God to hear their request. It was, after all, the first time they had mentioned it to Him, for they had been scrupulously cautious to whisper when they discussed it between themselves. Then she added graciously, "God, we know You can do it, and we want You to." She paused another long moment before solemnly intoning once again, "In the name of the Father, the Son, and the Holy Ghost." Suddenly she picked up a Mason jar of water that was sitting on the "altar" and poured it over Aimee's head. When she began to pour, she closed her eyes as tightly as she could and so did Aimee because the way they had it planned, this was the moment when God was going to do it.

After Rachel had emptied the entire Mason jar on Aimee's head, she kept her eyes tightly closed for another full minute. She couldn't bear to look because she just couldn't stand it if Aimee wasn't white. Finally she heard Aimee's timid voice, "Do you think we can look now?"

"I don't know," Rachel answered, her eyelids still tightly squeezed together. "I don't know how long it takes."

"I don't mind waiting a little longer," Aimee announced patiently.

"Well, I do!" Rachel blurted out, "but I'll wait anyway." So they waited another minute until Rachel finally complained, "I can't stand it any longer. Let's look."

"Okay," Aimee's voice sounded very unsure, "but you look first."

Rachel's bright blue eyes flashed open! Then Aimee heard one angry word, "Rats!"

Aimee's brown eyes popped open, and she looked down at her brown hands. "He didn't do it, did He?"

"He sure didn't!" Rachel retorted, "there's not a single white spot on you!"

"Maybe it just take a little longer," Aimee suggested hopefully.

"No!" Rachel flung herself despondently on the "altar." "He's not gonna do it. He just didn't go for it." Aimee joined her on the "altar," and the two girls sat in silent frustration until Rachel added gloomily, "Now you can't even go to school with me."

In time they moved their depression to the front steps of the huge old house. There they sat silently as the dark consumed the landscape. Even Lovey's offer of cookies and milk didn't tempt them from their posts. Finally Aimee speculated aloud, "Maybe God didn't like the Protestant part."

"Maybe He didn't like the Catholic part," Rachel suggested.

Another long pause occurred before Aimee added thoughtfully, "Maybe God ain't a Protestant or a Catholic. Maybe He ain't anything."

The two girls stared at each other in the growing darkness as this profound discovery sank in. Finally it was Aimee who added, "We ain't ever gonna figure *Him* out."

❧

I'm *still* trying to figure Him out, Rachel reflected as she snapped her attention back to the present. And still getting absolutely nowhere. Aimee, on the other hand, had better sense that I did. She put her mind on things she could figure out. Valedictorian of her high school class and straight through two degrees in math. And I barely made it through college algebra. Then she met her wonderful Joseph. How many high school kids the two of them must have influenced all these years! Oh, I can't wait to see her.

## SEVENTEEN

Grateful for her happy memories about Aimee, Rachel settled on the front verandah to await the workmen who were coming to repair the leaky roof and rain-soaked ceiling. Inevitably her thoughts returned to the journals of Marie and Jacques. Those journal entries have shown me something about the human condition that I never knew existed. There is an enormous schism in the human race. I know I'm generalizing and it's not this simple, but it seems to me that there are two types of people—those who feel good about themselves most of the time regardless of external circumstances and those who don't. I know I am a member of the second group. I am like Jacques. I also know that being that way has made me a very driven, very unhappy person.

I don't know how I got this way or what I can do about it, but when I consider the difference between Marie and Jacques or between Grandmere and me—well, I know I'm on to something. I'm on to something, and I *must* keep going! Even though I don't know exactly what direction to take.

By 11:00 everything was going smoothly on the house repairs, and Rachel decided she could afford to leave and take a quiet walk in the woods. Eager to get away from the noise of the repair work, she strolled deeper into the pine forest surrounding the lawn. It was a fine, autumn day with a bright sun filtering down through the pines. She stayed on an old path that she and her summer playmates had run up and down many a time in her childhood. Today she was alone with only the birds and the squirrels, who were busily harvesting the nuts and acorns. For the most part they ignored her and went about their business, but finally she invaded the territory of a cantankerous squirrel, and he paused to swish his tail wildly and give her a tongue lashing. He must be having a bad day, she surmised, as she stopped at a bend in the path to smile up at him.

Almost immediately she heard the voices of two girls, although the brush hid them for another minute.

"I ain't *never* going back to that school!"

"I ain't never going to *any* school again. I'm through with that stuff! Ain't gonna do me no good anyhow!"

Suddenly they stopped short as they nearly collided with Rachel.

"Good morning, girls," Rachel greeted them solemnly as she squashed the smile that had broken out on her face when she heard the two truants talking. "Are you playing hooky? No, no, I'm sure you wouldn't be doing that. Let's see. It's Friday. I bet the school is having a teachers' workshop day. That must be it. They canceled school. Right?"

"No Mam," they answered in unison as they ducked their heads and stared at their bare feet.

"Oh? School is not canceled? But you're not playing hooky. Well, well. You certainly look like truants to me."

"We ain't tru-u-u—"

"—ants," Rachel finished the word for the bigger girl who had bobbed up her head for just a second to defend herself and her friend. "The word is 'truant.'"

"Do they put tru-u-ants in jail?" the smaller girl whispered urgently to her bolder friend.

"No, they don't," Rachel answered her. "They just send them back to school where they can learn the meaning of the word 'truant' and know that it means playing hooky."

"I ain't going back to school!" the bigger girl snapped her head up just long enough to make her declaration.

"Sh-h-h-h!" her friend shushed her, then whispered, "You're gonna get us in trouble. That's Rachel D'Evereau. She owns this place."

"That's right," Rachel responded casually, "I am Rachel D'Evereau, but I don't want to get you in trouble."

The bigger girl sneaked a sideways glance at her to see if she was to be trusted.

"Besides," Rachel continued, "You are already in trouble if you skipped school. Now, let's start all over and do things differently. First of all, raise those heads of yours and look me in the face while I'm talking to you."

Neither girl spoke, but they raised their heads and looked at Rachel. "Now, that's better," Rachel approved. "Come on over here," she moved off the path toward a rock, and they reluctantly followed her, "I want to talk to you." She seated herself on the rock and invited them to join her, but they squatted on the ground instead and ducked their heads again.

"Now, what are your names?"

Silence.

"I won't have any trouble finding out, you know."

Silence.

"I'll just go up to the school—"

"Sassy!" the older girl called out, "my name is Sassy."

"I think your mama may have named you just right, Sassy," Rachel chuckled. "Now look at me and tell me why you left school. You sounded pretty fed up back there on the path, so I figure something bad must have happened."

"It sure did!" Sassy glared straight into her eyes as the suppressed volcano in her erupted. "That teacher told us we're stupid! Stupid! We're too dumb to learn anything, she said. We ain't gonna learn nothing, she said cause we're so stupid!"

"You don't sound stupid to me, Sassy," Rachel observed quietly, "I'm a teacher too, and I don't think you sound stupid at all."

"Well you ain't *my* teacher, and she said I'm stupid and gotta just sit still and don't bother anybody so I ain't going back there."

"I see, and what do you think your parents will say when they find out you ran away from school?"

"My momma don't care! She says I ain't gonna mount to anything anyhow. That's what she says. She says 'You ain't gonna mount to anything, Sassy.' She says it over and over. That's all I hear, all my life, 'you ain't gonna mount to anything'!"

"And your father?"

"I ain't got a father. Least ways, I ain't got one I know about."

Rachel silently considered what the girl had said.

"See," Sassy summed up, "there ain't anybody cares whether I go to school or not, and that teacher don't want me round, so what's the use of going?"

Again Rachel was silent for a minute because she knew she had no grounds for denying the truth of what the girl said. Finally she addressed the smaller girl, "Is it the same way for you too?"

"Yes'm," the girl sighed tiredly without raising her head.

"And what's your name?"

"Chelsy, Mam."

Rachel turned her attention back to the bolder Sassy. "Well, Sassy, what are you going to do with your life?

You're about thirteen, I'd say. What are you going to do from now on?"

"You mean you ain't gonna send us back?" the shyer Chelsy raised her head and stared in wonder at Rachel.

"I can't see any use in that," Rachel replied matter of factly, "you would just run away again. So what *are* you two going to do with the rest of your lives?"

"I'm gonna find me a man and get married!" Sassy announced.

"What man's gonna marry you?" Chelsy forgot Rachel and turned on Sassy. "Look at you! You ain't pretty, and you don't have any clothes or money. Who's gonna marry you?"

"Well, you ain't pretty either!" Sassy retorted. "Who's gonna marry you?"

Chelsy fell silent before gloomily responding, "Ain't any man gonna marry either one of us."

"I can get any man's notice I want to!" Sassy insisted. "They're only after one thing anyhow, and I got plenty of that!"

"Yeh! Then he'll run off and leave you with his baby! Then what are you gonna do? You'll be just right where you are now, only you gonna have a baby screaming all the time."

"I'll just get me another man!"

"And another baby. And before long you're gonna have screaming kids all over the place and no man's gonna stay round cause you're fat and old. And then you gonna die and go to hell just like Brother Ezra says!"

"What else are we gonna do?" Sassy demanded, and Chelsy fell silent. They both sat there engulfed in the gloom of their situation, having apparently long ago forgotten to worry about Rachel.

Rachel was silent too, but she was thinking intently. What else *are* they going to do? Their whole world is a mirror, and it's reflecting back to them a negative image of themselves. Apparently their teacher denounced them because they're ignorant. They're ignorant because no one has been able to teach them—for whatever reason. And their mothers don't care, most likely because they took the route Sassy suggested and started a chain of babies so long that they're just too worn out to be anything but abusive to these girls. What *are* they going to do?

Finally Sassy broke the silence. "Miz Rachel, if you ain't gonna take us back to school, can we go on now?"

"Yes, but you have to promise me something."

"What?" Sassy demanded, her voice filled with sudden, intense suspicion.

"That if you don't go to school Monday, you'll meet me here at ten o'clock."

They stared at her suspiciously and looked at each other. "What for?" Sassy demanded.

"Because I'm going to try to figure out a way to help you. I can't make any promises, but I'm going to try."

"Why?" Sassy's suspicion increased.

"Yeh, why?" Chelsy chimed in.

It was all too involved to explain, so Rachel simply responded, "Because I want to."

They looked at each other, their faces full of question, and then rose from the dirt, muttered "okay," and turned to leave. When they were far enough away that they thought Rachel couldn't hear them, she heard Sassy say, "She's weird."

And Chelsy responded, "Yeh, I heard she's been kinda crazy since her husband died, but I guess we're gonna *have* to come back."

For the remainder of the day Rachel pondered the plight of Sassy and Chelsy. She was haunted by the idea of their world being a mirror that reflected to them only a negative view of themselves.

After supper she built a fire in the fireplace of the music room and settled into a comfortable chair in front of it. It was her intention to stay there until she had figured out a way to change a little bit of that negative mirror in the girls' lives. However, the more she thought about the problem, the more she began to think about her own life and the lives of others she had known, and the more she thought, the more she recognized the truth of that basic concept of the mirror.

We are born with no view of ourselves at all, she reasoned, and slowly other people—parents, teachers, preachers, even other children—all the people we come into contact with create a mirror we see ourselves in. Each person reacts to us and that reaction, good or bad, becomes a piece of that mirror we see ourselves in. And events too, what happens to us—those things fill in the mirror and give us a piece of our view of ourselves. So, if we are treated kindly, if we are valued, we value ourselves. If good things happen to us, we think we are good because the adults in our world tell us that good is rewarded and bad is punished. If we find we are rewarded with good things, then we reason we must be good. But the reverse is true also; if bad things happen to us, we conclude *we* are bad. And the reverse produces girls like Sassy and Chelsy.

But for most people, I guess it's a mixture—some bad, some good—and we don't feel totally worthless, but we can't feel good about ourselves either. And if we can't feel good about ourselves, we're crippled. And if we're crippled, we can't help but cripple others. And so the madness goes on. Being crippled and crippling others. Seeing ourselves in the mirror others create and being a part of creating mirrors for countless others. How hopeless it seems!

She leaned back and tried to clear her mind of the despair she felt by listening to the crackling wood and concentrating on the soothing warmth of the fire. In time she relaxed so much she fell asleep and dreamed.

She dreamed of a long night of waiting up for Collins, a night she thought he was dead, a night she wished he were out of her life. She writhed in the chair, her face damp with perspiration. Then, Collins was there, but they were all standing around lowering something into the ground. They were all there—Collins and his mother and Jean and Shawna. She couldn't understand why they were burying something in the front yard, so she stepped forward to look into the hole. There she saw an open coffin, and Collins was lying in it. But no! That doesn't make sense, she thought as she recoiled from the hole. Collins is here at my side. But she turned, and Collins had become her father. Her father was there. He was holding her up, and suddenly Mammy Cassie walked through the crowd, pushing aside everyone, and she pointed her finger at Rachel and yelled, "Devil child! You's nothing but a devil child. You ain't never gonna be no good. You can't behave no matter how hard you tries. Now you's gone and made your mother sick again. Someday you's gonna kill her!" Mammy Cassie had her by the shoulders now, and Rachel had become a small child staring up at the huge woman who shook her. "Your mother ain't been happy since the day she knowed you was coming. Devil child! Devil child!"

"No! no!" Rachel screamed back at Mammy Cassie as she wrenched away from her, "you're a liar! No! I'm good! I'm good!"

"Miz Rachel! Miz Rachel! Wake up!" Rachel heard another voice as she ascended into consciousness again, and when she opened her eyes, there was sweet Lovey leaning over her trying to shake her awake.

"Lovey!" she gasped in surprise, "Oh Lovey! It's you! Thank God."

"You was having an awful dream, Honey," Lovey smoothed Rachel's hair as Rachel straightened herself up. "You want me to sit here with you a spell?"

"Yes, please," Rachel agreed gratefully. "Please stay a minute. I was dreaming about—about so many bad things, but at the last I was dreaming I was a little girl, and Mammy Cassie kept calling me a devil child. She used to do that all the time."

"That Mammy Cassie, she just plain mean!" Lovey replied angrily as she settled on the edge of another chair.

"Did you ever know her, Lovey?"

"No mam, and I's glad I didn't! I knows she be mean cause Miz Elinore say that Mammy Cassie is the onliest person in the world she ever want to kill, and Miz Elinore wouldn't kill a fly. So that Cassie gotta be something else!"

"Yes, yes she was. And still is! She was giving me the very devil after Collins died, before I came here."

"You don't say! She on you *then?*" Lovey clucked her tongue in irate disapproval. "Don't seem like *nobody* could be mean to a grieving wife that lost her husband. But then as I recollect you never come here once when you's growing up that you wasn't crying mad cause she done treated you bad before you left home."

"That's true," Rachel sighed tiredly, "but why, Lovey? That's what I want to know. I don't think I was any worse behaved than any other child."

"You was a perfect angel! You wasn't never bad! And neither was Mr. Justin."

"Then why would she treat me that way?"

"I don't know, Miz Rachel, but one thing I knows from my own experience is that they's always a reason.

They's always reasons why people does things, the good things and the bad things. They's always reasons why they does those things. Sometimes them reasons is real easy to see cause they's in the here and now and sometimes they's buried so deep in the past, for generations and generations, and it be real hard to see what them reasons is. But they's always reasons why people does what they does."

"You seem very sure about that, Lovey."

"I is sure. I's over seventy years old, and I's seen it over and over. I's seen the good reasons that make people do good things, and I's seen the bad things that causes people to turn ugly, to hate themselves. And once they hates themselves, they gonna have to bring everybody around them down, way down, way down to where they thinks they is, and so they gonna do something they don't even want to do maybe."

Rachel nodded before speaking slowly, cautiously, "Lovey, you told me you felt like dirt when you came here, that you felt like dirt cause you were living in dirt. I don't want to pry, maybe you don't want to talk about it, maybe you would just as soon forget, but is that—if you don't mind talking about it—is that how you know?"

"When I come here, I was about ten years old. Course I never did know exactly how old I was, don't know how old I am now cause nobody ever wrote it down when I's born. Miz Elinore, she just come to Belle St. Marie as a bride, just a shining, beautiful bride. I seen her come up the drive. I was in the woods special, waiting to see her. Everybody knew she was coming that day, that Mr. Alex was bringing her home. I heard she's beautiful, so I hid in some bushes cause I wanted to see something beautiful. There weren't nothing beautiful in my life, not in the people. But I knew there had to be something better, there had to be beauty in people cause there was beauty in the sky and in the trees just like there was storms in the sky and there was dead trees. I figured I'd seen all the mean, ugly people, and I wanted to see something beautiful, kinda like something to hold on to.

"I hid me in the bushes, and I waited for Miz Elinore to come, and she came, and she was shining like an angel, and I could hear her voice. It was like a little, gentle bell blowing in the breeze. She laughed real light like.

"Mr. Alex he picked her up and carried her into the house, and she's gone. From then on I watch Miz Elinore from the bushes everyday. I needed to see her. Then one day I got so brave I came and hid under them stairs out off the front verandah cause I knowed Miz Elinore, she always go for a walk in the woods before she go to morning mass. I hid under them stairs, then when she gone into the woods I followed her. I kept my distance, but I was as close to her as I could get, I figured. It was like being close to the sun. I just couldn't help but feel good. I just had to feel good when I's close to her.

"And Miz Elinore, she like you Miz Rachel, she talk to the birds and the squirrels. Why she even talk to the trees! How I loved to hear that voice. And she looked just like an angel with this special light coming out of her eyes."

"Oh yes, Lovey!" Rachel suddenly broke in. "I remember that light! And I can remember a lot of times when that light made me feel good. I know just what you mean. But how did you actually meet her?"

"Well, Miz Elinore, she wasn't no fool. Looking back I figure she knowed I was following her for a long time before she ever stopped and called me out of them bushes. Finally one day—it was a real, real bad day for me. It was early in the morning, and I'd been hiding in the woods all night."

"Hiding in the woods all night? Why?"

Lovey stared down at her lap for a long time and said nothing.

"Lovey, you don't have to talk about it. It's none of my business."

"No, I talk about anything that help you, Miz Rachel. And I think you needs to know. I's hiding in them woods cause my pappy he done fool around with me."

"Fooled around with you? Are you saying what I think you're saying, Lovey?"

"He fool around with me the way a pappy ain't supposed to fool around with his little girl."

"Oh. Oh, no!"

"Well I run off. It wasn't the first time it happened. I just couldn't take it no more, and I run off and hid in the woods. And I hid close to the path Miz Elinore liked, hoping she'd bring that light with her that she always brought. And she did. And I stayed closer to her on that walk that morning cause I needed that light more than usual. And it wasn't no time at all before she sat down under a big, old tree, and she was talking to a redbird and just in the middle of her talking to that bird, she just said real soft like 'Honey, why don't you come out of those bushes? Come on over here and sit with me.'

"I couldn't move any more than a rock could. I wanted to go, but I was so scared, I just couldn't even move. But Miz Elinore, with all that love and light in her, she just draw people to her. She just kept saying that, she kept saying, 'Honey, come on over here, come on over here and sit next to me. It's all right. Don't be afraid.' She never moved from under that tree, she never even looked in my direction. She just kept calling me, and there weren't no way I could stay away from her. So I edged me out of them bushes, and I crept up close to her. Finally she reached out and patted the ground next to her and said, 'Now, everything's okay. You sit right here, and let's talk. I want to know all about you because I think you and I are going to be special friends.'

"I couldn't help myself. I was as dirty as dirt could be, all tattered, almost didn't have no clothes on at all, but I sat myself down where she patted that ground. And she took my dirty hand in her clean one, and it wasn't no time at all before she had me telling her who I was and what had happened to me. I remember I had my head bent real low when I told her that part. I was looking down at the pine needles between my legs, and suddenly I felt an arm go around my back. I was too scared to look up, but then something was pulling me toward her. I looked up in surprise and saw her beautiful face up close, and there were tears running down that face, and she was pulling me over on her shoulder. She held me there, and I cried and cried. It was the first time I was able to cry about it. And she said over and over again, 'that will never happen to you again. I promise you. That will never happen to you again.'

"She brought me back to the big house. I was so filthy I's ashamed to tell you, Miz Rachel. There's even blood on me, but Miz Elinore, she didn't care. She took my hand and she put her other hand around my shoulder and she walked me right up them front steps and all the servants just stopped what they's doing and just stood and stared.

"When we got inside the main hall, Mr. Alex come walking out of the parlor and stopped short. He said, 'Elinore, what in the world?' But she stopped him short; she said, 'I will explain later, Darling.' She spoke in a sweet voice just like she always did, but there was something special about the way she said it, something that said she was not going to be stopped. He didn't argue with her; he just went on back into the parlor. Then Miz Elinore told the maid to fill a washtub with warm, soapy water, and before I knowed what was happening Miz Elinore was giving me a bath in the wash house. When I was clean from head to toe, she wrapped me in a towel and took me in and sat me down at the kitchen table. She said to the cook, 'This is Lovey. She will be staying here now. Give her a good breakfast and let her stay here with you. After mass, I'll go to town to buy her some clothes.' Then she did a real strange thing I didn't understand then. She raised her voice real loud and said, 'Anybody who mistreats Lovey mistreats the Lord.'

"She patted me on the head and started to leave, but I remembered my pappy and called out, 'But my pappy, he won't let me—'

"Do you want to stay here, Lovey?" she asked, and I burst out, "Oh yes, Miz Elinore!" Then she said, "I'll take care of your father, you leave him to me."

And she did just that. The servants told me she went into the parlor and told Mr. Alex that she wanted my pappy off this property before nightfall, that she would not tolerate children being abused. Mr. Alex, he tried to argue with her about how my pappy was a good worker and how he didn't want to mess into things, how he wanted to let the coloreds take care of their own business. She didn't argue a bit. She just said, 'Either he goes or I go. I will not stay here while children are abused.'"

"What happened to your father, Lovey?"

"I don't know. I never saw him again, and I was glad of it. Miz Elinore she had her way. Mr. Alex threw him off Belle St. Marie, and I stayed here with the house servants."

"That sounds like Grandmere, that sounds just like her! She would do that."

"She done it!" Lovey exclaimed. "She changed my life. She said flat out, 'Honey, you are good because you are God's beloved child, and nothing, *nothing* can change that fact. Now we just have to help you *know* that fact, help you feel it.' Then she started telling me good things about myself. Those bad things I heard those first ten years and the way my pappy treated me never went away totally, Miz Rachel, but Miz Elinore she kept telling me good things. And she told me to try to think on them. And that's what I did. I started thinking on the good things, the good things she told me about myself. I believed those."

"Why did your father act that way? Why do you think he did that to you?"

"I don't know for sure. As I got older, the other Negroes told me about what he was like as a boy, how mean his pappy was, always beating him. How his mama wouldn't even let him in the house. They told me how he started drinking real heavy after he married my mama, how he beat her. When I was good and grown, I began to see that he just done what was done to him. I come to see that most everybody is shaped by those things that happen to you when you's little. Miz Elinore help me see that, and it make it hurt less."

"But you had to choose to remember the good things," Rachel repeated what Lovey had said. "As much as you could, you chose to remember what Grandmere said. Not what your father did or said."

"Yes, Miz Rachel. That's the most important part. The most important part. We all does what we does cause of what been done to us, but most of us have had bad things and good things, and we gets to choose what we thinks on. We don't get no choice about whether bad things gonna happen to us sometimes, but good things they happen too. And we get to choose which one we gonna look at. Miz Elinore help me look at the good and she give me some good to look at and she see so much good in me, why I couldn't help but see it myself."

Rachel nodded thoughtfully. "Yes, yes, I remember her saying those things to me. Like you said before, every time I got here I seemed to be a bundle of broken pieces because of things that had happened in Texas, and as the summer progressed, Grandmere seemed to be able to make a whole person out of those pieces, a person who felt good about herself."

"Couldn't nobody help but think good of themselves around Miz Elinore cause she thought so good of them."

"I wish I'd grown up here, instead of in the clutches of Mammy Cassie," Rachel sighed.

"You was here a while with your Grandmere. Remember that too. And all that bad that's happened to you, you just got to let it lie. Just let it lie. They's reasons why that Mammy Cassie be the way she is. They's always reasons, Miz Rachel. We's just gonna have to leave that Mammy Cassie to the Lord. *He* know just what to do with her!"

Lovey sat silently a few minutes and stared into the fire. Rachel watched her worn face, watched as she settled into a peace Rachel did not understand. Lovey can leave Mammy Cassie to the Lord, Rachel thought. I suppose that's the privilege, the peace of age. As for me, I think I better figure out a way to deal with the impact Mammy Cassie's behavior has had on me. That's the burden of middle-age I suppose, trying to figure it out, trying to put it away for good.

"I guess I'll be going, Honey, if you's all right," Lovey roused herself from the chair.

"I'm fine, Lovey, I'm fine now. Thank you for staying with me a while. It was just like old times when you used to sit next to my bed while I fell asleep."

"And Miz Elinore be playing that piano," Lovey looked lovingly over at the baby grand in the shadows.

"Yes, those were good days."

"They's lots of good days ahead, Honey. Things is always changing, but that don't mean they's changing for the worse."

"No, not for the worse, not necessarily. Thank you, Lovey. What would I do without you?"

"You gonna do just fine no matter what cause you *is* fine," Lovey started to leave, but turned back and added, "No more of that thinking about Mammy Cassie."

"Yes mam!" Rachel watched her disappear into the shadows.

# EIGHTEEN

Once Lovey had gone to bed, Rachel turned back to the fire determined to take control of her thoughts and steer them into a positive path. "I'll think about those two girls. I'll think about Sassy and Chelsy and that negative mirror of theirs and what I can do—" Rachel's mind seemed to take an enormous leap as the idea of the negative mirror of the two girls collided with her memories of Mammy Cassie's meanness, and she suddenly realized that Mammy Cassie was a human being and had a mirror of her own, undoubtedly a negative one.

"A very negative one," Rachel announced emphatically, "only someone who felt terrible about herself could act the way that woman acts, especially to a child. Why would she feel so bad about herself? There must have been something that made Mammy Cassie so mean. Lovey says there are always reasons, things from the past. Now what do I know about Mammy Cassie's past?" She probed her memory, moving backward into time until she reached her nineteenth year, the year of her debut.

"Let me see," she spoke to the coals, "the house was a whirlwind of excitement. And no one was more caught up in it than Mother. She was in her element! A whole season of parties and dresses to consider. And Mammy Cassie was the worst I have ever seen her. We had fight after fight, and Mother ignored it as she always had. And then finally Mammy Cassie went for me, and I exploded and got really upset. Then Mother found out and turned on Mammy Cassie. That was the first time I'd ever seen her do that. But why did she do it then? I can't quite remember—wait a minute! Yes! It was the night of my presentation ball, and Mother was furious because Mammy Cassie made me so mad I cried, and Mother said my face was ruined!" Rachel laughed aloud at the thought. "My face was ruined! For heaven's sakes, how idiotic!"

Rachel rose and poked at the coals. "But that's not the important part. That happened the next day, after I had slept till noon and wandered into the kitchen. Mammy Cassie was there and she was in a mean mood," Rachel settled back in her chair. "And I found out things that day I never knew before."

❧❧

"So, you's finally up," Mammy Cassie snarled as Rachel pushed open the kitchen door.

Rachel ignored her and asked Florence for some breakfast, but Mammy Cassie was intent on a fight. "I hears you was the belle of the ball last night. Your daddy say you was the prettiest girl there. I guess he don't know what you's really like inside."

Rachel refused to take the bait; instead, she stared coolly into Mammy Cassie's angry eyes because over the years she had learned one lesson well—upsetting Mammy Cassie too much meant upsetting her mother. It was a simple equation she had figured out young: if her mother didn't have Mammy Cassie to coddle her, no one in the house would have a minute's peace. No one. And Rachel had finally managed to keep her mother happy for more than an hour at a time by embarking on a gala debut. She didn't plan to upset things the day after her presentation ball.

Mammy Cassie, however, had other plans. "Your daddy don't have no notion how selfish you is, how you takes the last thing a person got and leaves her standing there with nothing. He don't have no notion how spoiled you is."

Rachel's temper was rising.

"He don't know—"

"Mammy Cassie!" Rachel said, raising her voice, "What on earth are you ranting about?"

"I ain't ranting!" she insisted loudly. It was obvious she had worked herself up to an explosion and had just been waiting for Rachel to appear to set it off.

"I'd like to know what you call it!" Rachel retorted. "You're standing there talking about total nonsense. I don't go around taking things from people."

"You's took my Patsy away from me when you's had everything and I ain't had nothing!"

"What are you talking about?" Rachel demanded, and much to her annoyance, Mammy Cassie suddenly started telling her the story of her life in a seemingly endless, volcanic soliloquy.

"I's born in a one-room shack on Longwood land, not in a fine house like you was. That's what I's talking about. And I's born a nigger. I's born a nigger in a one-room shack, and they was older kids in that shack that stole my food, and they was more babies coming every year that I gotta take care of.

"*My* daddy didn't never say I was the belle of no ball. I never even knowed my daddy. I never even knowed who he was. All those kids in that shack, didn't none of them know their daddies—just Mama and whatever man be there at the time. Mama she always gotta have a man there, a field hand or some other no count. She couldn't do without no man. So one would come, and Mama would laugh and sing, and they'd be sounds in the night, but pretty soon the fighting would start up—the cursing and screaming. Then I have to just stand by and watch while my Mama be slapped down to the floor. Wasn't nothing I could do, I's too little. She just get up off that floor, and he go and slap her against the wall. Then finally he leave like all the others, and I be glad for a little while, but then my Mama's belly start swelling again, and I knowed there gonna be another baby for me to take care of."

"Hush, Cassie!" Florence broke in. "You just gonna cause trouble."

"I don't care no more! I's gonna tell her what she taken from me!"

Rachel was totally bewildered; she thought Mammy Cassie had finally lost her mind. She had always seemed crazy, but this was bizarre! Mammy Cassie rushed on before Rachel could think of anything to say.

"I had me two problems back then. One of them be keeping my share of the food and the other be not having to sleep too close to this big hole in the middle of the floor of that cabin. If I didn't stay right by my Mama's side until I gulp my food, one of the older kids, they gonna take it away from me, and it be a long time before more food in that cabin.

"One time that cabin be so crowded I gotta put my pallet down on the floor too close to that big, dark hole, and in the middle of the night I rolls over and falls all the way down to the ground. I's scared half to death. I land face down in the cold mud and filth under that cabin. I scream bloody murder when I hit the ground. I scream cause I fell on my face and the blood come gushing out of my nose. But my mama, you know what she done? She didn't rush into my pretty pink room and tuck me back into no clean, warm bed. No mam! She just shuffle over to that hole and jerk me out by grabbing that old tattered shirt I's wearing. I didn't have me no fancy night-gown, just a tattered old shirt some man done left behind. Then my mama she just take her foot and scoot my pallet over aways, drop me on it and scuff back to the only bed in the room, where some man I didn't know was calling for her. Didn't nobody pat my head and tell me everything gonna be all right. I just bury my face in my pallet, and my bleeding nose it run all over that shredding, moldy quilt."

She stopped, and Rachel noticed that Mammy Cassie's eyes had quit focusing as she remembered the incident. Rachel was totally confused. She resented Mammy Cassie's thrusting her life's miseries into the most special time of her life, but at the same time she felt sorry for her. She covered her confusion with an angry, senseless question.

"Well, if it was so horrible, why didn't you leave?" she demanded. "You were free; nobody was keeping you there."

"I's just a nigger girl! Where I gonna go? They ain't nobody gonna help me! What good's freedom to me if there weren't no place to go and nothing to eat when I got there? My mama was the cook at the Longwood big house, so at least I had a shack and some food where I was. Yeah, I was free, free to do without! As long as my mama work from six in the morning to ten at night, we could stay in that shack and eat anything nobody else would eat.

"I knowed they got a lot of food in that big house, so I always gets myself up when I hears my mama slipping out the door cause I wants to follow her and talk to her and maybe get some food. Besides, it be the only time I had her to myself. She don't pay no attention to me, but I just keep on jabbering, hoping I gonna say something she like. But when we get to the big house, she always just turn around and snap, 'Get back to them woods, Cassie Jo!'

"But one time she shush me and pull me into the kitchen. I never seen nothing like it! Everything was sparkling clean and just where it ought to be. And I ain't never seen so much food! And I says to myself right then and there, 'I ain't gonna settle for no filthy cabin when I's growed. I ain't gonna be like my mama.' I took me a vow right then and there that some day I's gonna marry me a man, *really* marry with a preacher and everything. And no matter how little I had, it was gonna be clean and all put up. So I bide my time till I growed some more, then when I start filling out, I starts looking for me a man to marry, a man that gonna work steady and let me stay home and keep my house and children clean and shiny."

Mammy Cassie had slipped so thoroughly into the past that she seemed to have forgotten her intention of quarreling with Rachel. In fact, she seemed to have forgotten Rachel was there. Rachel had become fascinated by what Mammy Cassie was saying. From the day of her birth, Mammy Cassie had towered over her, a huge figure with a face of fury and a tongue of perpetual denunciation. Rachel had never once thought of her as a person, never once realized that she had been a child, that she had had a life before Rachel was born.

"I just ignores all the young men around me, didn't give them no notice at all," Mammy Cassie picked up her story, "they wasn't fine enough for what I wanted. Then one day, when I's about fifteen, I seen Luther Wood for the first time. He be tall, real tall, and he had him some big broad shoulders. He was older than me, but I didn't care. He was the handsomest man I ever seen! And laugh! Lordy, that man could laugh! It make me happy just to look at him. He come to work in the Longwood fields, and I lean against the fence hour after hour watching his

strong shoulder muscles, glistening with sweat in the hot
sun.

"It didn't take Luther long to notice me neither; all
the mens was noticing me. I's only fifteen, but I's developed real good, round and soft, I was. They's looking at
me, them mens, but I never look back, not till Luther
look at me. So we starts courting, but Luther he say he
ain't interested in no marriage. He just want to mess
around. But me, I's determined, so I just keep on flirting
with him until he can't do without me no more and there
ain't no way to get me excepting to marry me. So finally
he did. We's married by the traveling colored minister; my
mama thought it was a heap of trouble to go to, but in
the end I had my way.

"The Longwoods, they let us live in one of the cabins
that was empty back in the woods, and I set about trying
to clean it up. It weren't no more than four log walls, a
rock fireplace and a dirt floor, but it was mine. I didn't
have to share it with no one but Luther. And he was mine,
too. And I made sure he gonna stay mine; I made sure he
ain't never gonna need to look at no other woman. And
I made sure ain't no other woman ever gonna look at him
neither. All my life I ain't never had me nothing, but
Luther was mine and that cabin was mine, and I made up
my mind ain't nothing or nobody gonna take nothing
away from me no more. I's gonna keep what's mine, and
it gonna be the way I wants it!"

Mammy Cassie fell silent suddenly, her eyes gleaming
with determination, the determination she had felt so long
ago. Then as Rachel watched intently and Florence stared
at the floor, Mammy Cassie's eyes darkened and filled with
rage.

"But that Luther! He ain't no good! No matter how
happy I makes him, he got to go looking for some other
woman. Over and over again! Pretty soon, all we does is

fights. He come in drunk, smelling of some hussy, just ready to fall in the bed with me. But I ain't gonna stand for that. No mam! 'You ain't gonna cheat on me!' I screams at him. 'I rather have you dead than messing with some piece of trash.' Sometimes when he sleeping I's so mad I look over at him and think of ways to kill him.

"Then I finds out I's gonna have a baby. I thought the world done come to an end. I's just going down the same path as Mama, nothing but dirt and hunger and more and more babies till I don't have no chance for no life at all. But then one day it come to me, I's lost Luther and there ain't no getting him back, but this here baby it gonna be mine. Ain't no way I can lose it to nobody else. I's gonna be its mama—its only mama. Can't no one ever take my place with my baby. Over and over as the days pass I keeps telling myself, 'Cassie Jo, this here baby gonna be all yours, you don't have to share it with nobody. This baby gonna love you, ain't never gonna quit loving you. Can't nobody make this baby quit loving you! Can't nobody take this baby away from you!' So I just lets Luther go his own way, and I thinks about my baby that's a-coming."

Mammy Cassie stopped talking and stood gazing over Rachel's head. There was the faintest smile on her face as her memories kept her captive. Then Florence moved, and that movement brought Mammy Cassie back to the present, and she lowered her gaze and looked into Rachel's eyes. Her face hardened in anger.

"Miz Longwood be expecting a little baby about then," Mammy Cassie's voice became harsher, "and my mama, she snook me upstairs to see the nursery they fix all up for the baby. They was determined on having theirselves a girl cause they already had three boys. They fix everything up in pink, everything was pink. I ain't never seen such a sight, all soft and light, and they's a cradle thing all covered in pink right in the middle of the room. It was the prettiest thing I ever seen, but Mama wouldn't let me touch it. She shoo me out of the room.

"About a month later Miz Longwood's baby was borned, and it was a little girl just like they wanted. After Mama told me, I sit myself down on the stoop of my cabin and dream about that little white baby girl in the fluffy pink cradle.

"I's sitting there on the stoop mixing dreams of the Longwood baby with dreams of my baby when I hear the first gunshot off to my left where most of the cabins was setting together. Then I hear screams and cursing male voices. All of a sudden there's a wild thrashing noise in these dense bushes close to my cabin. I jumps up cause I's so scared; then before I could move, suddenly out come Luther, naked as the day he's borned, staggering all over the place and clutching at his middle. There's blood all over his belly, oozing out between his fingers, and his face was all twisted up. He let go of his middle with one bloody hand, held it out to me and called, 'Cassie Jo! Help me! Help me!' Then I hear another shot, and my Luther, he fall to the dirt. I scream and run to his side, but he be dead. His blood is running all over me, but he be dead.

"That evening my water broke, and my baby start coming early. All night I screamed with them pains, and the women try to help me, and round about morning my baby was borned. My little girl she gulp in her first breath of air and cry and open her eyes for just a minute. Then she just stop breathing. She just take herself a good look at the world and she decide it ain't no fit place to be. So two days later I stood by two graves in the colored cemetery. I buried my Luther, and I buried my baby girl. I wanted to bury myself.

"For the next week—seven days and seven nights—there ain't no peace nowhere for me. Why? Why did this happen to me? That's all I can think on. I had to have me a answer. I had to! But no answer came.

"In the evenings I go to the edge of the woods, and I looks up at the window of the little white baby girl's room. They always this soft light glowing through that window, drawing me closer. Pretty soon I realize that baby need me, that baby a-calling me. I's sure that baby need me and weren't nobody gonna stop me from going. It was just like my own little girl was a-calling me.

"Finally on the eighth morning I got up good and early, washed myself in the cold creek and put on my very best clothes. Before anybody's awake, I slip through the kitchen door of the Longwood house and sneak up them stairs to the baby's room. There for the first time I seen Miz Patsy. It seem to me that my baby done come to life as an angel! God had took pity on me and made my little girl white and laid her here in this fluffy pink cradle just waiting for me to find her. Miz Patsy, she whimper just a little in her sleep, and I went on over and stroke the fine hair on the back of her head. She didn't cry no more. She just reach out and grab my finger and hold on tight as can be. She was mine! And she still is!" Mammy Cassie glared down at Rachel and stormed out of the kitchen.

Rachel sat and stared at Florence for a minute before commenting, "She's crazy! I always knew she was crazy, I just never knew *how* crazy!" Florence said nothing.

"Did all that really happen, Florence?"

"Yes, Miz Rachel."

"I still say she's crazy—and mean to boot!"

"Tell me all about your party last night," Florence wisely changed the subject.

It wasn't that simple, Rachel thought as she stood up to go to bed. It wasn't that simple at all. Mammy Cassie wasn't just crazy and mean for no good reason, but it never occurred to me to wonder back then. What an ugly image of herself she received from the mirror of her early life, a mirror pieced together by her mother's constant lack of concern for her, by whatever horrible things those transient boyfriends of her mother's might have said to her or even done to her. Even the few glimpses she had into the white world of the Longwoods must have impressed on her the idea that she was worthless. And then, when she had the sense and determination to try to make a better life for herself, it all came tumbling down on her because she was too young to choose the right man or too desperate to get away.

So she filled her world with my mother. Mother was her only ticket out of the hellhole she lived in. No wonder she hated me so! When I came along, she had to share Mother with me, and she certainly would not have wanted to share the only thing she had with anyone. Who would?

Lovey says there are always reasons why people are the way they are. I can see Mammy Cassie's reasons now. I couldn't when I was a kid and battling with her all the time; I doubt I would have wanted to.

Lovey also says that when you have a negative childhood and that negative childhood produces that mirror in which you see an unworthy you, then you have to choose to focus on the good things that have happened. You have to work at feeling good about yourself. Well, the only good thing Mammy Cassie seems to have had was Mother, the beautiful infant she was put in charge of. So she focused on Mother; she became obssessed with her because she lived through her.

And I suppose that now I can understand more about why Mother has been the way she has been. She had her own mother, of course, but she was one hundred per cent socialite. She just dropped in occasionally to spoil Mother.

So Mammy Cassie raised her; she molded Mother's character. Mammy Cassie is such a strong personality! She had to be to survive, to march into the Longwood nursery like that and take over. She could mold any infant into whatever she wanted. And she wanted the kind of relationship she had wanted with Luther, a mutually *exclusive* love. She wanted a child who would always love her, always need her to a neurotic degree, who would never leave her, who could never leave her. But her baby died, so she fulfilled her need with Mother.

Yes, she would definitely have grounds to hate me; I was a threat to her world. That's the way she would see it. And she would have reason to keep Mother dependent on her; otherwise she might lose her. And the fastest way to make a person dependent is to convince her that she is sickly, that she is easily upset and can only depend on one person—in this case, Mammy Cassie. Poor Mother! She never had a chance! And although I hate to admit it, neither did Mammy Cassie. She found a way out of the poverty she was trapped in, but not out of the fear and anger and hatred. She still lives in that.

Rachel turned out the lights as she walked through the house and upstairs to her bedroom. As had become her custom, she went out on the upper verandah and looked at the skies. "So what will you do with this new understanding, Rachel D'Evereau?" she asked herself quietly. "Will you forgive? Can you forget?"

She leaned against the pillar and stared at the stars for a long time. The feel of the sturdiness of that pillar sent her thoughts away from her own life and Mammy Cassie's back to the lives of those who had lived in this house through good times and bad so very long ago. She thought of Marie, of Jacques, of Cecelia, and especially of her grandfather, Alex. He was a motherless boy raised by a father who had nothing left but his ideal of Southern manhood, his land, and the prosperity he eventually produced. Alex would have been spoiled and very dogmatic about what constitutes manhood. And he would have taught Daddy that ideal of Southern manhood. It would have all worked fine because they were all cut from the same fabric—Jacques shaping Alex, Alex shaping Jack—until Justin came along. Justin wasn't a Jacques or an Alex or a Jack. He was an Elinore D'Evereau. He was like his Grandmere, only he was never allowed to be himself, never applauded for his uniqueness. Not by Daddy or the culture he was born into. But whose fault *was* that? Was it Daddy's, as I always thought? Was it Alex's or maybe Jacques? But wait a minute, according to Marie's journal, Jacques' father had excitedly escorted his son on the first mile to war. Did he start the insanity that ended in Justin's death?

"Dear God!" Rachel exclaimed. "We all act out what our mirror reflections of ourselves tell us we are, and those reflections are formed by others, who have mirror reflections of their own they are trying to live up to. We've all been victimized in the same way, some more than others."

She looked away from the stars and off into the direction of the family cemetery. "So will you forgive, Rachel?" she asked herself again, but she avoided her own question. "I don't want to forget, I don't dare forget," she whispered earnestly, "I must remember what's happened in order to make things better."

## NINETEEN

Rachel awoke early the next morning. Her mind was on Sassy and Chelsy. She had arranged to meet them on Monday, but she had no idea what she would do with them once she met them. She slipped out of the house quietly and walked to the plantation office to think about the girls. However, no matter how hard she tried, she couldn't keep her thoughts in the present. They kept drifting back to her first summer at Belle St. Marie. Then out of the corner of her eye she saw Lovey walk out the kitchen door with a bowl in her hands. It was part of Lovey's morning ritual that Rachel had forgotten about since she was usually fast asleep at this hour. There had been one morning, however, when she was seven, a magic morning when Rachel had awakened early.

❦❧

The sun was beaming through her windows, but there wasn't a sound anywhere in the house. Rachel waited impatiently for Lovey to come get her out of bed and help dress her, but no one came. Finally she slid off the side of the high bed and wandered down the stairs and into the center hall, still skimpily clad in her gown. The front door was closed, a sure sign that her Grandmere wasn't up, so lonely Rachel wandered back into the kitchen area looking for company.

There was no one there either, but the backdoor stood open to the sunshine, a sign that Lovey was up and around. Rachel walked across the large, cool tiles, occasionally feeling her toes fall down into a grouted jointure, as she headed toward the back door. There she paused and peered out through the screen door, but only Lovey's voice came to her ears. It sounded to Rachel like Lovey was crooning sweet words to the birds, "That's it! That's it! Just come get these here crumbs that Lovey got for you. You knows I never gonna forget my pretty babies. They's always something left for you. I sees to that." Rachel stepped eagerly out onto the porch, and from there she saw Lovey off to one side surrounded by wild birds, many of whom were so accustomed to her presence that they were eating the crumbs only a few inches from her feet. Lovey seemed to be in her own special heaven as the birds glided in from the nearby trees, sailing close by her head and landing at her feet. Rachel was delighted; she had never known anyone who had such rapport with wild creatures.

Slowly she crept forward in her nightgown, eager to be a part of the enchanted scene but afraid of disturbing it and making the birds disappear. Finally Lovey caught a glimpse of her and motioned for her to sit on the grass. Rachel settled into the warm, scented lawn. Slowly Lovey began to move toward her, continuing her soothing talk to the birds, changing the words but not the tone. "Let's you and me go on over here and see Miz Rachel," she crooned as she took one gentle step at a time in Rachel's direction. "That's it. You not afraid of Miz Rachel. She just a sweet little girl who love you a lot. She never hurt nothing in her whole life. She just like Lovey—just like your old friend Lovey." By now Lovey was standing directly over Rachel, and the birds were flying in from all directions to find the crumbs. Rachel was delighted and almost too excited to sit still, but she managed to remain motionless, only moving her eyes around to watch the graceful birds.

Most of them were brown or gray birds, but occasionally a geranium-red cardinal or a bright blue jaybird would swoop in, and Rachel's heart would leap with a special joy. Over and over they came, gliding in from every side and in every imaginable flight pattern. Seven-year-old Rachel wondered, how does she do it? She's just old Lovey. Yet there was an indescribable peace in that backyard, a rightness that Rachel had never experienced. Her heart was flooded with a new kind of happiness, a happiness no one else had ever given her.

At last the crumbs were gone, and Lovey moved over to a bench under an oak to enjoy the birds' final cleanup campaign in the grass. Suddenly Rachel's only desire in life became to sit next to this remarkable woman, to touch her. She rose and hurried over to the bench, and Lovey automatically gathered her to her side as she continued watching the birds.

"Which bird do you like the most, Lovey? Which one do you think is the prettiest?" Rachel whispered.

"Oh, I like's them all, Honey. They's all just fine, just fine with me." Rachel was startled when Lovey spoke very loudly.

"But you must think one is the prettiest, Lovey," Rachel insisted. Then she realized that Lovey had raised her voice intentionally, and Rachel knew why. She leaned over in Lovey's lap and looked up into her face as she whispered. "You do have a favorite, don't you, Lovey? You can tell me; I won't tell anybody." Lovey said nothing so Rachel continued persuading, "You can whisper it in my ear so they won't hear."

Lovey paused a moment longer, looking out at the mass of birds of different types on the grass. Then she smiled ever so sadly, leaned close to Rachel's ear and confided, "I likes the sparrows the best, Honey."

"The sparrows?" Rachel whispered back. "Which ones are they, Lovey?" She peered out into the swarm of birds, trying to pick out the most beautiful ones, certain that the sparrows must be the most beautiful birds out there.

"They's the little brown ones, Honey. All them little brown ones." Startled by Lovey's response, Rachel stared up at her intently, but Lovey just quietly patted Rachel on the head, and there was a strange look in her eyes that Rachel had never noticed before.

"But why do you like the brown birds best?" Rachel earnestly inquired, for she could not imagine anyone choosing the flock of common brown birds as a favorite over the bright red and blue birds. "They're not pretty; they're not special, Lovey!" Rachel persisted applying her world's value system to the situation. "They're just plain old brown birds."

"That don't matter none to God. He just interested in the insides of them birds, and to God them brown birds is just as pretty inside as them redbirds."

"Are you sure, Lovey, *really* sure?" Rachel was having a hard time believing that appearances didn't count.

"Yes mam, I's sure. God love all them birds the same just like He love all people the same. He made every one of them, and He made every one of them special. We's the ones that always judging, always worrying how much somebody owns or what family they's born into or what they looks like. God He don't bother with none of that. He know He made us *all* special." Lovey was absolutely definite about this point, so Rachel turned her face back to the birds and pondered Lovey's words.

There was another long pause while Lovey watched the

few remaining birds take their various flights into the trees. Then she broke the silence, "Well, I best be getting your Grandmere's tea up to her so she won't be late for mass. She got a busy day ahead of her what with all them meetings about the school for colored childrens." Lovey rose to her feet and headed slowly back across the yard.

"What school for colored children?" Rachel demanded as she tagged along.

"Best ask your Grandmere about that, Honey," was all Lovey would respond.

So a few moments later Rachel skipped along happily, still clad in her scanty nightgown, as Lovey climbed the staircase with Grandmere's tea tray. She had no problem outdistancing Lovey and burst into her Grandmere's room after just the barest of knocks on the door. When Lovey arrived a moment later, Rachel was already sitting cross-legged next to her Grandmere in the huge bed, plaguing her with questions about the school.

Grandmere laughingly addressed Lovey as she came across the room, "What on earth have you been feeding the child this morning?"

"I didn't feed her nothing yet—she just wake up that way," Lovey chuckled.

Rachel's questions continued until Grandmere finally broke in with, "Just let me drink this cup of tea, Darling, and I'll tell you the whole story." She sipped at the steaming liquid, while Rachel waited as patiently as she could.

Finally Grandmere began, "Way back in the late 1700's, Rachel, the first D'Evereaus came to Louisiana from France. Since they were devout Catholics, when they arrived to take possession of the enormous tract of land that they had inherited, they immediately built a small chapel on their land, even before they built a house. In time the chapel was replaced by the church you see now. After the War Between the States, when the D'Evereaus had regained some of their wealth, they built the convent and the school next to the church. But the Negro children were not allowed to go to school there."

"Why not?" Rachel asked the obvious, but painful question.

"Because they had been slaves for a long time," Grandmere explained sadly as she glanced at Lovey, who was intentionally busying herself straightening the room, "and the white people at that time did not think that they should be educated. In time, pressure came from the government, and schools were established for the Negro children, but they were separate schools from the schools for the white children, and they weren't very good. In fact, no one even encouraged the Negro children to come to the Negro school, and many of them never went to school at all."

Rachel considered her Grandmere's words for a moment before inquiring, "Then how did they learn to read and write and do arithmetic?"

"They didn't." Grandmere sipped the last bit of tea from her cup and fell silent a moment. "That's the problem."

"Well—" Rachel reached for Grandmere's cup and gaily pretended to sip tea from it, "why don't you just send them to the white school now?"

There was a grave silence in the room as Grandmere's pained eyes sought out Lovey's sad ones. "Because the law will not allow them to go." The anger in Grandmere's tone halted Rachel's questions.

The day continued according to the usual Belle St. Marie pattern, but Rachel was a changed child. She had never even wondered what it was like to be someone other than herself. Certainly she had never considered what it was like to be a Negro. Now, quite suddenly, because of her love for Aimee and the shocking thought that Aimee was forbidden to go to school with her, she was forced into a heightened perception of reality, a painful perception. As a result, many things crashed in on her troubled mind as the day progressed. Aimee was well treated at Belle Saint Marie, but even here she didn't sleep in a grand room like Rachel's. She slept on a couch in Lovey's rooms over the garage. Rachel ate in the dining room; Aimee ate in the kitchen. Aimee didn't have the beautiful clothes Rachel wore. And even though Grandmere stubbornly took both Lovey and Aimee to mass with her, Rachel had seen the disapproving glares. But worst of all, Rachel remembered all the little Negro children she had seen on the downtown sidewalks when her mother took her shopping. She remembered their bare feet and shabby clothes and how they stared at the pavement when her mother walked by, her nose in the air, her eyes straight ahead.

That's what it's like for Aimee when she's home, the thought plagued Rachel all day. That's what it'll always be like. Just because she's colored.

By evening she was a much quieter child, saddened by what she had discovered about the world that day, and when she and Grandmere settled on the front verandah for Grandmere's evening coffee, Rachel broached the subject that haunted her the most.

"Grandmere, does Jesus love colored people?"

Grandmere stared at her for a prolonged moment before answering. "Yes He does, Darling." There was another long pause as Rachel stared back at her. She did not believe what Grandmere had said, but she knew she shouldn't argue with an adult.

Grandmere sighed and asked quietly, "Is something bothering you, Darling?"

"Does Jesus love colored folks as much as He does white folks?" Rachel demanded.

Grandmere looked worried, but she insisted firmly, "Jesus loves all His children the same."

"Then why are colored folks so poor?" Rachel demanded angrily, "and why can't Aimee go to school with me? And why doesn't Aimee live in a big house? And why doesn't Aimee have pretty dresses like mine?" Rachel's questions indicted the entire white, adult world so surely that there was no need for a trial.

"Rachel, questions like that have bothered me all my life. I can't give you answers that will bring peace to your heart because I've never found them for myself. All I can tell you is the historial facts. Negroes are poor because a long time ago white men brought them here from Africa and made them slaves, and even though they were eventually freed, they have never learned how to change things for themselves, how to make things better for themselves."

"But how can they learn to make things better if they can't even go to school?" Rachel's straightforwardness shot straight to the heart of the matter.

"They can't," Grandmere concluded firmly.

"Why doesn't God help them Himself? Why doesn't He change things?"

"Darling, many bad things happen in the world, and I have often asked God why. Many times I never receive any answer, but this situation is different, it seems to me. We made this bad situation. Human choices have caused the Negro children to have a bad education, and God expects *us* to fix this problem. If we do our part, God will work with us." She paused and watched Rachel before she asked cautiously, "Do you understand?"

Rachel nodded her head angrily. She understood all right. She understood that it was another one of those things about God that she didn't understand. There was getting to be a growing list.

※

"Is you gonna stare out that window all day, or is you gonna come in and have some of my pecan pancakes?" Lovey demanded.

"What?" Rachel was startled back to the present and surprised to find herself an adult sitting in the plantation office.

"What's you doing up so early, Honey? Ain't nothing troubling you, is there?"

"I can't seem to figure out how to help those two girls I ran into. I know there's no use in sending them back to school because they'd run away again. They say the teacher doesn't want them and their mothers don't care whether they go to school or not."

Lovey sighed. "They's lots of kids around here like that."

"You and I know what's going to happen to them if they don't learn enough to make a living of some kind."

"So, you's gonna teach those two, aren't you?"

"I guess I am, although I'm not sure I had made up my mind until this very minute. I guess it's my experiment in hope." Lovey nodded knowingly, and Rachel continued. "After reading those journals and learning more about Daddy's life and thinking about all the things you said—well, I just can't get that idea of the mirror out of my mind, of how we grow up thinking we're what people tell us we are, and of how others create that mirror we see ourselves in. And it's wrong, Lovey! Most of the time that mirror is a liar; it doesn't tell us the truth about ourselves. It tells us we're no good."

"That talk with your Daddy about Mister Justin and about you and Mammy Cassie, that give you something to think on too."

"How did you know about that?"

"I ain't deaf! You two wasn't whispering."

"No, I guess we weren't," Rachel laughed wryly. "Yes, it helped. I even tried to remember what I knew of Mammy Cassie's youth."

"And now you got some idea of why she turn out like she did."

"Yes. And understanding Mammy Cassie a little helped me see why Mother is the way she is." Rachel paused and stared at the floor. "But, Lovey, I've been angry so long. I don't know if I can stop."

"You's already started stopping that anger."

"But they made me feel so worthless! Even if I can forgive them—now that I know why they treated me the way they did—how am I ever going to feel good about me?"

"That mirror of yours ain't just got bad things in it. It got your Grandmere in it too telling you you's wonderful."

"I know! I know! You're going to tell me to choose. To choose to look at the good. But I don't know if I can. I don't know if it will work."

"Then why you gonna work so hard to give them two colored girls a good view of themselves?"

"Because they deserve it."

"You just wasting your time. Fine lady like you with a fine education wasting your time on two ignorant, colored girls. How come you gonna do that?"

"Because they're worth it! Lovey, what on earth is wrong with you, saying such a thing?"

"Ain't nobody round here thinks they's worth anything."

"I do! I think they're worth something! And I'm going to see to it that they have a chance, come hail or high water!"

"Then tell me this, Miz Rachel, if you can see they's

worth something no matter what their world telling them about themselves, why can't you see how worthy you is?"

Rachel could think of nothing to say.

"God don't make no trash, Miz Rachel," Lovey spoke with quiet firmness as she stared into Rachel's eyes. "He don't make *no* trash, and He made all of us."

Rachel added thoughtfully, "But we take over and persuade children they're trash because we've been persuaded we are."

"Until someone come along and give them a good picture of themselves and teach them to choose it," Lovey insisted.

"That's what I want to do for those girls!" Rachel rose and faced Lovey, her eyes full of commitment. "I want to help them choose to stop this horrible cycle. The trouble is how do I get *them* to try?"

"It gonna take some powerful persuasion."

"Lovey, you sound like you've got an idea. What is it?"

"Food."

"Food?"

"And something from the J. C. Penney catalogue when they's worked real hard."

"You think they're hungry?" Rachel demanded.

"I knows they's hungry. They lives back in them shacks in the woods, and there ain't no food back there, and they ain't never owned nothing to wear they could call their own."

"I don't believe it! Not here!"

"You's been in the city too long, Miz Rachel."

"I guess so," Rachel murmured. "I just don't know what to do. In all my years of teaching I've never run into kids like these and—wait a minute! Where are my brains? Aimee! I'll call Aimee; she'll know just what to do. She's worked with disadvantaged kids all these years."

"My Aimee will know for sure," Lovey agreed proudly.

"Yes, for sure, and certainty is what I need. Do you think she's up this early? It is Saturday morning."

"You know Aimee. She's up and about, probably getting ready to take them boys of hers to some kind of ball practice."

"And I'd better catch her before she's gone for the day. I'll just tell her what I want to accomplish and give her some time to think about it."

"Aimee won't need no time; there ain't nothing new in this to her."

"You're right," Rachel called back as she left the plantation office for the house.


"Aimee?" Rachel sat at the telephone desk in the main hall as she talked, "It's Rachel."

"How are you?" Aimee demanded. "And tell me the truth, Rachel D'Evereau."

"I'm fine. I can't wait to see ya'll at Thanksgiving."

"I wasn't sure you were ready for us to descend on you. Three boys can be pretty noisy, you know."

"They've always been good kids, Aimee. I'll take them any time."

"How about this morning?" Aimee laughed. "We've got one soccer game and two practices scheduled. The car smells like sweaty tennis shoes all the time now."

"Well . . ."

"I didn't think so!" Aimee teased.

"Actually I've got something else on my mind."

"How very convenient! What is it?"

"I met these two girls wandering around in the woods," Rachel quickly gave Aimee the details and then ended with, "I don't know how to handle this, Aimee. I know what I want to accomplish, but I don't know how to go about it. I'm not even sure how to get started. Lovey says to start with food and a bribe from the Penney's catalogue.

The thought of those girls hungry sends me into shock."

"If you're going to get into this, Rachel, you're going to have to be realistic," Aimee warned. "Grandma is right. Those girls are sure to be hungry. We have kids who come to school everyday hungry. You know that; you've had your student teachers in inner city schools, I know."

"Yes, of course I have. I guess I just didn't want to see that part of the problem."

"Who does?" Aimee asked. "But it's reality. The idea of getting them to work for a reward, like something from the catalogue, may not be theoretically appealing to an educator, but it will work. And that's what you're facing—finding something, anything that will work."

"It's just that it makes me sick to think about it being that way. This is my plantation now, and I don't want anybody on it to be hungry."

"You can't afford sentimentality, Rachel, not if you want to help them. You're going to have to make them work *hard* for every bit of bread you give them," Aimee warned. "I know it sounds mean, but you won't help them a bit if you don't make them help themselves."

"I know *they've* got to choose to change their lives—"

"And they've got to *work* for it! You're too softhearted, Rachel. You'll have to toughen up for their sakes."

"I know. I just feel so sorry for them."

"Then help them the right way," Aimee insisted. "Make them work hard for a good meal and when they've done a good job, give them something from the catalogue. Before you know it, if you're lucky, their self-esteem will emerge, and you won't have to bribe them to perform. Then nobody can stop them."

"Okay, I'll try it," Rachel agreed. "But what about the local school board and some books?"

"You better see their principal first thing Monday morning. My guess is you'll have no problem with the schools.

They've probably done their best and just given up. Kids like this are hard cases. As for books, you know what to get. Just think elementary level even if they are thirteen. They probably can't read, so of course you'll start there. I wouldn't be surprised if the principal is willing to loan you some books to get started."

"You're probably right," Rachel agreed. "I'm going to make it very plain to the officials that my goal is to get them back into the public schools. To catch them up as much as I can and get them reinstated in the schools."

"I think you'll find them very cooperative. Call me later and tell me how it's going."

"I will. I can't wait to see you—and thanks, Aimee."

"Be tough, Rachel!" Amiee warned again. "Don't let that soft heart of yours get in the way."

"I'll do my best. See you soon." Rachel hung up the phone and went to find Lovey.

"You're right, as usual!" Rachel hugged Lovey. "How did you get so smart?"

"Wasn't in no school; I just live a long time. How many sandwiches you gonna need?"

"How many do you think they can eat?"

"About ten times as many as you can!" Lovey declared with absolute certainty.

Rachel laughed and explained her plan. "I'm going to meet them in the woods on Monday and bring them back to the storeroom here in the plantation office to work."

"They ain't gonna like this! You gonna have to be mean."

Lovey was right about the girls' reactions. When Rachel met them in the woods on Monday morning, they were hanging their heads as usual, but when she told them they had to go to school at the plantation office for two hours a day, they came to life.

"No way!" Sassy jerked her head up and stared defiantly at Rachel. "I ain't going to no school!"

"Okay," Rachel replied calmly as her mind raced, looking for some way to make the girls cooperate. Finally she thought of something. "Just run on home and tell your mama to start packing."

"Packing what?" Sassy demanded.

"Everything she owns," Rachel kept her voice even as she stared coolly into Sassy's eyes. "She should be able to get off my property in two days, but I don't want to be unreasonable, so I'll give her three before I call the sheriff."

"You gonna throw us off your land?" Chelsy's head had popped up, and she was staring at Rachel in disbelief.

"So far it's only Sassy's mama who has to leave, Chelsy. You haven't said yet whether you're going to come to my school or not."

Chelsy looked at Sassy for a long time; then she swallowed hard and said, "I'm coming with you, Miz Rachel!"

"No you ain't!" Sassy insisted before turning to Rachel. "My mama has told me all my life that Miz Elinore wouldn't throw nobody off this land."

"I'm *not* Miz Elinore, Sassy," Rachel hardened the tone of her voice. "Your mama has three days before the sheriff comes after her. Come with me, Chelsy." Rachel started back toward the house with Chelsy reluctantly following her. By the time they reached the plantation office, Sassy had caught up with them.

Rachel took them into the storeroom and sat them at a small table. "Now, we'll begin by seeing how well you can read. Chelsy, read the first page from this book," she handed the girl a copy of *Heidi* she had found in one of the bookcases. "This story was one of my favorites when I was a girl."

Chelsy stumbled through the first paragraph, missing about half the words, before Rachel stopped her. When she told Sassy to read, Sassy just stared down at the table in angry silence.

"Sassy, read the next paragraph!" Rachel commanded. Sassy didn't open her mouth.

Rachel hated herself with every word she uttered, but she remembered Aimee's warning to be tough so she said sternly, "Sassy, either read the paragraph or go home and help your mama pack."

"Please, Miz Rachel," Chelsy broke in, "she can't read!"

Sassy jumped out of the chair and ran toward the door, but before she could leave, the door was blocked by Lovey and Alice. Alice was carrying a large tray heaped with sandwiches, and Lovey had a pitcher of milk and two glasses.

Sassy stopped in her tracks at the sight of the food, and Chelsy jumped up in excitement.

"Here's the dinner you wanted for the girls, Miz Rachel," Lovey announced. "Where you want us to put it?"

"I'll take it!" Sassy exclaimed.

"No you ain't!" Alice moved past her. "Not till Miz Rachel say you can have it."

"Just put the food over there on that table, please, Alice. We're not ready for it yet, but thank you for bringing it out." When they had gone, Rachel continued, "Come sit back down, Sassy. The reason we're having this school is to teach you to read, so there's no reason to be embarrassed if you can't read on the first day."

"Miz Rachel," Chelsy spoke just above a whisper, "I'm awfully hungry. I guess I forgot to eat breakfast or something, and it must be close to 11:00. Do you think we could eat now?"

It was the hardest thing Rachel had done in her life, but she steeled herself and said, "No, Chelsy. We're going to eat at noon every day *after* you finish your lessons. Now let's get to work."

In the next hour Rachel tested the girls' abilities in various ways. All the time the food, which Lovey had had the good sense to bring early, was in the girls' sight. When the clock in the plantation office finally struck noon, Rachel was as delighted as they were, although she forced herself to appear nonchalant.

"Well, girls, you may take the food out on the porch and begin eating. We don't eat in the schoolroom." Both girls jumped for the food and hurried out to the porch. Rachel followed them and found them sitting on the edge of the porch with their legs swinging off the side. They were gobbling down the sandwiches and gulping the milk. When they were both full, Chelsy tried to take another sandwich and put it in her pocket.

"Chelsy, what are you doing?" Rachel demanded.

"I'm gonna take this to my baby brother, Miz Rachel. He's only three years old, and the big kids get all his food."

Rachel felt like fainting, but she managed to keep her voice even. "You'll have to study an extra half hour tomorrow for that sandwich, Chelsy."

The two girls looked at each other, and Chelsy mumbled, "Yes mam." Then both girls put a sandwich in their pockets.

"Well, I'll see you tomorrow; be here at ten," Rachel dismissed them briskly. When they were out of sight, she took the dishes and dragged herself across the yard to the kitchen.

"How'd everything go?" Lovey was waiting for her at the door.

"I hate myself," Rachel put the dishes next to the sink,

"and I'll never be able to look at myself in the mirror again."

"It gonna be uphill for a long time, Honey, but the hardest part's over. You just got to remember what you's trying to do for them girls. They ain't never gonna have any life without somebody help them. Now you go wash up, and wash *real good*. Tomorrow I's gonna give them girls a bar of soap, and you's gonna tell them they gotta use it. That's part of education too."

"Yes mam!" Rachel saluted her as energetically as she could manage.

After three days Rachel knew she had the girls hooked. She met with the principal of their school, Mrs. Butler, to report her progress. Mrs. Butler had given her tentative approval early Monday morning. She was now delighted with Rachel's success and sent her home with workbooks for the girls.

"As you know, Rachel, home schooling is perfectly legal," Janet Butler said. "The most important thing is to get these girls to learn, to want to learn. I'll back you up. There may be some technicalities to handle along the way, but we'll handle them. These woods are full of truant kids who for one reason or another have been lost by the system."

Rachel left the meeting invigorated by the support she had received. When she met the girls the next morning, she took the Penney's catalogue with her and showed them how far they had to go in their workbooks to earn $10 worth of merchandise. The girls were flabbergasted and plunged into their lessons with a gusto that Rachel had never seen in all her years of teaching. During their lunch time they poured over the catalogue, planning and scheming about what they would buy. Then they demanded to work an extra hour. After that, it was all downhill. Rachel found she could start them on their lessons and watch them through the door as she worked in the plantation office.

By Thanksgiving week Rachel's biggest problem was that the word about her special school program had spread, and other girls had come to the office and wanted "to take lessons." Rachel started a list of prospective students to discuss with Janet Butler. She wanted to find out which girls had been truant so much that the school system couldn't handle them.

Aimee, Joseph and the three boys arrived from Shreveport early Thanksgiving Day, and the weather was so warm they all ate their turkey on the east verandah. Rachel and Aimee talked late into the night about old times and new times, about the pains and the joys of the last year. Over the years of their adulthood they had seen each other many times, but being together again at Belle St. Marie was special.

# TWENTY

The Christmas season was a time of both sorrow and joy for Rachel. It was her first Christmas since Collins' death, and the thought of him brought tears to her eyes and forced her to remain silent a moment, while she relaxed her throat and regained control of herself. She had thought she was incapable of such an emotional reaction to his death because he had betrayed her in so many ways. However, she found that with her growing understanding of why so many people see themselves in a negative way and thus act in ways that hurt themselves and others, she felt less angry toward the significant people in her life, especially Collins. Her anger had always been her way of defending herself from her other emotions. When that anger was stripped away, as it now was with Collins, she had to deal with her grief and hurt.

Since her confrontation with her father in October, she had a new understanding of why he had behaved the way he had toward Justin. She wasn't sure she had forgiven him for his behavior, but she had come to admit to herself and to him that she had mixed her anger about Justin's death with her hurt feelings from her childhood, from the years she had felt abandoned by her father to Mammy Cassie's damaging care. With her growing understanding came mixed emotions: some new-found peace, regret that they had lost so many years, and a longing that they could come together as a family, especially at Christmas. She had no illusions that such a reunion was possible. First, it was simply too soon. Second, she had never been close to her mother, and even if Mammy Cassie were somehow removed from the picture, she doubted that her mother, who had been so sheltered and brainwashed from birth, could or would choose to change her pattern of thinking after nearly sixty years.

These sorrows were heightened by the painfulness of spending the Christmas season at Belle St. Marie without her Grandmere. Many years had passed since her death, but they were years during which Rachel had refused to set foot in this house. Only once had she returned to the plantation, and that was for Justin's burial. Even then she had refused to enter the house itself because Grandmere would not be there.

On the positive side, there was new understanding, and understanding brought hope. Her father had visited several times, and with each visit she was happier to see him come in the door, and they had been able to have more frank discussions about the past. She thought she now had a clear idea of what his life was like in his twenties, of his emotional state after being wounded in the Normandy landing and then the death of his father so soon after. She could now easily understand how he could have met her beautiful, charming mother and fallen in love too quickly. And by the time Rachel had been born, her father must have been in quite a mess because Patsy and the atmosphere she produced were so different from Grandmere and the atmosphere he had grown up with. As early as Rachel could remember, her mother had thrown tantrums. How would her father know how to deal with such things? Or with Rachel, when he became a father?

She had written to invite both her parents to visit at Christmas. She had no real hope her mother would come;

she had never once set foot on Belle St. Marie soil. When she had been healthy enough, she wouldn't because she hated her husband's ethnic and religious background. Since Justin's death she hadn't been well enough to go anywhere unfamilar. Her father, Rachel knew, would come back to his boyhood home for midnight mass on Christmas Eve. She had never known him to miss that service here, not even if he had to drive back to Texas before dawn on Christmas Day and not even after her Grandmere had died.

Lovey was aching for Rachel to host the traditional D'Evereau Christmas open house, a time when the D'Evereaus had always invited their family and friends to an evening of festivities. Rachel remembered the custom well, for she had been present for Grandmere's open houses from the time she was seven until Grandmere's death, when the receptions had ceased. It was too soon for Rachel, however. She did not feel emotionally capable, and she did not think it appropriate so soon after Collins' death.

She wanted to have a quiet Christmas; however, party invitations were beginning to come in from some of her D'Evereau relatives in the area and other prominent families, and she was unsure how to handle the situation. People had been very sympathetic to her plight when she had arrived in June, and they had accepted her wish to have solitude to heal and had only sent notes of condolence. Now they seemed to be eager to know if Rachel D'Evereau was going to be a recluse the rest of her life. Unsure what to do, she consulted her father by phone.

"Do you want to go to any of these parties?" he asked.

"No, definitely not."

"But you will want to know your neighbors later, Rachel," he warned. "And you mustn't insult the D'Evereaus who are left there."

"I know Daddy, but surely a widow can—"

"That's the key," he broke in. "You haven't been widowed very long really, and in that culture you can plead that excuse. I'll tell you what you do. Refuse all the private invitations graciously. Then attend only the church functions. I know you don't believe me now, but in another six months you're going to want to be a part of society."

"If you say so."

"I do. Oh, by the way. Collins' estate is about to go through the first stages of probate."

"I don't want to hear one word about that! I told them to keep every last penny—"

"I know. I know. I'll handle it; I just thought you ought to know. I'll be sending you some papers you have to sign."

Rachel sighed but said nothing.

"Just sign them. You don't even need to read them; my lawyers and I are watching everything. Just sign them and send them back to me. Then forget it."

"Right. Forget it."

"I know that's not easy, Baby, but be as good as you can to yourself, and I'll talk to you soon."

"Okay, Daddy. Thanks, and give my love to Mother."

Rachel hung up the receiver, picked up the invitations she had stacked next to the phone, and went to her desk in the music room to begin answering them.

Sassy and Chelsy were now working four or five hours a day on their schoolwork. Both of them were determined to order bright new blouses for Christmas from the J. C. Penney Catalogue, and both were near their goals. Although they would never have admitted it, Rachel could see that they were motivated by more than the thought of the bribes she was holding out. They had developed a sense of pride in being able to conquer every academic challenge Rachel put before them. Their self-esteem was growing enormously; for the first time in their lives they could do something that the rest of the world considered important. Rachel had already begun to overhear snatches of conversation between them that suggested that they were setting higher goals for their lives and that their values were changing for the better.

One day she heard Chelsy telling Sassy about a conversation with a girl named Sally.

"You know what Sally said to me? She said I'm stuck up, going around with my nose in the air. Well, I just told her that I need to keep my nose in the air cause she never takes a bath and she stinks."

"She's just jealous," Sassy said, "they're all jealous cause we're the smart ones, and now they know it. Wait till they see our new Christmas blouses! We're gonna have every boy in the place looking at us."

"Well, I ain't looking back at any of them cause most of them are just sitting around all day doing nothing. I'm gonna find me a boy that's gonna go on with his schooling."

"You are?"

"You better believe it! I ain't gonna settle for anybody but the best! They're plenty of black boys in the high school, and I'm gonna find me one of them. They're the ones that are gonna go somewhere and be somebody, and I'm gonna go along with them. I might even find me one that is gonna be a doctor or lawyer."

"There ain't any black doctors and lawyers."

"Yes there are! Miz Rachel says there's lots of them in the cities."

"You're crazy! How are you gonna find you one of them? You're just a backwoods—"

"What I am now is not what I'm gonna be!" Chelsy declared. "I've got it all figured out. I'm gonna learn enough from Miz Rachel to get me some clothes and to get back into the regular school. You gotta be in the right place to meet the right boys. I ain't gonna end up like my mama!"

"It sounds like too much work to me," Sassy grumbled. "That Miz Rachel is already working me to death!"

"I ain't tired! I just keep thinking about the clothes in that catalogue. I've already reached chapter ten in our reading book!"

"You ain't!"

"Yes I have! I'm gonna get an education and a good man, and I ain't gonna be poor the rest of my life!"

"Well, I ain't either!"

Rachel called the girls in to their studies and resolved that she would go into town that afternoon to speak to Janet Butler about the other girls who had asked to join her school. So far no boys had expressed an interest, a fact that Rachel considered a blessing at this point in her experiment.

When she returned to Belle St. Marie late in the afternoon, she had four more students in mind. They were girls who had been totally uncooperative with the town school. Even though she brought their school supplies home with her, she didn't plan to make it easy on them, so the next day she sent word to the four girls through Sassy and Chelsy that she wanted to "interview" them.

The four girls came out of the woods the next morning. It was hard for Rachel to believe that Sassy and Chelsy had looked so undernourished and dirty just a few weeks before, but she knew they had. She explained the rules of the school and then "interviewed" each girl privately for about five minutes. She could tell that that five minutes was an eternity to them, but when she announced that they had all been accepted, they hugged each other and chattered with excitement. Rachel gave them each a bar of soap and ordered them to report the next day.

As she watched them hurry off, she realized that a new phenomenon had occurred. Sassy and Chelsy had become the elite of their group and had thus set a new fashion to be followed. Rachel had every intention of helping as many girls as possible to follow that new fashion. Aimee and Lovey had been correct when they had warned Rachel to be tough on the girls. They needed an authority figure to set a high standard for them and to insist that they meet it, as well as to assure them that they could.

Just as Rachel and Lovey expected, Jack D'Evereau drove up in plenty of time for midnight mass on Christmas Eve. Rachel had insisted that Lovey rest all afternoon, and she herself had taken a nap, for she knew the night would stretch into the next day before they returned home. Jack escorted them both to the beautiful old church for one of the happiest occasions in the church's calendar.

When Rachel entered the sanctuary, which was decorated with greenery and lit only with candlelight, she felt the presence of her ancestors, especially those she had so recently learned about. It was easy to imagine Marie coming here with Jacques before the Civil War. She would have been a happy young bride or perhaps a new mother come to make her prayers of thanksgiving. And how many times she must have come here for solace during the war!

Rachel thought of Jacques, his anger with God, the many years he, no doubt, denied this church of his ancestors. And she thought of tragic Cecelia, losing her first love in the war, waiting so long for a second chance for happiness with Jacques, then living only long enough to give birth to Alex and continue the D'Evereau line.

Most of all she thought of Grandmere. In Rachel's mind this church was as linked to Grandmere as was the remarkable blue color of Grandmere's eyes. Rachel prayed fervently that somehow she could do justice to the trust her Grandmere had left in her hands. In the last two months she had come to understand that inheriting Belle St. Marie was inheriting its people as well as its land and buildings. The old house had nurtured her through the trauma of the summer months. The former inhabitants, through their journals, and Lovey, through her own words and her memories of Grandmere, had enabled her to see that her opinion of herself could and must be improved, that the past need not define her. They had given her the courage and the hope necessary to walk through whatever swamp there was that kept her from knowing her worth.

As Rachel knelt at this midnight mass, celebrating the coming of Christ into the world, she felt better about herself than she ever had. After working with Sassy and Chelsy and the other girls just a short time, she was positive that God wanted all His children to know their worth, and she realized that the inheritance of Belle St. Marie carried with it the responsibility of working toward that end. It was a responsibility she gladly embraced.

At the end of the mass, the congregation knelt in the candlelight and sang "Silent Night." Then, awestruck by their experience, they quietly left the church. When the church was still again, Jack and Lovey knelt to pray. Rachel slipped out of the pew quietly and walked out.

When she closed the church door behind her, she discovered that the bright moon was filtering through the pines. Her eyes were drawn to a particularly bright spot a little distance from the church. There she saw that the pines had been cleared, and thus the moonlight could shine down like a soft spotlight. In the middle of that spotlight, she saw a small building. It was the old Catholic grammar school, closed down some time back. She knew instantly that now it was her school.

"I have a lot of work to do," she announced joyfully.

"What's that, Baby?" her father walked up behind her.

"Oh, I'll tell you later," she promised.

"Now, I know you're going to fight me on this," Jack's tone suggested he was ready to do battle and win an argument, "but I really think you ought to do it. I want you to go with me to Cousin Phillipe's house for the traditional Creole breakfast after midnight mass. I know what you said about socializing, but your cousin Phillipe is your closest relative here and—"

"I'd love to go!" Rachel abruptly announced. "Yes indeed, I really want to get to know my relatives here; in fact, I want to get to know all the population. Merry Christmas, Daddy!"

"Merry Christmas," Jack responded a little dumbfoundedly.

# TWENTY-ONE

The day after New Year's Day Rachel was at St. Mary's for morning mass. As hard as she tried, she couldn't concentrate on the short mass because her mind kept flying ahead to the appointment she had with Father Timothy after the service. Finally Father Timothy blessed the few faithful who were present and announced, "This mass is ended. Let us go in peace to love and serve the Lord." After he had left the sanctuary, Rachel and the others gathered their things together and left also. Outside the church Rachel paced on the steps, impatiently waiting for Father Timothy to take off his vestments and meet her.

Finally he appeared. He was a young priest, who had come directly from the seminary in Rome to this small, out-of-the-way parish the previous summer. Rachel knew him more by reputation than on a personal level since she had rarely attended the church. From what she did know of him, she knew he was an intellectual who probably belonged in a university, serving either as a chaplain or a professor. However, as the church so often did, they had sent him here to spend some years working with the people.

As she followed him over to his office in the rectory, Rachel felt confident that Father Timothy was going to be a kindred spirit in the venture she had in mind. And indeed, when she had told him of her plan to start an after-school remedial program for all children who needed help, an excited gleam lit up his eyes.

"Great!" he responded, "no one can argue with the fact that there are many children in this area who need tutoring of some kind."

"Good, I felt certain you wouldn't argue with that part," Rachel pushed on, "but my problem is that I need a building, and I want to use the old school building. What do you think about that part?"

"I think it's the perfect location, but the building is a mess."

"But will you let me use it? I'll clean it up, repair it, whatever it needs. Will you let me use it?"

"That's a request only the Bishop can grant."

"Oh no, the last thing I need is red tape! How do we get him to give us permission—and in the shortest possible time?"

"We show him this," Father Timothy tossed a newspaper across the desk so Rachel could see the lead story. Quickly she scanned the headline, "Learning Club Launched for Needy Youth" and read the first paragraph of the article. Surprised by what she had read, she looked back at Father Timothy.

"I hope you don't have a lot of ego involvement in the idea that you were the first one to think of this concept," he grinned at her.

Rachel started laughing and shook her head. "I should have known some nun would get there first. It's okay, just so we help the children here."

"It's more than okay actually. The fact that they have started this program in the diocese in Pennsylvania is certainly going to help the Bishop decide we need one here. Particularly if you come up with the finances."

"I will!"

"I've no doubt of it, Rachel. This is a small town so

there are few secrets. From what I've seen, you're a less-than-enthusiastic Catholic, but from what I've heard, you've walked through difficult times with unusual courage. Today it is obvious to me that you have also retained your love for God and your fellow human beings in spite of your own sufferings."

"*Because* of my sufferings would be more accurate, Father," Rachel responded quietly.

"Yes, that's the way it's supposed to work I'm told," the young priest murmured thoughtfully.

"Father, I'm not going to promise to be a better Catholic, but I am going to promise to support a Learning Club here. How do we get started?"

"We contact the Bishop."

"Could you call him?" she requested, "or can't we just drive down and see him tomorrow?"

Father Timothy laughed, "Are you sure you don't want to drop in on him for supper?"

"No, I think that would be pushing it a bit, but I see no reason why we can't have breakfast with him in the morning."

"I can think of several. I have to say mass at 8:00, and we have to be sure he is in town and can see us."

"Father, I don't want to wait a month to see the man," Rachel warned.

"You don't want to wait an hour! I'll do the best I can, and if that doesn't get the job done, I'll turn you on the poor man."

Rachel tried to look innocent, but failed miserably so she replied bluntly, "In the meantime, I want to see what condition that building is in."

"Why not?" He got up and dangled some keys in front of her.

"You knew what I came for!"

"Let's just say that when a wealthy teacher, who is

known to be tutoring black children, turns up on church property and starts poking around the old school building, I start praying. Let's go see what's really over there.''

"You think the Bishop is going to approve this, don't you?" Rachel asked.

Father Timothy tapped the newspaper still lying in front of Rachel and smiled at her, "What do you think, Rachel?"

"I think if I ever run for governor, I'm going to make you my campaign manager."

Rachel left Father Timothy and the old school building with excited confidence. She had found a kindred spirit in Father Timothy, and the old building was in better condition than she had hoped. It was Saturday so she drove home to pick up Lovey and drive her into town for their weekly shopping expedition. Rachel talked non-stop all the way to town, and Lovey smiled and listened. They bought the needed groceries, and then Rachel drove into the old townsquare and parallel parked in front of the drugstore. It was their last stop.

They stepped out of the car onto the old, red brick streets and climbed the high curb. Rachel pushed some coins into the parking meter, and they went into the drugstore.

Their business completed a few moments later, they started to leave. Rachel was looking back over her shoulder, calling back cordial good-byes to the owner, whom she had known for years, while she pushed open the glass door and stepped out onto the sidewalk.

Just as she had cleared the door, Lovey, who was right behind her, suddenly jerked her back and exclaimed, "Watch out, Miz Rachel!" Struggling to regain her balance and overcome her confusion, Rachel heard Lovey plead in a frightened voice, "Oh Lord, help us, help us!"

However, before Rachel could turn to her, she was assaulted by a screaming voice coming from the direction of the sidewalk.

"You cussed fool!" a man yelled, then added a jumble of obscene words. "Watch where you're going!"

Rachel wheeled around in time to see an obviously drunk man stagger against the wall of the store and nearly sink to the ground. "What do you think you're doing?" he demanded. "You nearly killed me! Can't nobody even walk on a public sidewalk no more without getting killed by a cussed fool!"

Rachel had no problem sizing up the man with a single glance. In short, he was not the sort of person a lady—or anyone else, for that matter—would willingly speak to. His obscenity-filled mouth was matched perfectly by his appearance. He was covered with greasy sweat, spilled alcohol, and drooled chewing tobacco.

Without speaking a word, Rachel turned to go. Suddenly the man staggered forward, blocking her path, and leered down at her face. "Well—l—l," he drawled out. "I'll be! If it ain't Miss Rachel D'Evereau!"

Revolted by the man's smell and appearance, Rachel simply stared straight through him, but for some strange reason she couldn't merely dismiss him as a drunk who happened to recognize her. She was positive that she knew him although she couldn't place him.

"Let's go, Miz Rachel," Lovey pleaded at her side. "We gotta go now!"

Automatically reacting to Lovey's request, Rachel started to step around the man, but once again he blocked her path. Her mind raced into the past, digging deeply into her memory, searching for the man's identity. However, all she could dredge up was an unexplainable, but scalding anger, an anger entirely out of proportion to the man's present disgusting behavior, an anger that was filling her stomach with acid.

"Hey! Look everybody!" the man turned his head to yell at the passersby as he continued to block her path. "It's Miss Rachel D'Evereau! One of the high and mighty D'Evereaus come to honor us with her royal presence!"

Silently, Rachel continued to stare straight through him, resolved not to lower herself by speaking to him, but her peripheral vision revealed to her that his loud words had accomplished their purpose. Everyone moving about on the square had stopped to stare. Still Rachel did not recognize him.

"Let's go, Miz Rachel," Lovey tugged at Rachel's arm as she pleaded. "Please, let's go!"

"Shut up, nigger!" the man suddenly snarled at Lovey. Something snapped in Rachel; the man's attack on Lovey had turned the situation into a different game. Her external cold disdain turned into the fury she had been feeling inside.

"Don't call her that!" she ordered the man. "She's worth a thousand of your kind!"

"I'll call her anything I like!" the man shouted in Rachel's face. "You're a nigger lover just like your grandmother, ain't you? Ain't you?"

"Please, Miz Rachel," Lovey begged, and this time there was unmistakable panic in her voice. "We gotta go!"

"Shut up, nigger! I told you to shut your mouth!" Raising his hand to strike her, the man staggered toward Lovey. "But seems like you need to be taught your place!"

In an instant Rachel jumped in front of him and hit him across the face with the back of her hand. The force of her furious blow and his drunken state combined to send the man stumbling backwards. He slipped off the high curb and would have fallen into the street if he hadn't caught himself on a parking meter.

"You'll pay for this!" he snarled, then called Rachel a

series of vulgar names. "I took care of your nigger-loving grandmother, and I can sure take care of you!"

Suddenly the pieces fell together for Rachel, and she finally recognized the man. He was Garth Gunner, the hate-filled drunk who had killed her Grandmere. Her long-carried hatred for him scorched through Rachel's whole being, and she would have given her very life for a gun.

As the drunk turned to stagger across the street, Lovey grabbed Rachel's arm and tried to drag her toward the car, but Rachel turned back into the store to call the sheriff.

Driving home, neither one spoke a word. The same memory kept repeating over and over in Rachel's mind, repeating with the irritation of a recording that replays a single measure of music until one's nerves are rubbed raw. She was nineteen again, home from college for Easter vacation, and she heard the sound of broken glass crashing and crashing, over and over again in her parents' living room. Panicked, she flung open the double doors, and there was her father throwing every breakable object he could find, shattering them against the fireplace. She stared first at his face, which was wet with tears, and then, as he continued to throw things at the fireplace. There she saw the telephone, ripped from the wall, surrounded by broken glass and porcelain.

In time his violence ceased, and he sank to the floor and held his head. Rachel rushed to his side, begging him to speak. By the time he had composed himself enough to utter the words she was desperate to hear, the whole household had gathered in the room.

"Your Grandmere is dead," he muttered. "She was run down by a no-good drunk named Garth Gunner."

It was much later that night before Rachel had learned the circumstances of her beloved Grandmere's death. Her driver, old Solomon, had been helping her out of the car in front of the grocer's when the drunken Garth Gunner had sideswiped her car and killed her and Solomon instantly.

It was even later, as her father tried to have Gunner convicted of murder, that Rachel learned of Gunner's intense hatred of her Grandmere. It was his type who hated the blacks the most and despised anyone who tried to help them. His type had nothing because of their shiftlessness, but rather than admitting to their own responsibility for their condition, they preferred to blame it on the blacks.

Garth Gunner had hated Grandmere for years because of her support of the blacks, and he had often threatened her. When he saw her on the street that day, he had taken his revenge. Jack, however, could never send him to the gas chamber because Gunner had been so drunk the day he had killed Grandmere that there was no way to prove premeditated murder.

When Rachel and Lovey drove up to the kitchen entrance of the plantation house, Rachel turned and angrily demanded of Lovey. "How long has he been free?"

"I don't know," Lovey looked at her lap as she spoke.

"You knew he was free, didn't you?" Rachel demanded. "You knew it!"

Lovey nodded. They sat in silence for a tense moment until another thought suddenly struck Rachel.

"Has he been out here?" she demanded. "Has he?"

"Once." Lovey's single word spoke volumes to Rachel's imagination.

"How he must have loved it!" she spit the words out bitterly. "How he must have loved seeing the house all closed up, seeing the life taken out of the place!"

Lovey merely nodded sadly as she brought her tired, old eyes to meet Rachel's, but she found no resignation in the younger woman. Instead, Rachel's eyes glistened with anger. "He'd better not come back!" she spat out. "Because I'll kill him!"

Rachel slammed out of the car and jerked a bag of groceries from the trunk. As she marched off in the direction of the kitchen door, Lovey caught her by the arm.

"I get the groceries, Miz Rachel," Lovey said.

"I need something to do!" Rachel shouted at the woman for the first time in their relationship. "Don't you understand? I have to *do* something!"

Lovey stood mute before her, her loving eyes focused squarely on Rachel's face. Rachel instantly hated herself for directing her anger at Lovey, but before she could make amends, Lovey raised her own voice just slightly and spoke with great firmness.

"I *do* understand, Miz Rachel. I understands exactly how you feel. I's been down the same road you's traveling right now, and I gots to tell you, it don't lead nowhere. It lead to the swamp! You gonna drown in that hate you got for that man. You gotta let go of that hate or it gonna kill you. There ain't no two ways about it—it gonna kill you!"

"I don't care! I do hate him!" Rachel was yelling again in spite of herself. "He shouldn't be walking around free while Grandmere is—is—"

"Buried under the ground," Lovey quietly finished the sentence for her.

"Yes! Buried! Buried!" Rachel flung the bag of groceries to the ground and plopped down on a bench. Her eyes were filled with tears of anger, but those tears were soon replaced by tears of grief as she looked around her and realized that she was sitting on the bench where she and Lovey had watched the birds so very long ago. So long ago. Such a peaceful time. She and Lovey on the bench, the birds gathering the crumbs from the grass, and Grandmere still asleep in the house.

Lovey joined her and put her old arms around her, as she had done so many times, and pulled her to her bosom.

"Grandmere's really gone, isn't she?" Rachel cried quietly on the woman's neck.

"She's free, Child," Lovey soothed. "She's free."

Rachel's quiet tears turned to sobs. "But she's not here! And I miss her! And I need her! Oh, Lovey, I miss her! Don't you miss her? Even though it's been so long, don't you miss her too?"

"I misses her, Honey," Lovey was stroking Rachel's hair as she spoke. "Ain't a day gone by I ain't caught myself looking for her somewhere in the house. Then I grieves all over again."

"Then how can you *not* hate that scum?" Rachel sat up and stared at Lovey in wonder. "How can you not hate him?"

"Oh, I hated him at first. All I could think of was finding him and killing him. But I's older than you, and I knows how hate eat away at everything good inside you till there be nothing left but the hate. Miz Elinore done taught me that about my Pa and what he did to me. She done taught me that I was full of love and not to let the hate make me different. So finally it come to me that I already lost Miz Elinore, and I didn't want to lose the good in me that she helped me see. So I asked God to help me, and He did."

"How?"

"He remind me of all the times Miz Elinore say God love all His children. He love them no matter what, she say. She used to say that all the time. So I knowed God love Garth Gunner even if he kill Miss Elinore, so I couldn't hate him no more. I couldn't love him cause I ain't God, but I couldn't hate him. Then I was free just to grieve—not to hate—to grieve."

Rachel stared thoughtfully at the shady lawn for a long

time. "The trouble is, Lovey," she finally spoke, "I have to hate him. Look what he *did*. In my book, he's worthless. He's proven himself to be worthless. No man who did a thing like that could be worth anything to God or anyone else!"

•Lovey rose stiffly from the bench to go after the groceries, but after she had taken several steps, she turned back to face Rachel.

"I's glad God don't play by your rules, Miz Rachel," she smiled peacefully as she spoke, "I's glad God don't judge my worth on what I done or ain't done cause I wouldn't have no chance in the world of making it to heaven."

## TWENTY-TWO

Rachel sat on the bench for half an hour trying to cool her temper. In the end, she gave up and admitted to herself that the only thing she had accomplished was to realize that she had been awful to Lovey and owed her an apology. In regard to Gunner, she hadn't changed her feelings at all.

She found Lovey in the kitchen.

"Lovey, I'm sorry," she blurted out as she walked toward her. "I have no right to yell at you for any reason. Certainly I shouldn't be yelling at you about this mess."

Lovey continued stirring something on the stove and said nothing. Rachel's heart sank, but all she could do was try again. "I shouldn't have yelled at you. Please forgive me."

"Is yelling at me going to get that hate out of you?" Lovey demanded as she suddenly turned and faced Rachel. "Cause if it is, you just yell your head off at me or anybody else."

Rachel walked to the kitchen table and sat down with a sigh. "I don't think yelling is going to help. I don't think anything short of killing that man is going to make me feel any better."

"Then you sure is up a creek with no paddle," Lovey shook a wooden spoon at her, "cause you can't kill him, that's for sure."

"No, he would have been dead long ago if I could have gotten to him."

"Well, I's glad neither you nor your daddy got here before they caught him and got him in the jailhouse cause you and your daddy would have killed each other trying to decide who was gonna get to kill Gunner."

"Are you trying to say I'm like my father?" Rachel demanded.

"I ain't trying to say it, I *is* saying it. You got your father's temper. You got your Grandpere's temper." Lovey strode to the table and leaned over close to Rachel's face and demanded, "What you mean hitting that man like that? Miz Elinore gonna turn over in her grave."

"Did you expect me just to stand there and let him knock you to the ground? Is that what you wanted?"

"That be a heap better than you hitting him. I could of got up off the ground. Now you gotta live with hitting that man."

"It's not bothering me one bit!" Rachel retorted.

"Well, it bothering me plenty." Lovey returned to the stove.

"I'm sorry, Lovey. I'm sorry it's bothering you, and I'm sorry I yelled at you, but I'm not sorry I hit Gunner. Now are you going to forgive me or not?"

"Course I is, but you gotta promise me you gonna stay away from that man."

"I promise. I didn't exactly go looking for him this time."

"I know. I know."

Rachel left the kitchen and went upstairs to compose herself as best she could.

By tea time she had returned downstairs to the music room. Just as Lovey came in to say the water for the tea was boiling, the phone started ringing in the hall. "That gonna be Mr. Jack calling," Lovey announced.

"Daddy? Why would he be calling?"

"Cause he done heard what's going on over here." Lovey called over her shoulder as she walked toward the hall.

"That's ridiculous, Lovey, it just happened," Rachel waited while Lovey answered the phone.

"She right here," Lovey said into the receiver and then called Rachel, "Your daddy want to talk to you."

When Rachel said "hello," her father's voice came booming through the receiver. "Rachel D'Evereau, what in tarnation do you mean slugging Gunner? Haven't you got any sense at all? That man would just as soon kill you as look at you. I'll be over there in two hours, and don't you stir from that house until I get there!"

"Daddy! Stop yelling a minute and listen to me. I'm not the least bit afraid of that man, and I don't need you to come over here and rescue me. How did you find out anyway?"

"The sheriff called me, of course. He's on his way over there right now. Don't you dare leave the house! I'm on my way!" Rachel heard a dial tone and knew he had hung up.

As she replaced the receiver, she glanced out the beveled glass that surrounded the front door and saw the sheriff's car approaching the house. She met him on the verandah and demanded, "Did you call my father?"

"Yes Mam, I did."

"Don't do it again," Rachel warned. "I'm not a child. I run my own business."

"Miz D'Evereau, you ain't gonna like this, but if it comes to choosing between tangling with you and tangling with Jack D'Evereau, I'm gonna tangle with you every time cause I don't *ever* want to tangle with your daddy.

Now please cooperate with me like your daddy wants and stay in the house until he gets here. Otherwise he's going to skin me alive."

"Okay, okay. I don't want you skinned alive—at least not at the moment."

"My deputy's gonna be here in a minute, and I'm gonna leave him here and go get things started. In fact, here he comes now."

"Okay, Sheriff, I'll be inside."

When Rachel re-entered the hall, she found an anxious Lovey hovering there. "What they gonna do?" she asked.

"They're going to try to find him, but they won't get much done tonight. We might as well calm down, if we can. Let's have some tea, and in a little while we'll send Alice out to see if that deputy wants some coffee. He's staying here to guard us."

"And your daddy coming?"

"You know the answer to that, Lovey."

"Good. It gonna be just fine then." She hurried off to make the tea, and Rachel settled down in the music room and fumed about the whole situation.

By the time her father arrived, it was pitch dark. He waved aside offers of supper and paced the front verandah, with the deputy trying to keep up with him, until the sheriff came tearing up the drive. Rachel joined them, determined to be a part of anything to do with catching Gunner.

"Evening, Mr. D'Evereau," the sheriff began amiably, but he was immediately cut short by Jack.

"Have you found Gunner?"

"No sir. He seems to have disappeared off the face of the earth, ain't nowhere in town, but we'll get him. Don't you worry. We'll get him."

"You can count on it!" Jacks eyes glowed with frustrated anger. "If he isn't in town, he's taken to the woods, probably these woods. What we need is a massive manhunt. Plenty of dogs and plenty of men."

"With all due respect, sir, I don't think Gunner really wants to tangle with you. I think he's slipped out of town. He's a coward through and through; he don't want no trouble."

"He threatened my daughter's life this afternoon! And you seem to be forgetting that he killed my mother!"

"He tried to slap Lovey to the ground!" Rachel added.

"Yes mam, I heard something about him trying to hit some old woman that was with you—"

"She is not 'some old woman'! She is my dearest friend, and she's worked in this house since she was ten years old!"

"Yes, mam, sorry about that," the sheriff mumbled and turned to address Jack. "Well, Mr. D'Evereau, it's still my judgment that he's long gone, and we can't mount a manhunt and go through these woods on a night like this."

"Then be ready at dawn," Jack ordered. "If you haven't found him by then, we're searching every inch of these woods in the morning, and I expect your full cooperation."

"Yes sir! You'll have it! We'll be here. Good night, Mam."

Rachel spent the evening working in the plantation office. To divert her mind as much as possible, she planned the girls' lessons for the month of January and made lists of things that needed to be done to the old school building before she could open it. As her mind jumped from Gunner to the school and back to Gunner, it began to dawn on her that Gunner was once a child. Inevitably she began to wonder what his life had been like, and it was pretty easy to guess. Even after she had envisioned the probable horrors of his childhood, however, she was still in no mood to forgive him. Nevertheless, thinking about his childhood made her think of the many poor white children in the area who were dropping out of school, and she began to expand her vision of the school.

By the time Lovey came out around 9:00 to check on her, Rachel had decided to reach for the stars and plan for a summer school that would be open to any child who needed help. She was confident the Bishop would let her use the building. All she needed was money to renovate the necessary space, cooperation from the school district to help her locate the students who needed help, and teachers.

When she explained what she was thinking to Lovey, Lovey responded, "I's glad your mind's on that, and I knows where you can get two real good teachers."

"Where?"

"Aimee and Joseph. They didn't want me to tell you, but they's both gonna have to go out and get extra summer jobs cause they can't make ends meet."

"Perfect. Absolutely perfect. Now all I need is money."

"That gonna come too."

"You know, I think you're right."

The next morning Rachel awoke later than she had planned because there was no sun. She walked to the French doors in her room to check the weather. It was a gray, foggy day, and the mist hung in the air like smoke. She dressed as quickly as possible in the cold room and walked across the hall and found her father's door open. She hurried down to the warm kitchen where she found Lovey standing over the stove and stirring some kind of hot cereal.

"Good morning," Rachel stifled a yawn as she spoke. "Have you seen Daddy?"

"He gone down to the stables to look around." Lovey kept stirring.

"Boy, this is a good day to just sit in front of the fire. I wish we could."

"We gots to go to mass," Lovey responded without turning around.

It was unusual for Lovey to be so distant. Rachel watched her a minute and then asked, "Lovey, are you all right? Do you feel okay?" Rachel took a few steps to the right to catch a glimpse of Lovey's profile, but Lovey briskly turned away and busied herself at the sink.

"I's just fine," Lovey said as she turned on the faucet. "Just don't want to be late to mass."

"It's two hours until mass," Rachel walked up behind Lovey and put her hand on Lovey's shoulder. "What's wrong?"

"I told you everything's fine," Lovey whirled around irritably and tried to move away.

"No, it's not." Rachel took the woman's shoulders in her hands and peered into Lovey's face. There she found two eyes brimming with tears. "Tell me," she demanded. "Tell me what's wrong."

"I ain't gonna tell you cause—"

Suddenly the back door banged opened. Scared by the sound, Rachel turned around to see Alice standing panting in the doorway. "Is you okay, Lovey?" she demanded as she marched across the kitchen toward Lovey. "He didn't hurt you none, did he?"

"Go home, Alice," Lovey raised her voice in an uncharacteristic fashion, and Rachel's heart began to race. "You can't come in here bothering Miz Rachel. How many times I told you—"

"She's not bothering me," Rachel broke in. "What's going on, Alice?"

Alice opened her mouth to speak, but Lovey stepped

toward Rachel and started babbling as if she were out of her mind. "You ain't supposed to be in the kitchen anyhow. You's supposed to be a lady, and ladies don't come in no kitchen. What your Grandmere going to say? You get on in the music room till I calls you for breakfast."

Confused and filled with anxiety, Rachel stood her ground and waited for Lovey to stop fussing. When the old woman grew silent, Rachel put her arms around her and spoke quietly, "Lovey, either you're going to tell me what's wrong or Alice is going to tell me. Which is it going to be?"

Lovey sighed and seemed to crumple against Rachel. "Promise me, you gonna go to mass with me before you does anything else," Lovey begged.

"What?"

"Promise me. I's done a lot for you, and I ain't never asked for anything." She lifted her head and looked into Rachel's eyes. "Promise me."

Rachel was torn between the tears streaming down Lovey's face and her certainty that whatever Lovey was going to tell her was going to drive her into action, not into prayer. However, she could not ignore those tears. "I promise," she said firmly. "Tell me what's happened."

"I went to see about Miz Elinore's grave," Lovey began and halted suddenly.

"And?" demanded Rachel.

"Somebody been in the graveyard and messed things up a little."

Rachel tried to look into Lovey's eyes, but she ducked her head. "What do you mean 'messed things up a little'?" Rachel demanded.

"You remember you made a promise to me, Miz Rachel—"

Suddenly it was all clear to Rachel.

She dashed out the kitchen door and raced across the lawn

and through the woods until she came to the D'Evereau cemetery. When she reached the wrought iron gates, she stopped in her tracks. Her heart pounded away in her chest as she faced the graveyard she had avoided ever since she came. Then staring through the gates she searched wildly for the statue of Jesus that had always risen above the crypts. His pedestal was empty. A fury like Rachel had never known rose from within her. She banged the gates aside and marched into the cemetery straight to the pedestal. There she saw the figure of Christ, that had stood above the D'Evereau dead for over a century, lying on the ground in the mud. Someone had taken a crowbar or something and beaten on it, trying to destroy it, but he had only managed to gouge it here and there.

She turned and ran to the crypt of her Grandmere. There she found that the intruder had done his best to smash the statue of Mary holding the infant Jesus; it was still standing, but it was almost unrecognizable. Rachel stared down at her Grandmere's crypt and found the answer she knew she would find. There, crudely carved in the moss that covered the crypt, she found the name "Gunner." Tears splashed down her cheeks as she knelt next to her Grandmere's crypt, but they were not tears of grief. They were tears of fury.

With Alice by her side, Lovey came rushing into the cemetery as fast as her age would permit and soon reached Rachel's side. "You promised me, Miz Rachel," she panted out. "Right here in front of your Grandmere's grave I claims that promise. You ain't going after that man cause he gonna kill you."

Rachel stood and faced her. "Lovey, I am going to stop that man, and if I have to kill him to do it, I will. Did you see him?"

"You promised me!" Lovey cried out as she staggered into Rachel's arms. Until that moment Rachel had been determined that nothing would stop her, not even her promise, but when Lovey collapsed, her anger was instantly cooled.

"I will keep my promise," she managed to say the words. "Let's get you back to the house."

"Thank you, Jesus," Lovey whispered as Rachel put her arms around the woman's shoulders and with Alice's help supported her toward the house.

When Rachel and Alice had settled Lovey in front of a warm fire and gotten her a cup of tea, Rachel knelt down beside her chair. "Lovey, I must call the sheriff." She waited for Lovey to protest, but instead she smiled serenely at Rachel. "I have to do it, Lovey, because that man is dangerous." Lovey continued to smile. "He is capable of hurting anyone here. I can't let that happen."

Lovey reached out her weathered hand and stroked Rachel's hair. "You go ahead and call him. Everything gonna be all right now."

Rachel stared at her, wondering if she had lost her mind, but Lovey's eyes were alert and confident. "I don't understand, Lovey. You made me promise not to do anything until after mass."

"That was *before*, Honey. It gonna be all right now cause love has overcome the hate in your heart. Hate has lost the battle for you; love has won you."

Rachel stared at the fire, unable to comprehend and unsure whether to tell Lovey she still hated Gunner or just to keep her mouth shut. She decided on the latter.

"I knows what you's thinking," Lovey spoke with quiet confidence. "You still hates him and wants to kill him. You still thinks he's nothing but a worthless no good that ought to be shot down, but you don't want to upset me." She reached out, took Rachel's chin in her hand, and lifted it until their eyes met. "You's gonna feel that way for awhile, but I's telling you that when you forced that anger out of your mind long enough to love me, you made your choice. Love has won the war." She put her hand back in her lap, and closed her eyes. "I's gonna rest me a spell before mass," she murmured.

Totally mystified, Rachel rose and told Alice to stay with Lovey. Then she went into the hall and called the Sheriff. Just as she put the receiver down, she heard her father on the back porch. She dashed off to meet him, and when she found him coming in the back door, she pushed him back outside to tell him about the damage at the family cemetery.

His response was predictable. Seconds later he bolted off the porch and ran in the direction of the cemetery. Rachel went back to the music room and sat next to the dozing Lovey. When she heard her father on the front verandah, she hurried to meet him in the hall. He was white with fury.

"Did she see the scum?" he demanded.

"I don't know."

Her father grabbed the phone, "We've got to know how much time he has on us."

"I've already called the sheriff, Daddy, and Lovey is asleep. I think she may be in shock. I'm going to call the doctor."

Jack put the phone down and stared at Rachel.

"Miz Rachel," Alice peeked around the door, "Lovey getting up."

Rachel and Jack reached her at the same time.

"Lovey, sit back down," Rachel commanded.

"I's gonna fix breakfast," she insisted in a dazed voice.

Jack echoed Rachel, "Sit down, Lovey." Lovey sat back down. "Rachel is going to have the doctor look at you, and we both want you to take it easy. But I've got to know one thing. Did you actually see Gunner?"

"No sir, I just seen his hate."

"He could have been here any time last night then. Lovey, you do what the doctor tells you now. I'll take care of Gunner."

"I's gotta go to mass," Lovey protested, "and there ain't gonna be no breakfast."

"Alice can fix breakfast," Rachel insisted. "I'm going to call the doctor. You stay in that chair until he comes and tells you that you are able to get up." She walked out into the hall, with her father following her, and called the doctor.

As soon as she put down the phone, her father picked it up and started calling the D'Evereau cousins to join in the search. Rachel started out the front door.

"Where are you going?" he called after her.

"Down to tell the people to spread the word to be careful." She ignored his protests and kept walking. In a minute he had caught up with her.

"Rachel, go back to the house. I'll do this."

"No," she kept walking.

"Rachel D'Evereau!" he grabbed her by the shoulders, "I'm telling you to go back to the house."

"I can't!"

"Why not?"

"Because I own Belle St. Marie. They know that. I have to *act* like the owner. You're not going to be here all the time; I am, and they have to know they live on my land and work for me and that I care about them. They have to know I won't hide in that big house and leave them in danger."

Jack released her and ran his hands through his hair in frustration.

"Daddy, every plan I have for the future depends on these people believing in me."

He nodded slowly. "It wouldn't be a sign of weakness to ask one of the men to walk you back, you know. It's supposed to be a mutual thing in a place like this. You take care of them, and they take care of you."

"Sounds like a good idea," she hugged him and hurried on.

The day crept along as the sheriff and the men of the neighborhood fanned out in the woods searching for Gunner. Rachel stayed in the house, a frustrated non-participant in the search. She still wanted to be the person to find Gunner and deal with him, but she wanted more to keep Lovey quiet and resting in bed, and she knew she had to choose. So she spent the slow hours helping Alice make coffee and food for the men. Occasionally she walked out onto the front verandah and looked down the drive at the sheriff's car. The sheriff was always standing near the car, sometimes talking into a walkie-talkie, sometimes talking to someone on his patrol car radio, but mostly staring off into the woods. Always, he looked at her and shook his head. Rachel scanned the woods herself and returned to Lovey's bedside or the kitchen.

Shortly after noon Father Timothy arrived with communion for Lovey and Rachel. Rachel's anger kept her from accepting it, but Lovey gratefully received it. Rachel left them alone and went back out on the verandah. In time Father Timothy joined her and said simply, "I won't lecture you; I know it won't do any good. However, I will plead with you to follow your highest thoughts."

"With Lovey lying in there, I can hardly do anything else!" Rachel retorted.

"That's right," the priest agreed. "It appears that God has forseen your difficulty with your anger and blessed you with an insurance policy that will keep you from acting out that anger. But He won't remove anger from your heart, Rachel. You'll have to do that."

"I thought you weren't going to lecture, Father."

Father Timothy smiled. "Good day, Rachel."

She watched him walk to his car, then she scanned the woods for the twentieth time and returned to the kitchen.

Rachel was standing out on the verandah late in the afternoon when she saw the sheriff reach into his car and snatch the radio to his lips. His movements propelled her off the verandah because it was obvious that something had happened.

"What is it?" she demanded when she reached his side. "What's happened?"

Above the crackle of the radio, he announced, "Gunner's been spotted in Alabama."

"Alabama! Are they sure?"

The sheriff waved her aside and asked the dispatcher a number of questions. When he returned his attention to her, he said, "Yep! It's him. No doubt about it."

"Have they got him?"

"Not yet. They're just watching him."

"What?" Rachel exploded. "What's wrong with them? Why don't they stop him?"

"They will, they will! If we want them to."

"What do you mean 'if'? Of course we want them to!"

"I ain't so sure. I'm gonna call your daddy in." He picked up his walkie-talkie and started calling Jack.

"I want him stopped!" Rachel raged at the man. "I don't care what Daddy wants. I'm a taxpayer too, and I want him picked up!"

"He ain't gonna get away, Miz D'Evereau. We gotta think what's best for the future. Now just calm down. Go on back up to the house—"

"Forget it! I'm not going anywhere!"

"Okay, okay, but don't worry; he ain't gonna get away."

It seemed like an eternity to Rachel, but her father finally came, and the sheriff explained that Gunner was in Alabama. "He's heading due east, Mr. D'Evereau, in a pick-up truck. Don't seem to have any idea of stopping."

"Pick him up!" Jack ordered.

"Thank God!" Rachel exclaimed. "At least I don't have to fight with you."

"Now," the sheriff drawled out his words, "I'm gonna do whatever you want, Mr. D'Evereau, but let's think this thing through."

"There's nothing to think about," Jack responded coldly.

"Maybe not, sir, but it won't hurt to listen to me." He paused to see if Jack would listen, and when Jack said nothing, he continued. "The way I see it, the man's done what he came to do. He don't have the guts to do anything worse. Now we can haul him back here and prosecute him, but he won't get more than a year in the pen. When he gets out about a year from now, he's going to be good and mad. And he ain't gonna settle for just messing up your family cemetery."

"So what are you recommending?" Jack demanded.

"I recommend we keep him under careful surveillance and see where he goes. If he settles in some place a long way from here, I recommend we leave him alone. The man's crazy, but he don't really want to tangle with you. He just wanted to cause you a little grief before he left."

"Bring him back!" Rachel demanded.

"Miz D'Evereau," the sheriff pleaded with her, "at least think about what I'm saying. If the court won't put him away for killing your grandmother, they ain't gonna do much to him for messing up a gravestone or two."

"*You* didn't see his face when he threatened me in town," Rachel insisted. "He will come back!"

"I don't think so, Mam."

"At any rate," Jack broke in, "you can call off the man-hunt. Rachel and I will discuss your proposal. Come on up to the house when you've finished. But you be sure that Gunner is watched!" Jack took Rachel's arm and started walking toward the house.

"I want him brought back, Daddy!" Rachel insisted. "I won't tolerate knowing that man is free, living it up, after what he's done."

"You want him brought back so you can kill him. I know because I feel the same way," Jack admitted. "But the truth is neither one of us will ever get that chance. And even if one of us did get the chance to kill him, he's not worth going to jail for."

"I don't care! I want him!"

Jack opened the door for her as he spoke. "Let's sit down and talk this over."

"It won't do any good," Rachel warned as she took a seat in the music room.

"Yes it will because you've also got your Grandmere in you. Her part of your heritage is pushing you beyond yourself, pushing you to reach out to others who need you. What you're doing and planning to do with the needy children of this area is worth more than having your revenge on Gunner. Isn't it?"

"Yes, if I have to choose. But do I have to choose?"

"I think you do. I think the sheriff's right, even though I hate to admit it. I know Gunner wouldn't be in jail long if we prosecuted him. Then he would be after you and doing his best to stop your school. The only way to win this thing is to let him think he's won. It infuriates me, but it's the truth."

"So we just let him go?"

"We have him watched, and if he settles in some place, we leave him alone."

"Okay, Daddy," Rachel agreed reluctantly and rose to go check on Lovey, "do it your way, but I want to say one thing. This plan won't settle things. It doesn't change the way I feel about him. And it doesn't change the way he feels. He *will* be back!"

Jack stayed at the plantation for the next three days. During that time Gunner was tracked as he drove toward South Carolina. When he arrived in that state, he headed for a coastal village where he moved in with a woman who had been awaiting him. He had apparently settled in, so Jack felt free to return to Texas.

In spite of her misgiving about her father's decision, Rachel accepted it as best as she could and turned her attention once again to the school she was trying to begin.

## TWENTY-THREE

The remainder of January was a confusing time for Rachel. She had acquiesced to her father's judgment about Gunner very reluctantly and only because the school she was trying to start was so important to her. However, the decision she had made was a rational one; her heart was still full of hatred for the man. Law enforcement officials had watched Gunner for several weeks, and when he took a job on a fishing boat in South Carolina, they assumed he had settled there, content with the level of revenge he had taken on the D'Evereaus. Rachel still believed he would be back, but she disciplined herself to think only of her plans for the school. The Bishop had been out of town for weeks, so she still had not received permission to use the old school building.

In early February she was drinking a cup of tea in the late afternoon of a rainy, windy day when she heard a car drive up. When she opened the front door, she found Father Timothy standing on the front verandah and shaking himself like a wet dog.

"Does it ever stop raining in this place?" he demanded as she drew him into the hallway. "This is definitely not Rome!"

Rachel laughed at him as he shed his soaked raincoat. "No, this is not Rome," she agreed as she continued with a laugh, "and you're no longer a seminary student. Did you decide to swim a bayou or something? Your coat is wet through!"

"I have been swimming in the graveyard for your information!" he retorted. His tone made Rachel stop laughing and take a close look at his face. There she saw the features of an upset young man.

"Come in by the fire and dry off," she coaxed as she drew him into the music room. "I'll get you something hot to drink. Tea or coffee?"

"Whatever," he walked to the fire and turned his back to her so he could warm his hands.

When Rachel returned five minutes later with a hot pot of tea and another cup, she found him still staring gloomily into the flames. Without a word she poured his tea and handed it to him. She studied his face as he gulped down the hot liquid. He is so young, she thought, no more than twenty-five or twenty-six. Straight from the seminary in Rome to this backwoods parish. He's got guts.

"Who died?" she asked quietly as he handed her the empty cup.

He turned back to the fire and muttered, "Betsy Wilson."

"I don't know her, I'm afraid."

"Of course not!" he whirled to face her. "She was poor and thirteen years old and overdosed on some drug. Why would you know her? Why would anyone know her?"

Tears burned Rachel's eyes as she thought of the girl and saw this young man's anguish. "Come sit down, please."

"Priests are not supposed to want to kill people, Rachel, but I want to kill whoever got her started on drugs!"

"That sounds like a perfectly normal reaction to me, normal for any human being. Come sit down."

"I'm supposed to be a priest!"

Rachel grabbed his arm and directed him toward a chair.

"Sit down," she ordered quietly as she pushed him into the chair. She stood and looked down at him for a minute. He bore no resemblance to Justin, but she felt as if she were addressing her brother. "You are a human being, Timothy," she dropped his title intentionally just this once, "who is trying to be a priest of God. I'm no expert, but I suspect that for the rest of your life you will continue to be a human being who is trying to be a priest of God. I suspect that every day of your remaining life you will succeed as a priest and you will fail as a priest because you will continue to be human until you die. But you *are* trying. I'm no theologian, but I don't see how God could ask more of you or of any of the rest of us than that we try our best to love Him and our fellow human beings."

Father Timothy continued to stare at the rug, and Rachel turned her gaze from him to the fire. She had said all she knew to say.

Finally he spoke. "We lost Betsy; we fumbled the ball."

"I know, and I'm grieved by our loss, by our failure. But Betsy's fate is now in God's hands. What about the millions that are left? What about the hundreds here in this parish? Have you heard from the Bishop?"

Father Timothy reached into his pocket, pulled out a crumpled sheet of paper and handed it to her. It was the Bishop's letter giving them permission to use the building for the school.

"Now we can begin, Father. Betsy is in God's hands, but there are hundreds left in our hands. We can help them; I've seen it happen already with the girls I'm working with. They have developed some pride in themselves; they are beginning to know they are worth something, that they are precious gifts to the world. Why, Chelsy even wants to return to the regular school and come after school to be tutored. She is determined to work her way out of the hole she was born into, and I don't believe anyone, *anyone* could talk that girl into taking drugs."

"We lost Betsy!" Father Timothy exclaimed.

"We saved Chelsy!" Rachel countered. "If Lovey were sitting here with you, she would ask you which girl you were going to concentrate on. I know because she's been asking me that same question about problems in my life ever since I got here. So now I'm going to borrow Lovey's wisdom. Which girl will you focus on? Betsy or Chelsy?"

Father Timothy stood and strode to the fire. He grabbed the poker and aimlessly jabbed at the log while he reached up and brushed something away from his eyes. Suddenly he turned, his eyes still glistening from unspilled tears and cried out, "Oh Rachel! I don't want to bury any more children who died because of, because of—"

"Their feelings of worthlessness? Their ignorance of their worth?"

"Yes! I want them to know that they're worth more than a needle of cocaine and a six-foot-deep hole in the ground."

"Then let's talk about the school," Rachel urged gently.

"How do we know that's the answer?"

"How do we know it's not? We know it's a way to begin. Undoubtedly there will have to be many answers; we can't wait until we have the whole battle plan beautifully laid out in front of us. The war is on top of us right now, and we are losing it. This school idea, this Learning Club as it's being called elsewhere, is the fastest way to give these kids a feeling of success. It's also the fastest way for us to see into the problems the kids are facing and find solutions."

"Are you so confident we will find solutions?"

"We certainly won't if we don't try. Look, Father Timothy, I can't promise you there won't be more Betsys for you to bury; in fact, I can promise you there *will* be Betsys.

But I also can promise you there will be Chelsys, many Chelsys. And I think there will be more Chelsys than Betsys."

Father Timothy stared at her for a long moment; when he spoke, his voice sounded confidently efficient. He seemed to have conquered his doubts about the school. Rachel could not help wondering if he had not also been struggling with doubts about himself and his suitability for his chosen vocation. "How do we begin?" he asked.

Rachel invited him to stay for supper, and for the next several hours she told him her plans. She explained that she had six drop-out students now who studied in the plantation office. She did not want to increase that number. Instead she wanted to renovate the school building as much as necessary and start a Learning Club. This club would be open only to students who stayed in school; she was fearful that the reward system she had in mind might encourage students to drop out if she didn't make this stipulation. She wanted to work closely with the school system, seeking their aid in spotting students who were falling behind.

"When do you want to start this Learning Club?" Father Timothy asked. "Next fall?"

"No," Rachel grinned, "March 1st."

"March 1st! This is February!"

"Father, I only need one classroom because I only have one teacher—me. Surely we can manage that."

"Well, I suppose—"

"Of course we can!" Rachel hurried on. "But we'll need more space by summer because I want to offer a summer school for anyone who wants to come."

"Now I know you're crazy. You really think kids will give up their summer vacation and come to school?"

"If I make it worth their time, they'll come."

"You're going to bribe them, the way you've bribed those six girls?"

"I am."

"But they'll just take advantage of you. They won't care about learning."

"But they *will* learn or they won't get their rewards. Father, I'm not trying to fill the graduate schools of tomorrow. I'm trying to stop functional illiteracy so these kids can go to public schools and succeed and feel good about themselves. And they can graduate someday and get some kind of job. I'm perfectly willing to bribe them. I'm perfectly willing for them to snicker behind my back, and I recognize the fact that many of them will never be motivated by anything but the material rewards I offer. Some of them, however, will be like Chelsy; they'll move from working for the things they can acquire to working for the worth they can feel."

"I hope you're right."

"What have we got to lose?"

"Just time and money, I guess."

"Well, we have the time, and I'll come up with the money."

"How?"

"I'll take personal responsibility for the first years," Rachel promised. "After that, I believe we'll have good enough results to get community support and grants from foundations."

"What about teachers? If you're right that the kids will come to a summer school, you're going to need help. You can't teach a mob of kids all on your own."

"I'm going to ask Aimee and Joseph Bonet to come down from Shreveport for the summer. They both teach in the public schools; they'll be perfect, and they need summer jobs."

"I had no idea you were thinking this big," he shook his head in amazement.

"It has to be big," Rachel insisted, "big and important. We want it in the newspapers and splashed everywhere. We want people to take it very seriously so the kids will, so their parents will, if they have any parents around."

"But the money, Rachel—"

"It will be available, I promise you."

"I don't want you to bankrupt yourself."

"I've come as near to being bankrupt this past year as a person can come, Father, but I was never short of money. Real bankruptcy has nothing to do with money; it involves only the spirit."

## TWENTY-FOUR

Rachel was sitting on the top step of the front verandah, leaning back against a massive pillar. This was a favorite spot of hers for watching the sunset, and tonight the day's farewell was magnificent.

"God putting on quite a show," Lovey observed reverently as she walked out the front door.

"Yes, He is!" Rachel agreed. "Come sit down and enjoy it."

"I oughta get going on supper," Lovey reached for Rachel's extended hand and slowly sat down beside her. "But they's plenty of suppers ahead of me and only one of these."

"Incredible creativity. Every sunset different, but there's something especially beautiful about this one."

"They's been lots of special sunsets lately. Your mind's just been so tied up with getting the school ready that you ain't had time to see them."

"I can't argue with that," Rachel admitted. There was a long silence between them as they watched the colors deepen. "It's all ready now, Lovey. The building is ready, the first students are signed up, and the workbooks came in today. Maybe that's why this particular sunset seems so special. Because I feel so good about getting all this done. Because I feel so hopeful about the results."

"You sure ain't the woman who come dragging in here last June."

"No, thank God! I don't think I would even recognize that Rachel if she came walking through the door."

"That's the Lord's healing, Honey, and your choosing."

Once again there was a long silence between them as they watched the changing color.

"Isn't it amazing," Rachel mused aloud, "how a sunset like this makes everything beautiful? Even a broken, bare limb bathed in that light is transformed into a beautiful creation. I hate to see it end, but I know it will."

"Light don't ever end."

"No, I guess not, not really. We just have a few hours every day when we can't see it."

"That's why the Lord give us faith. And just in case our faith get to dragging in the middle of the night, He give us the moon and the stars."

Rachel turned her gaze from the sunset to Lovey's face. It was wrinkled and worn and had withstood all the usual assaults of time, but it was aglow with light that did not come from the sunset. I wish I saw that light she sees, Rachel thought. It was in Grandmere's eyes too, but she didn't give it to Lovey. She only encouraged Lovey to find it for herself. That's the best anybody can do for another person. And for almost a year now Lovey has been encouraging me. In turn, I have been tentatively encouraging Sassy, Chelsy, and the other girls to start their journey toward that light. And now it's almost time to expand my efforts.

She looked back at the sunset and found it was fast fading and disappearing behind the pines. A surge of anxiety ran through her. It hasn't been that long since Collins died, she worried. Have I learned enough? Am I really ready to light a lantern for the many children I hope are about to enter my life? Will they be drawn toward the light? Will they continue a lifelong journey toward an eternal light by learning to believe in themselves and their Creator's love for them?

"The Lord give us a full moon tonight," Lovey murmured.

"He has?" Rachel had been so caught up in her thoughts she hadn't noticed that the sunset was gone, dusk had come, and the moon was rising. "Yes, I see, He has. Good."

"And lots of stars, too. Course we gonna see them better in a few days when the moon ain't so bright."

"Yes."

"You ever miss the city, Miz Rachel? Must have been mighty pretty at night with all them sparkling lights ever color of the rainbow."

Rachel thought of the many times she had stood, high in a city building, and looked down at the lights of the city spread out before her. Back then she had thought of them as jewels, every kind of sparkling jewel.

"No, Lovey, I never miss it." Rachel leaned over and hugged her. "Here all the lights in the night are diamonds."

"Miz Rachel! Miz Rachel!" the serenity and joy of the moment were smashed by a hysterical scream.

Rachel jumped to her feet and ran down the steps toward the frantic voice. Just as her feet touched the walk, Chelsy came tearing around the side of the house and threw herself into Rachel's arms. "Miz Rachel! It's Sassy!" she sobbed uncontrollably and couldn't go on.

Rachel dragged her up the steps, and Lovey hurried to open the door into the entry hall. "Lovey, turn on some lights," Rachel called as she continued to drag the sobbing girl into the music room. With Lovey's help she settled

Chelsy on the loveseat and stared into her face. The girl's eyes were full of panic.

"What's happened to Sassy?" Rachel demanded. Chelsy reached out and grasped Rachel's skirt and buried her face in it like a frightened child and continued to sob hysterically. "Chelsy, talk to me! For heaven's sake talk to me! What's happened?"

"You gotta tell us what's happened, child," Lovey tried to pull the girl away from Rachel enough to communicate with her, but Chelsy held on for dear life.

Rachel's professionally disciplined mind flipped the necessary switch, and her own wild imaginings were buried under the weight of reason. She grabbed both of Chelsy's shoulders and shook her as hard as she could. Chelsy was stunned into silence.

"Chelsy, tell me this instant what has happened to Sassy!" Rachel commanded before the girl could become hysterical again.

"Gunner got her! He pulled her into the woods! She's hurt real bad!"

Rachel's fury blew off the weight of reason she had clamped on her emotions. She had been ready for every catastrophic announcement except this one.

"Get Alice!" she commanded Lovey as she gathered Chelsy into her arms.

"I's here!" Alice called from the dining room. "I heard the noise—"

"Alice, come help me with Chelsy," Rachel interrupted her. Then she turned her attention to Chelsy, who was sobbing again. "You're safe, Chelsy, and I'll take care of Sassy. Whatever has happened, I'll take care of it. Do you understand me? I want you to stay here in the house. I'll take care of Sassy. I promise you."

"But Gunner!" Chelsy sobbed out.

"I'll take care of Gunner!" Rachel felt like her whole body had turned to steel. "You can count on it!"

"What you gonna do?" Lovey demanded.

Rachel ignored her. "Alice, take Chelsy into the kitchen with you and call the doctor for Sassy. Tell him I said to come immediately." Alice hurriedly pulled the girl away from Rachel and helped her walk toward the kitchen. When they were gone, Rachel looked Lovey squarely in the eyes and for the first time in her life ordered Lovey to do something. "Go help Alice, Lovey!"

"I ain't going nowhere, and neither is you." Lovey stared back at her. "You gonna call the sheriff."

Rachel answered by striding into the hall and opening the closet that contained her father's guns. She grabbed a rifle, fumbled on the shelf for some bullets, and loaded it.

"What you doing with that gun?" Lovey demanded as she blocked Rachel from leaving. "You don't even know how to use that gun. That man gonna kill you."

"I know how to use it, Lovey! Daddy taught me, remember? During one of those beautiful summers before that monster killed Grandmere."

"And now you gonna go try to kill that Gunner? You gonna remember Miz Elinore one minute and go out to kill a man the next? No you ain't! You gonna call the sheriff."

"The sheriff will do the same thing he did last time. He'll say 'let him go; we can't keep him in jail very long anyway.' "

"No he won't. This time Gunner didn't attack no grave; he attack a person. He attack Sassy. The sheriff gonna put him in jail for the rest of his life. You just wants to kill Gunner cause you hates him."

"Yes, I hate him! He killed Grandmere! They didn't keep him in jail but fourteen years for that. How long do you think they'll keep him in jail this time?"

Rachel pushed past Lovey, but before she could get out the open front door, a small black boy came darting across the porch, saw her and yelled, "Aunt Sally told me to come tell you the men have caught Gunner at the old stables, and they're gonna kill him!" Then the boy dashed away in the direction of the stables.

Rachel stood in the doorway, her back to Lovey, and looked in the direction of the stables. After a moment she turned, walked past Lovey to the closet and put the gun away, but she couldn't force herself to turn back and face Lovey.

"You gonna let *them* kill him," Lovey said quietly.

"What will the sheriff do to the men if they kill Gunner?" Rachel stared into the closet as she asked.

"You knows the answer to that."

Rachel jerked up the rifle and ran past Lovey. "Call the sheriff, Lovey!" she yelled as she bounded down the stairs.

Rachel ran as fast as she could toward the old stables, the rifle gripped in her right hand. "Dear God! Don't let them kill him!" she cried out into the night. When she saw the stables, she saw a mob of people. Her heart sank with hopelessness, but she raced on.

As she came up behind the mob, she climbed the first fence she came to, and over the heads of the people, she saw Gunner backed up against the wall of the stables. Some of the men were hitting him, and she saw him fall to the ground. The night was full of the screams of the crowd's rage as the men began to kick him.

Rachel raised the rifle to her shoulder and fired three shots into the roof of the stables above the men's heads. There was instant silence as the men jumped back from Gunner and the crowd turned to see where the shots came from. Rachel had not waited for their reaction. As soon as she had fired, she had jumped down on the other side of the fence and begun running around the edge of the mob. As they, surprised and afraid, turned to look back, she raced to the stable wall where Gunner lay and turned her rifle on the men she had known for years.

"Get away from him!" she ordered. "I mean it! Move back!"

"We gonna kill him, and you ain't gonna stop us!" Tom, one of the field hands, yelled at her as he started moving toward her.

Rachel knew she couldn't hesitate. She aimed close to his feet and shot. He stopped in amazement.

"Why in the name of God are you gonna try to save the trash that killed Miz Elinore?" he demanded.

"Because he's white!" someone from the crowd yelled.

"No! Because I'm afraid for *you*." Rachel shouted back without taking her eyes off Tom or lowering her rifle. "I mean it! Get back!"

Slowly the crowd began to move back, but the men who had been beating Gunner stood still. There was total silence as Rachel and the men stared at each other.

"Why you really doing this?" Tom yelled at her.

"Because you're worth it!" Rachel shouted back. She felt her arms weakening. She knew she couldn't hold up the rifle more than a few more seconds, so she shouted at the crowd, "You are *all* worth it!"

"You can't hold that rifle up like that for long," Tom taunted and took a step forward. "Your arms gonna give out."

Rachel's exhausted arms were forcing her to lower the gun, and Tom jumped forward and took it from her. "He's all ours now!" Tom raised the rifle triumphantly in the air.

The crowd was silent, still. Rachel turned and looked at Gunner. He's unconscious, she thought. He's no more than a bloody mass that has curled itself into a fetal position. This man who killed Grandmere is nearly dead. This man who attacked Sassy is nearly dead. He's going back to God in the same position that God sent him to us. He was a baby once, an innocent baby. He was a little boy, a child who could laugh and run in the woods. Dear God! What happened to him? What abuse drove him to hate so much?

"Let's finish him boys!" Tom called and took a step toward Gunner.

"No!" screamed Rachel as she ran and threw herself on the ground in front of Gunner. "No! I won't let you! Don't you see, if *you* are worth something—and you are— then he *has* to be worth something too. If Grandmere was worth anything, so is he. If Sassy is worth anything, if any of us is worth anything, we all are! He's one of us!"

"But what about all the evil things he done?" a woman called out. "We ain't done none of them things."

Rachel stood, faced the crowd, and spoke with passionate decisiveness, "We are not what we *do*! We are what God created!"

They stared at her, not able to comprehend—or not ready to comprehend. Rachel gave up trying to explain. After all, it had taken her whole life to come to this point of understanding. She said firmly, "God did not make any trash. I know it's hard to believe that fact sometimes, but it *is* a fact. God did not make any trash! Now go home. The sheriff is coming. I don't want you here when he gets here."

The crowd started hurriedly dispersing, but Tom and several of the men who had beaten Gunner stayed behind. Lovey pushed her way up to Rachel, "Oh Miz Rachel! I heard what you said, but I couldn't get through the crowd and—" She stopped short when she saw the men. "What's you waiting on?" she demanded of the men.

"They're waiting to see if we need any help," Rachel answered for them. "And we do."

It was several hours later before Rachel could drop into the loveseat in the music room and finally rest. The doctor had done what he could for Sassy. Then he had ridden back to town in the ambulance with Gunner, with the sheriff following close behind. Rachel had gone to see Sassy and held her hand until she had fallen asleep under the influence of the sedative she had been given. Chelsy had been escorted home, Alice had gone for the night, and the house was finally quiet.

Lovey came in to check on her, and Rachel reached out and pulled her down beside her.

"I's so proud of you, Miz Rachel," the old woman's eyes misted, "and I know Miz Elinore as proud as can be."

"Thank you, Lovey. Not just for tonight. For this whole year and for all the times before when you tried to head me in the right direction."

"I knows you went down there to save the coloreds, Miz Rachel. How come you decide to save Gunner?"

"I did go down to save the blacks because I thought Gunner was just too worthless for those men to go to jail for killing him. But when I saw him lying on that ground, all curled up like a baby, it just came to me that he was probably like Mammy Cassie, that his past had made him see himself as so worthless that he acted like he was worthless. Even if there had been some good in his life, there must not have been anybody around to help him choose to look at the good instead of the bad he was enduring. All of a sudden he just didn't seem like the devil incarnate to me. He was just a pitiful creature fighting off the world with the only weapons he knew he had—anger and hate. He seemed like someone who had walked down the same road we all had. He seemed like me! I've been angry all my life and for less reason than he has. He seemed like me, and he seemed worth too much to die at the hands of an angry mob."

"So you saved him," Lovey concluded proudly.

"I did my best. He was worth saving. The men who were going to kill him were worth saving."

"You could have been hurt real bad, Miz Rachel, maybe even killed."

"They were all worth the risk."

"And you?" Lovey asked quietly. "What is you worth?"

"It's like you've told me over and over, Lovey, 'God don't make no trash.' *No* trash. I must be worthy too."

"Praise the Lord! You finally got hold of the Truth. We gotta have us a celebration!"

# Also by Thomas Nelson

An excerpt from *A Safe Haven* by Summer Allman:

The twin-engine plane banked left, leaving behind the last fragment of civilization she would contend with for a long time. Katherine kept her eyes to the window to avoid encouraging conversation with the pilot and to drink in the source of her solitude. Giant emerald firs, dusted in mist, pointed to her, reaching, welcoming. This would be good place to hide. *And good hiding places don't come easy,* Katherine thought. If it didn't work out, perhaps the peacefulness of the outside would squeeze the inside torment into a small compact emptiness.

At the edge of fifty, life had become for Katherine Allen a cruel exposure, an accumulation of explanations, justifications, and criticism, etched into every wrinkle and bit of sagging flesh—identifying marks betraying a truth within.

For the past nine months Katherine hed felt hidden in someone else's dream. Nothing mattered because it wasn't real. It wasn't hers. She had tried her best to bury herself in church work and exercises of faith and praise, but the joy never came. Instead, each succeeding day was a steady slide into a gray nothingness.

John had died the night the tea roses froze.

**DON'T MISS**

*A Safe Haven*
by Summer Allman

**Available June 1996**